PLAYA DUST IN
MY SOUL

By Sarah Marshall

Visit the Official Website at: Operations-Architect.com

Printed in the United States of America
First Printing: December 2025

Sarah Marshall Publishing
Hardcover ISBN: 979-8-9940197-0-2
Paperback ISBN: 979-8-9940197-1-9
Audiobook ISBN: 979-8-9940197-2-6

This book may be purchased for educational, business or sales promotional use. Special discounts are available on quantity purchases. For more information, please call or write.

DISCLAIMER

This book is a tapestry of memory: true threads, frayed threads, and threads rewoven for clarity, rhythm, and meaning. It is a work of recollection and imagination, shaped by the limitations of memory and the necessities of story.

People, places, conversations, and events have been altered, combined, obscured, or invented outright. All names have been changed. Certain details have been softened or sharpened to protect privacy. Any resemblance to actual individuals, living or dead, or to real events is coincidental and unintended.

What follows is *emotional truth*, not documentary record. Memory is imperfect, perspective is personal, and time distorts all things. This is the author's experience as the author remembers it... filtered through hindsight, interpretation, and the desire to make sense of what once was.

Readers are invited to hold these pages as story, not evidence; as impression, not transcript. The author and publisher make no claims regarding factual accuracy, nor any guarantees or warranties of any kind. They assume no responsibility for any consequences arising from the reading or use of this material.

Acknowledgements and Authors Note

This book began more than twenty years ago with an idea I could convince absolutely no one to take on. Not friends, not writers, not even the very patient people who listened while I waved my arms around describing "a surreal Burning Man story but also not really about Burning Man, and also a coming of age but not exactly, and also maybe a myth." Sensible people ran. The rest smiled politely, the way you do when someone insists they have seen a coyote riding a tricycle on the playa at dawn.

So I had to learn how to write it myself.

To get from that early spark to the pages you are holding, I had to learn to tell stories, build worlds, and revise sentences so many times that some of them have been through existential crises and come out better for it. In the years between, I have been shaped and supported by a truly enormous constellation of teachers, mentors, peers, and readers. There were so many drafts that I could have used them to build a reasonably sturdy shelter in a storm. And through it all, a small army of readers gave their time, their notes, their raised eyebrows, and their encouragement.

I am deeply grateful to the Burning Man event itself, to the organizers, and to the people who make that temporary city rise out of nothing every year. I am especially grateful to the thousands of villagers I have camped with over the years. You built my home in the dust long before I built one on the page. Many of you read early manuscripts. Many of you gave feedback that made the story sharper and truer. Some of you gave me materials that I still cannot identify, but which absolutely inspired entire chapters. All of it mattered.

Among this desert sized village, two people stand above the rest for their unwavering support.

First, Michèle Lamarre. Michèle has read every version of this manuscript. That means she has endured sentences that no longer exist, characters who no longer exist, and at least one entire subplot that I cannot fully explain even now. She gave invaluable critique, encouragement, and clarity at every turn, and she never once told me to give up even when that suggestion might have been quite sensible. She has been the best kind of cheerleader, the one who hands you water, tells you the truth, and keeps you running long past your own doubts.

Second, my daughter, Rebecca Marshall. Rebecca has been a true collaborator in every sense. She inhabited each character, pushed me to keep their arcs honest, and reminded me when someone was doing something they would definitely never do unless I had lost the plot. She saved me from countless wrong turns with gentle insight and the occasional pointed look. The art throughout this novel is entirely hers, and if you love the visuals, you have her to thank. It is not an exaggeration to say that she co developed the narrative and heart of this story. Without her nudging, grounding, and enthusiasm, this book would not exist.

To everyone who walked alongside me during this long, dusty, improbable journey: thank you. You helped me finish the story that began with a wild idea no one else wanted. You helped me earn the ending.

And now I finally get to give it to you.

BLACK ROCK CITY

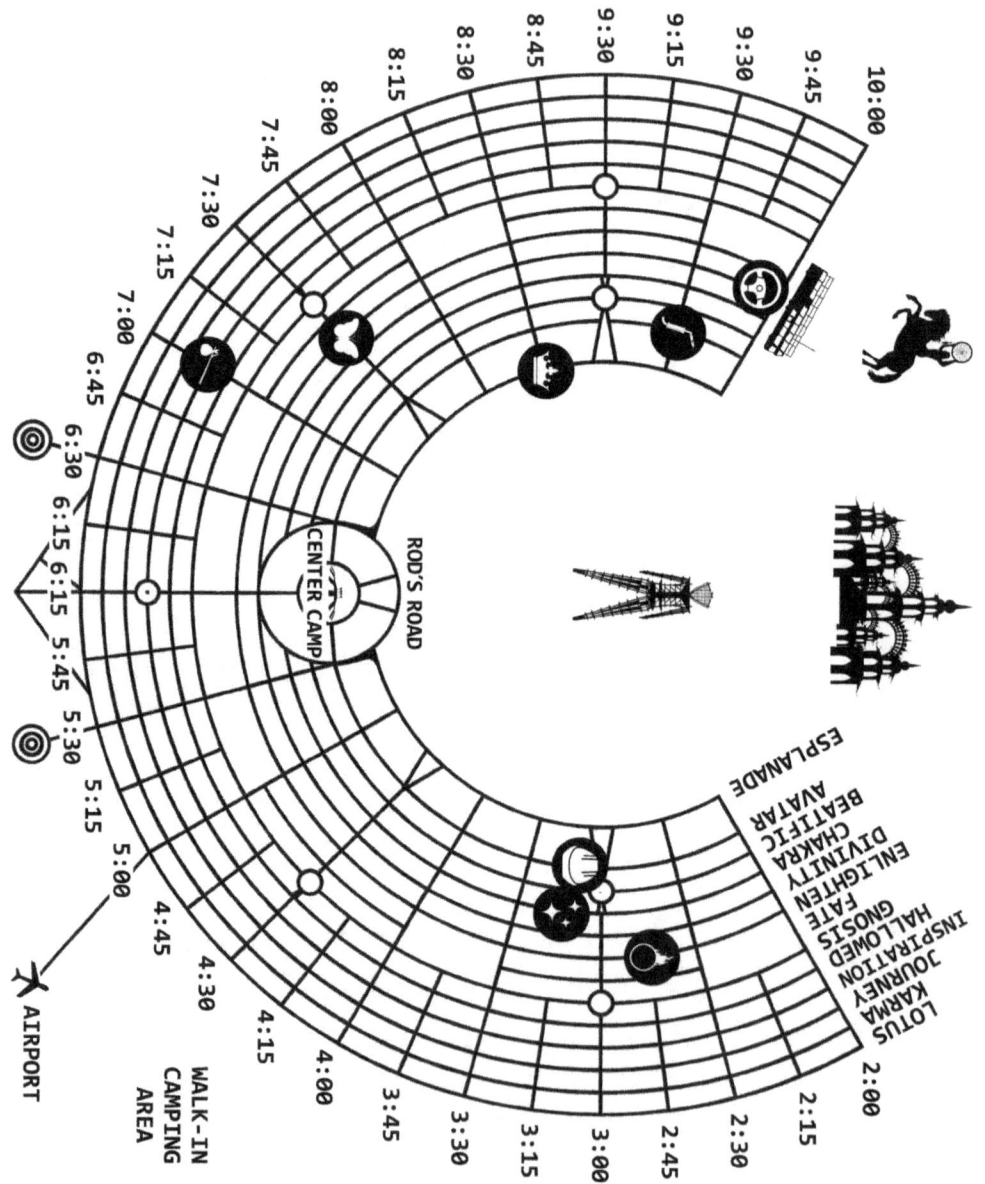

RUBEN

HARLEY

CRAWFORD

EMILE

JUSTINE

RACHAEL

CYPHER

SPARKLEVILLE

THE TEMPLE

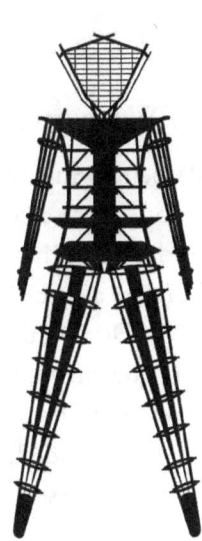

THE MAN

ATARAXIS WARRIOR

CENTER CAMP

MAGRATHEA

28 Spins Until the Man Burns

DPW Ghetto, 3:10 and Avatar, BRC, 4:32 PM - Ruben

Ruben hadn't seen open space like this in years. Beyond a friendly park or an open stretch of road, this was raw and vast and blinding, an ocean of dust under a sun that didn't know how to blink. The desert rolled out in front of him like a dare.

"Drink this, Ruben. And keep drinking," said the driver, passing him a bottle of warm water. Her voice was bone-dry, no-nonsense. "You get careless out here, the playa will chew you up."

He nodded, unscrewed the cap, and took a long swig of the tepid liquid. It tasted like second chances.

The bottle was warm, almost hot against his palm. Four years of drinking what they gave you, when they gave it to you, had trained him not to care. But this? This was different. Nobody was going to count how many times he drank today. Nobody was logging his movements. The thought made his chest tight.

He screwed the cap back on slowly, testing the simple freedom of deciding when to stop.

The truck groaned over a rise in the dirt road, tires spitting up clouds of fine grit. Then, without ceremony, the world fell away. A vast, bone-colored lakebed spread before them, so flat it felt unnatural. On the far side, nothing but distant high desert and baked, granite ridges. On the near side: a crooked clutch of trailers and skeletal structures, half swallowed by heat shimmer.

Ruben squinted. "I don't see much out there."

"That's because you're looking the wrong way," she said, jutting a thumb out the window. "We're headed thataway."

He turned his head. The playa stretched to the ends of the earth, chalky, endless, and absurdly empty. But there, miles away, a scatter of strange shapes broke the nothingness. Too far to identify, too weird to ignore. He raised his eyebrows.

"Yep," she said. "That's home for the next month or more. By the end of it, a whole city will rise up out there. Parties, temples, towers, art cars of unusual size. Then, poof. Gone again. Like it was never here."

Ruben let out a short laugh. "Thud, my friend, I'll take that over my last home any day."

She grinned. "I feel that."

The truck rolled off the road and onto the hard-packed playa. But there was no water, just cracked earth and space and sky. Thud cranked the fan to full blast.

"Windows up. Let's make some time," she said. He complied, rolling up the window with a creaky whine as the truck surged forward, kicking up a wake of almond-colored powder.

"Seriously, drink water all night. And take some ibuprofen before bed. We're at altitude, and this place is bone dry. You'll get your ass handed to you if you don't stay ahead of it. You're now a member of Burning Man's Department of Public Works. DPW for short. If you fuck up, including taking care of yourself, DPWers are merciless."

He could tell this was not a gesture of maternal concern. She wanted to make sure he wouldn't flake, wouldn't fail. She was taking a chance on him, and he knew it.

The old truck glided across the playa like it was skimming glass, dust boiling out from under the truck in an ocher wake. Ruben marveled at how quickly the strange shapes on the horizon came into focus – trailers, tents, a partial wooden structure. The edge of something.

"I'm loving the speed out here," he said.

"Enjoy it while it lasts. When the event starts, it drops to five miles an hour."

The truck pulled up alongside the trailers. Thud hopped out, boots hitting the dust with a signature thud. Ruben followed, less gracefully.

Thud gestured to trailers and crude structures. "Welcome to the DPW ghetto. Our home on the playa."

They made their way to the tailgate. She handed him another bottle of water. "Finish that in the next twenty minutes," she said. "Trust me."

The crew appeared as they unloaded the truck, stepping out from the shadows and shade. One familiar face grinned.

"Ruben. My man!"

"Hey, Lenny," Ruben smiled, embracing him in a dusty back-pounding hug.

Thud gestured to the group with the force of a general. "You know Lenny. That's Squeaker, Bunny Boy, Snag, Stitch, and Shakespeare."

"Fuckin' right," Shakespeare said.

"The name's ironic," Lenny offered.

"I'm getting that," Ruben replied.

"Want a beer?" Bunny Boy asked.

"Nah," Ruben waved him off. "Budweiser let me know four years ago, I hit my lifetime limit. They revoked my license."

Laughter rippled through the group as the message landed. Ruben would not imbibe. They accepted him, at least for the time being.

Thud glanced up at the sun. "It's starting to cool. Get settled. Tomorrow you build. And you'll need to keep up."

She nodded toward a half-built structure. "I thought you lot would have the living room done by now."

"We were pacing ourselves," Bunny Boy smirked. "You'll have your palace by nightfall."

"Good," Thud said. Then she turned to Ruben. "You'll be tempted to help tonight. Fine. But take it easy. The playa breaks people who try to prove something on day one."

Ruben's hand snapped up in an automatic salute, which triggered laughter throughout the crowd.

Thud cleared her throat and scanned the horizon. The sun hung low above the jagged ridge to the west. The heat was fading, replaced by a warm breeze that hinted at the coming night.

Ruben took in the desolate beauty. The bigness of it. The ridiculous promise.

Speaking to no one specifically, Thud declared law. "I want the living room up tonight. We have bigger fish to fry and need it up and operating."

The crew was silent. "I'm happy to jump in and work on it," Ruben volunteered.

"There you go, ignoring me right out of the gate," Thud's jaw jutted out. A slight lopsided grin pulled at the corner of her mouth. "You'll fit right in here."

Chuckles erupted from the crew. Thud clapped Ruben on the shoulder. "Don't fuck up."

Ruben's eyebrows raised. "Consider me warned."

DPW Ghetto, 3:10 and Avatar, BRC, 9:18 PM - Ruben

Ruben pounded the nail in with three swift blows. His swing was confident, strikes precise. He examined the hammer with satisfaction, as if he had encountered a long-lost friend.

"You know your way around construction, eh?" Ruben turned to see Squeaker watching him.

"I've pounded a nail or two," he replied casually.

"Did you do that with Lenny?" Squeaker asked.

Ruben felt the interrogation. It was not subtle. He had a sense that nothing about Squeaker was subtle.

He furrowed his brows, "No. Lenny and I were friends in another life. We were closer to garbage men than construction workers back then."

"Did you just come off a build job?" Squeaker plowed on.

"Not exactly. I've been an indoor pet for the last few years." Ruben changed the subject with a question of his own. "This is a living room?"

The plywood structure around them was the size of a cargo container. It was enclosed on three sides with a door-sized egress opening toward the crew trailers, while one side remained entirely open to the road.

"Sort of," Squeaker replied. "Balcony up top, couches and rugs down here; enough shade to keep us alive. Back wall gets a bench for water jugs. Functional, not pretty."

"Shit. I'll need to find something to put water in," mused Ruben.

Squeaker walked to his tool pouch, pulled out a quart Nalgene bottle, and tossed it to Ruben. "You can have that one. I have another."

Ruben examined it. It was scuffed and dinged but serviceable. "Thanks." Ruben looked at Squeaker and smiled, genuinely appreciative.

"Sure, mystery man. Can't have you die on my watch. Thud would have me on shit duty for the rest of my life. Which reminds me, drink some fucking water."

Squeaker laughed to himself as if he had made a hilarious joke. Ruben set the Nalgene down, grabbed the two-by-four, and swung the hammer hard, each strike an answer in itself. For now, he'd let the work speak louder than his past.

14 Spins Until the Man Burns

DPW Ghetto, 3:10 and Avatar, BRC, 5:22 AM - Ruben

Ruben sat on the edge of the hard, narrow cot in his tank top and boxers, rubbing his face. He looked around the small, spare room. It was little more than a closet, yet the space had become his sanctuary, his quiet country.

His eyes fell to the unopened letter on the nightstand. Flamingo Girl had brought it days ago with the mail. He had shoved it in a drawer, not ready for the weight of whatever it held. Now, the not knowing pressed harder than the fear itself. He tore it open.

At the top, the blue seal of the **Superior Court of California**. His eyes skimmed the stark lines: conviction vacated... exonerated of all charges... unconditional release.

The words blurred, then steadied. He exhaled a breath, one he had not realized he had been holding. Every moment since stepping onto the playa, he had braced for the mistake, for the letter that would drag him back into the cage.

But this was proof. He was free.

A chill ran down his spine. Freedom was one thing. The more complicated question whispered in the back of his mind: *Can I keep it?*

Ataraxis Warrior, 11:00 and Outer Playa, BRC, 7:05 AM - Harley

The diesel engine growled as the early-90s Dodge Power Ram crawled across the cracked playa. Head out the window, Harley scanned the vast dust sheet, shaggy raven hair snapping in the morning breeze. He leaned further, brow furrowed. Then, there. He eased the truck to a stop. The engine coughed, then died.

The creaking door protested as he stepped out, landing with the quiet grace of an aging athlete. His weathered face, carved deep by sun and time, held a grim focus until his boot nudged a faded ribbon nailed into the playa. He exhaled, satisfied.

Ice-blue eyes in a face the color of red clay scanned the horizon. First east, to where the sun edged above the ridge. Then south, a mile and a half away, to the ghostly frame of Black Rock City's first skeletons rising from dust.

He was alone. Just the way he liked it.

The silence pressed against his ears like hands. Not empty, full. Full of space he didn't have to share, air he didn't have to explain himself through. Out here, no one was waiting for him to be someone he used to be. No one was disappointed yet.

He closed his eyes and let the morning heat touch his face.

Then opened them. The work was waiting.

The pickup and camper hunkered behind him like old warhorses. He had maybe two hours before the flatbeds rolled in with the pieces. Time to set camp. Time to work.

Center Camp, BRC, 10:03 AM - Ruben

Two heavily laden flatbeds groaned in the distance, heading out past the man. Their cargo was metallic yet undiscernible. Regardless, it was massive and heavy. Ruben's curiosity was piqued.

He grunted as he hoisted the four-by-four beam off his shoulder onto the ground.

"Jesus, man. What are you, the Energizer Bunny?"

Ruben turned to see a man in khaki pants, which were cut roughly into shorts that ended at awkward angles above his knobby knees. His dirty khaki shirt was buttoned down to his wrists. His face wore the kind of facial hair that demanded attention, but not respect. From his jawline downward, twin curtains of lamb chop sideburns framed his cheeks like shaggy punctuation marks from another era. They clung to his face with the defiant pride of someone who had chosen a style and made it law.

Ruben grinned. "Hey, Beef. What's up?"

"Thud thought Superman might need a sidekick, so I'm reporting for duty," Beef said.

"You know this shit far better than me. Feel free to jump in," Ruben responded.

Beef pulled a four-by-four beam out of the back of the pickup. "I'll see your beam...," he said, hoisting it onto his shoulder, "and stick with the beam." He walked it over to where Ruben's beam lay and dropped his next to it.

"You seem to really like it out here," Beef noted.

"Yeah. This is about the opposite of my last four years. Kind of chaotic. I actually like most of you assholes. Lots of fresh air. And the work is sort of... meditative."

"You sound like one of those burner hippies." Beef quipped as he dropped another four-by-four on the ground.

Ruben smiled. "What, someone who actually comes to Burning Man for the experience?"

"Fuck off. You know what I mean. The sparkle ponies. The ones who show up for the party we built."

The two men continued to unload the truck while chatting. Ruben had taken Beef's measure during the past two weeks. The man's approach to socializing was to bait his targets to provoke a reaction. Talking with him was less of a conversation and more of a jousting match. Ruben's strategy with him was to act like they were having an everyday conversation and not give him the satisfaction of a reaction.

"Are you one of those recovering Silicon Valley tech dudes? Finally free of the office? On a spiritual journey to find your roots?" Beef was being provocative, but his tone conveyed a sense of real curiosity.

Ruben smiled. "Not exactly. But I was isolated from both nature and people for a long time. I am enjoying dealing with the elements and the hard work, despite the marginal company."

"You fuckin' talk in riddles, man." Beef complained. "I feel like I'm talking to a politician."

Ruben dropped the four-by-four he was carrying and straightened up, looking Beef in the eye. The man was clearly frustrated. This was not Beef's typical prickly banter. Suspicion, bordering on paranoia, laced his tone. Ruben's opaqueness was breeding distrust. If Beef was voicing it, others were likely thinking the same thing. Time to lance the boil before it creates a wedge between him and the rest of the crew.

"Three weeks ago, I was in San Quentin serving time for armed robbery. I was exonerated and released without notice. I was way fucked. No place to go and no means to do it. Thud took mercy on me and gave me a job. Now I'm here with you, for my sins. That's the whole fucking story." Ruben turned away from Beef and walked to the truck to retrieve another four-by-four.

"Fuuuuck," oozed out of Beef like a tire deflating.

Ruben took quiet pleasure in the stunned silence that followed. They worked in silence until they finished unloading the truck.

There was a certain quality of stillness out here that was comforting to him. It was like a balm for the years of confinement and unwelcome noise he endured. He gave up that stillness reluctantly to be social with the crew.

He dropped the last timber, his shoulder giving a satisfied pop. From his tool belt, he drew a water bottle, took a long pull, then wiped his brow with a sun-warmed kerchief.

In the distance, the playa shimmered like spilled mercury. A week ago, it had been nothing. Now Center Camp bristled with life — timber skeletons, shade canopies, dust-worn humans crawling like ants over a living machine. The Man's base structure was rising, awkward, unfinished, sprouting wooden columns like stubborn weeds still deciding what they wanted to be.

Half a mile beyond, the Temple was taking shape, hushed even at this distance. But what caught Ruben's eye was farther out: massive steel ribs sliding off a flatbed near the city's edge. Not part of the builds he knew. Not in any plan he'd heard.

He squinted, shading his eyes. "No idea," he murmured, more to himself than to Beef. But his gaze lingered on the distant steel. Something was unfolding out there; raw, unscripted. And for the first time in years, he had the freedom to follow it.

Ataraxis Warrior, 11:00 and Outer Playa, BRC, 11:19 AM - Harley

The semi growled away, dragging an empty flatbed, leaving Harley surrounded by what looked like the scattered organs of a fallen beast. Massive awkward segments.

"Good luck, Harley," the driver had called with a laugh. "You've got all the pieces. Now just put 'em together."

Harley stared at the field of steel and sculpted parts. A small tracked excavator, on caterpillar tracks, squatted near the camper, sun glinting off its arms. Harley's sweat had already soaked through the collar of his shirt.

He muttered, "What the fuck was I thinking?"

The scale of it all hit again; four and a half days to bury the tanks, build the base, and get the stallion's hindquarters raised before the crane showed up. He had turned down help. He wanted solitude, wanted control.

Now, solitude was all he had.

He dragged the first panel toward the placement marker. It scraped with a metallic groan across the hardpack.

As dust curled around his boots, Harley stopped, bent over by the weight of the metal. The silence out here wasn't empty. It pressed on him. The years of anger and absence that had preceded this moment had taken their toll. Now he was more than a little worried that this grand gesture, the peace offering to his past, might be undermined by his own stubborn desire to go it alone.

He straightened slowly, squinting into the sun. No one to help. No one to stop him. Only the Warrior and the work.

Center camp, BRC, 8:04 PM - Ruben

"The days of this being our little wonderland are coming to a close," bemoaned Squeaker.

"What do you mean?" asked Ruben.

The skeleton of Center Camp was rapidly emerging from the playa as if some great hand, wielding a mighty paintbrush, had applied the first, tentative brush strokes to the canvas of painting that would eventually be a masterpiece.

"You know that song by Dire Straits, 'Telegraph Road?' The lead-in lyrics are pretty apt –

A long time ago, came a man on a track

Walking thirty miles with a sack on his back

And he put down his load where he thought it was the best

He made a home in the wilderness."

"That's us. We're the men who made a home in the wilderness. But, while we set the table, this place quickly ceases to be ours when the diners show up. The next part of the song goes:
Then came the churches, then came the schools
Then came the lawyers, came the rules
Then came the trains and the trucks with their loads
And the dirty old track was the Telegraph Road."

"That's the love-and-light-fuckers that are coming for the event." Squeaker spat the last comments out with disgust. "They may fill in the blank spaces of the city. But the cost to us is that this place becomes civilized and ... fuckin' nice."

"In the next several days, the early camp builders are going to show up. Then the game starts to change. I'd rather keep things wild. But, want in one hand and shit in the other."

Ruben chuckled. "That was quite a rant. I think that's the most words I've heard you say since I've been out here. And, kudos on your command of Dire Straits lyrics."

Ruben stared at the rising ribs of Center Camp. He wanted to agree with the romanticism, but the truth was simpler, the chaos still made him uneasy. He liked building, he liked rules, steps, order. That would disappear soon. While Squeaker saw civilization coming, Ruben saw it as letting the hordes of chaos join them. When it did, he didn't know if he could hold up against the chaotic onslaught.

"Didn't you know that Squeaker is our resident DPW philosopher and poet laureate?" They turned to see Thud standing with her fists on her hips, a wry grin spread across her face.

"C'mon dickheads. Early Man waits for no one."

Squeaker let out a "Fuck yeah," and leaped into the back of the pickup.

Ruben opened the passenger door and slid into the truck's cab, as Thud did the same on the other side. She turned the key, and the reluctant engine turned over for several seconds before roaring into a loud idle. She eased up the clutch, but the truck still jerked forward into motion.

"What's Early Man?" Ruben asked.

"Oh shit. No one told you?" She asked incredulously.

"Uh, I guess not," Ruben replied.

"Early Man's our private rebellion. We burn our own man," Thud said, grinning. "A real burn. No stage show. Just us pyros and the dark."

"As opposed to the rest of the nights I've been here?" Ruben gently ribbed her.

Thud laughed. "We do go pretty hard. That's for sure. But tonight is our little celebration before the camp builders start to filter in."

"Fair enough," said Ruben.

"Some folks struggle with the shift once the 'civilians' roll in," Thud said. "But to me, this place is a living production. We build the stage. The artists dress the set. Then the hippies, sparkle ponies, and yahoos show up and turn it into the wildest play you've ever seen. The Man-burn is the grand finale, and after that, we strike the stage. Our part just takes longer than most."

They pulled up to a gathering crowd, coagulating into small knots of DPWers, Man crew, Temple crew, and folks wearing Bmorg badges.

Ruben squinted at one of the badges as they passed. "What's Bmorg?"

"Burning Man Organization," Thud said. "The suits. Well, dusty suits. They sell the tickets, handle the gate, wrangle permits, coordinate rangers, deal with the gendarmes, and handle the stuff that keeps this circus legal."

Beyond them, Early Man stood proud, holding a large coffee cup constructed of a 55-gallon steel oil drum.

Thud threw the truck into park and killed the engine. They all clamored out. Ruben and Thud met in front of the truck. He stayed closely in tow as she circumnavigated clots of dusty, work-grizzled people, many of whom he now recognized. A few he knew by name. Thud's fingers dug into his bicep. "Come on. I want to introduce you to somebody." She grunted in her version of friendly warmth.

He allowed himself to be pulled along with her to a knot of laughing women and men. As they approached the group of DPWers, Thud's callused hand reached out and gently slid across the shoulder of a thin, ropey woman in a leather halter and Utilikilt. Her hair, braided into a long ponytail, appeared brown under the dust. The woman turned to see Thud and lit up with a broad smile.

"Hi, honey!" the slender woman exclaimed, throwing her arms around Thud's sturdy neck, planting a long kiss on her lips. After a prolonged moment, their lips parted, and the new woman withdrew just far enough so that they could stare happily into each other's eyes. Eventually, Thud broke the connection. "I want you to meet someone," she said, turning her head towards Ruben. The woman drew her eyes away from Thud's to meet Ruben's gaze.

"That's Ruben... the new kid I told you about." Thud hooked a thumb toward him.

The new woman's smile widened again as she said, "Hi, Ruben. Welcome." She let go of Thud and moved to embrace him in a warm hug.

"Thanks," he muttered, a bit embarrassed. No one had shown him this much affection in five years. Thud introduced them as they hugged, "Ruben, this is Sunshine. She's the black sheep of the DPW family. All friendly, huggy, and shit. It's annoying, but I've learned to live with it."

Sunshine laughed as she slid back into Thud's arms. "You do more than live with it, my dear. You thrive on it." She said, kissing Thud's neck and ear.

Thud looked at Ruben with a sheepish grin and shrugged her shoulders as if to say, *'What can I do?'* Then followed up with, "Oh yeah... Sunshine is my girlfriend."

Ruben smiled back at Thud. "I... uh... get that." He felt his cheeks flushing and was in real danger of an outbreak of crimson when the drums sounded.

"Early Man is about to deflagrate!" Thud yelled.

Flames were already licking the man's feet from the base. Disjointed hoots, hollers, and whistles filled the air. Then a most wonderful thing occurred. Slowly, the arm with the burn-barrel-sized coffee cup began to rise.

The arm continued its arc upwards. The screams and curses built in anticipation as the cup traveled above Early Man's head. Ruben watched in rapt awe as the flames captured the man's legs. The onlookers around him cheered.

A bear-sized man in a greasy vest and tightly bound durag put a conch shell to his lips and let loose a mournful blast. Early Man burned on. Ruben did not know what could make this moment better. And then it happened. The cup, as it reached the peak of the arch, began to pour its contents onto Early man's head, dousing his wooden head and shoulders with dark liquid.

"That's the blackest coffee I've ever seen," Ruben said out loud to no one in particular. The cup continued to drain as the liquid slathered Early Man's chest and hips. Long rivulets of dark goo slowly worked their way down the legs until, ultimately, they found the flames. The meeting of liquid and fire resulted in an explosive burst of flame, so bright and violent that the onlookers fell back, shading their eyes. A loud whoosh silenced the cheers for a moment. Then, the crowd went wild. The smell of burning petroleum permeated the air. Early Man burnt to the ground in haste.

Cheering and shrieking whistles ushered his rapid demise. Backs were clapped. Knowing smiles of appreciation were passed.

Yet, as the others celebrated, Ruben stood still. The embers held him.

In prison, fire had meant lockdown, meant danger, meant controlled burns in the yard that reminded you the walls could contain even that. But this? This was different. This fire had been an offering, a gift given freely and consumed with joy.

His throat felt tight. He didn't understand why watching something burn could make him feel less broken.

And then, as quickly as the event had started, it was over, leaving in its wake a pile of flickering embers.

"That was a treat," Sunshine declared.

Ruben passed his hand through his short-cropped hair. "I really liked that."

Then he turned to Thud and Sunshine. "I need my beauty sleep, ladies. I'm heading back to the DPW ghetto." Sunshine gave him another long, warm hug. Thud followed up with a brusker, back-clapping version.

Ruben took a long, last look at the Early Man embers, then turned to make his way home, striding past the stalwart fire watches framed in the glow of the dying flames. He felt both exhausted and content; for now.

But even in the warmth of this camaraderie, a seed of unease had begun to sprout inside him.

His sobriety had been scaffolded by routine: prison, then the playa, then build assignments. But now, as the chaos gathered on the horizon, he felt the edges of his sobriety fraying. The city was about to get loud.

With the DPW work ending, he felt chaos coming. And without structure, he wasn't sure he could remain strong.

Despite the coolness of the evening, sweat clung to his neck. The work crews' private burn was over. But the test was just beginning.

11 Spins Until the Man Burns

Center Camp, BRC, 3:15 PM - Ruben

Ruben leaned back against the freshly mounted plywood, its rough edge biting into his sweat-slick shirt, though the desert air dried him faster than he could soak through. Sunshine slumped beside him in the sliver of shade.

"Jesus, it's a hot one," she muttered, handing him her water bottle.

He took a long pull, catching a hint of Southern twang in her voice. "Yeah, I'm not getting much done between shade breaks. We should slow down 'til it cools, then give it hell."

She nodded, ass against the wall, bracing her upper body on her knees. "Not sure I can walk back out into that oven."

Her flushed face said the rest. Assessing her, Ruben said, "Shit. You've got heat exhaustion."

"Maybe," she muttered, dropping her face into her hands.

Ruben grabbed a box from the truck and slid it beneath her legs. "Sit. Drink." He dumped electrolyte packets into her bottle and shook it until frothy. She drank without protest.

"Better," she murmured after a few minutes.

"You're fine. You just need a minute." He handed her a refill, then crouched beside her. "Thud'll kick your ass, but she'll understand."

"She's a marshmallow under that scowl," Sunshine said, grinning into her hands.

With her resting, Ruben took in the shifting city. The playa shimmered like a giant abalone shell, now scattered with half-formed art. He'd spent weeks heads-down on work, but now the city tugged at him with its mysterious promise. He was yearning to explore it in its wild expressions of creativity.

However, one installation in the deep playa kept calling to him. While others had crews, this one – massive, skeletal, magnetic – was being built by a lone figure, mostly at night, under halogen glare. Always alone. Always working through the night.

"How the fuck is he doing it?" Ruben muttered.

"Huh?" Sunshine mumbled.

"Nothing," he said, eyes locked on the far horizon.

He couldn't explain it, but he needed to get closer. Something about that piece, about the man, was starting to get under his skin.

Ataraxis Warrior, 11:00 and Outer Playa, BRC, 9:23 PM - Harley

Things were not on schedule.

The tank was buried crooked. He'd spent half the day clawing it back out of the earth and resetting it. Sweat, dust, and hours wasted colluded to fuel his frustration and anxiety, leaving him half a day behind schedule.

Now, in the long amber exhale of dusk, Harley should have hit his stride. But instead, his limbs felt heavy. The light was going, and his drive with it.

He dropped onto the camper's doorframe, his ass using the floor as a seat, cracked open a ration pack, and spooned food into his mouth with mechanical effort. The water from his container was warm, metallic, and contained errant playa grit.

The ache in his back was nothing compared to the grind in his chest.

He stared at the unfinished framework, the shadows growing longer against steel. The impossibility of the effort confronted him.

The crane will be here in three days. There'd be no do-overs. No extra days. When he had scheduled the crane, they had made clear that his window for use had a hard stop.

No savior coming. He had planned it this way. Chosen it. In retrospect, his carefully devised schedule had no slack to start with. It now became an ever-tightening noose.

But now, alone with dusk, unforgiving hardpack, and deadlines, he could feel the old pressure creeping in, tightening behind his ribs like it used to before the bottle numbed him to his pain.

I'm fucked. The only question is how fucked?

The thought hit hard, jarred him.

And still, no answer. His growing anxiety accompanied an emerging lightheadedness.

Only the silent wind and the unfinished bones of the Warrior stared at him in the halogen glare, with the usual disappointment.

3:00 and Espanade, BRC, 10:47 PM - Ruben

Ruben stood alone at the center of the intersection, staring out into the dark of the open playa. He was not ready for sleep. Nor was he in the mood to socialize. He had been heads down since he arrived, focused on the immediate tasks at hand and on navigating his place with the DPW crew. Now, metaphorically and literally, he was raising his head, looking beyond his narrow world to the galaxy of activities surrounding him.

The inky cloak of moonless night was marred by blotches of harsh light, marking the builds emerging throughout the cityscape. The Man and the temple lights shown brightest, like larger planets in an endless cathedral of stars. However, the lights that drew him, that tickled his deepest curiosity, were the halogen glare on the massive shapeless installation deep in the outer playa.

Over the past few days, his interest had grown into an obsession. Something about it had unbidden flipped a switch in him, woken something in him that had been sleeping over a decade, something not yet defined. But, it harkened to a time of creativity and joy long since forgotten. An image of a small sculpture flashed in his mind, a memory from another lifetime. With it came a deep sense of sadness, regret, and loss.

He needed to, almost as much as taking breath, go out there, reckon with whatever was igniting inside of him. Fear kept him from making that journey at the moment. However, he knew that even fear would not hold back his desire for much longer.

10 Spins Until the Man Burns

Ataraxis Warrior, 11:00 and Outer Playa, BRC, 10:16 PM - Harley

Harley mashed his thumb into the controller button. The winch groaned as it rotated, taking up the cable slack. The top of the hindquarters section shifted and began to rise, making a slow arc to a standing position. Just as it was reaching its apex, he heard a groaning screech. He looked back at the truck. The backend suddenly jerked off the ground. His eyes widened as the hindquarters rocked back and forth, finally settling upright in high tension. It was then that dizziness took him. He felt himself losing consciousness.

He slumped onto the truck's bumper, dizzy and breathless. Even the three steps to his lawn chair felt like a marathon. He dropped into it, his body a sandbag collapsing under its own weight, his breath short, limbs buzzing, vision narrowing to the shape of the chair.

"Harley Longknife, you're a giant asshole." He had taken to talking to himself out here. He took a long pull on his electrolyte-laced water, then pushed himself to standing.

He blinked, staring at the work before him. The five-foot-diameter hooves, positioned to be tacked onto the platform, taunted him. What gave Harley even greater angst was that those hooves were the easy part. Beyond them, the massive equine hindquarters, an intricate layering of stainless steel, bronze, and copper, hung from a set of industrial pulleys extending down from a fifty-foot-tall pyramid frame. The chains holding the section were under high tension, anchored to the truck's undercarriage. The back end of the truck was no longer solidly on the ground.

In this precarious moment, Harley needed his wits about him. There were a hundred ways that he could get maimed or killed standing the section up. And, he was in no condition at the moment. He had pushed himself harder than he should. His careful planning to make this a one-man installation had failed to take into account that he was human.

The knot of anxiety was growing in his belly. Harley prided himself on his go-it-alone approach to life. But, at the moment, he was afraid that he might have bitten off more than he could chew. He kept his anxieties at bay. His rational brain warned him that he would pay for a burst of work now with an even longer convalescence. He let the weariness swallow him, eyes closing before he could fight it.

When he blinked awake forty minutes later, the world was sharper. The hooves were still waiting. The desert felt still — too still, as if waiting for him to move. He took another large swig of the electrolyte mix.

You ever try welding while your bones mutiny? Harley silently mused, shaking out his arm as he reached for his gloves. That's when he heard a throat clear.

He scanned the lighted area. A figure materialized from the darkness into the lighted area from the city side.

"I didn't want to startle you." The man was a stocky fellow with close-cropped hair. Tattoos decorated his arms. He looked tough but not particularly threatening.

"I appreciate that," Harley replied. "I really don't want to be surprised with everything I have going on here." Harley waved vaguely at the perilous setup.

The man took in the hindquarter and the gerryrigged lift. "Goddamn. I'll say."

He smiled at Harley as he approached, thrusting out a hand. "I'm Ruben."

"Harley," he responded as he took the hand and shook it.

"I've been thinking about coming out here for a couple of days. I'm not sure if it's the piece you're putting together or the fact that you're doing it by yourself that was the biggest draw."

Harley chuckled. "Yeah. I think my inclination to work by myself and my ambition just might be at odds with each other."

Harley felt the call of the work to be done. "Look, I'm piss-poor at social niceties and am running behind. I need to get the hind quarters mounted before the crane gets here."

"Can I help you?" Ruben asked.

Harley cocked his head, wrinkling his forehead. "You just wander out on the playa looking for a project?"

Ruben laughed self-consciously. "Uh... no. I'm with the DPW. We have a few more days of work ahead of us, and then we wind down. I wouldn't mind doing some double duty for those days."

Harley continued to scrutinize Ruben, as if staring at him long enough would provide answers. Finally, he blurted out, "Why?"

Ruben blushed, looking embarrassed, as if he had been caught in the act of something. It made this hardened man look like he was eight years old. "I... uh... let's just say that I abandoned art a long time ago and replaced it with stupid. Helping you would make me feel like I'm back in the game, in a way."

Harley blinked for a few seconds, turning Ruben's comment over in his mind. "I understand that more than you know."

His gaze wandered the perimeter to give himself a moment to think. Then, he turned and locked eyes with Ruben. "Here's the deal. I am shit to work with. I'm not what you'd call a conversationalist. I'd rather do things myself than spend time explaining them to someone else. Normally, I would politely beg off, but I'm behind. So if you want to help and you're not a drag on my productivity, I could use a hand."

He let out a breath, then remembered something. "Oh, and I know that you DPWers are hard partiers. You show up here boozed up or high and we're done."

Ruben was grinning ear-to-ear. "You offer quite a bargain. I'm sober – eh, recovering – so that won't be an issue."

Harley's face softened. "Okay then. What are you doing right about now?"

Ruben laughed. "Working on an art installation."

Harley nodded, then jerked his chin at the hooves. "By sunrise, that behemoth needs to stand tall on those feet."

Ruben glanced at the massive form swaying in its chains and gave a slow, reverent nod. "Then let's raise the beast."

Harley grinned; not wide, but real. "Grab the chain guide. You're on."

As they worked through the night, Ruben felt something shift. The rhythm of the work (measure, cut, weld, test, repeat) was familiar, meditative. But more than that, watching Harley move with such fierce intention around this monumental piece awakened something in him. This wasn't just construction. This was devotion. The kind of single-minded commitment Ruben had once poured into his own small sculptures, back before everything went to hell.

He gripped the chain guide tighter, steadying the massive section as Harley welded. In the halogen glare, surrounded by the vastness of the playa, Ruben realized he wasn't just helping raise a sculpture. He was remembering what it felt like to create something that mattered.

09 Spins Until the Man Burns

Ataraxis Warrior, 11:00 and Outer Playa, BRC, 5:03 AM - Harley

Harley finished the tack while Ruben held the piece steady. Staring at the welding tip as the slag cooled, he noticed that, for the first time in days, his hands were not shaking. Pulling up his visor, he looked at the work with satisfaction.

Looking at Ruben, he said, "I'm not comfortable with how comfortable your help has been."

For the first time since he'd landed on the playa, Ataraxis Warrior was ahead of schedule. The top section stood on its pre-built blocks. The base and hindquarters were secure, well on their way to full assembly. Fuel lines and tanks were buried. Harley felt confident they'd have the dream catcher installed and all the plumbing hooked up with time to spare.

"I need to go get ready for my day job," Ruben said, clapping the dust off his gloves. "See you tonight?"

The real question hung in the air: *Did I do good enough to come back?*

Harley nodded. "Thanks to you, we're ready for tomorrow's fuel drop and Saturday's crane lift. If you've got the juice to return, you've got an open invitation." He paused. "You gonna get enough rest?"

Ruben smiled. "I'll get all the rest I need when I'm dead."

Harley chuckled. "You're as stupid as I am."

Ruben turned and started his long walk toward Center Camp. Sunrise was still an hour off, but the ridges to the east glowed faintly. In the distance, the outlines of the Man and the Temple stood tall, well on their way to becoming whole in the days ahead.

He watched Ruben shrink into a silhouette against the lightening sky, then turned back toward the sculpture. His mouth twitched. He was grinning like a damn fool.

Something stirred in him, unfamiliar and persistent – optimism.

"So much for being a stoic red man," he muttered, shaking his head.

He looked at the half-built colossus before him, then to the soft edge of dawn.

For a final time, he looked at the tiny dot that was Ruben, looking forward to the man's return.

Center Camp, BRC, 5:27 AM - Ruben

Ruben let out a huge yawn that ended in a smile. He was good-tired, happy-tired. The long walk in from the Warrior to the staff area behind Center Camp as sunrise broke was a revelation. It gave him a sense of what freedom might feel like.

"Where the fuck are you coming from, dingle rod?"

Ruben looked over his shoulder but already knew who was asking. "Hey, Shakespeare."

He stopped, letting Shakespeare close the distance between them. Once he caught up, the two continued together, joining others in ones and twos, stumbling in a casual migration.

"Looks like a lot of us need coffee," Ruben observed.

"I sure the fuck do," acknowledged Shakespeare. "Thank god for the commissary."

The commissary provided meals for staff, including Bmorg (the abbreviation for the Burning Man Organization), the DPWers, the Man and Temple crews.

The pair drifted in behind a woman that Ruben was pretty sure was a Bmorg computer jockey, catching the open tent flap and ducking into the large hall within. They stepped into line, inhaling the aromas wafting from the service line.

"I didn't realize how hungry I am 'til now," Ruben noted.

"My goddamn stomach hasn't even woken up," Shakespeare responded. "So, where were you? I walked from the ghetto, and you weren't there. You gettin' laid?'

Shakespeare nudged Ruben's ribs, wiggling his eyebrows.

Ruben laughed. "You writing another play, Shakespeare? Leave my story out." Ruben clapped Shakespeare's shoulder.

"Fuck you, man." Shakespeare pouted.

Ruben gave him a lopsided grin. Truth be told, he did not want to admit what he had been doing. Admitting what he was doing felt like he was exposing his soft underbelly.

"Only a few more days and we're free." Lenny grinned wistfully, holding a plate heaped with breakfast in one hand and a steaming coffee cup in the other. Ruben had never been so relieved to be interrupted.

Thud joined them similarly laden. "Gentlemen, and I do use that term in the loosest possible way." They all chuckled. "Come join us. We'll plot the day. I think we can finish up the build by tomorrow night if we work smart."

The pair began to move away, then Thud turned back to them. "Ruben, thanks for taking care of Sunshine. She fucked up."

Ruben shrugged. "She was exuberant and wanted to show off for you."

Thud went somewhere inside. Smiling, she said, "She is my cutie patootie."

"What are you? From the '50s?" Shakespeare asked.

"Hrrumph, a lady needs to maintain some mystery, Poet." With that, Thud spun and clomped away in her work boots, knee-length cargo shorts of vague color, and a dark tank top.

"The lady makes a point," Ruben observed.

"She's a real princess. And, if I said anything different, she'd like to knock me the fuck out," Shakespeare said.

Ruben grabbed his shoulder. "That she would, my friend. That she would."

Ruben loaded his plate, chasing away the afterglow of the Warrior walk. The calm that had filled his chest was slipping, replaced by the dull throb of dread.

Two more days of structure. After that, nothing but noise, neon, and glitter.

He carried his tray toward the others, but his gaze drifted out past the commissary flap; toward the horizon where camps were multiplying.

He was no longer building a sculpture. He was building a shelter for his soul.

Gordian Knot, Esplanade and 8:30, BRC, 10:14 AM - Crawford

Crawford paused in the RV doorway, letting the blast-furnace heat confirm what he already knew: he looked good. The Ray-Bans caught his reflection in the window: the careful curl, the pressed shirt, the posture of a man who'd rehearsed confidence until it became reflex.

He stepped onto the hardpack, boots finding purchase on the dust with the deliberate grace of someone always aware he might be watched.

"Never let them see you sweat," he muttered.

He glided across the playa with a self-possessed saunter, part general, part showman. His sandy curls were flawless, his 'work uniform' pristine. A satisfied smile crept across his face as he surveyed the scene before him.

Jimmy's got the layout flagged already, he thought. *He's a damn fine lieutenant. I know how to pick 'em.*

Two forklifts danced across the site, lifting crates off long flatbeds and easing them into place. A lanky man with a neat ponytail and a fastidious goatee directed the ballet, his gestures efficient, his gaze sharp. Around him, crew members hustled, relocating gear, hammering stakes, laying cable.

Crawford made his way toward him. "Jimmy."

Jimmy turned and nodded. "Crawford. You're up."

The two clasped shoulders – firm, efficient, masculine.

"Got in late last night?" Jimmy asked.

"I was late out of L.A., lost time on the drive. I crashed hard when I saw the RV was already set up." Crawford gestured back toward his rig. "Looks like you rallied the troops."

Jimmy's mouth twitched in acknowledgment. But before he could respond, Crawford's mood snapped.

"What the fuck? What are they doing with the vent piping?"

Jimmy placed a hand lightly on his arm. "Don't go full ass-ripper. They'll fix it."

"They better. A little public shame sharpens focus."

"Or breaks morale," Jimmy muttered, letting his hand fall. "Remember, these aren't employees, they're volunteers."

A voice interrupted. "Jimmy?" They both turned.

Penelope approached, sundress clinging to her curves, eyes shaded beneath a wide-brimmed hat. Her expression was relaxed yet assessing, as if she had already calculated the social dynamics of the scene.

"Penelope," Crawford said, voice like a slow pour of bourbon. He stepped toward her, swept her into a hug, a decisive, practiced, lingering choreography that was just a breath longer than necessary.

"You're here," she said, smiling. "Wasn't sure when you'd land."

"In the flesh," Crawford grinned, gesturing at himself.

She turned back to Jimmy. "I could use a hand with setting up the common area."

Jimmy opened his mouth, but Crawford cut in, "I'd be happy to help you sort it out."

A flicker passed over Penelope's face, reluctance or curiosity, hard to tell.

Jimmy's eyes lingered on her for a moment longer than polite. Then his gaze shifted to Crawford, unreadable and coolly assessing him.

"Thanks, Jimmy," Crawford said, already steering Penelope away. He clocked Jimmy's stillness, the first sign of emotional weather from his usually stoic lieutenant.

Interesting.

As they walked, Penelope looked up at Crawford. "How's it feel seeing your baby come to life out here?"

Crawford tamped down his residual irritation, reshaping it into a brighter mask. "Many's the slip between the cup and the lip, but Jimmy and I'll get them through it. We're going to blow Black Rock City away."

"That sounded suspiciously like something you'd say to your board. Are you always this rehearsed?" she teased.

He gave her his best roguish smile. "Only when it works."

She chuckled, but it wasn't wholehearted. "I think you've built something impressive. The crew's hyped. The maze pics from the pilot looked insane. I'm excited to see it."

Then she chimed in, "You may have a challenger for coolest thing on the playa. Have you seen the Ataraxis Warrior?"

"What's that?" he asked.

"It's a big, metal sculpture being erected in the outer playa. I saw it as we were driving in. It's half up and already looks awesome," she replied.

"Hmm. Nobody's going to out-cool Gordian Knot," he declared.

They stepped into the circle of RVs. Penelope turned slowly, taking it in. "This is literally the inner sanctum."

Crawford smiled. "It's good to be king." His gaze lingered a second too long, enough to make her blush and stiffen.

He pivoted, gesturing toward a pile of tubes and a tarp. "I designed the shade structure as a hexagon. It's stable, secure. It assembles fast on the ground, then we raise it as one piece."

"You engineered the shade?" she asked, genuinely surprised.

"I don't just run the show. I built the stage," he replied, then flashed her a grin. "You, my dear, are lucky enough to be in the best camp on the playa."

She smiled, then glanced back toward Jimmy's silhouette across the compound, thoughtful.

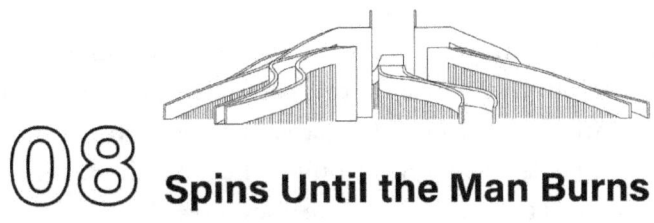

08 Spins Until the Man Burns

Gordian Knot, 8:30 and Esplanade, BRC, 9:34 AM - Crawford

Crawford bit into the watermelon slice, pulling the remainder away while leaning forward to avoid wearing any juice drips. He surveyed the gathering around him. Since they had set up the common area tent within the nest of RVs, the crew had assembled a couple of food prep tables, a camp stove, and a mismatched collection of camp chairs under the protective shade. Crawford was uncomfortable with the motley aesthetic but would generously let it be for the next few days. Build was always a chaotic period.

As far as he could tell, the entire crew had gathered in the area, eating, sipping coffee, and quietly chatting among themselves. Crawford envisioned them busting ass to bring his vision into existence.

I need these people in gear building so I can plan our next moves to be the coolest thing on the playa. The thought made him smile. *It's good to be king*, he thought to himself.

He took a long sip from his electrolyte-laced water bottle and swallowed. "My friends," he announced in his finest stentorian voice, commanding their reluctant attention.

In unison, five of the crew held up blown-up versions of a *Fortune* magazine cover. Crawford's photo stared back, his torso angled to the right, arms folded, wearing a Thomas Pink vertical-striped shirt, the top two buttons unbuttoned, sleeves rolled up his forearms. His face cocked toward the camera with a satisfied smile. The caption read, *Next Digital Media Titan?*

The crew began chanting, "Titan, titan, titan."

He smiled, clearly enjoying the acknowledgment. After a moment, he held up his hands to wave away the chanting. "Alright, alright. You know, we don't bring outside-world business to the playa. We're here in service of Black Rock City's greatest ever camp, the Gordian Knot. Maze to put all mazes to shame."

The crew cheered... mildly. Crawford ignored the restraint.

"We have four days to erect the best maze ever designed, the best Esplanade attraction ever to hit the playa," he said, savoring the weight of his own words. He let the moment build. "Let's finish up here in the next twenty minutes and get at it. If you have questions..."

Jimmy stood up abruptly, cutting him off with a practiced ease that could pass for enthusiasm. "Come see me," he projected over Crawford's last word. His wiry frame practically vibrated with intent.

"You all did amazing work yesterday staging the materials. We're ahead of schedule. That gives us space to work smart."

Jimmy's eyes flicked to Crawford before continuing. "Just a reminder. This is high desert. Over 4,000 feet. If you're from sea level, that's gonna hit different. Hydrate, take breaks. Heat exhaustion sneaks up fast out here. If you don't have electrolytes, I've got extra."

He smiled warmly. "A few more folks are arriving each day. Treat 'em like reinforcements. Keep yourself sharp, and the rest will fall into place."

A weak "Woo" escaped from someone in the crowd, followed by a ripple of chuckles.

Crawford clenched his jaw. Jimmy had undercut him, gently, but deliberately.

If you give people room to breathe, they'll stop running.

Crawford made a mental note to course-correct Jimmy later.

Just now, Penelope's gaze was on him, and it was soft. Adoring. He did not meet it.

Let her wait.

The best way to capture a wild animal is to pretend you haven't seen it. Let it circle closer. Let it need you.

The king will have his princess.

Ataraxis Warrior, 11:00 and Outer Playa, BRC, 11:01 AM - Harley

Harley squinted at the flanges, checking that the stud bolts from the top section lined up cleanly with the holes below. This was the most delicate moment in the build. If they missed alignment, even slightly, it could mean damage, and with no wind to fight them, now was their shot.

He raised a fist and slowly lowered it. The crane operator responded, lowering the top section. As the gap vanished, Harley flashed an open palm to halt the descent.

"Hold tension," he shouted. "I'm tacking the sections before I bolt them."

Thumbs-up from the cab. Harley dropped his visor and struck the arc. The welds were quick, just enough to keep things steady if the wind kicked up. Then he lowered the cherry picker, jumped from the cage, and slipped into the belly of the beast.

Inside, the heat hit like a furnace. He climbed to the joint, grabbed the nut bag and drill, and spun each nut down the bolts. They'd need tightening in passes. Sweat poured. He wiped his brow with a dusty sleeve, then tied a bandana across his forehead.

Christ. I wish Ruben were here.

He paused, blinking in surprise at his own words.

"What the hell?" he muttered. "Next thing I know, I'll be writing poetry about my feelings." He exhaled a dry laugh.

Still... if that bastard's sticking around, maybe I ought to figure out who he is.

Then Harley shrugged, uncomfortable with the idea of leaning on this stranger. He set himself to work to, if nothing else, prove to himself he could still go it alone.

Center Camp, BRC, 11:09 AM - Ruben

"Tighten that bitch down, dude. We're done when you're done, and I very much want to be done." Lenny yelled from below. "Get your head out of the clouds, asshole."

"Technically, my head is through the canopy," Ruben yelled back down to Lenny.

Ruben had paused his work to ease his head through the hole in the middle of the Center Camp shade structure. He felt like a kid at Christmas, needing to take a peek at the presents before he burst. His stolen glance confirmed that the stallion's top section was now in place.

He was crouched high above the cable trusses, head poked through the circular opening at the crown of Center Camp's immense shade structure. A coarse wind tugged at his bandana, already crusted with playa dust. From this vantage point, the city shimmered, albeit muted by dust and a lack of finishing splashes of color. Over the past few days, the bare bones of the city sprouted emergent camps like stubborn green shoots pushing through charred earth, raw and improbable.

Off in the deep playa, the massive stallion sculpture gleamed, its top section newly installed. A half-mirage of steel sinew and coiled rebar, the thing reared up out of the cracked alkali, a stoic warrior gracefully balanced on its back.

"Alright, alright,... I'm getting it done. When am I going to get this view again?" Ruben asked rhetorically.

Lenny answered practically, "Never again if I let go of this ladder.

"Point taken," Ruben replied.

He finished tightening the replacement clamp on the shade cable.

He made quick work of descending the long ladder. Once earthbound, he helped Lenny collapse the ladder and fold it up.

"What were you looking at up there?" Lenny asked, elbow on the steering wheel, squinting through his grime-smeared sunglasses.

Ruben hesitated. His face flushed. Lenny wasn't just another crew dude. He had vouched for Ruben with Thud, bringing him into the fold. They had a shared history that gave the relationship weight. Lenny deserved better than evasive quips and deflection.

"Hmmm... I uh," Was all that that came out.

They climbed into the truck cab. Lenny swung them around, heading toward the DPW ghetto. With streets filling in at five miles an hour, there was time to fill. Lenny broke the silence.

"You're a mystery, man. I've been thinking about Arizona. We had a good time, and even made death cleaning halfway fun. But I don't know shit about you."

"To be fair, I don't think you ever saw me sober back then," Ruben said.

Lenny gave him a look. "Drunk people usually overshare. From what I remember, you just got quieter."

Ruben exhaled. "I thought you preferred to keep things light. Didn't think you cared."

"Well, I do now." Lenny responded.

Ruben ran a hand through his hair. "You're right. I don't like talking about my past. There's a lot in there I'm not proud of. Stuff I left behind for a reason."

Lenny nodded slowly. "You're preaching to the choir. I've fucked up plenty. You're in ... fucked up company."

He chuckled, having amused himself.

"I'm not generally one to share. And, in this case, I am less than interested in providing ammo to the DPW wolves because I'd never hear the end of it."

"Spill it, mother fucker." Lenny was getting impatient.

"Alright, alright." Ruben let out a sigh. " You know that big installation going up way the fuck out in the deep playa?"

"Yeah, that horse's ass?" Lenny asked, smirking.

Ruben's shoulders tensed, but he nodded. "Yeah. That's what I was looking at. I've been helping the artist. I knew the top was going up today."

"No shit," Lenny said, stunned. "So, you've been pulling double shifts?"

"Just the past few days. And I'm not partying like you guys every night," Ruben added, half defensively. "But yeah. I've been sneaking off after our builds."

Lenny turned fully toward him. "Why?"

Ruben stared ahead at the emerging camps along the road.

"I used to be an artist. Like, seriously. Fabrication, small and medium-scale installation. Before Arizona. Before I disappeared into... whatever this became. Helping out there it's like tasting the rainbow again. Even if it's not mine."

Lenny's expression shifted. No jokes. Just the slow realization of something deeper.

"Damn," he said. "You did a good job of keeping that under wraps. I had zero idea that you're an artist."

"'Was' is the operative word. I buried it. That part of me's been layered under so much bullshit, I wasn't sure it still existed."

As they neared the makeshift living room, dilapidated couches, overbuilt scaffolding, with a plastic flamingo nailed to a plywood wall, Ruben broke the silence again.

"You didn't just get me a gig out here. You gave me room to breathe. Space to remember something I thought was gone. I owed you the truth."

Lenny reached out and clapped him on the shoulder. His palm was dry and gritty with playa. "Don't worry, man. Your secret's safe. I won't throw you to the wolves."

Ruben nodded, a weak smile playing at the edge of his lips.

But now that he'd named it, ... *artist...* something stirred inside. Not a memory. A growing, clear, and present hunger. It stretched beneath the dust and ash, that old fire, waiting for oxygen.

And it would not be satisfied with borrowed glory for long.

Magrathea Base Camp, 10:00 and Divinity, BRC, 1:23 PM - Emile

The laden tires crunched along the virgin playa. The bus driver imagined that they were leaving deep grooves in their wake. As he brought the bus to a halt, the crew behind him had their faces plastered to the window, nearly dancing with excitement. They had arrived.

Emile stood up from the driver's seat, stretching. He opened the bus's accordion doors, allowing the hot, dusty desert air to mix into the very human odors that had compounded and soured during the past three grueling days of travel. He slid out of the driver's seat and was first out the door onto the playa. "This is one small step for man..." His Neil Armstrong impression was undermined by his light Eritrean accent. The crew chuckled as they filed out behind him.

"So fucking good to be here, Emile!" He flinched slightly at the sensation of the woman's hand clapping his smooth, muscled shoulder. "And, as much as I love Magrathea, so fucking good to be off the bus. As much as I love our crew, three grueling days in close quarters is plenty, thank you."

Emile looked over his shoulder at the woman behind him. "No truer words have been spoken, Beth."

As the crew stretched and shook out their stiffness, the relief was palpable. An SUV pulled in behind the bus. The SUVers joined the bus crew, equally excited. There was much whooping, dancing about, and hugging.

Emile ran his hand along the side of the bus, admiring the custom mural painted along its expanse.

"Perfect," he said aloud.

He quickly made his way to the belly doors, opened one of the bus's cargo holds, and pulled out a milk crate. Dropping it onto the playa, he stepped up on it. The seventeen crew members coalesced around the makeshift dais.

"We have lots to do over the next few days to get the bus ready, to be the coolest thing on the playa. But remember that you are acclimating. As we unload this afternoon, please drink plenty of water and take breaks when needed. Shimmer, Bart, I'd like you to set up a couple of pop-ups for shade near the SUV as soon as we pull them out. Any questions?"

"We're here but to serve, your imperiousness." Wisecracked one of the men. Emile smiled at the man, belying the cringe he felt in his chest.

"Gabe, could you grab a couple of folks and start unloading the trailer?"

The wisecracking man nodded. "Sure thing." He moved off toward the rear of the bus.

A handsome man stepped out of the crowd toward him, extending an open palm toward Emile. "Come down from your box, my love. Give everyone a moment to shake off the trip." His words were lilted with a light Irish brogue. Emile stepped off the box without taking the extended hand.

"You're always so protective of them, Liam. Are you their mother?" Emile asked.

"More like yours," Liam chuckled. "Keep remembering that only you operate at your level of intensity. The rest of us are mere mortals."

Emile rolled his eyes in a slow orbit, the physical embodiment of the monologue he wisely kept inside. "I need to check the bus to see how it fared. He moved away from Liam, circling the front of the bus on his way around to the far side adjacent to the 10:00 road. Liam followed him.

Emile gazed up at the massive beast of a vehicle. The double-decker bus rose up two levels. On the bus's roof, a custom-built platform extended its height, creating the foundation for a third level. The rear of the bus was nearly sixty feet away. The smooth walls were bisected mid-length by an articulated hinge, making the bendy bus the largest ever made. The rear of the bus was extended, with a storage platform added. Behind the platform was a large enclosed cargo trailer, extending the massive bus by another eighteen feet. It was a sight to behold on the highway.

"Jesus Christ. That is a massive bus." Liam and Emile turned toward the voice. It belonged to a dusty, ropy man, dressed for work in boots, shorts, and a vest. "What kind of bus is this?"

"It's a Neoplan Jumbocruiser, an articulated, double-decked colossus super coach. This one was built in 1976. We call her Magrathea's Final Answer. Magrathea, for short. Catch a ride with us. We're the largest traveling party on the playa."

"I will, my friend, I will." The man continued along the road, shaking his head.

Liam threaded his arm through Emile's elbow. "Ever the promoter."

Emile glanced at him and then back at the bus. "She's perfect. I can't wait to get the railings and stripper pole up on the roof deck. She'll be even bigger."

"Yes, dear. It's your monument. And, since you're perfect, by extension it's perfect too," Liam said, his tone a mix of admiration and sarcasm.

Emile looked at the bus for a moment longer and then smiled. He looked at Liam. Allowing his native Eritrean accent to thicken his practiced English, he said, "Well, you're not wrong."

Liam looked out past the 10:00 road out into the deep playa. "Jesus Christ."

Emile turned his head to see what caused Liam's reaction. His eyes went wide. "Whoa."

In the distance, a large metal rearing stallion and warrior dominated the panorama. Even in its construction phase, it was breathtaking.

"I definitely know one art installation we'll be visiting," Liam declared.

"Definitely," Emile confirmed.

They both chuckled. After a moment of appreciation, they continued along the length of the bus, inspecting it for road wear. They had much work ahead to ready the beast for the greatest moving party that the playa had ever seen.

Gordian Knot, 8:30 and Esplanade, BRC, 8:11 PM - Crawford

"It's really shaping up."

Crawford turned to see Penelope gliding toward him in the dusky, dying light. He flashed a bright smile, feigning delighted surprise.

Facing the gaping, dark maw of the entrance, he said, "I'd love to be further along."

"Are you kidding?" she asked, incredulous. "The external walls are up. Center hub's started. Interior's underway. Lighting kicks off tonight now that it's cooler. You're a taskmaster SOB," she teased.

As if on cue, a halogen lamp flared to life deep in the structure. Jimmy was setting up for night work. Shadows danced as he placed lights to mark the evening's assignments.

"Oh, by the way, you have a new contender in the competition for coolest thing on the playa. The biggest bus I've ever seen drove onto the playa this afternoon. I think it's going to be an art car."

Crawford's eyebrows raised. "Once we have the Gordian Knot up and running, it will outshine art cars and statues alike."

His stomach clenched. "I'm famished. Care to join me for grilled cheese and tomato soup?"

Her eyes lit up. "Gawd, that sounds amazing." Then, hesitating: "But I'd feel guilty leaving while everyone's still working."

"Things are flexible during build. No group meals. People peel off when they need to, as long as they pull their share of the weight. You'll have all night to get stuff done. Come eat something fresh, recharge, then dive back in."

She still looked hesitant, so he continued. "What have you eaten today?"

She looked sheepish. "Granola bars and watered-down Gatorade."

"Real warm food?" He tilted his head toward his RV.

Her resistance melted. "Okay, but let's not take too long."

"Of course not," he said smoothly, leading the way. Over his shoulder: "The Gordian Knot demands attention. We'll be better able to give it to her once we've fed the crew captains."

Inside, they pulled off their shoes at the door. Crawford moved to the kitchenette. Penelope collapsed into the booth, stretching her legs out with a sigh.

"Damn, this feels good. I thought it would be stuffy in here, but it's cool."

"I ran the air conditioner earlier," Crawford said matter-of-factly. The statement was a subtle reminder to Penelope of the luxury she could enjoy with him.

Crawford handed her a tall glass filled with fizzy water, fresh lemonade, electrolytes, ice, and a sprig of mint.

She took a sip, eyes going wide. Then a long gulp. "Oh my god, this is wonderful."

"I call it a Mint Juplaya."

He pulled a quart-sized Ziploc from the freezer and rummaged in the fridge. Glancing back at her, he said, "A friend of mine's an executive chef. Couldn't make it out this year. But he gifted me frozen meals. Tonight's soup is his. The rest is mine."

He sliced dill bread, buttered it with garlic, and laid it on the hot flat iron. Cucumber with lemon pepper. Gruyère stacked thick. Pear slices dusted with gorgonzola. Two small glasses of pinot noir.

On the booth table sat a *Fortune* magazine bearing his photo. "Next Digital Media Titan?" blared the headline. Crawford had set it there earlier. A silent reminder to both of them.

When he placed the meal on the table before her, the effect was immediate. He had artfully plated her sandwich and soup.

"Jesus, this smells amazing," she said, biting into the sandwich with eyes closed. "Tastes even better."

"Simple things feel elevated out here," he said, pleased.

"Jesus, Crawford," she said after her first bite, "this is fit for royalty."

"Of course it is," he said, voice honey-smooth. "You're eating it."

She rolled her eyes, smiling despite herself. They ate in companionable silence, savoring the richness.

Penelope set her fork down. "Crawford, you've been great to me. I appreciate how welcome you've made me feel."

"My pleasure. My little contribution to a playa newbie."

"So... when does your wife arrive?"

He clocked the question instantly. Tone casual, interest sharp. His answer mattered.

"She gets in on Sunday. We'll have a flood of reinforcements by then." He pivoted gently. "We'll need them. The early crew's already logging serious hours."

"Do you miss her?" she asked, softly.

"She's my best friend. Of course I do. But we also give each other space. Time apart's as important as time together."

"Jimmy said you have an open relationship." Her tone stayed curious, but Crawford heard the probe.

"Yeah. We've been exploring that for about a year."

"How's it working?"

"So far, so good. Honest communication is everything. We've agreed: if a sweet connection shows up, we have permission to follow it." His tone was measured, sincere. The statement was both true and a lie. He loved having the freedom to play around. Vicky, on the other hand, had been pressing to return to monogamy. He knew his window, and plausible deniability, was closing.

"What's going on with you and Jimmy?" he asked.

She blinked. "Jimmy? He's just a friend. Nothing more."

Crawford had seen Jimmy's look. He knew better, but he said nothing.

They finished in silence, save the occasional satisfied moan. Crawford gathered the plates.

"Let me clean up," he said.

"Let's clean up together. I'll wash. You dry," she replied.

They stood side by side in the tiny sink area, hands brushing as they worked. When they touched again, there was the briefest pause. Then again, longer this time.

Still touching, Crawford turned. She was staring at their hands.

Let the seduction unfold.

He reached up slowly, fingers grazing the side of her jaw, tilting her face toward him.

No resistance.

Their hands lingered, and the warmth spreading with each contact sent shivers down her spine, and he was aware of her subtle parting of her lips. Time seemed to stand still as they both waited for the other to make the next move.

Then, he leaned in. She closed the distance. Their first kiss was long and intense, tongues probing in discovery. He pressed her to him until he felt her body relax and surrender to him. He kissed her again, this time taking command, pulling her into him.

She let out a small sigh.

He leaned back, suppressing a smile of satisfaction.

Closer... just stay with me.

On cue, she leaned into him. He gathered her to him, almost pulling her off the floor. She stood on her tiptoes leaning against him. He felt her emotional guard evaporate. Sliding an arm around the bottom of her ass, he lifted her effortlessly, feeling the quickening of her heartbeat against his chest as she leaned into him. Every brush of her skin made his pulse race as he carried her toward the bedroom.

Ataraxis Warrior, 11:00 and Outer Playa, BRC, 11:19 PM - Ruben

"You want some coffee?"

Ruben looked up, startled, not by the question itself, but by what it implied. Until now, Harley had spoken only in task-specific barks and nods. No personal talk. No pleasantries. That quiet boundary had been a comfort. Now it was dissolving.

"You want some coffee?" Harley repeated, patiently.

"Yeah," Ruben wiped his hands on his pants. "Thanks."

He walked over to the tailgate kitchen setup. Harley poured a stream of tar-black brew into an enamel mug.

"Want anything in it?"

"Nah. Don't want anything messing with the caffeine." Ruben took a sip. The bitterness hit like a slap. "Jesus. This coffee has an opinion."

Harley chuckled. "You passed. That's the test."

They dropped into the two lawn chairs beside the truck, both facing the massive silhouette of the Warrior in the halogen light.

Ruben let out a slow breath. "This isn't just an art piece, Harley. It's a masterpiece. That you dreamed it up, built it, hauled it here... I'm kind of speechless."

"I obviously overplayed my hand," Harley muttered. "That you're here means I needed help."

"Even with a full crew, this would be incredible. You've gotta feel some pride."

Harley scanned the sculpture, then looked away. "It's not pride. It's penance. A way to live with the mess I've made of things."

Ruben nodded slowly, staring into his mug. "I get that. I'm still sorting through mine. Haven't made it to the forgiveness part yet."

The silence between them was steady, comfortable.

Harley broke it. "You've surprised me. We're ahead of schedule because of you. I'm not used to leaning on people and not regretting it."

Ruben smiled faintly. "Ain't my first rodeo."

"DPW veteran?"

"Nope. First year. First Burn. Actually..." he hesitated, then went on. "I got out of federal prison three weeks ago, exonerated for wrongful conviction. Basically, I've been on the playa since then."

Harley turned slightly, assessing Ruben. "You bitter?"

Ruben kicked at the dust. "Not really. It probably saved my life. I was a wreck when they hauled me in. Being clean and sober now? Might not've happened otherwise."

Harley gave a short nod. "Fair enough."

More quiet.

Then, almost offhandedly, Harley said, "I've spent most of my life rejecting my Indian blood. Didn't want it. Didn't claim it. I even went by my white name, Logan. Ataraxis Warrior is me reclaiming who I am."

Ruben turned toward him, brow raised. "Wait. You're Harley Logan? *The* Harley Logan?"

Harley gave him a sheepish nod.

Ruben's mind reeled. The scale of the sculpture. The welds. The gravity in Harley's posture. It all clicked. "Holy shit. I idolized your work in the '80s."

"Yeah, well... that guy died a nasty death in the '90s," Harley said. "Drugs, booze, self-sabotage. These days I weld fancy security gates for rich assholes. But this," he waved at the Warrior, "This is mine. For my people. For me."

Ruben studied him. "Looks like your comeback."

Harley shook his head. "It's not a comeback. I don't want the old life. I want wholeness. I went back to the Rez last year. I did a sweat. I had a vision. This sculpture... It's part of that."

Ruben frowned. "Wait. 'Sweating'? You mean like... running a marathon?"

Harley chuckled. "No, man. A sweat lodge. It's a spiritual ceremony we do together, purifying the mind and body. That experience changed everything for me. "He paused, voice thickening. "I didn't build it for recognition. I built it to make peace. Doesn't matter if the people like it or not."

Ruben raised his mug. "To making peace."

Harley clinked his gently. No speeches. Just that quiet pact.

A breeze stirred a small dust devil in the halogen glow. The Warrior loomed, silent and steady.

Ruben took a final sip. "I think this is changing me."

Harley stared out into the dark. "Let's hope it's enough for you."

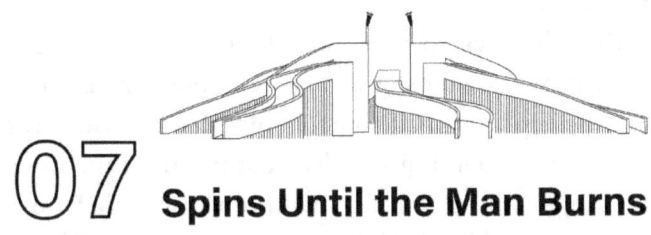

07 **Spins Until the Man Burns**

Ataraxis Warrior, 11:00 and Outer Playa, BRC, 6:20 AM - Harley

Black Rock City offered many awe-inspiring, soul-stirring, and superlative moments. Some of those moments were ushered in loud, brash adornments of cacophonous noise, swirling motion, and lurid color. Other such moments crept in quietly, sublime and delicate as a butterfly's wing. This was one of those latter moments. The desert was entirely still except for the lightest of breezes, which stirred in playful greeting to the dawn. Harley stood, hands in his jacket pockets to ward off the chill, quiet and motionless, watching the crimson blush intensify over the eastern ridge. Night's cloak had gracefully retracted over the last half an hour to expose the playa's bare shoulders.

The rudimentary city slumbered in exhaustion. Harley was happy to have these few moments to himself, enjoying an intensely personal experience. Gone were the anxieties that had attached themselves, lamprey-like, to him since the project's inception. Gone were niggling concerns about life beyond the playa. There was simply him and this moment. Here. Now.

Harley's feet were solidly planted on the hardpack. He felt like a tree that had sprouted from the depths of the playa, bearing witness to the endless possibilities that can grow from this dusty landscape.

The playa insinuated itself into everything and everyone that ventured onto it. Equipment, electronics, and fabric, once exposed to the cement powder-like dust, were forever tainted. No amount of cleaning could remove all of the playa. Pristine condition, after exposure to the playa, meant something different.

The same was true for people. Skin and hair carried a constant layer of dust. Even as a playa denizen stepped from a shower, dust was already coating all parts and places. However, these were merely superficial manifestations. Playa dust was much more insidious. It went far beyond dust in cracks, pores, fabrics, and hair.

Harley thought back to that first playa morning when he first met Claire. He remembered what she said to him about the nature of Burning Man, how it gets deep inside you. She told him that she had playa dust in her soul. He did not understand quite what that meant at the time. Now, two years later, staring at the ridge, his mammoth installation hulking behind him, preparing to enjoy his third burn, he understood completely.

"I have playa dust in my soul," he whispered, just as the sun crowned the ridge, lighting up the city, the sculpture, and the man who was no longer the same.

DPW Ghetto, 3:10 and Avatar, BRC, 9:11 AM - Ruben

The lace snapped mid-pull. Ruben stared at the frayed end, caught between his thumb and forefinger.

"Shit."

He bent, fishing out the slack and tying a neat, tight, improvised square knot. Like everything lately. The kind of fix that would not last, but would get him through today.

Chainsaw wandered in, wearing nothing but sunglasses, pink panties, and a thousand-yard hangover stare. She didn't say a word until she'd chugged half her Nalgene.

"Ruben."

"Chainsaw."

As Ruben finished re-lacing his boot, the young woman topped off her water bottle. She took another long draw from the bottle, then turned toward Ruben.

"Hangover?" he asked.

She nodded, "Fuck your sobriety." Not waiting for a response, she turned and made her exit out of the opening in the back of the living room.

Ruben smiled to himself in her wake. He did not miss that part of drinking. "Knock wood," Ruben said out loud, using his fist to knock on his forehead.

"Cheshire, you ugly bastard. How the fuck are you?" Ruben turned his head toward the gravelly voice to see an upside-down head staring at him. A massive upside-down grin covered the man's face. Bunny Boy was being... Well, Bunny Boy.

"Cheshire?" Ruben asked.

"Yeah, man. You're quiet and smile all the time. You look like the Cheshire Cat. You needed a playa name anyway. Consider yourself named."

"It's that easy? No ceremony? No trial by fire?" Ruben asked.

"Some never get one. Some get one right away. Playa names just come to you. Yours is Cheshire. That's just who you are."

Ruben laughed, but something in him shifted. Cheshire. Quiet. Smiling. Watching. The name fit better than he wanted to admit.

Bunny Boy, grabbing the 2x8 board that marked the edge of the balcony underfloor, flipped over and smoothly dropped himself gracefully to standing on the hardpack at the edge of Avatar. The front end of the living room area was open to the street. He sauntered into the living room and dropped onto the couch perpendicular to Ruben's.

"The ladder is the easy way down from the balcony." Ruben noted.

"Since when did I do anything the easy way?"

"That's incredibly self-aware and accurate," Ruben chuckled.

"Cheshire, eh?" Both men swiveled to see Thud at the edge of the living room. "Bunny Boy, I think you nailed it."

"I do have a way with words." He gloated.

"Do you have a way with work? I have one last job. Then we put a bow on DPW preparations."

"Shit. I'm out, man." Bunny Boy came off the couch as if he had a spring on his ass. "My mom's calling. I have an appointment at Center Camp." He grabbed a day pack and headed out to Avatar, exiting stage left down the street.

"Whatever black magic that is, teach it to me so I can get him to fuck off like that," Ruben said as he watched Bunny Boy scamper down the street.

Thud cackled. "Cheshire, my man, you're running uncharacteristically late."

"Sorry, I was fixing my boot," he said as he stood up. She closed the distance between them stone-faced, coming close enough that he could feel her breath on his chest. She scrutinized his eyes. Then a crooked smile seeped onto her face.

"Well, at least you aren't hungover." She laughed, slapping him on the shoulder. "Come on. We've got a lot to do, and I want to take a pound of flesh before you turn into a pumpkin."

Thud turned and walked to the pickup.

Ruben lingered a beat. His fingers played with the knot on his bootlace, tugging it gently to test its hold.

The Warrior would be finished soon. The event was about to tip from labor into abandonment.

And Ruben? He was not sure who he would be when there was nothing left to build. That thought was terrifying.

Magrathea Base Camp, 10:00 and Divinity, BRC, 10:30 AM - Emile

A steady breeze worked its way across the playa. Most of the time it was gentle, but now and again, it gathered its strength and kicked up a gust that teased the edges of a dust-up. Nothing serious. Just enough to raise a light haze that hovered at knee height, making it harder to spot the gear scattered across the ground. Still, the air was cool, and the light dust cover tempered the sun's burn. It was a good day to be working on the playa.

Emile finished his progress inspection on the street side of the bus. They were on schedule, but he felt the crew was lackadaisical in their approach. Too much camaraderie and not enough focus on making Magrathea perfect. He shook his head. As he turned to walk back to the camp side of the bus, a dark shape caught his eye. The dark horse and warrior sat deep in the outer playa, yet it dominated the landscape.

He had brought all of his architectural talents to bear in designing Magrathea's 'wow factor'. He had designed it to be the most noticeable thing in Black Rock City – moving, loud, and eye-catching. Yet that inert hunk of metal silently gave Magrathea a run for its money in an elegant sweep of twisted metals. He stared at it with a mix of admiration and envy.

Finally, he looked away, inspired to make Magrathea even more perfect. Time was flying by. They had much to do and little time to get it done. He navigated around the back of the bus, letting his eyes wander up the levels of the bus until they reached Magrathea's top.

A tall, neatly groomed man with a lean Nordic frame stepped to the edge of the bus's roof platform. Lifting his arms like a Shakespearean spirit, he declared, "Magrathea is no longer a hauling van. But she is not yet the party bus she will become. Conversion season is upon us."

With theatrical grace, he slid a railing post into its sleeve on the roof deck.

From below, Liam shaded his eyes with one hand and called up, "Oh, Django, master of the roof. By day's end, our street-legal machine will be a full-on art car."

Django chuckled.

Dobbs emerged from the trailer with a massive bass speaker balanced on one shoulder. His towering frame made it look like a lunchbox. His voice rumbled. "So we just spent eight months building an art car conversion kit. Think there's a market for that?"

"Dobbs, my friend," came Beth's voice, low, amused, commanding, "do not sully our burn contribution with commodification."

Dobbs grinned, "Sure, Beth. Did not mean to corrupt the purity of our jalopy."

"It is DJ Bedlam out here," she corrected, with mock menace.

He bowed and tipped an imaginary hat. "M'lady."

The crew was in high spirits. Too high, Emile thought, as he stepped up into the bus. He crossed the open floor and dropped onto the bench seat Liam had just dusted off.

"They are too chatty," he muttered. "They need to focus. There is too much at stake here. We're debuting her tomorrow night. She has to be ready."

Liam appeared at his side almost instantly, crouching and taking Emile's head in both hands. "Darlin'. Let them be. They know what needs doing. Right now, we are just moving the big rocks. There will be time to fine-tune Magrathea once she is on her feet."

"They are too casual. If they just did it right the first time, there would be nothing to fix."

Liam's eyes crinkled with both affection and exasperation. "You are a god among the anal retentive, my love. But these mortals need breathing room. Give them that."

He kissed Emile on the forehead and stood. "Now go find yourself a project before you start micromanaging people into therapy."

Emile let out a long sigh. "Fucking fine."

He crossed the dance floor and bounded up the spiral staircase two steps at a time. As he ascended, he allowed himself a flicker of satisfaction. The extension to the stairwell had been a seamless addition, just as he had envisioned.

Up on the roof, Django had finished locking in the final section of railing.

"Django, my man. Want to help me mount the side panels and set up the LCDs?" Emile asked as he reached the top.

Django froze. His face was composed, but Emile caught the faint tension in his jaw.

"Uh... sure. Give me a minute." Django stepped toward the edge of the roof and peered over.

Below, Dobbs and DJ Bedlam were working on the speaker mounts. Dobbs caught Django's eye and shrugged with exaggerated flair. DJ Bedlam snorted. Django turned back around, resigned to his fate.

He joined Emile, hands already moving toward the tool bag.

Emile nodded, already plotting the alignment of brackets in his head. Around him, the crew hummed with effort and chatter, a rising tide of motion and noise. He could feel the rhythm building, even if no one else seemed to notice it yet. By nightfall, Magrathea would begin to resemble the monument he envisioned.

And maybe, if the crew held it together, it would be perfect.

Gordian Knot, 8:30 and Esplanade, BRC, 1:30 PM - Crawford

Crawford surveyed the bustling activity two stories below, a critical eye on his rapidly emerging kingdom. Time was slipping by too quickly. He was committed to a Sunday night opening so that the Gordian Knot would already be established as the go-to attraction as the bulk of the burners arrived during the early days of the week. He needed to inspire the troops with extreme prejudice to redouble efforts.

He felt thumping vibrations under his boots, signaling that someone had dropped off the ladder onto the bridge that crossed from the outer radius of the maze to his current perch at the center of it. Crawford turned to see a short, muscular man in a pressed shirt and khaki pants making his way carefully along the bridge. To Crawford's chagrin, the man's shirt looked quite similar to the one he wore for the cover photo. He waved at the approaching man. "Hey,` Ganesh. Did you just arrive?"

"Yeah, man. I wanted to check on my investment." Ganesh winked as he stepped off the bridge to join Crawford on the platform.

They moved to the railing where Crawford had been overseeing the action below. "This is where your investment went." Crawford gestured at the partially built maze below.

"What is this, a guard tower?" Ganesh asked.

"We call it the hub. The two floors below act as access points between the four sections of the maze. If the maze wanderers don't find the shortcuts between sections, they end up going the long way, which brings them back to a different hub portal than the one they entered. To complicate things, we can rotate the inner rooms of the hub, so even if they figure out one path from section to section, we can change it up. It's pleasantly sadistic." The two men chuckled.

"We call this top part the crow's nest. It's only accessible via that ladder and bridge you just used. Only those of us in camp have access to it. Not so much a guard tower as a lifeguard tower. From here, we can see if anyone is in trouble in the main parts of the maze." He clapped Ganesh on the shoulder. "We tried to think of everything."

Ganesh leaned on the rail. "All of that effort down there is moving to Jimmy's choreography," he observed. "He's playing the same role here as he does for the company. Thank goodness we have him. We need him."

Crawford tightened but said nothing. Jimmy was his creation, just as the maze was. He was the visionary. Jimmy was just an executor.

"Look, I need to go check on a couple of the special experience sections. They're a little tricky to put together and require guidance. You're welcome to stay up here. I recommend you change before you join the working crews."

"What?!" Ganesh exclaimed in mock indignation. "I have to invest my manual labor, too."

Crawford, halfway along the bridge, turned and shrugged his shoulders, his open palms facing upwards. "It's part of the new cruelty, my friend. Time for me to rub shoulders with the teeming masses."

He climbed down the ladder and made his way to the hard wall that separated the maze sections. Crawford had to search for the panel with the recessed latch. When at last he found the panel, he jammed his hand into a waist-level grooved hollow in the frame, tripped the latch with his index finger, and slid the door open. He stepped through muttering with satisfaction, "If it was that hard to find now, it will be impossible for the uninitiated once we are up and running."

Lost in thought, Crawford collided with the ladder, catching it with both hands to keep it from toppling. Above him, a surprised Jimmy jolted, reaching to steady himself, but the sudden shift caused the drape guide in his hand to slip free. It spiraled downward, grazing Crawford's shoulder with a metallic scrape before clattering to the ground. Crawford grunted, stumbling back and clutching his arm.

Jimmy scrambled down the ladder, wide-eyed with concern, until he realized it was Crawford. Then his face became a mask. Jimmy, on a good day, took the Asian stereotype of inscrutability to a new level. As he stared at Crawford now, Jimmy's face was blank. Crawford was bent over, cursing and clutching his shoulder.

After a moment, Jimmy asked without enthusiasm, "You okay?

Crawford swore under his breath, inspecting the tear in his sleeve and the shallow scratch beneath.

"Let me see." Jimmy stepped close to Crawford and pulled away the torn fabric to examine the wound. An inch-long scratch decorated the top of Crawford's arm. The scratch oozed a light, seeping bleed. "I think you'll live." Jimmy turned back toward the ladder.

"My shirt's ruined," Crawford snapped. "And I'm bleeding."

Jimmy leaned in and peeled back the torn fabric. "Hm. Flesh wound. You'll survive." He turned back toward the ladder.

"Wait," Crawford rasped. "What the hell's going on with you? We haven't talked in days. You've been low-key undermining me in meetings. Don't pretend you don't know what I'm talking about."

Jimmy side-eyed Crawford for a moment, then turned toward him. Jimmy paused. He picked up the drape guide, turned it in his hand, then removed his glasses and began cleaning them with unusual calm.

Crawford stood frozen. His reflex was to attack. Yet, he recognized the moment for what it was, something rare enough from Jimmy to demand stillness.

After a quiet beat, Jimmy slipped his glasses back on. His voice, when it came, was even. So quiet that Crawford had to lean in. "You know, Crawford, I've tolerated a lot over the years. Your compulsion to introduce yourself via résumé. The way you repackage my ideas with just enough polish to call them your own. Your belief that praise is a zero-sum game, you always deserve to win. You're more well-behaved when your ass is fully kissed. So I always let you get full credit, just to limit your tantrums."

Crawford opened his mouth, but Jimmy raised a finger, signaling he was not finished.

"I let it slide. Because you're good at what I hate, navigating egos and wrangling money. We made it work. I let you have the spotlight, you let me do the work uninterrupted. That was the balance."

Jimmy took a step closer.

"But no amount of adulation is enough for you. And you started believing the applause meant you could do anything to anyone. That charm is a currency that never depreciates." He paused, gazing flat. "You always saw people as chess pieces. I am tired of...no, that's not right. I'm done with being moved."

Crawford stood rigid. Jimmy's voice dropped a register.

"You bulldozed Vicky into an open relationship, something you dressed up as freedom, but was just another way to have your cake and eat it too. And Penelope? You knew I cared for her. But of course, that made her a more interesting challenge."

Jimmy sighed, almost pitying. "You thought so little of me and our relationship that you never even checked in with me. That's the part I can't ignore anymore. Not the taking, but how naturally you erase everyone else in the process."

He paused, letting the silence settle between them.

"You know, for someone so obsessed with being seen, you're blind to the people holding you up. You talk about vision, but you never look. Not really."

He held Crawford's gaze now, steady and unsparing.

"I've watched you make people feel disposable. Brilliant people. Loyal people. You use admiration like oxygen, but you forget who breathes life into the room when you're not on stage."

Jimmy's voice was quiet but steady. "There's a difference between being admired and being trusted. You chased the first so hard, you never learned how to earn the second."

Crawford could not help himself. "I only borrowed Penelope, man. I wasn't planning on keeping her."

Jimmy stared at him in a long silence that stretched.

His reply was quiet with finality: "I'll finish this build, run the maze, tear it down. For the camp and the crew that worked so hard to create it. Not for you." Jimmy slipped the guide into his toolbelt. "When we're back in L.A., I'll tender my resignation. You might want to start building a new narrative. The one where you did it all alone."

Crawford was off-balance, not a place that he was used to being in. "You can't do that, Jimmy. We're at a delicate point with the company. Everything is on the line."

A grim smile emerged on Jimmy's face. "Oh, but I can, Crawford. I very much can."

He walked back to the ladder and climbed steadily, not waiting for a response.

BRC Airport, BRC, 3:16 PM - Justine

"We're almost home," the pilot's tinny voice crackled through the headsets.

The young woman in the passenger seat squinted at the bright beige landscape unfolding beneath them. The world below broke abruptly from desert scrub into a flat, stark, unbroken expanse. It looked like a grand, otherworldly canvas stitched between two jagged mountain spines and stretching endlessly toward the horizon. The Black Rock Range to the west rose in fractured defiance – ash-gray ridgelines and dark volcanic scars – while the Jackson Mountains shimmered to the east in dusty layers of rust and bone, catching the sun like worn copper.

Ahead in the dead center of the bone-white plain lay the city. The smudge that she had seen moments ago was resolving into lines and structures. From this height, as they closed on the burgeoning mass of Black Rock City, the lines partitioned into a radial grid scratched into the playa. Tents, structures, and vehicles dotted the shape like some stubborn petri dish culture taking hold.

"Let's take a city tour before we land," the pilot said, angling the plane west toward the far side of the city. Justine reflexively braced herself with one hand and clutched her pendant with the other.

The pendant's delicate elegance stood out against her dusty gear: a silver pillow shaped like a bisected heart, divided by a soft S-curve rather than a sharp line. Its beveled surface rose gently to a center peak, forming a heart-shaped yang. Set in the center was a brilliant blue stone that glimmered like a captured piece of sky: the yin within the yang.

It had been a gift from her mother. The woman had given it to her without a word, and when Justine asked about it, her mother simply said, "It was given to me in another life. It fits you better now."

"Justine, since this is your first time out here, you're getting a very special treat," the pilot said, turning to smile. She returned a wan smile, but her grip on the armrest gave her away.

"The Esplanade is filling in nicely," said a voice she thought belonged to Garrett.

Justine raised an eyebrow at the unfamiliar word, she grasped its meaning once she turned toward the inner ring. She watched it thicken with settlements, camps blooming along the curved street like desert flowers claiming their territory.

Below them, the city's grid revealed itself more clearly, doughnut-shaped with the northernmost quadrant missing. As Garrett had said, the inner streets were already thickening with settlements, with some open pockets scattered among the shapes. The further out the rings stretched, the thinner the population became.

"The whole city'll be filled by Monday," Garrett said.

"Wow," Justine muttered. "That's damn organized for a giant desert party."

"Yes and no," he replied. "BMorg builds the skeleton. The magic? That's what the camps bring. That's what *we* bring."

"What do you mean? Isn't that just... where people camp?"

"Yes and no. All the 'placed' camps, those inner-city ones, got that real estate for offering something to the rest of the citizens," Wendy explained. "Art, food, music, lectures, shade. That's the gift economy. That's the magic."

Jim dipped the starboard wing, offering a better view; and spiking Justine's anxiety. Her stomach flipped as the horizon tilted.

"This place grows like slime mold," said Elise, another passenger. "Give it two days. It'll double in density."

"There's Center Camp," Jim said, pointing to a huge circular shade structure at the doughnut's heart. "Behind that are trailers for BMorg staff."

"There's the Man." A tall structure stood at the center of the city's doughnut hole, teeming with ant-sized workers swarming its base.

Jim banked again. "Up ahead's the temple."

Another crowd of those same tiny people scurried over its skeletal frame, cherry pickers reaching skyward like robotic limbs.

"Look at the size of that fucking bus at 10:00," Justin heard Garrett exclaim. Parked along the final street, before that open playa, was an accordion bus that was so long that it covered most of a block. She had never seen a bus that size.

Then, just as they reached the northern arc, Justine gasped.

A massive steel sculpture rose from the dust, hoisted by a crane: a man astride a rearing horse, arms flung overhead, holding something high in his grasp. It was impossibly detailed, breathtaking in scale, at least a hundred and fifty feet tall.

"Holy shit."

"Right?" Garrett's mic clicked on. "That sculpture's incredible."

Whatever else I do this week I'm spending time at that sculpture, and maybe that bus too. Justine had just had her first positive thought about the time she would spend at Burning Man since she had agreed to attend the event.

As the plane circled back toward the landing strip, the pilot snapped back into business mode. He exchanged clipped radio commands with ground control, pointed his nose into a gentle headwind, and landed with almost theatrical smoothness.

Justine finally exhaled.

"I ain't gonna lie, Captain Morgan," she said. "I was white-knuckling it. Never been in a private plane before. But you made it fun."

The plane rolled into its parking spot beside six other aircraft, all tethered like patient horses to pad eyes on the tarmac. Between the polished landing and the crisp tour, Justine found herself almost impressed. Maybe the chaos she'd feared wasn't as bad as she thought.

Jim helped them unload bags. The passengers, already animated, walked toward the airport gate, buzzing. They hugged. Exchanged contacts.

"Thank you, Jim," Justine said. "And nice to meet you all." She meant it.

Jim gave her a wink. "If you want another ride later this week, stop by Sparkleville."

"I might take you up on that."

By now, the rest of the group was flashing credentials to enter the city. Justine followed suit, sliding her ticket across the counter to a platinum-blond woman whose tattoos danced down both arms in inky spirals.

"You've got to have your work pass," the woman said flatly.

"Work pass?" Justine blinked.

"You need one to enter before the official gate opening. No pass, no entry." Her tone could've qualified for a desk job at the DMV.

"Oh wow. So I flew into the middle of the desert just to be turned away at the door. Delightful."

"Technically," the woman said, "you're not even supposed to be here. You can't enter Black Rock City until midnight."

"Really?" Justine arched an eyebrow. "The glittering gates of bureaucracy don't open early for charm and optimism?"

"Yep. Really." The woman didn't even blink.

Justine tried again, sweetening her sarcasm. "Isn't that just a touch arbitrary? Not like I can pop over to the nearest Starbucks."

"First burn?" the woman asked.

Justine sighed. "Yeah. My first."

The woman's expression softened a half-shade. "Okay, then I'll withhold my irritation. Listen, BMorg pays BLM based on pre-event headcount. If we fudge the numbers, they get fined. So no. You gotta wait. Bench is over there."

Justine glanced at the bleached-out plank in the sun. "Fantastic." She gathered her things with the air of a silent-film heroine wronged by fate and trudged over to her assigned exile.

"Hey, need a ride?" Jim called from the passenger seat of a dust-covered sedan.

She looked up. The others were squeezing in.

"Apparently, I'm too punctual for Burning Man," she said. "Sentenced to bench jail. Parole pending paperwork."

"That sucks," Jim said. "Catch a ride later this week. I'm doing city tours."

"I'll book one between dust storms and existential crises." She smiled, gave him a wave, and watched the car dissolve into the shimmering emptiness.

The sun beat down, deliberate, unrelenting. She rummaged through her pack, pulled out a tube of sunscreen, and covered every exposed inch. She found a linen scarf, wetted it with precious sips from her half-empty water bottle, and draped it over her short-cropped hair before sliding her hat into place.

She sat on the bench and folded her arms. Studied the planes. The fence. The peeling wood. The silence.

Her watch read 4:31 PM. It was going to be a long wait.

The bench radiated heat through her jeans. She shifted. The new spot was just as hot. She shifted back. A fly landed on her arm. She watched it clean its front legs with the focused deliberation of someone with absolutely nothing else to do.

"How the hell are you alive out here where nothing grows?" she asked to fly. Rather than respond to her the fly launched off of her arm and disappeared into the vast nothingness.

To keep herself busy, she studied the map. The three-quarter doughnut from the air, now labeled with streets and landmarks. Clock-face grid, alphabetical rings. Her camp: 2:45 and Enlighten. When midnight came and she was finally allowed in, it would be a hike.

She folded the map and stuffed it into the back pocket of her pack. Then pulled out the event guide, but her eyes skimmed without seeing. She was too road-weary, too heat-wilted to absorb it. With a sigh, she dropped it back into her bag and retrieved her water bottle. One measured sip. No more. The rest was for later.

The heat pressed in. She slathered another layer of sunscreen onto her neck and arms, then dampened the linen scarf with what little water she could spare, draping it over her shoulders and the crown of her head. Her hat followed, pulled low.

At last, she slumped back onto the bench, arms folded tight across her chest. She scanned the planes, the fence line, the skeletal office trailer. Even the grain of the bench held her attention for a moment. Nothing moved.

She tilted her head back, hat brim shading her face, and tried to find shapes in the scattered clouds. A rabbit. Maybe. Or a deformed shoe. Her mind was already going soft from the heat and boredom.

She checked her watch. 4:48 PM. *Fuck.*

She tilted her head back against the bench, pulled her hat down lower, and closed her eyes—willing the sun to pass faster and unconsciousness to come like shade.

7:30 and Enlighten, BRC, 5:26 PM - Rachael

The lumbering moving truck ahead slowly lurched off the provisional road onto the virgin hardpack, swaying back and forth as it slowed to a crawl. The woman driving the lagging car followed suit, contemplating, not for the first or last time, making a U-turn and heading home. The truck navigated between scattered tents and a few ambiguous structures, slowly coming to a halt, leaving a fifty-foot gap between the vehicles. The doors of the moving truck cab swung open in unison, signaling to the woman that they had arrived. She let out a long, slow breath that became a guttural sigh. She punctuated the end of the sigh with a whispered, "Fuck. I do not think I belong here."

Pushing her door open, she hoisted herself out of the car, standing on stiff legs, one hand braced against the door frame as her boots hit the playa with a distinct crunch. She looked down, kneading her toes. Her feet, uncomfortable in the unforgiving leather, were emblematic of her general discomfort with everything here.

The truck driver bounded toward her, beaming, his wrestler build buzzing with excitement. "Welcome home, Rachael." He crushed her in a happy embrace.

She forced a smile and returned the hug as she surveyed the litter of tents, structures, and the occasional lethargic camper. She felt the sweat on the man's back and released him, grasping his shoulders. "I don't think I've ever seen you this happy, Nathan."

He stepped back, gesturing expansively with one arm. "This is my happy place."

She again surveyed the Spartan scene before her, a brow raised skeptically. "I'm happy to not be driving."

He laughed. "You'll come around." The sound of the truck's roller door raising interrupted the exchange. Rachael looked over to see a crowd gathering at the back of the truck. Nathan smiled. "When you bring the supply truck, you're very popular. Let's get the truck unloaded and sort out our camping spots. Once we're set up, I'll take you for a wander."

"What's the schedule for the camp?" Rachael asked, expecting to be gainfully employed.

Nathan smiled at her. "You don't really have one. You're free to play all week."

Rachael furrowed her brows. "Really? I don't have any camp responsibilities?"

"Well, our main contribution is Jiffy Lube." Nathan gestured at a large, ranging army tent, looking as if it were stolen from a M.A.S.H. unit, on the corner of the lot. "It's a kind of giant gloryhole for the boys. Shifts are covered by the bear camp. So you have no responsibilities."

She suddenly felt at sea. A week to frolic with no responsibilities, that sounded like her version of hell.

"I'm used to people inviting me to places for the utility I bring," she said to Nathan, consternation lacing her tone.

Nathan put a sympathetic hand on her shoulder. "I invited you just because I like you. I just want you to enjoy this place I love so much."

"I question your discernment," she replied.

Nathan laughed. "Your job this week is to enjoy yourself."

"That sounds horribly non-productive. I don't really do anything non-productive," she mused.

"Think of this week as a necessary system reboot for you. Black Rock City is your oyster. Make the best of it."

"I'll see what I can do," she said skeptically. "Frolicking is a foreign concept to me."

Freetime represented too much time to think for her. *Responsibility is my refuge.* She thought to herself. She said nothing more to Nathan.

Rachael took another look around the barren, alien landscape. "Shelter would be good." She muttered, more to herself than Nathan. Sweat dripped into her eye, stinging intensely. "Fuck it's hot."

Nathan turned back to her. "Put on a hat and hydrate like a motherfucker." He pulled a water bottle off his belt and reached out to her.

"I'm good." She said, turning, she leaned through her open car door to extract a store-purchased water bottle. She took a long pull from the bottle, emptying half the contents.

"The faster we unload and set up, the faster we can explore." Excitement permeated Nathan's voice.

"Let's do it." Rachael's false bravado attempted to mask her ambivalence.

BRC Airport, BRC, 6:22 PM - Justine

Justine was sore and cranky from loitering. She'd been camped on the bench beside the airport gate, her last barrier to Black Rock City, for hours.

Her meager travel supplies were long gone, her water had been polished off, and her nerves were dulled by heat and monotony. On a very thin positive note, the sun had finally begun its slow descent toward the western ridge, taking the edge off the heat.

She consoled herself that she would eventually be able to perform almost every day this coming week and make her way out to that amazing sculpture. However, her emergent happiness was foiled by her current situation. She still had nearly a quarter of a day left in airport jail.

At shift change, the blonde woman from earlier passed by on her way to the DPW car that had brought her relief. She tossed her bag into the back seat, then leaned in, rummaging. A moment later, she returned with two large bottles of water in her hand.

She walked straight over to Justine. "You running low?"

"I'm out," Justine said, her voice dry in more ways than one.

"Take these," the woman said, handing her the bottles without fanfare.

Justine accepted them, blinking. "Thank you."

"I'm Sparrowhawk," the woman added, almost as an afterthought. "You've only got a couple more hours. Then you're in."

She didn't wait for a response. Just turned, climbed into the car, and drove away down the long straight access road..

Justine watched the dust swirl where the car had been, clutching the cool weight of the bottles. She had been simmering in the belief that her bench incarceration was a sign that Burning Man was rejecting her. However, that small act of kindness began to chip away at her well-developed wall of cynicism.

7:30 and Esplanade, BRC, 8:21 PM - Rachael

The group reached the inner edge of the city, backlit by the dying reds and oranges of the setting sun. Nathan led the way with a furtive energy, scanning the playa like a kid let loose in a toy store. Rachael lagged a few steps behind the cluster of men, who chatted cheerfully as they surveyed the wide open space.

"What was that installation about here last year?" one of them, Todd, she thought, asked.

Nathan looked back, stepping off the road onto the unmarked hardpack. "Poseidon's Folly."

"Yeah, I loved that one," Todd said, his eyes fixed on some memory.

All three men were shirtless, chiseled and glowing in the low light. To their right, the city swept out in a long arc, encampments clumped and scattered, wide gaps between. Ahead, the playa stretched open and spare. Half a mile off, a dark, spindly structure loomed, swarmed by tiny figures and glaring construction floods.

"That's the Man," Nathan said, suddenly beside Rachael. "He'll be our landmark until we burn him Saturday."

Rachael took it in, then turned, scanning the expanse, city curve, endless hardpack, the distant, jagged mountains. She whispered, mostly to herself, "I'm already overwhelmed."

"It's a lot," Nathan said. "Take it at your own speed."

She gave him a lopsided smile. "I don't know if my wiring is made for this."

Nathan laid a gentle hand on her shoulder. "We all felt that way the first time."

Something in his voice grounded her. It helped. "In Nathan I trust," she said quietly.

He grinned. "Let's reconnoiter."

They veered across the playa, cutting close to the Esplanade. Rachael stayed in the rear. With darkness settling in, the vastness became even more mysterious. There was little around, but the flat terrain made for easy walking. The heat had broken, and the chill evening air wrapped her skin like a balm.

She noticed her breath was shallower than expected. "It's so flat you forget we're at elevation," she said aloud.

"Takes a few days to acclimate," the man she recalled as Cyril said. "Hydrate."

She realized she hadn't brought water. Noted it. Fixable.

After a while, Nathan pointed right. "Let's check that out."

A low-slung structure, bottom-lit with soft, ground-level glow. As they neared, it resolved into a narrow wooden bridge spanning a glowing light stream. Nathan climbed up first, the others trailing.

Rachael followed, looking down. Below the bridge: a video display mimicking a swim lane. A lone swimmer looped silently, perfectly formed. It was eerie. Calming. A mirage of fluidity in this desert.

"If only we had a pool out here," Nathan muttered.

"Project for next year," Cyril said. Laughter.

Rachael paused at the crest of the bridge. She admired the tech and design, which were elegant, simple, and durable. A contradiction to the raw surroundings.

Todd pointed. "Let's go over there."

She turned to the flashing light in the distance. Silhouettes. Movement. Curiosity stirred in her chest.

They approached. The flashing resolved into a large open ring surrounded by figures. As they drew near, Rachael's perspective warped. Arms, heads, torsos appeared to rise out of the playa itself, swimming in place.

"What the fuck?" she muttered.

Closer still, she crouched instinctively. From the new angle, the mystery clicked into place: paper-mâché figures mounted on a giant spinning disk, each frozen in a moment of the freestyle stroke. The strobe made them move. Swim.

"It's a zoetrope," she breathed.

Cyril nodded. "Simple. Low-tech. Perfect."

"Seems like swimming is a theme," Rachael said.

Nathan grinned. "Tonight's theme. Tomorrow's a new story."

A quick thrum of anxiety pulsed through her. She exhaled a drawn-out, sarcastic, "Cool."

"Let's dip into the city," Nathan suggested.

They headed toward the Esplanade. Camps glowed faintly with setup activity. Rachael shivered. The air had cooled fast.

"Trampoline," someone called.

Across an empty lot, a trampoline sat unattended. Boots came off. The guys scrambled on. Rachael hesitated, then followed.

They bounced and laughed. Rachael joined, giggling mid-air, feeling the bounce lift something heavier than her body.

After ten minutes, they collapsed, breathless and grinning.

"Jesus, I'm out of shape," she wheezed.

"Elevation," Nathan said.

"Right." A beat. "So much for revisiting childhood."

They lay there a while, then laced boots in shared silence.

"What the hell is that big thing out there?" Todd pointed toward a dark shape in the outer playa, framed by the halogen glare of work lights.

Cyril moved up next to him. "I read about that one. I think that it's called Ataraxis Warrior. It's a stallion rearing with a native warrior on its back. Made of different metals."

"We'll have to make a trip out there when they're done working on it." Nathan declared.

"There are two other things that I read about, that I can't wait to see," Todd said. "Some camp is building a giant maze on the Esplanade, and there is a giant bus art car, traveling rave. I can't remember what they are called, but both should be easy to find."

Rachael remained quiet. Seeking out the novelties in this weird hellscape seemed frivolous.

"Enough recon for night one," Nathan said.

"Agreed," Rachael said. This time, the relief in her voice felt earned. "I have to admit, this place is insane. It's like landing on another planet. Everything's off-kilter."

"That's typical. It takes time to integrate. You'll grow to love it."

Rachael's brows furrowed. "We'll see."

She realized that she was thirsty. *I should have brought water with me. I can't afford to be stupid.*

They set off down the Esplanade, the city flickering to life around them. Rachael looked out again into the unknown. "We'll see," she repeated, but this time quieter. And not entirely unhopeful.

Ataraxis Warrior, 1:00 and Outer Playa, BRC, 10:16PM - Harley

"Okay, go."

Harley heard Ruben's voice, muffled and metallic, echoing from deep inside the sculpture's gut. A beat later, a low mechanical whir answered. He toggled a sequence into the control panel.

The Warrior stirred.

One of the massive forelegs lurched upward, clawing toward the stars. Hydraulic joints hissed, settling, then reset as Harley punched in the next sequence. The opposite leg rose and curled in a fluid mirror of the first.

"We're looking good here. Come on out," Harley called, shielding his eyes against the low halogen spill.

Above him, the sound of boots clanking against steel moved closer, echoing through the sculpture's interior ribs. Then two legs dropped through the portal between the stallion's hindquarters and dangled for a moment, comically awkward, before the rest of Ruben followed, sliding out and dropping onto the scaffolding.

Harley grinned. "So that's how you DPWers are born. Straight out of a horse's ass."

Ruben adjusted his pants and shirt, brushing dust from his sleeves. "No argument there," he said with a tired smile, climbing down to stand beside Harley.

They turned together to face the Warrior.

The sculpture loomed, still and enormous, a silhouette against the moon-dusted playa. Inert for now, but barely. Alien-blue halogen lights skimmed the curves of steel: sinew, flank, spine. Even in the dark, the musculature rippled with intentionality. The wild flare of the stallion's nostrils. The powerful tension in the warrior's thighs. Shadows danced across the contours of hammered copper, brushed aluminum, bone-white steel.

By day, the piece would be a monument of static, sculpted elegance. But now, in the breathless desert night, it promised something more: fury, fire, transformation.

Harley tilted his chin toward the panel. "The parts all work separately. Now we just need to bring them together. You want to bring it to life?"

Ruben blinked. "Seriously? Me?"

"You've earned it."

Harley nodded toward the control podium, a welded plinth like a sacrificial altar, and Ruben stepped up.

"Punch in one-seven-zero-pound," Harley said.

Ruben keyed in the sequence. A low growl trembled through the frame as the Warrior reared back. The stallion's front hooves slashed at the empty sky. The warrior's upper body counterbalanced, leaning forward with the grace of a dancer.

Ruben took an unconscious step back. "Whoa," he breathed.

Harley chuckled. "Oh, we're not done."

He flipped the first of three switches. The eyes of both the stallion and the warrior sparked to life — and then, from each face, fiery tears began to slide down. Slow, molten rivulets that fell into the stainless steel catch-pond below, hissing as they extinguished on contact.

Harley flipped the second switch.

A diamond pattern of vertical tubes embedded in the pond fired off with synchronized sparks. Thin flares shot up in waves, lighting the underbelly of the Warrior like an inferno stage show.

"And now..." Harley's eyes gleamed, "...for the pièce de résistance."

He flipped the final switch.

A guttural roar ripped from the stallion's throat as a massive tongue of fire exploded from its mouth. The flare blasted 150 feet into the night sky, a searing arc of white-hot breath.

Cheers erupted in the distance. Whistles. Screams. Applause rising from the scattered edges of Black Rock City. The playa had noticed.

"Jesus Christ," Ruben whispered. His mouth hung open as he stared.

Harley allowed himself a satisfied smile. "I think we've made our point."

He toggled the system off. One by one, the components powered down. Flames guttered. Sparks fizzled. The catch-pond settled into stillness.

Harley stepped back from the panel. "Tonight was the dress rehearsal. Tomorrow we premiere. I'll show you how to run the sequences. You'll be the conductor."

Ruben gave him a slow shake of the head, half in disbelief. "You're a hell of a showman."

Harley shrugged. "Gotta earn my keep somehow."

He motioned to the chairs by the truck. "Let's have some coffee while she cools down. I want to check the nozzles after. Oh, by the way, now that we have the Warrior up and running I'm moving my shit over to my base camp at 9:30 and Avatar. If you can't find me here, I'll probably be there."

They sat side by side, faces lit by the warm afterglow of metal and ember, cups steaming in their hands.

Ruben was quiet for a long time. Then: "Harley, whatever you have or haven't done in your life... I think this makes up for a lot."

Harley stared at his boots. "I appreciate that. But I don't agree."

He sipped, swallowed, and let the cup rest on his thigh.

"This," he waved toward the Warrior, "is a gesture. That's all. A way to embrace my roots; the good, the brutal, all of it. But it doesn't make up for absence."

Ruben turned to him, puzzled. Harley's face was still.

"I quit on everyone who ever loved me," Harley said flatly. "I left my father and the Reservation with no goodbye. Didn't speak to him for thirty years. I didn't leave my wife and daughter, but I disappeared anyway. Into a bottle. Into silence. I became every cliché I hated."

He looked up at the Warrior again.

"Last night I told you that I don't care what people think about this piece. But that's not strictly true. There are three people whose opinion matters; the three Cs in my life: Clarence, my dad, Cyan, my daughter, and Claire, a woman in my life who is both the hardest and softest person I know. I've kept them all in the penalty box. Now I need to let them out."

His voice cracked, but he kept going.

"This piece won't fix that. But maybe it's a start. If I can reconcile with who I've been... maybe I can give something back. Maybe I can be someone worthy of the love and support that I have."

Silence settled between them.

Ruben reached out and laid a hand on Harley's shoulder. No words. Just heat and contact.

Harley let out a long, uneven breath. Rubbed his eyes. The steel in his posture slackened.

Ruben didn't speak. He stared at the Warrior, motionless now, but still radiant with potential.

A part of him had started to see Harley as something solid. A man with time under his belt, his shit together. A mentor. Now he saw it clearly. Harley was still in the middle of the journey. Still lost, still rebuilding.

It hit Ruben like a gut punch. The road ahead was not something you ever finished. It just kept going.

The thought overwhelmed him. So much damage. So much to repair.

He took a breath, grounding himself in the moment.

I just need to stay upright through the next fire cycle, he thought. *One more breath. One more bolt tightened. One more morning.*

The Warrior glinted in the darkness, as if waiting.

BRC Airport, BRC, 11:58 PM - Justine

In the hours since she'd talked to Sparrowhawk, Justine had drained one of the large bottles and worked her way through most of the second. Now, her watch read midnight straight up. She blew out a breath and stared into the dark expanse of the city.

The road from the airport vanished into that darkness long before it reached anything that resembled a structure. From her daytime recon, she knew the airport road was a half-mile straight shot to Karma—the outermost ring of Black Rock City.

A long walk. In the dark. Schlepping sucked. But, schlepping would take her into the city, to her camp, to a week of performing and exploring.

She'd have to stick to the roads to avoid getting lost. The idea of wandering through an unfamiliar desert in the middle of the night made her skin crawl. But the alternative, sleeping the night on that scorched bench, was unthinkable.

Sighing, Justine shouldered her bags, gripped her oversized valise, and pushed through the gate. She stepped onto the road, resigned to an hour's walk through silence and sand.

About two hundred yards in, she spotted a slow-moving truck turning onto the airport road. Its headlights cut through the darkness, flooding the path ahead, and her.

A chill shot up her spine.

She glanced around desperately. No one. Nothing within a hundred and fifty yards. No shelter. No cover. If whoever was in that truck meant her harm, there'd be no flight. Only fight.

The truck slowed as it neared her. Then it rolled to a stop beside her, engine idling.

She squinted through the glare.

There, on the driver's side door, the Burning Man logo. She looked up into the cab.

Sparrowhawk was grinning down at her.

"Welcome wagon. Need a lift, sassy bitch?"

Justine let out a huge sigh of relief. "Oh Jesus, thank you. I'll manage my sass."

Sparrowhawk laughed. "You paid your dues. Now it's time to come on in."

Justine slung her bags into the bed of the truck, circled around, and climbed into the battered passenger seat.

"Slam the shit outta that door," Sparrowhawk said. "It doesn't like to latch."

Justine gave it a hard yank. It clicked.

"Where to?"

"Uh, 2:45 and Enlighten," Justine said.

"As you wish, m'lady."

Sparrowhawk turned the truck around in the airport lot and eased it forward, the headlights casting long beams into the dark ahead, slowly driving Justine to her camp, and what her campmates arguably called home.

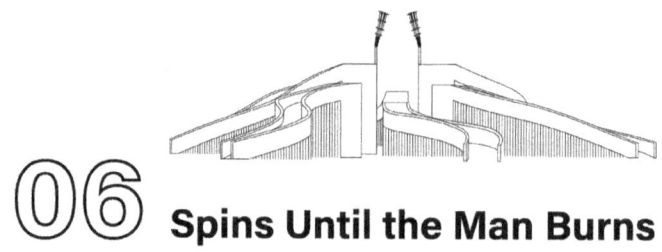

06 Spins Until the Man Burns

Gordian Knot, 8:30 and Esplanade, BRC, 8:12 AM - Crawford

Crawford studied the sheet lying on the dining nook table before him titled, 'FINAL DRAFT FOR APPROVAL'. The body read:

FOR IMMEDIATE RELEASE
Contact:
Investor Relations
press@nexmuse.com
+1 (818) 555-1903

NexMuse, Inc. Debuts on NASDAQ Under Ticker Symbol "ZYNQ"

Burbank, CA – [Insert Date], 2007 – NexMuse, Inc., a pioneering force in digital media personalization and immersive content discovery, announced today the pricing of its initial public offering of 55 million shares of Class A common stock at $18.00 per share.

Shares begin trading today on the NASDAQ Global Select Market under the symbol **"ZYNQ."** The company has granted underwriters a 30-day option to purchase up to 8.25 million additional shares.

Crawford Thorne, NexMuse CEO and co-founder, remarked:

"We built NexMuse to spark curiosity, elevate creativity, and reinvent how people interact with content. Going public accelerates our mission to build the most intelligent, intuitive media platform on the planet."

Jimmy Lau, NexMuse CTO and co-founder, added:

"From our first prototype to our global architecture, NexMuse was designed to evolve with our users. Today's IPO marks the next chapter in scaling our technology and impact."

The offering is led by Goldman Sachs & Co. LLC, Morgan Stanley, and Allen & Company LLC as joint book-runners. Baird, Needham & Company, and William Blair serve as co-managers.

Founded in 2002, NexMuse connects over 150 million monthly users with digital experiences. Its patented adaptive media engine powers dynamic storytelling for audiences worldwide.

For the official prospectus and further investor information, please visit investors.nexmuse.com or email ir@nexmuse.com.

Ganesh was quiet next to him, patiently waiting for Crawford to finish working through it.

Crawford took his time, making sure every jot and tittle was correct. He looked up, giving Ganesh a cursory nod. "Looks good. Ship it."

Ganesh clapped his back. "It will be champagne time when you and Jimmy get back to L.A. my friend."

Crawford smiled unconvincingly, clapping Ganesh's back in turn. "You're only returning a few days before us. Just enough time to put the champagne on ice."

"Okay, I'm going to grab some breakfast before I start my slave labor shift." Ganesh winked. He slid his shoes on and opened the RV door to a bright sunny morning.

Crawford stared at the door long after Ganesh shut it.

"Jimmy, Jimmy, Jimmy... you need to calm your shit," he said to the silence. Half of him would not accept that Jimmy would fuck up this IPO. Too much invested for too long. Half of him was terrified by a side of Jimmy he had never before experienced. He needed to develop a strategy over the next few days for reigning Jimmy in and bringing him to his senses.

Then there was the matter of these spoilers he had heard about. They must be shown up no matter how hard he had to drive the crew to deliver. After spending time perusing the 'Who, What, When, Where Guide', he had identified them. The art piece was the Ataraxis Warrior and the big bus would debut as Magrathea's Final Answer. Hearing crew members speculating about them in the dining area, had left him prickly and irritated.

He ran his fingers through his hair, considering various approaches, when he heard a firm knock at the door.

"It's open," he yelled. "Did you forget something Ganesh?"

The door cracked open and Penelope stepped up the stairs onto the landing, firm, shapely and bare shouldered.

"Hey," he smiled genuinely. "I was just thinking about you."

Irritation clouded her face. "You borrowed me?"

"What?" he said, feigning innocence.

"That's what you said to Jimmy yesterday. You borrowed me." She declared it quietly, yet emphasizing each word in a way that might as well have been a shout.

"I'm not sure what nonsense Jimmy is giving you..."

She cut him off, "I heard you say it. I heard the whole exchange. Not only that, Jimmy told me that Vicky made it clear to you that she wanted your open relationship closed."

"She and I were going to discuss taking it off the table when she arrived," he countered.

She arched her eyebrows. "Are you planning to die on that hill?"

She shook her head slowly looking at the floor. Then she looked up at him. "Your borrowing privileges have been revoked." She turned, opening the door as she descended the stairs and swung the door shut without looking back. The door shut with a thump. She did not slam it, but the thump sounded final, without drama.

He sighed. He would have to broaden his Jimmy strategy to finesse Penelope as well.

2:45 and Enlighten, BRC, 9:34 AM - Justine

Justine woke in a sauna of her own making. Her snug, one-person tent had turned into a sweatbox, and her limbs felt poached. She kicked herself free from the twisted remnants of her sleeping bag, the air so thick it was like trying to breathe through a wool blanket.

Pushing to her hands and knees, she fumbled at the tent zipper. It jammed. She cursed under her breath, wrestled with it, and after several excruciating minutes the teeth finally relented. The zipper screamed in protest as it slid open, the flap falling away to reveal a wash of cooler air.

She inhaled sharply, relief hitting her lungs like a gasp of freedom. Scooting forward, she parked herself in the narrow slice of shade beneath the awning and laced her shoes with groggy determination. Stepping outside, she blinked at the sun, already asserting its dominance, and turned to glare at the tent that had slow-roasted her like a foil-wrapped potato.

She grabbed her water bottle, took a swig, and turned in a slow circle trying to get her bearings. A few cars were parked at irregular angles nearby, their shadows warped in the morning light. Tents of every shape and absurd color huddled next to the vehicles, many cloaked in camouflage netting. Beyond them, a portable carport stood like an oasis, populated with camp chairs and a card table.

There sat Susan, her boyfriend Max, and their friend Zig.

Justine rubbed her eyes with the heels of her hands and willed her feet forward, each step reluctant, her body greasy and sour with sleep and sweat.

Susan spotted her and lit up. "Well, well, look who's among the living! Someone made it through the night."

Justine offered a lopsided smirk. Susan popped out of her chair and gave her a quick hug, the kind that said *you smell awful but I still love you.* Justine returned hugs from Zig and Max with the enthusiasm of a damp rag.

Susan handed over her thermos with exaggerated flourish. "Here you go, girl. Wake up and smell the playa. Notes of dust, regret, and barely functioning infrastructure."

"We'll get some shade over your tent," Max said. "And cut down on the solar oven effect."

"That would be amazing," Justine muttered. "Because waking up basted in my own sweat was a spiritual experience I didn't ask for."

"Why'd you get in so late?" Zig asked. "Thought your flight landed mid-afternoon?"

"It did," she sighed. "But apparently, if you don't have a work pass, the desert becomes a velvet rope situation. I had to wait until midnight to be allowed into the city, like some dust-covered Cinderella."

Zig winced. "Shit. Right. Forgot about the work pass rule. Didn't think your alternative means of transport would land you in early-bird purgatory."

"Yeah, well," she said, dry as talc, "lesson learned. Bureaucracy doesn't stop for sparkle."

She took a sip from the thermos and handed it back, then cracked open her water bottle like it was a precious treasure. After a long drink, she scanned the street: little pockets of chaos blooming into structure as camps emerged from the playa canvas. Beyond them, the endless expanse of playa shimmered. A small dust devil pirouetted into view and vanished in a puff.

The breeze lifted the sweat from her skin. The world remained broken, hot, and absurd, but at least she no longer felt like death by microwave. She slumped into a chair and stretched out her legs with a groan.

"This place is such a weird mix," she muttered. "Half government logistics, half post-apocalyptic circus."

Zig laughed. "Magic happens at the nexus, baby."

Justine raised an eyebrow. "Yeah, well, I'd trade a little magic for a nap and a pleasant microclimate."

Susan waved her off like a Broadway diva dismissing bad press. "Oh hush. It'll look totally different to you tomorrow. You just got here. Breathe a little before you spiral."

Justine nodded, unconvinced but willing to fake it. "Fine. Consider me acclimating. Slowly. With sarcasm." She glanced upward. "Lovely morning though. If you're into light dehydration and airborne grit."

They lifted their drinks, whatever vessels were within reach, in a toast to the new day. Dust, sweat, sarcasm, and all.

"Oh, I saw a huge installation during our fly over that I definitely want to see up close," Justine declared.

"Ataraxis Warrior," her campmates said in unison. Then Susan followed up. "It's the talk of the town, so to speak. It's not just a pretty face. It shoots fire."

Justine let out a slow breath. *Maybe I just need to get my feet on the ground here. Get acclimated. Rough start, but it could even out.*

For the first time since landing, Justine reluctantly let the smallest smile settle on her face.

Sparkleville, 3:15 and Chakra, BRC, 11:21 AM - Rachael

Rachael leaned to the right and veered smoothly around a knot of people congregating in the intersection, noting the cross street as Beatific. Almost there. She leaned slightly to her left. The bicycle obeyed her subtle direction veering back to the left. She smiled. She was pretty sure that this was the first time she had smiled since she parked her car on the playa.

Acclimation was not coming easily. She was quickly adapting to the elevation and harsh environment, as was typical for her. Less easy was for her to be untethered in the raucous environment, without responsibility, leaving her with a sense of being ungrounded. She would have preferred to labor away in the gay boy camp, on something that had no charge for her. As much as she yearned for responsibility, the thought of having to engage others and secure responsibility was repellent. For the moment she would just enjoy riding her bike.

Her petty joy was short-lived. She had arrived. She knew she was in the right place because of the cluster of Vanagons parked away from the cross-streets. Directly in front of her was a primitive camp frontage that left much to be desired. A portable carport provided limited shade. A tarp covered the ground beneath it. Centered under the carport roof was a kiddie wading pool. As she rolled up to the structure she swung her right leg over the handlebar and onto the pedal next to her left foot. She stepped her left foot off of the bike pedal into a walking step bringing the bike into a halt in front of the carport.

"Fancy dismount." Rachael turned to see a lanky straw haired woman strolling toward her.

"Riding my bike, after all these years, is well, like... riding a bike." Rachael retorted with a wry smile.

"Where the fuck is your car, bitch?" The woman wrapped Rachael in her arms and hugged her.

Rachael tensed reflexively then relaxed. "You fucking huggers." She mumbled into the woman's neck, then drew back and grasped the woman's upper arms. "I'm not camping here, Elise."

"Fucking why not?" Elise's face registered genuine confusion. "Bea said you were bringing the kitchen."

"That's what she wanted me to do. I never committed to it." Rachael tried to attenuate the defensiveness in her voice. "I'm camping with my friend Nathan over at 7:30 and E."

"Nathan, the political aide?" asked Elise.

"That's the one," Rachael said.

"What's their camp?" Elise asked.

"Uh, hard to tell. It's three hundred gay boys in a big open space. Jiffy Lube is on the corner." Rachael responded.

"No shit. Are you going to get some gay boy sex tent action?" Elise was amused.

"Nah. I'm just camping in the gayborhood. Sex tenting is not my style." Rachael felt embarrassed.

"Well fuck. You still have to spend time with us here." Elise insisted.

Rachael smiled. "Ipso facto here I am."

Elise wrapped an arm around Rachael's waist. "Let me show you around."

Rachael splayed her hands, gesturing toward the primitive structure. "Sparkleville?"

Elise laughed. "Naked and shiny as god intended. You'll have to come get glittered."

"Can't wait." Sarcasm dripped off of Rachael's response.

"Cmon." Elise tugged at Rachael's hip. Rachael reluctantly stepped forward with her.

The two women walked past the carport, deeper into the camp, approaching the skeleton of a partially erected geodesic dome. The bottom section was complete. Next to it, a lanky man in khaki shorts and a maroon sleeveless shirt squatted, assembling the next level section, a wrench in one hand while squeezing three struts into a connector with the other hand. The women watched as he bolted the assembly together. Once fastened, the man let the assembly drop to the ground standing to get more parts.

"KangaRay." Rachael said. The man looked toward the women.

"Rachael." he said casually as if she had been there all morning. He closed the distance between them and hugged her. She felt his sweaty back. She'd usually pull away right away, but she was uncomfortably aware of her own poor hygiene. "Did you just get here?" he asked.

"I arrived yesterday afternoon. Just made my way over here." Rachael responded.

"Oh, I thought you were camping with us." KangaRay looked puzzled.

"I think Bea was trying to make that happen by force of will. I'm over in the gayborhood." Rachael said.

"Oh, okay." he said, looking at the partially built dome.

"You're clearly in the middle of things. We'll leave you to it." Rachael said, noting his distraction.

The two women moved on, heading toward the cluster of Vanagons. "That was pretty social for KangaRay," noted Rachael.

Elise laughed. "He really opens up out here." Both women chuckled as they approached the Vanagon cluster.

The Vanagons were parked in a rough arc, and rugs were laid in front of them, as if they were suites off of a common living room. Several haphazardly placed pop-up canopies provided living room shade in 10'x10' squares. The canopy shadows stretched away from the noonday sun. The Vanagon in the center of the cluster had a canvas-covered arch serving to shade the side door entrance to the van. As the women approached the arch they saw a man sitting on the doorstep in deep concentration working on something laying in his lap. The man was a counterpoint to KangaRay. He was squat, furry, with a thatch of thick curly hair and a well groomed beard. The makeshift vestibule gave the impression that they were approaching a throne.

"Hey there, Leon." Rachael hailed. The man looked up from his work, which Rachael could now see was a frayed leather utility belt.

"Ha. Rachael." He jumped up and quickly covered the distance of the vestibule, throwing his arms around her and squeezing her warmly. "Did you just get here?"

She cleared her throat and sheepishly responded. "I came out with another crew. I got here last night."

"Oh." he was genuinely surprised. "You're not camping with us?" he asked rhetorically more to himself than to Rachael. He grabbed her shoulders and stared into her eyes. "Well, I'm so glad you're here. Let's definitely do some playa adventuring together."

She awkwardly smiled. "Of course." She endured his gaze for a few beats, then cleared her throat again. "We'll leave you to it. I just swung by to say hi."

"Yes, yes," he said. Then he followed up. "Most of the crew arrives either later today or tomorrow. Come to dinner on Tuesday. We'll have a plate for you."

Rachael let a light breath out. "Sure. Tuesday night is a date."

"Great," he said and turned back into the vestibule and the repairs at hand.

Elise hooked her arm through Rachael's as they walked in silence back to her bicycle. Rachael put her free hand on the seat and looked at Elise. "I'll see you Tuesday if not sooner."

"Are you sure that you don't want to camp here? We have room for you." Elise asked.

Rachael smiled warmly this time. "I"m good. See you soon." With a smooth economic movement, she mounted the bicycle and set it in motion, swinging back around toward the Esplanade and the playa beyond.

As she navigated the divots and a knot of coagulating early burners, she let out a sigh of relief. The Sparklites were friendly and welcoming. But, she felt repelled by it. As if she were a trinket, they enjoyed having around just to show how cool they were. The short visit reinforced her choice to stay with Nathan. She might have been a stranger in a strange land, camping with a bunch of gay boys. But, she knew where she stood. There was no pretense. In that gay field of corn, she was a tomato plant.

2:45 and Enlighten, BRC, 11:37 AM - Justine

"Okay. I think I'm ready." Justine jogged over to where Max stood, wagon handle in hand.

"Cool. Let's go get ice," he said, stepping into the street. The tinny rumble of the wagon filled the silence between their footsteps. "Travel with me, my dear, down Rue de Dust. I'll show you the wonders of Center Camp and Camp Arctica."

She rolled her eyes but smiled. "Oh, a sunstroke march with promised refrigeration? Be still my heart."

Falling into stride beside him, she muttered, "I can't believe the friggin' effort it took to leave camp. Sunblock, hat, sunglasses, water, snacks... all this prep just to walk a mile and back. Feels like I packed for a summit attempt."

Max chuckled. "You'll get the rhythm soon. Nothing out here is simple, but it all matters. Thriving is in the details. This may be the flattest place on earth, but it's deceptively high in the mountains, pushing a hundred degrees. Every little thing takes forethought."

"Mmm, yes. Dust, dehydration, and discipline. My three favorite D-words." She shot him a sideways grin.

He didn't bite, just kept walking with that easy smile and a patience she was starting to appreciate.

"You make it sound so dire," she pressed.

"That's vague. Give me an example?"

Max pointed at a man smoking, catching ash in an Altoids tin. "Everything you bring, you take. Cigarette butts, pee bottles, car drips. MOOP is the ultimate sin."

"MOOP?"

"Matter Out Of Place." He grinned. "You'll be fluent by week's end."

"Okay," she said slowly. "That's... actually kind of beautiful. In a militant, eco-monastic way." She gave a wry shrug. "You're like a sexy desert Boy Scout."

Max laughed. "Guilty as charged. And you're gonna love how prepared you'll be by then"

"I already hate how much I don't hate that." She paused. "Who knew I'd get misty-eyed over waste sorting?"

Camps buzzed around them like surreal desert blooms – music, shouts, someone offering popsicles from a cooler on wheels.

"This place is changing fast," she said, more to herself. "Feels like it's waking up... and dragging me with it."

"That's the magic," Max said. "It builds. Then it blooms."

Just then, a wiry young man in a vest and top hat trotted toward them. "Hello, hello, my friends! Are either of you, perchance, a virgin?"

Max jerked a thumb at Justine. She scowled with mock betrayal. "Et tu, Maximus?" Then to the stranger: "Define virgin, and I'll decide whether to deck you."

"Playa virgin," Max clarified.

"Oh. That kind." She flushed. "Yeah. First burn. Proceed with your ritual."

The man grinned and produced a watch and a compass. "May I offer you tools to keep you found?"

Before she could object, he strapped the watch on her wrist and hung the compass lanyard around her neck.

She glanced down. The watch face bore no numbers, just the bold word:
NOW!

She opened the compass. No needle, no bearings. Just the word:
HERE!

Justine blinked, then laughed. "Wow. I came for the art and fire and got clocked with mindfulness." She looked up. "Honestly? Weirdly love it."

The man tipped his hat and vanished into the crowd.

"Okay, real talk," she said. "I thought this would be wall-to-wall rave chaos and poor decisions. But people are... kind. Weird as hell, but thoughtful. Not what I expected."

Max smiled. "Welcome to Black Rock City."

She hesitated, then said quietly, "I think I might... be starting to get it. Well, something."

"That's the thing about this place," Max said. "It doesn't ask you to get it all at once. Just to show up. The rest unfolds."

"Get off my fuckin' lawn, hippie." A voice cut through the air, gruff and grating.

Both Max and Justine turned to see a cranky gnome of a man with shaggy mutton chops. He stood deep in the shade of a plywood-hewn living room with multiple couches, yet completely devoid of aesthetic touches. Utility was clearly the only consideration.

Justine screwed up her face in confusion. The man squinted menacingly. "Get the fuck off my lawn."

Max tapped her shoulder and pointed at her feet. She was standing on a square of astroturf.

She looked up at the man, amused. "Relax, I'll leave before the HOA fines me."

The man was not prepared for snark. He had no comeback, so he shrugged.

They continued down the street. "That was a shitty looking camp," she observed.

"DPW," stated Max without explanation.

"What the fuck is in DPW?" she asked.

"They built the city – the street grid, Center Camp, and such. They'll tear it down when we're gone. In the meantime, they have nothing to do but fuck with us. But, no one prepared that poor fucker for Little-Miss-Sassy-Pants." Max poked her shoulder.

Her crooked smile was a mix of pride and embarrassment.

Justine walked on, silent for a beat, eyes flicking down to the bold words on her new gear. **NOW. HERE.**

The snark was still there, always would be, but something underneath it was shifting. Not melting. Just... warming.

"You know," she said, "if the rest of this week keeps going like this, I might have to eat some of my own cynicism."

Max grinned. "Don't worry. We'll pair it with ice."

She giggled. "Hey, can we come back on the Esplanade? I need to find the stage I'm performing at later today."

"It's your oyster. Playa on a half shell. We'll put that on ice, too."

DPW Ghetto, 3:10 and Avatar, BRC, 12:22 PM - Ruben

Ruben made his way to the rear "door" of the living room, crossing paths with Beef, who was coming from the opposite direction with a laugh and a piece of astroturf clutched in his hand. Ruben had questions, but knowing Beef, they were not worth asking. He needed to replenish his water. As he approached the opening, he heard two women talking to each other in the living room area.

"Are you sure that you want to venture into the lion's den?" asked one. "Last time I asked to borrow something from a DPWer, she gave me a speech about radical self-reliance. They're cranky bastards."

"We need a post hole digger. They definitely have one. Gotta take my shot," said the other. "If they kill me, burn me with the Man."

Ruben grinned to himself. He paused for a moment to plaster on a serious face and stepped into the living room area. The two women were standing together near the couches. They radiated that love-and-light Burner vibe, soft clothes, bright eyes. The event was coming, and this was its first ambassador.

He nodded at them and bee-lined toward the five-gallon water jug. He held up the mouth of his water bottle and flipped the spigot lever, watching the bottle fill.

"Hi. I'm wondering if we can borrow a post hole digger from you." One of the women crossed the space to join him at the jug station.

Rather than looking at her, he held up a finger to signal that she should wait. As the water hit the neck of the bottle, he twisted the spigot lever shut.

He looked up at her as he screwed the top onto the water bottle. "We don't lend out our tools."

Thud had drilled that into him – *Don't loan out our tools. Especially don't loan out our tools to those love and light motherfuckers. You'll never see them again.*

"Let's start over," said one of the women, undeterred. "I'm Elise. This is Bea. We're part of Sparkleville at 3:15 and Chakra. We fucked up and didn't bring a posthole digger. We can't put up our sign unless we dig the holes for the signposts. I understand that you don't want your tools to walk off, and I don't blame you. I'd be happy to leave my driver's license with you as collateral until I return it. And, I promise I will have it back to you within two hours."

She added, "We're two short blocks behind you as the crow flies. You can see our camp from the back of yours." She gestured through the back of the living room.

Ruben's face was impassive. His head slowly shook from side to side. His empathy for them battling with DPW policy, as it was. "Tools walk off."

"You're right, of course. And, I don't want to fuck you over when you're doing us a solid. My ex was a DPWer. I know how you guys feel about us. How 'bout you come with us? We'll feed you, dig the holes fast, and hand the digger right back to you."

He was quiet for a moment, assessing. Then he asked, "You say it's a straight shot from the back of the camp?"

"Yep", Elise nodded.

"Cmon," he said and led the way out of the back of the living room through the back of the DWP encampment to a small Bobcat-style four-wheeler with an auger mounted in front of it. He slid into the seat and started the engine. "Show me the way."

Elise and Bea trotted out in front of him, leading him across Beatific and through the still-open block across Chakra and the assembled Sparkleville sign lying on the ground. Divots, in front of the supine signposts, marked the locations for the desired holes. Without extracting himself from the four-wheeler, he augered out two three-feet-deep holes for the signposts. The entire effort took less than five minutes.

He whipped the four-wheeler around, aimed at the DPW Ghetto, turned and nodded at Elise, and was in the throes of leaving when Elise yelled out. "Hey," as she approached the four-wheeler. As she reached his side, she said, "You're a lifesaver. Thank you so much. What's your name?"

"Ruben. Well, I guess I have a playa name now, so Cheshire."

"You hungry, Cheshire?" she asked.

"Nah. I'm good," he replied.

"Would you like a flying tour of the city? We have a pilot in our camp who's brought out his private airplane. He's going to do a fly-around of Black Rock City on Wednesday?"

"A fly-around," he repeated. "Huh. That might be interesting."

"Be here at 5 pm on Wednesday. We'll head out to the airport as a group," Elise directed.

"Alright. See you on Wednesday," he said.

"Thanks again," Elise said.

Ruben throttled the four-wheeler forward, quickly returning to the DPW Ghetto back area. As he stepped out of the four-wheeler, he looked back to see that a small crowd had gathered around the Sparkleville sign and was in the process of sliding the posts into his holes.

"A fly-around." Ruben stared after them.

He'd spent weeks with his boots in the dust, head down, body aching. But up there? Maybe he could see the whole thing at once.

"Today I'm a DPWer. Wednesday I'll be... something else."

Watching the sign stake its claim in the hardpan, he understood he'd been wrong about the "love and light fuckers." The DPW stories had painted them as fragile idealists, but these people had steel in their spines, just wrapped in softer packaging. They were evolution in action, adapting to the playa while slowly reshaping it to fit their vision. He felt something shift in his chest, part fear, part fascination. What happened when an unstoppable force of kindness met the desert's immovable indifference?

7:30 and Inner Playa, BRC, 4:53 PM - Rachael

Rachael walked beside Elise in silence, her elbow lightly hooked in Elise's arm. The warmth of the contact was unfamiliar, almost alien, but not unpleasant.

"I'm glad we ran into each other at Center Camp," Elise said, smiling sideways. "Nothing like an impromptu playa date to make my day."

Rachael cocked an eyebrow. "Is that what this is, a playa date?"

"Sure," Elise replied easily. "Playa dates come in all shapes. This is one of them."

Rachael laughed softly. "I thought we were just friends... sharing a coincidence."

Elise gave her a wink. "Out here, the line between coincidence and magic gets pretty thin."

They reached a gathering crowd clustered around a small raised stage. The structure was bare-bones: wooden planks, stairs at each end, a few paper lanterns strung from poles. A performer near the base of the stairs was strapping on stilts with the practiced focus of a dancer before curtain call.

"Oh. Showtime," Elise said, tugging Rachael toward a better vantage. "You know, 98% of Burning Man is spontaneous. The other 2% is miracles. You have to make peace with the fact that you'll miss most of it."

Rachael glanced sidelong at her. "That's not in the guidebook."

"No," Elise grinned, then added more softly, "but I wish I'd known that my first year. I spent a lot of time chasing the perfect moment. Missed a lot of great ones that way."

7:30 and Inner Playa, BRC, 5:02 PM - Justine

Justine made quick work of strapping on her stilts. She pulled her poi and fire gear from the backpack. Finally, she grabbed her hoops and bounced toward the stairs, gracefully mounting the stage. Susan followed discreetly behind her, carrying poi, spinning gear, and a fire extinguisher, crouching into her firewatch position at the top of the stairs.

With calm precision, Justine set a hoop spinning on her hips. It looked effortless, even on stilts. She added three more, tossing them into the air. Each arc grew higher until one hoop slid off track — cattywampus. Or so it seemed. It landed cleanly around the upturned stilt of her vertical split. The crowd cheered.

Justine stepped through the hip hoop, letting it drop to the foundation leg's knee. She spun more hoops on her arms and neck, all in sync, never missing a beat. The control was breathtaking.

Susan handed her the lit poi. Justine didn't falter. She spun them smoothly while maintaining her hoop rhythm, closing with what she liked to call *hoop flambé*. The crowd erupted.

Justine dipped into a stilted curtsy and climbed down, her breath catching as she collapsed onto the stairs and unbuckled her stilts.

"You were perfect, babe, as usual," Susan purred.

Justine shot her a self-conscious smile. "No thanks to the breeze, dust, and wobbly stage. It's hard to perfect myself in these conditions."

Susan scrunched her nose. "That imperfection gives back, too. You can..."

But she was cut off by an adoring fan. "That was amazing!" said a woman leading several others toward her.

7:30 and Inner Playa, BRC, 5:24 PM - Rachael

"That was objectively perfect," Rachael said, eyes fixed on the performer. "But..." She hesitated. "I didn't feel anything."

Elise turned to her. "What do you mean?"

"I mean, it was beautiful. She was brilliant. But I didn't feel her. There was no... soul in it." She looked away, suddenly self-conscious. "Not that I'd know what that looks like."

Elise shook her head gently. "Perfection doesn't always mean connection."

Rachael nodded slowly. "Yeah. It reminded me of... me. Doing the right things, hitting the marks, but..."

"Empty?" Elise offered.

Rachael smiled, thin, cautious, barely touching her eyes. "Yeah. Empty. Automated. Soulless."

She watched the petite woman basking in praise. A flicker of envy. And recognition.

If Burning Man is about this, Rachael thought, *I definitely won't last the week.*

But Elise was still next to her. Solid. Warm. Rachael felt the brush of her arm again and didn't pull away.

They let the moment settle. Then, as if by silent cue, they turned back toward the Esplanade.

"Let's go get our bikes," Elise said.

Rachael nodded. "Yeah," she replied, voice quiet but a little less hollow. "Let's."

Magrathea Base Camp, 10:00 and Divinity, BRC, 6:12 PM - Emile

"You're a fucking twat, Emile. I don't need a backseat DJ." DJ Bedlam's eyes were cutting holes in him. "Go be king of the bus. I'm the empress of beats right now and don't need your... thoughts. Your version of perfection sucks the soul out of the music. Fuck off. Leave me to it."

She flicked him away like a pesky fly, her focus snapping back to the control board and the mix in her headphones. Emile glared at her. Eventually, she glanced sideways without turning her head. "Go."

Her tone was final.

He huffed, impotently. A sword stuck in its scabbard, sharp, gleaming, utterly inert. He seethed at his own failure to move her. With the subtlety of a matador in rush-hour traffic, he whirled around and stomped off, each step a full-volume footnote to his indignation. He mounted the spiral ladder, pounding up the steps with a force that might screw the staircase into the playa itself. He burst onto the roof deck, his fury uncoiling like a firehose gone rogue, brutal force without aim, all velocity, no clarity.

A man with a greying beard stood mid-deck, a large speaker propped between his hip and the railing, trying to untangle a cable wrapped around both his leg and a shade pole.

"Stanton!" Emile shouted.

The man flinched as if electrocuted. The speaker, suddenly unsupported, crashed to the deck.

Emile froze. His breath caught, not in rage, but in grief. This wasn't just equipment. This was him: cracked, sputtering, coughing static. He approached the speaker like a parent to a wounded child.

He looked up at Stanton, frustrated tears welling. "What were you thinking?"

"Emile, you're done here." Liam appeared, stepping between them. His voice was calm but firm.

Emile turned his ire on Liam. "Complacency. Lack of discipline. Lack of reverence for this masterpiece of an art car is sabotaging what we can be."

"Walk with me," Liam said it quietly, but the command was unmistakable. They crossed to the front of the deck in silence.

"They don't unders..." Emile started.

"Stop." Liam's voice remained calm, but steel-threaded.

"Wish as hard as you want, you can't transmogrify the crew into nineteen Emiles. You need to rein in your shit. The crew vacillates between calling you Captain Bligh and Jekyll and Hyde. That broken speaker? That's on you. You scared the shit out of Stanton. And you're pissing everyone off with your kibbitzing, including me."

"If you want to examine the single greatest threat to Magrathea's success," Liam said, "go down to our suite and stare into the bathroom mirror."

Emile blanched, "You want the same mediocrity the rest of the crew is striving for?" He felt betrayed. He was certain Liam would be on board with providing the ultimate experience.

Liam blinked, almost incredulous. "Mediocrity and Magrathea don't belong in the same sentence. This bus was destined for the history books the moment we drove onto the playa."

He took a breath.

"That said, this is Burning Man. The crew is made up of humans. Brilliant, fragile, unpredictable humans. You've made this a hostile environment. They're also artists in their own right. And they'll only commit to your vision as long as they're still getting something joyful from the ride."

He stepped closer.

"Your way is not the only way. Each of them deserves the chance to snatch perfection in their own way. That's leadership. Stop being a tyrant. Start being a leader."

Emile's glare didn't drop, but the fire behind it flickered. He stood, tight-lipped, suspended between righteousness and the first sting of shame.

"Now go for a walk. Calm down before you do real damage to your relationship with these good people. I'll get Misha, we'll fix the speaker. Just... get off this bus. Let the crew do their thing."

Emile stared a moment longer.

"Now," Liam repeated, with quiet finality.

For the second time in five minutes, Emile had been shut down. He turned, walked across the roof, down the spiral stairs, across the main floor, and out the door onto the playa without seeing anyone.

The bass still throbbed behind him, but out here the city felt quiet. He headed down the 10:00 street, away from the lights, away from the bus, and away from anyone who knew his name.

Magrathea Base Camp, 10:00 and Divinity, BRC, 8:33 PM - Emile

Emile stood just far enough away from the bus to fully take it in. The bus's lights glowed against the deepening dusk. A broad grin spread across his lovely face, making it all the more beautiful. He shook his head, hoping to impose order on his stubborn, sculpted dreadlock nubbins. They were the one part of his choreographed life that resisted order.

It had taken him a long walk to cool down after the speaker incident. And while the crew was operating below his idea of perfection, they had rallied well. Well enough for him to keep himself in check. He considered that a reasonable concession for the moment. He would ramp things up after their maiden voyage.

In the past day, the full complement of Magrathea's crew had arrived and acclimated. Nineteen excited crew members bustled about the bus, fussing with various aspects of the now fully customized rave mobile. The crew themselves were colorful in their own right, representing both a broad artistic and queer spectrum. There were even a few straight members sprinkled in for good measure. He watched them moving about, rapt in preparation. He could make out DJ Bedlam in the second-floor DJ booth, pumping out a premix wallpaper to underscore and motivate the crew's efforts.

"She's magnificent," he muttered to himself.

"Yes, she is," Liam agreed. His voice came from just behind Emile's right side.

Emile reached back and clutched Liam's shoulder, his eyes shining. "It's time." Liam could see the child that Emile had once been in his excitement.

He quickly covered the distance to the bus, bounding through the door to the first level. He moved across the lounge space, with speed and economy, to the circular staircase leading to the second level. He took every other step like a schoolboy. Three long, jumping steps put him in front of the DJ booth. He caught DJ Bedlam's eye as he approached.

When he came within speaking distance, he said, "It's time. Let's gather the children." She winked at him and did her best lounge lizard finger gun with a wink. She cranked up the thumping to rave level for a few seconds, then brought it down to conversation level. Flipping a switch on the console, she leaned into the standing mike. When her lips were all but kissing it, she said, "Gather on the second level, my children. Magrathea's about to get her groove on." Her clipped British accent lent a sense of gravity to the announcement.

They heard whoops from the bus roof. Liam appeared coming up the stairs. Dobbs, who had been working on a lighting problem at the front end of the dance level, wandered back and collapsed on one of the upholstered benches. Within a few moments, the whole crew was gathered on the second level.

Emile made a long, slow sweep from left to right, catching each campmate's gaze. He spotted a few of his favorites. Misha, a squat Filipino man sporting a ponytail and wispy beard. He had custom built Magrathea's sound system. Gina and Kathy, a dyke edgy couple with a Portlandia aesthetic, looked so much alike that they were hard to tell apart. Gina was the bus's electrician. Kathy had coordinated all of the crew meals.

There were a few new crew members as well, guests of the main crew. He ended with DJ Bedlam, then started into the brief speech that he had framed up as he waited for everyone to gather. "My friends, my campmates, my comrades in par tay..."

Whoops, whistles, and screams rose up. Emile let them die down of their own accord before he went on. "Most of you have been pouring yourself into this little project, heart and soul, for the better part of the last eight months. For the last two days, we've all been eating, sleeping, and drinking preparations to get this mule playa ready. Now, our time has arrived." Another, louder burst of whoops and whistles erupted. Emile grinned as they let loose.

"I see a few new faces, so let me give a quick Magrathea operations breakdown for the uninitiated. Magrathea is designed for three modes on the playa. The first mode you are about to experience is as an art car. We'll be raving in motion and transporting Black Rock Citizens from destination to destination in style. We will be the finest in motion party on the playa."

The crew hooted and hollered. DJ Bedlam cranked up the music for ten seconds and then took it back down.

"The second mode is fixed position rave. Once or twice each night, we will drop anchor and rave in place at select, strategic locations. When we do that, there is some setup to do, mostly around shifting the front and back speaker platforms to angle into the dance area. Veterans know how to do it, but will need your help."

He purposefully caught the new member's eyes to let them know he meant that last comment for them.

"The final mode is home base. When we close down and park back here at base camp, the bus becomes the camp's common area. And," he pointed to the closed door at the back of the bus behind the spiral stairs, "Liam and my master suite."

Laughs and suggestive whistles broke out.

"Tonight, we will make a tour of the inner playa around the man. It's a simple show of force to our fellow citizens of Black Rock City. We are announcing that Magrathea's open for business."

The crew jumped up, cheering. DJ Bedlam gave them another quick dose of music. Everyone was excited and anxious to take the behemoth for a tour.

"Before we leave on our maiden playa voyage, I just wanted you all to know how much I appreciate what you've done. But for your love, creativity, and effort, Magrathea's light would not shine the way it will this week. I love each and every one of you. You are my family. This amazing creation is nothing without you all to provide its heart." He took a breath, paused, and finished, "and, what a mighty heart you have."

The campmates let loose with another wave of whoops. This one was the loudest. When it died down, he went on.

"Remember, we are here to serve Burning Man, both the event and the individuals we will host and entertain."

As if by instinct, the crowd rushed together in a chaotic group hug. After a few minutes of friendly groping, cheek kisses, and extended hugs between individuals, they slowly began to break up. Emile worked his way to the top of the stairs. He turned in front of the stairs and yelled, "Road trip." He turned back, braced himself with stiff arms on the handrails, and slid down the circular stairs as laughter and whistles followed behind.

He quickly crossed the lounge area and dropped into the driver's seat. Without ceremony, he engaged the clutch and mashed the starter button with his thumb. The diesel engine roared to life. This time, the yells and whistles were muted by the engine noise. He pulled the telescoping microphone to his mouth and announced, "Hang on, my lovelies. Magrathea's Final Answer is now departing for destinations known and unknown."

He eased out the clutch, and the bus shuddered, vibrating for several seconds, then started to move slowly forward. Emile's eyebrows raised in alarm, and he quickly scanned the gauges. Nothing appeared to be wrong, but the vibration lingered longer than it should have. "What the hell was that?" he muttered, gripping the steering wheel tighter. The bus crept forward, the vibration gradually dampening but not disappearing entirely.

They had traveled the length of 10:00 and reached the Esplanade before Emile felt the tension in his shoulders ease slightly. The shuddering had smoothed to an occasional tremor, barely perceptible unless he was listening for it. Which he was. Once the bus had fully cleared the Esplanade, he gently turned right and aimed the vehicle across the inner playa, threading the space between the outer ring and the Man, heading roughly toward Center Camp. For this pilot run, they would stay within the inner perimeter of the city, completing a counter clockwise tour. They would save the outer playa for tomorrow.

Emile scanned the playa in front of him, illuminated by the bus headlights. He then scanned, as best he could, the surrounding playa currently cloaked in darkness. All was reasonably clear, which made sense. The crowd on the playa this evening would be sparse, relatively sober, and somewhat more cautious than the evening dwellers starting tomorrow night, when the event was officially open.

The bus was now running smoother, though Emile kept one ear tuned to the engine's rhythm. His campmates were sharing time between finishing their projects and sightseeing. DJ Bedlam had cranked up the music. He could feel it thumping in his chest. The grin slowly returned to his face, though it felt more cautious than before. He shrugged his shoulders and charted a meandering course never exceeding three miles per hour.

His confidence was growing that he could deliver perfection to Black Rock City. But the memory of that initial vibration nagged at him like a splinter he couldn't quite reach.

Gordian Knot, 8:30 and Esplanade, BRC, 9:22 PM - Crawford

"Fuck, Crawford. That entrance is a magnet to partying Burners." The middle aged woman turned toward him and patted him on the shoulder. Her long greying blonde hair was swept up into a french braid. Her flowing robe gave her a mystical appearance.

Crawford shot her a quick glance, then snapped his attention back to the entrance. "That's the plan, Delores. Woo them in like a boardwalk attraction and give them the biggest challenge on the playa."

He glanced at her again. "No one would guess that you're an entertainment lawyer."

She grinned. "That's the plan."

The broad entrance provided a funnel into the guts of the maze. The marquis lights blinked on the letters one-by-one until they spelled out 'Gordian Knot'. Then they shut off and repeated the sequence. The sign was so large and garish that it could be easily read from the Man.

City dwellers were wandering into the maze in ones and twos. Sunday night, and they were already getting serious traffic.

Tiësto's "Adagio for Strings" had made its way into Crawford's consciousness. He first assumed the noise came from a distant sound camp, but as it grew louder, it felt as though a rave were rolling straight toward him, burrowing into his mind. Delores and Crawford turned, trying to locate the source. A massive reticulated bus rumbled past about a hundred yards off the Esplanade. A tangled, eye-catching sign stretched across its roof announcing, "Magrathea's Final Answer." Colored lights pulsed along its sides, and spotlights swept from both ends of the upper deck. The whole thing was a spectacle.

Crawford glanced at Delores. Rapture pooled across her features as if she'd just glimpsed eternity breathing in color. Her lips parted, her eyes wet with joy so naked it felt indecent to witness.

Crawford's fury was immediate. *Fucking posers. That superficial display can't touch the intricate engineering feat that is the Gordian Knot.*

"I need to check the traffic in the maze from up top." He turned without waiting for a response, making his way around the perimeter of the maze wall to the ladder placed adjacent to their common area. He climbed the ladder, stepping off of the ladder onto the bridge. He strode purposefully across the bridge to his favorite vantage point in the crows nest, surveying the activity in the dying light.

People dotted the maze. He stood leaning against the rail, like the ship's captain on his quarter deck. The light breeze blowing across the playa whipped up the tails of his long coat, lending drama to his visage. He was impressed that a few of them had made it to the third section. He wondered if they had cheated. Perhaps they had been in there for the entire three hours since they had opened for business.

He smiled to himself. *I can still turn this around. Butter up, Jimmy. Make him feel indispensable. I know his buttons.* He became aware that he was talking out loud. He shook his head, relieved no one was here to hear him talking to himself.

The maze was shadowed in the descending darkness. However, the strategically placed lighting in the maze provided enough ambient illumination that he could still track the people in the uncovered maze runs. He assumed that there were even more folks in the enclosed sections, but could not monitor them. He had designed the lighting to be generally atmospheric, giving the maze an aura of mystery.

He felt a thump from behind him and turned to see a heavy man clinging to the bridge rail, catching his ragged breath.

"What's up, Caleb?" Crawford asked.

The rotund man gasped for another minute, then looked up at Crawford. "Delores told me that you were up here. Vicky just got here."

Crawford rubbed his face. "Thanks, man."

He pushed past the man and turned as he mounted the ladder. Clamoring down quickly, he jumped off the last several rungs, planting himself squarely on the ground into the crew-only gallery. Then he quickly circumnavigated the perimeter of the RVs to the parking area. He wanted to catch Vicky before she talked to Jimmy.

He arrived at the parking area to find Vicky's Mercedes closed and dark.

"Shit." He spat the words out without pause and moved toward the gap between the RVs, heading straight for his own. The windows of his RV glowed, a welcoming light. Or so he hoped. As he neared, Crawford slowed, gathering himself. He paused at the door, steadying his breath, forced a casual smile, stepped onto the metal step, and swung the door open.

Stepping up into the living quarters, he surveyed the chaos. The pristine room he had left was replaced by one occupied with a sprawl of boxes, bags, and suitcases on all the horizontal surfaces. He suppressed the irritation that always welled up when faced with Vicky's mess in "his" space.

"Nice timing, Bud. I just finished unloading the car." He turned to see Vicky framed in the bedroom doorway.

She was radiant, clearly happy to see him. As usual, she was beautiful. And she seemed happier than Crawford had seen her in a long time, making her all the more beautiful. She had donned her full-length zebra striped party coat over her casual travel clothes. The juxtaposition made her all the more endearing.

She had used 'Bud,' her pet name for him. She had not used it in years.

"I've been upgraded. Reinstated to 'Bud'."

She covered the distance between them and threw her arms around his neck. He slid his arms inside the coat and pulled her slim, gym polished body to him. They kissed for a long while. Her familiar lips felt like home to him. She smelled fresh and clean as only someone arriving from the outer world can.

Their lips parted. "You're never far from 'Butt'. Mind your Ps and Qs."

"You want a Mint Juplaya?" he asked, moving quickly into mixologist mode.

"Sure," she brightened.

"Jesus Bud. The Gordian is amazing. You've really outdone yourself," she gushed as he worked.

"It does have a certain je ne sais quois, does it not? Wait until you see it from the crow's-nest," he said as he completed the finishing touches. He turned and handed her the drink.

She took a long sip. "Mmmmm. As tasty as always."

"Luring in those production artists to the maze crew really paid off. I drove past the entrance before I parked. It's over-the-top fabulous," she said, then added, "theme park quality."

"Hey," he gently protested. "It's my design."

"Yes dear," she mocked. "We all know you're a genius."

She looked around at the mess. "Wanna help me get all this stuff put away?"

"Sure," he replied, then ventured on, "I haven't seen you this happy in a long time."

She smiled and looked up from the groceries she was unloading. "I've spent a lot of time thinking about us and where we've been for the last few years. I don't want it to be difficult for us anymore. I'd really like to treat this burn as our do-over. Wanna have a do over with me?" She smiled up at him with puppy-dog eyes.

He raised his eyebrows, knowing there was only one answer. "Sure."

She fell into him and they kissed again, long and hard. She stepped back and grabbed him by the lapels, pulling him toward her and the bedroom behind. "Let's break a bottle of champagne over the bow of our new relation - ship."

He let himself be pulled into the bedroom, surprised by the unexpected turn of events. Things were looking up. As he stepped through the doorframe, he continued to ponder how he would steer the conversation with Jimmy.

Ataraxis Warrior, 11:00 and Outer Playa, BRC, Sunday, 10:34 PM – Harley

Night had fully claimed the playa, painting everything in deep indigos and quiet shadows. The sky above stretched wide and velvet, constellations watching the unfolding city, the occasional star blinking in solidarity. The wind had calmed to a whisper. The soundscape was soft; an occasional distant bass line, the hiss of a propane torch, yet the event was still young and only beginning to awaken.

He noted the blinking giant bus cutting between the Man and the Temple, relieved that it was not coming this way.

The *Ataraxis Warrior* loomed in its full fiery, shining majesty, its sinewed body washed in its own candescence, the faint gleam of copper and steel catching light like breath. Around its feet, visitors circled in quiet curiosity. Not a crowd, not yet. Just drifting clusters: early-week pilgrims wrapped in fleece and dusters, still calibrating to Black Rock City's rhythm.

Harley stood near the control station, checking fuel pressures, adjusting fuel timing, and scribbling notes in a beat-up pad. His sleeved arms were in constant motion as he worked the controls. It was a soft run, meant more for calibration than spectacle.

People came and went. A few offered thanks or praise. Harley nodded, sometimes muttering a polite "Appreciate it." He didn't linger in conversation.

A little girl in a butterfly cape broke from her parents and padded up to the sculpture's hind leg. She placed a palm on the steel hoof, eyes wide with solemnity.

"Does he sleep?" she asked.

Harley glanced down at her, then back at the control gauges. "Sometimes," he said.

She nodded as if that made perfect sense, then ran off, the cape trailing behind her.

Later, a tall woman in a glittery jacket paused to take a photo. "This is the most powerful thing I've seen out here," she said, almost reverent.

Harley shook his head. "The build crew deserves the credit," he replied. She smiled, not quite believing him, and wandered on.

A young artist lingered longer. He stepped forward tentatively, his eyes dancing over every welded joint, every muscular line.

"Can I ask," he said, "what it means?"

Harley didn't look at him. He watched the Warrior instead, flicking his pen once between his fingers.

"It's a mirror," he said.

The artist blinked. "A mirror of...?"

But Harley was already scanning the feed ratios again, making no effort to clarify.

The young man eventually nodded, half to himself, and drifted into the dark.

Minutes passed. The crowd ebbed and flowed. No two interactions were the same. One woman wept quietly as she touched a leg. A trio of DPWers cracked beers beneath the hindquarters and toasted the thing like it was a war memorial. Someone lit sage and muttered a prayer. Someone else shouted, "Is this the fire-breathing one?" and was shushed by an older couple sitting cross-legged nearby.

Harley stood back, arms crossed. Watching. Listening.

And something began to turn.

He saw the way people moved around it, some reverent, some giddy, some broken open. He realized the Warrior had already become something he could not control. It was no longer a sculpture. It was an experience, refracted through every stranger who stood in its play of flame and shadow. They saw what they needed. It had stopped being *his*.

The thought should have twisted in his gut. But it didn't.

He stepped back from the panel, rubbing a palm against his jeans.

A woman in an EL wire robe knelt at the Warrior's base, eyes closed, whispering something to the wind. He didn't hear what she said. He did not need to.

It hit him like a low roll of thunder:

It's not mine anymore.

And instead of fear, he felt something like breath finally let go of his ribs.

Relief.

Ataraxis Warrior, 11:00 and Outer Playa, BRC, 10:56 PM - Justine

Justine tucked her wrap more tightly around herself, leaning into the shield of Susan's body. The air was cool, though not cold, and Susan bore the brunt of the breeze. Justine nestled in close, finding shelter on Susan's downwind side.

"This is one of those moments I'm so grateful you're taller than me," she mumbled into Susan's armpit. Susan chuckled.

"I wasn't planning on this extended trek. But when we saw it lit up..." Susan admitted, trailing off. "I couldn't say no."

Ahead, drawing steadily closer, stood *Ataraxis Warrior*, alive with flame. From a distance, the first thing Justine had seen was the great, flaming hoop suspended impossibly high, over a hundred and fifty feet, she guessed, and the streams of fire flowing like tears down the figure. The warrior's eyes glowed red in the dark. Even from afar, the sculpture radiated power.

But now, as they approached, the details emerged with more clarity, like a dream sharpening into focus.

The massive hoop was a dreamcatcher, gripped in the extended hands of the towering Native American warrior. Not just the rim but the webbed lattice itself was ablaze. Fire danced in both the warrior's and the stallion's eyes, flickering behind their metal irises. From those eyes, streams of flame leaked downward, fiery tears slipping onto the warrior's chest and vanishing into the body.

Susan quietly said, "If someone was on a particularly bad hallucinogenic trip, they could confuse that dream catcher for the eye of Sauron."

The stallion wept too, fire tears flowing down its broad chest and into a large basin on the playa, extending from the stallion's chest past its nose. Sparks pulsed periodically from beneath the pedestal, spraying the stallion's legs and belly, flaring from the warrior's back like breath from a sleeping volcano.

Then, when they were within a hundred yards, the stallion suddenly reared, mechanical and majestic, and belched a gash of flame into the sky. Both women halted, stunned.

"Holy shit," Justine murmured, awe-struck.

Susan's response was more laconic. "Fire," she intoned, equal parts reverent and gleeful.

A small knot of people stood at the base, equally enthralled. Justine and Susan didn't move to join them. The distance felt right. They were content to witness, quiet, still, folded into the inky vastness of the playa.

Justine leaned against Susan and let herself be absorbed by the moment. The installation was wild and monumental, and somehow intimate. In its surreal, mythic beauty, it made sense, maybe more than anything else had in days.

"Our primal urge is to gather with the tribe," Susan said softly. "To sit around a fire, sharing stories and art. For all our accomplishments, science, cities, conquest, this is still where we're drawn."

Justine had never heard her wax so poetic.

But the words struck a chord. This experience, this quiet awe, this surreal communion, offered something deeper than spectacle. And for the first time since arriving, Justine *felt* it. Not just intellectually, but viscerally. Something in her unlatched.

Her eyes stung, not from dust, but from the slow rise of something uninvited. Emotion. She blinked, hard. A strange, unwieldy gratitude rippled through her. The moment tugged at something deep, something she thought she had armored and buried long ago.

Her mind flickered, unbidden, to the hush of a studio back home. Mirrors. A barre. A practice schedule. That was the structure, precision, discipline, and safety for which she yearned.

Here? Chaos. Wildness. Fire leaking from the eyes of a god.

Yet this chaos moved her. That terrified her as much as it thrilled her.

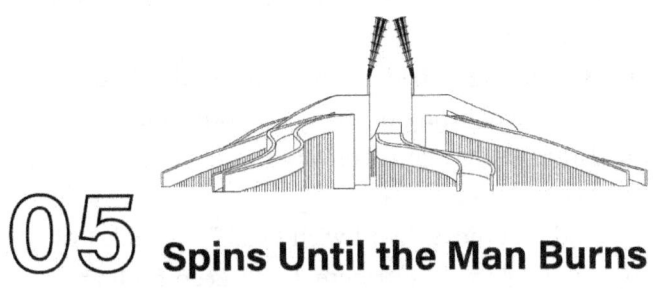

05 Spins Until the Man Burns

Ataraxis Warrior, 11:00 and Outer Playa, BRC, 1:56 AM - Harley

Harley rubbed his face. The Ataraxis Warrior had performed flawlessly all evening. He was satisfied, or as close to it as he ever got. The knot of anxiety that usually lived between his ribs had loosened. Now, he was just tired. Tonight would not be an all-nighter.

He shut off the main program. The stallion dropped slowly into its resting position and stilled. Harley moved through the shutdown process, first closing the LP gas and kerosene master valves, then the local ones as the fire subsided and the tears stopped streaming. The last of the flames flickered in the basin before dying, dimming the area until only the low solar garden lights remained, tracing the perimeter in quiet warning.

From across the flame pond, he saw a petite woman with a pixie cut approach, weaving along the border of the installation. He kept one hand on the final valve as she came closer. When the last ember went out, he turned the lever with finality and looked up to meet her.

They stood there, facing one another in the hazy ambient light.

"Hi," she said.

"Hi," Harley replied, offering a faint smile.

"I was going to offer help shutting things down," she said, glancing toward the now-silent sculpture, "but it looks like you've got it handled."

"Yeah. I tried to build it so one person could manage the shutdown. Just in case."

"Makes sense," she said, studying the towering silhouette. "This is my first time out here. I'm not sure how I feel about all of it yet, but... what you've made here would be amazing anywhere. Thank you. This gave me a place to land while I figure out what this place means to me."

Harley nodded. He looked past her into the deep darkness of the open playa. Then back at her.

"It's just something I had to do," he said. "You're welcome. But honestly, you're just benefitting from my compulsion."

She smiled at that, though there was a softness in her eyes, a shadow of something familiar.

"I understand that more than I wish I did," she said. "Still, I'm grateful. There's plenty I struggle with out here, but I keep finding myself drawn to this." She gestured toward the darkened form. "What I'm awkwardly trying to say is... thank you."

She looked down, her toe brushing the dust, then stepped back. "Alright. I'll let you get some peace."

"Hey," Harley said gently. She paused and turned.

"What's your name?"

She flushed a little. "Justine. Sorry. Should've started with that."

"I'm Harley." He extended his hand, and they shook—warmly, without pretense.

"Nice to meet you, Harley," she said.

"Nice to meet you, Justine. I'm glad the Warrior anchored you. I hadn't thought of it that way when I built it, but... yeah. It grounds me, too. I guess I needed that more than I realized."

Justine smiled again, this time with less self-consciousness. "I'll definitely be back."

"Say hi when you do," Harley said.

"I will."

She turned and walked off into the desert night, her silhouette swallowed by the dark, the memory of flame still etched into the air between them.

Harley stood there a while longer, alone now, listening to the silence hum. The Warrior rested behind him, still and massive, a monument born of obsession. And maybe, just maybe, connection.

DPW Ghetto, 3:10 and Avatar, BRC, 7:12 AM - Ruben

Ruben blinked into the dim light. The craving had crept in hours ago.. Now, it roared. His body buzzed with want. *A drink. Just one.* It'd be so easy. Any trailer in the ghetto could pour him salvation in under two minutes.

Nodding to the pointlessness of laying there basting in his desire, he crawled out of bed, threw on shorts and a sleeveless sweatshirt, and stumbled out to the otherwise empty living room. He sat, taking in the silence of the sleeping city and managing a growing sense of dread.

He stared at the water jug as if it were filled with whiskey. Hands mid-tremor, he leaned forward and rubbed his face, "Fuck, fuck, fuck."

"Some other time." Ruben stiffened and brought himself upright, eyes bulging. Toucan Girl stood at the edge of the living room by the street, arms full of bags.

"Here's your shit." She dropped the load onto the couch next to the overstuffed chair where Ruben sat."Your laundry, mixed fresh fruit, and a gallon of milk. Just like you asked," she said as he stared at the bags. "Thank you, " he said, shocked that his entire order was filled. Most of the time, when someone was making a grocery run, his list was aspirational.

"If you tell anyone that I did this for you, your body will never be found." she said.

Ruben smiled a crooked, knowing smile. "You'd rather have the crew think that you were selling me drugs than know that you did me a favor."

"If they get wind of it, I'll be doing 'favors' every time I make a run into Reno until I die. That was a special offer only for you."

"I'm honored. And you have my word on discretion," he said.

"Oh, I know. Partially because you're the rare decent man here. And mostly because you have a healthy fear for your own mortality," she replied. "Now stow that shit away and say nothing more of it."

He nodded and made to get up. "Whoa, whoa, whoa!" He looked up at her. She had her arm aimed toward him, hand up in a halt sign. "First, tell me about that shit you were doing when I got here. I've seen that look before."

He slumped back in the chair and sighed. "Every recovering drunk has their way of dealing with sobriety. Mine is routine. Today, I am released from my DPW routine. I have no real structure now. Without structure, chaos wins. And, this place is about to be the most chaotic place on the planet."

Toucan Girl nodded. "You know that there are sober camps out here. Find yourself a "Who, What, When, Where Guide" and look up their locations and times. Make that your routine."

Ruben looked down at the ratty area carpet laid down to keep the dust at bay. He nodded and looked up at her. "Thanks. That's a good idea."

"Okay, now go hide that shit before I have to kill you." She turned abruptly and left.

He laughed. *That was a well-disguised act of kindness.*

He stacked the supplies in the mini-fridge by his bed and sat in the dim light, heart still racing. He sensed the tectonic shift from focused work to festive diffusion. The tide had rolled in.

The thirst hadn't passed. It never passed. It just waited.

One AA meeting at a time, he told himself. *One Ataraxis shift at a time.*

The rest? He would have to play jazz.

3:00 and Divinity, BRC, 9:14 AM - Justine

The streets had shifted overnight, more celebratory now, pulsing with foot traffic, bikes zigzagging like caffeinated insects, and vehicles rumbling in like dusty nomads. Black Rock City was officially open for business, and business was booming in entropy.

Justine made her way along Enlighten toward the long line of portapotties stationed on 3:30 between Chakra and Divinity, what she privately called the *Temple of Mildly Controlled Suffering.* Even at their best, portapotties were a balancing act of survival and denial. At their worst, they were a full-blown existential reckoning with heat, stench, and the delicate illusion of modern plumbing.

She loathed them to near phobia. Deeply. The thought of peeling off layers in a sun-baked plastic coffin while hovering over a dark mystery hole ranked somewhere between "snake pit" and "nuclear waste" on her list of horrors. To Burning Man's credit, they'd been shockingly tolerable so far. Still, her optimism was measured in quarter-teaspoons.

Rounding the corner at 3:00, she joined the slow pilgrimage toward the neat row of blue-green thrones, glowing ominously in the morning light like cheerful little biohazards. She was almost there, close enough to taste the chemical bouquet, when a bike cut her off.

Instead of pedaling past like a normal human, the rider slowed to match her pace, clearly gearing up for a full charm offensive.

"Good morning, my lady," he intoned.

She glanced over. Of course.

A lean, smugly confident Burner in a pinstriped vest, calf-length pants, and a fedora, complete with a green feather, because of course it had a feather.

He was cute. Damn him.

But he'd also just inserted himself directly into her path like a pop-up ad, and he wasn't done. "Might I escort you to yon domiciles of refuge, yea that you may, in your own privacy, perform your morning ablution?"

Oh great. A Shakespearean pickup line at nine in the morning.

Justine turned her head just enough to side-eye him, equal parts *nice try* and *nope*. "I think I can manage on my own," she said, voice dry with amusement and sharp around the edges. "But ten points for using 'ablution' before breakfast."

"I've no doubt of your capability," he replied smoothly. "Yet the sojourn is sweetened by fair company and pithy conversation."

She stopped abruptly, watching him nearly crash trying to brake. "You're like a Renaissance fair and a thesaurus had a baby," she muttered.

She stepped around the back tire and made a clean break toward the toilets. As she rounded the stalls, she tossed a glance over her shoulder, a razor-thin smile in place.

"Keep workshopping that rap. By the end of the week, you might even land a mildly dehydrated yoga teacher." And with that, she vanished behind the blue doors.

A flicker of guilt caught her off guard. He *was* clever and attractive. Maybe she didn't need to verbally disembowel every flirt with a pulse.

Maybe.

Six stalls down, she found one that was clean, stocked, and mercifully dry. "Score," she muttered.

For several minutes, her attention narrowed to basic logistics. When she emerged, blinking into the sunlight like she'd just re-entered Earth's atmosphere, she made a beeline for the hand sanitizer. Nothing says rebirth like ethanol gel and disgust.

As she scrubbed her hands, she heard a familiar voice crooning again from the street.

"Mademoiselle, may I offer you an early morning libation?"

She turned. There he was, mid-performance with a new target, already presenting a tiny bottle of Jägermeister like it was a rare jewel.

Add creative pivoting to his villain résumé, she thought. *Our little Casanova's doing A/B testing now.*

She shook her head, half-smiling in spite of herself. "Jesus, I hate being cynically right."

Then, she turned back toward camp.

As she put one foot in front of the other, she couldn't shake the interaction. The guy had been harmless, even charming in a try-hard kind of way. So why had she gutted him? She knew why. Every attempt at connection felt like an invasion here, every kindness like a setup for disappointment. She'd learned young that if you never let anyone in, they can't let you down.

She watched three desert goddesses stride across the playa in sculptural metallic armor and radiant headdresses; one crowned in copper sunbursts, another in crystalline rays, the third in silvered light, their bodies adorned with intricate metalwork that catches the harsh Nevada sun and transforms them into living art. She wondered:

What if that armor was exactly what was keeping her from experiencing what this place promised? The thought made her deeply uncomfortable. She shoved it down and kept walking.

2:00 and Chakra, BRC, 11:05 AM - Harley

Harley pushed the door open with his shoulder and stepped into the bright mid-morning glare. The air, dry and searing as it was, still felt twenty degrees cooler than the fetid heat box he'd just escaped. By late morning, the porta-potties transformed into full-blown torture chambers. He'd trained himself to breathe as little as possible in those personal saunas.

People were everywhere. The party was on. While he did not care for it, he resigned himself to its inevitability. He headed toward the sanitizer station, pumped the lever. Nothing. He tried again. Still dry.

"Here, I've got some," came a warm, lightly accented voice. Harley turned to see a tall Black man holding out a small bottle of gel. Harley stepped over, took it with a nod, and worked the sanitizer into his hands.

"Appreciate it," Harley said, returning the bottle. "I'm Harley."

The man smiled, offered a hand. "Emile."

They shook, then both looked toward the heat shimmer rolling across the playa.

Emile looked up and shaded his eyes. "I think this will be the hottest day since we've arrived."

"Been here long?" Harley asked.

"Nah, just a few days." Emile responded with a smile

"I've been out here a few days longer, and it's still the hottest day." Harley laughed.

"You with the DPW?" Emile asked.

"No. I came out early to put up an art installation."

"Oh, really? Which one?"

Harley pointed past Emile's shoulder out towards the playa. "That one." Ataraxis Warrior dominated the landscape in the distance.

"No shit?! I haven't been out there yet, but it sure is impressive from a distance... day and night."

"Thanks." Harley was embarrassed.

"You know what would be great?" Emile asked and then answered. "You could come over to my camp some morning, and we can take my art car out there. You could give us the nickel tour."

"That's doable." Harley smiled, "Where are you camped?" Emile pointed off to his left. "Right there." Harley turned to see the bus parked two blocks down.

He turned back to Emile, confused. "Behind that bus?" Emile smiled but said nothing. Harley's eyes widened. "That bus is yours?" Emile broke into a large grin.

"Jesus, I've been wanting to take a closer look at it since I first saw it." Harley was almost giddy. "It's a deal. I'll come over to your camp one of these mornings. If you show me your bus, I'll show you my warrior."

"Deal. You show me your warrior, I'll show you my bus."

Just then a wiry man in mirrored shades joined them. Emile slung an arm around him and handed over the sanitizer.

"This is my partner, Liam."

Liam looked at Harley and said hello. "I'd shake your hand but..." Liam's voice trailed off as he waved his sanitizer-slicked hands.

"No problem." Harley smiled as he responded.

"So, would Wednesday work, say 11 AM?" Emile confirmed.

"I'll be there."

Harley turned and walked off, the sun at his back, dust rising around his boots.

Liam leaned in. "Who was that?"

Emile nodded toward the distant sculpture. "The man who made *that*."

Liam whistled softly. "No shit."

"No shit," Emile echoed. "And come Wednesday morning, we've got the tour from the man himself."

7:00 and Inspiration, BRC, 11:32 AM - Cypher

The dilapidated RV creaked down Inspiration, groaning to a halt with a long, stuttering squeal of the brakes. The door swung open, and a young man stepped down onto the warped metal step, every possession he owned strapped to his back or rattling in a small cooler at his side. His hand-sewn pants, baggy and bulging with pockets, looked like they'd been stitched together from a dream half-remembered by a child. He wore no shirt. Just a sun-scorched torso and the grin of someone who believed he was exactly where he belonged.

He took a few paces from the RV, turning in a slow, lopsided 360, scanning the wide-open playa like a monarch arriving in exile.

A second figure emerged in the doorframe, stooped and shadowed, then stretched to full height. He was gaunt and towering, almost skeletal. His red ten-gallon hat scraped the top of the door frame. He looked like a three-way collision between a cowboy movie, a flea market, and a psychedelic circus. The red alligator boots. The paisley pink yoga pants. The thick belt cinched like armor. The dinner-plate-sized buckle. The threadbare ruffled shirt. The long denim duster hung off his wiry frame like a magician's final flourish.

Despite his creaky movements, the old man's eyes twinkled with life.

"Cypher, my boy," he called, arms spread in a generous arc. "You're in for a treat. The revelry has begun. Back here, at the edge of the fiesta, you can pitch up anywhere that's open."

Cypher bounded over and grabbed his hand in a confused hybrid of a high-five and a shake. "Thanks, Captain Dusty."

Dusty clapped him on the shoulder. "Have fun and burn well, my boy." Without waiting for a reply, he climbed back into the RV. It coughed back to life and rattled off down the road, leaving Cypher alone.

He waved until it disappeared around a bend. Then he turned to face the emptiness.

A broad patch of open playa stretched before him. The closest camp in either direction was over 200 feet away. Unclaimed, unstructured, unjudging.

He crossed the road, his gear jangling with each step, and dropped everything into a shallow dip in the ground. It landed with a clatter that echoed farther than he expected.

He stood still. Scanned the horizon again. Big sky, dry ground, the faint pulse of distant music. "Jesus, it's hot," he muttered, squinting.

He shook out his tent, knocked it together in a few practiced motions, and shoved his belongings inside. He brushed off his hands and exhaled with satisfaction.

"Baby, I'm here," he said, looking up. "I *got* this."

His stomach rumbled. He ignored it.

A brief pause, just long enough to notice that he was, for the moment, absolutely and completely alone.

No crowd to impress. No social cues to dodge. No distractions to interfere with the purity of his ideas.

He swallowed, hard. Then grinned.

"Better here than boxed in," he said, not entirely convinced.

He tilted back his head and let out a long, uneven howl. Not for show. Not for anyone else.

A declaration. A deflection. A dare. If anyone heard, no one responded.

He had nothing more to do in camp. Nor did he know or need to answer to anyone. Time to explore this crazy place and take in everything he can.

Still grinning, he nodded to himself. He wasn't just surviving. He was winning. Right?

Gordian's Knot, 8:30 and Esplanade, BRC, 11:38 AM - Crawford

Crawford cupped his hands under the faucet and caught the water in his palms. He pressed his face into the pooled liquid, letting it cascade down his bare chest as he gazed out the window over the sink. A sly smile crept across his face, remembering the night of torrid passion he and Vicky had shared. She hadn't been that zealous in years. Their evening together put an exclamation mark on the transition from toil to celebration. Time to take advantage of the party.

"I'll have more of that. It's good to be king." He caught himself talking to himself again. That needed watching.

He studied the shaded common area through the window, instinctively assessing what he might be walking into. Vicky sat just outside their RV, her bare feet soaking in a water-filled pan. Crawford grabbed a bowl of diced melon and hooked a finger through the loop of his water bottle. With his other hand, he opened the door.

As he stepped onto the playa, he froze.

Penelope was hugging Vicky.

"Isn't this amazing?" Penelope said.

"You build-crew heroes outdid yourselves," Vicky replied.

Crawford willed his deer-in-the-headlights reaction into a casual saunter and forced a smile onto his lips. He would not lose control, not here, not now.

"Do you mind if I join you?" Penelope asked Vicky.

"Please do," Vicky said. "You should try the foot bath."

"Foot bath?" Penelope tilted her head.

"Yes, it has vinegar in it. Neutralizes the alkali dust. Helps keep your feet from cracking, it's the best way to avoid playa foot." Vicky explained.

Vicky looked over. "Good morning, love. Ah, you brought the melon. Good man."

She settled back into her chair, wiggling her toes in the shallow bath.

"Good morning, Crawford," Penelope slid into the chair beside Vicky without looking at him. She kicked off her shoes and plunged her feet into the water with a squeal. "Shit! That's so fucking cold."

"Bracing, isn't it?" Vicky said, smiling just out of Crawford's line of sight. "It's ice-melt from the cooler."

"Crawford, come feed me." Vicky batted her lashes theatrically.

He dropped a piece of melon into her open mouth, then set the bowl and water bottle on the table between their chairs. Sliding off his own shoes, he dropped into the third chair and dipped his feet into the bath. No way in hell was he leaving the two of them to talk unsupervised.

"Where's Jimmy?" Vicky asked. "I haven't seen him since I got here."

"He's in the maze doing minor repairs," Penelope said, slipping easily into a Jimmy impression. "'The opening night attendees provided fault testing.'"

Vicky chuckled. "You have him down to a tee."

"I don't know how long the repairs will take, but I do know he'll be at the camp dinner tonight," Penelope continued.

"Oh yeah. We're having a camp meeting, aren't we?" Vicky asked.

"Yep. Now that most of our camp is here, we're reviewing the monitoring schedule and talking about maze adjustments. Right, Crawford?" Penelope looked directly at him, smiling lips, deadly eyes.

He matched her with a flash of charm. "As planned. We've got to make sure the maze stays tight."

"I can't wait until dinner," Vicky said. "I'm looking forward to seeing the whole gang."

Crawford eased back into his chair, sliding his sunglasses down over his eyes. So many pieces on the board. So many loose ends to tie up. Nothing he hadn't handled before.

You got this, he told himself.

He pretended to doze, but his ears were wide awake, tuned to every word exchanged between the women beside him. He wasn't the king of this game because he took chances. He was the king because he listened, especially when no one thought he was listening.

Gordian's Knot, 8:30 and Esplanade, BRC, 8:03 PM - Crawford

Crawford walked across the common area to the kitchen stationed at its center, his bowl, dining ware, and cup clutched in one hand. Chairs and small tables had organically gathered beside the kitchen, creating a dining area of sorts. Crawford would have preferred the area to be more organized. He added that to the list of discussion points for their meeting.

A rough line of diners had formed, skirting the perimeter of the dining zone. The smell of grilled spices and roasted vegetables hung in the air. The folks at the front were already scooping food onto their plates.

As Crawford stepped into the dining area and joined the back of the line, a subtle ripple passed through the group, a tightening of posture, a sudden hush in conversations. He felt it like a shift in atmospheric pressure. He made eye contact with no one.

Someone's been talking out of school. This party has taken a turn for the worse.

He clenched his jaw. He'd spent the afternoon glad-handing the crew members he could corner, laying the groundwork for a community coalition to pressure Jimmy. During the sunlit hours, it felt like momentum. But here, in the cooling dusk, he sensed the terrain had shifted.

Jimmy is running a campaign of his own.

No one approached him. Nor did he attempt to engage anyone. Instead, he stood, scanning the crowd. *No Vicky.*

When his turn came, he ladled food into his bowl without registering what it was, just the right volume. He had just settled into a chair when he heard Jimmy's voice from across the dining space.

"Hi folks! Welcome to all of you new arrivals. We're so happy you're here," Jimmy called out.

A cheer erupted, loud and heartfelt. Crawford's eyebrows twitched. *That was my line.* Jimmy was making a power play.

Jimmy continued, gesturing toward the maze. "Let's hear it for the build crew. Their collective heart and soul is now standing as a Black Rock monument."

The cheer exploded. Some of the new arrivals stood, clapping. A partial standing ovation. Crawford's eyes narrowed. *What is this, the Tonys?*

He half-expected someone to throw a bouquet. Jimmy had omitted his name deliberately. But the crowd was all-in. This wasn't the moment to assert ownership.

"How 'bout the dinner crew? Gourmet food in the desert, served tonight!" Another round of cheers and claps. The dinner crew bowed and curtsied. Crawford watched in disbelief.

Jimmy is charming them. Outshining me. Becoming a rival in plain view.

"The schedule is posted on the community board." Jimmy pointed to a large whiteboard-and-cork combo. Half was covered with a foam-printed schedule; the other, already blooming with dry-erase scribbles.

"We've divided ourselves into six-hour, three-person crews — a gate barker, an observer, and a runner. The gate barker hooks them in. The observer watches the maze progress and radios issues. The runner helps participants in distress. If you want a tour of the DIAPs, discrete intervention access points, A.K.A secret passages, Linny and Millie have you covered." Two women stood and waved.

Crawford bristled. *The team structure was my idea.*

"We've kept shifts light. Most of you are only on once, so be on time and prepared. Your crew is counting on you. We serve dinner nightly for those into the group meal thing. For tent campers, we've set up showers behind that RV." Jimmy gestured vaguely toward an electric-blue-trimmed Mercedes RV.

"Any questions, find a build crew member. Build crew, hands up!"

Hands shot up around the dining area. Crawford kept his in his lap.

"Alright, folks. Have a great Burn." Jimmy sat down, swarmed immediately by animated campers.

No one approached Crawford. It was as if he'd become invisible.

He stood with quiet rage, his movements precise. He smoothed his shirt, set down his bowl, and walked away, each step clipped and controlled, as if his fury could be folded neatly into posture and pace.

So many pieces on the board. So many people who think they know how this ends. Let's see what happens when the king decides to move.

3:00 and Esplanade, BRC, 9:21 PM - Justine

The crew of five clustered just off the Esplanade, at the gaping mouth of 3:00. They bunched together, gazing out at the surreal 360-degree panorama.

"I was not, nor let's be real, was it remotely possible for me to be, emotionally prepared for this spectacle," Justine said, eyes wide, voice somewhere between wonder and disbelief.

The city stretched before them in a mad deluge of color and light, like a post-apocalyptic theme park curated by Salvador Dali and a rave DJ with a god complex. Everything pulsed and flashed—LEDs, LCDs, neon, fire, spinning sculptures, and art cars lit up like mobile hallucinations. A cacophony of music swirled around them, genre boundaries dissolving into something closer to sonic warfare.

Justine slowly turned in a full circle. "This fiesta doesn't go to eleven. It starts at eleven and then lights itself on fire."

A sudden wave of explosions lit up the skyline, fireworks bursting across the Esplanade in a thunderous cascade. Justine flinched. "And there's the part where the sky tries to give me a heart attack."

"Oops, forgot. Happy Monday," Sasha said, entirely unfazed.

Justine turned, eyebrows raised. "Wait. This is just Monday? Casual thermonuclear Monday?"

"Monday fireworks are the starter pistol," Sasha replied. "We're off to the races now."

Justine rolled her eyes. "Fantastic. Because clearly the crowd was holding back before."

"Seems like every year the kickoff is bigger," Max said. "This Monday night feels like the Friday night of my first Burn."

"Word," Zig added, nodding like a desert philosopher.

Around them, Burners cruised by on foot and bike, adorned in glimmering costume chaos, neon fur, gold lamé, bedazzled masks, and body paint that shimmered like bioluminescent jellyfish. Justine, who had always filed glitz somewhere between hollow nonsense and a desperate cry for attention, found herself unusually speechless.

Max gestured at the crowd. "After my first few Burns, I realized it didn't matter how outlandish I dressed, I was going to be chronically underdressed next to most of these crafty artist-types."

As if summoned, a woman floated past dressed as a pastel butterfly, her lycra suit lit in looping el-wire, her mechanical wings flapping with dramatic grace.

Justine blinked. "How in the hell do people sleep through this? The lights, the noise. It's like trying to nap inside a blender."

Susan smiled and gave her shoulder a squeeze. "Like everything else out here, you adapt. Silence is a rare commodity. I've got extra earplugs if you need."

They wandered slowly along the Esplanade, drifting clockwise toward Center Camp. No destination in mind, just strolling through the surreal.

"Seriously," Justine muttered, "how do you keep your brain from melting with this much stimulation? I feel like the place is trying to enter me through all five senses at once."

Zig nodded. "You need a strategy. Right here, it's sensory overload. But head out a few hundred yards into the inner playa, and everything drops off. It's a different vibe."

To prove it, he veered off the Esplanade into the open playa. Justine followed, and sure enough, the chaos dimmed. Music faded to a murmur.

Lights shifted from garish to alluring glow. Noise softened from abrasive to a manageable pitch.

Zig turned, walking backward. "If we were deeper out in the great beyond, it would be almost meditative."

"The great beyond," Justine echoed. "Sounds like a place where hippies go to die or nap. Honestly, I'd take either."

They passed 6:00, the artery stretching from Center Camp to the Man. The stream of people was endless — leather-clad toughs, drag queens in full Disney regalia, and a man who had clearly spent six months perfecting his Dune stillsuit.

And somehow it all worked. These weren't just costumes. They were declarations, at least for the night.

They passed jugglers spinning flaming bowling pins while hula hoops blazed around their waists. Then a digital oasis, a hollow in the playa playing a video loop of a full-sized swimmer gliding through pixelated water. A few steps farther, they encountered a metal beast with seven flame-throwing heads that screamed notes like possessed pan flutes.

Eventually, they made their way to the Man, towering above a multi-level structure cordoned off for final prep. He beamed down in halogen judgment.

As they turned back toward camp, Susan slipped an arm around Justine's shoulders. "How you doing, baby girl?"

Justine exhaled, not quite laughing. "Somewhere between awestruck and emotionally concussed."

Susan chuckled. "If you'd said anything different, I'd know you were lying."

Justine smirked. "Good. Lying is extra work, and I didn't pack the energy for it."

She fell quiet as the buzz of the Esplanade returned to full volume as they approached it. Every instinct in her wanted to analyze, to assign meaning, to pin this place down. But none of it held still. It felt like stapling spaghetti to a wall. She wasn't sure what she felt, only that it was more than she expected. And that unnerved her.

Inside, something tugged. She walked on, hamstrung between resistance and surrender

Gordian's Knot, 8:30 and Esplanade, BRC, 9:52 PM - Crawford

Caleb had stationed himself at the maze entrance, fully immersed in his role as barker, heckling passersby, luring them toward the Gordian with exaggerated flair. Crawford stood across the Esplanade on the open playa, taking in the entire frontage. The external walls flanking the entrance pulsed under theatrical lighting, painted in motifs of explorers groping through shadowed passageways, carnival funhouses, and arcane sorcery. The visuals drew them in. Caleb was just the icing.

Maze-goers trickled in every few moments.

Crawford, uninterested in banter with Caleb, skirted the frontage and followed the length of the wall to its far edge. He cut across the Esplanade and slipped into the narrow corridor between the maze perimeter barrier and the line of parked vehicles.

He climbed the ladder to the crow's nest. Empty. A fresh wave of irritation rose.

This team needed to get its shit together.

Deciding to check the shift assignment, he descended, heading for the camp's common area. The dining space was deserted. He crossed to the community board, bracing to hand out a verbal reckoning.

"Hi, Crawford."

He jolted, spinning. "Jesus Christ! You scared the shit out of me."

It was the woman from the dinner meeting, one of the volunteers he hadn't bothered to remember.

"Sorry," she remained unfazed. "You looked deep in thought. I was trying to give you a heads up."

He gave her a curt nod that landed somewhere between dismissal and insult.

"I'm surprised you didn't go out with everyone."

"I have no interest in herding cats," he spat. The bitterness surprised even him. In truth, no one had asked.

"I hear you." She paused. "Well, I finally got my shit together and I'm heading to Opulent Temple over at 2:00. One of my favorite DJs is going on at half past ten. You're welcome to come with me."

Crawford hesitated. On one hand, she was a nobody. He wasn't sure he wanted to be seen with her. On the other, this might be his last invitation of the night, and maybe, just maybe, a way back in. He could spin it. Reintegrate with the crew. Reframe the narrative.

Jimmy won a few battles. I'll win the war.

"Yeah, why not?" He stepped to his RV and pulled his CamelBak from a nearby chair. "Let's do it."

As they walked toward the edge of camp, he stopped, realizing he didn't even know her name.

"What's your name again?"

She turned to him, wearing an amused smile. "Millie. My name's Millie."

He nodded, registering it. They had been introduced. More than once.

Xaraland 2:10 and Esplanade, BRC, 10:28 PM - Rachael

"So this is what clubbing looks like in Black Rock City." Rachael tried to sound nonchalant. But the casual bravado buffered a welling anxiety.

Todd stepped off his bike. "No bouncer. No cover charge. Free drinks as long as they have alcohol. Great music. What more could you ask for? This is my perfect fandango."

"All good points," she replied. *Why was she anxious? Clubs weren't really her thing, but they usually didn't scare her.*

As Nathan locked the bikes together. Todd, Cyril, and Rachael stepped away, onto the Esplanade, to get a better view of the 'club.'. It was massive.

The "club" loomed ahead, a flat-topped pyramid draped in black shade cloth, half a block wide. Its entrance arched boldly, flanked by torches, silver letters spelling 'Xaraland' overhead.

"You know what a really big door means?" Cyril wiggled his eyebrows suggestively.

Rachael snorted a little too raucously. Then frowned at the snort. Then it dawned on her. "Fuck. I'm high."

Cyril squinted at her. "How much of that brownie did you eat?"

"All of it?" she offered, shrugging.

Cyril's jaw dropped. "Dude. That was forty milligrams."

"Okay. Translate. I haven't been high in twenty-five years, and that was from smoking a joint."

"You would've been baked off a quarter." His tone sobered. "If it gets intense, find somewhere calm. We got you."

His gaze locked with hers to make sure she understood. She nodded

Soulful trip-hop EDM welled up and oozed out of the entrance, enticing them like a sensual, ethereal siren. The dark interior beckoned to them.

Costumed burners navigated around them, making their way into the din. Rachael felt the night chill on her face as she took in a deep breath of dry desert air. Nathan came up from behind them, slinging one arm over Rachael's shoulder and the other over Todd's. "We promised you a real adventure tonight, and here it is."

The group moved forward into the dim interior. After they passed the torches, it took a moment for Rachael's eyes to adjust. They stepped into the ruckus. A crowd pulsed on the dance floor ahead, lit by moody LED ropes.

To their right and left was darkness and dark shapes. As her eyes adjusted to the dim light, the dark shapes resolved into shrubbery walls flanking the vestibule leading to the dance floor. She reached out and touched the closest bramble. Real leaves. Real branches.

She trailed her hand along the hedge until she found a gap, shoes neatly lined up. Without hesitation, she unlaced her boots and stepped through. Her foot sank into cool whispering silk, startling against her skin. It was a quiet shock. "Whoa."

She looked back at her crew. "It's grass."

Her crew peeled off their shoes and joined her.

The four of them giggled like children as they danced from foot to foot , squeezing their toes in the turf. They were standing in an indoor park that was larger than the dance floor. The lawn was littered with people in small groups, luxuriating on the sward. For a moment, she felt grounded. Not high. Just here. The quiet resilience of the grass beneath her felt impossibly alive.

The music shifted, a low, sensual rhythm, the singer's voice a slow chant.

"That's my cue." Nathan slid back into his boots in preparation for the dance floor, Todd and Cyril close behind.

"I'm going to stay here and commune with nature." Rachael said as they shuffled toward the dance floor.

"We'll be back." Nathan said over his shoulder as he disappeared into the crowd.

Alone now, Rachael wandered deeper into the greenspace, carefully stepping around huddled and sprawled bodies. At the far end of the space, she approached the perimeter hedge. Here it towered over her, reaching up toward the top of the wall.

She wandered deeper, dodging sprawled bodies. At the far edge, the hedge rose high, at least ten feet deep. She ran her open palm along the cool, dew-slick leaves. It felt soothing, like dipping her fingers in memory. "God. I am so high," she whispered, but didn't sound alarmed.

She was beginning to think it might be good to sit down. A small opening appeared in the hedge, a hobbit hole. Rachael crouched, peeked in. A dim space stretched beyond. She crawled forward, knees brushing turf.

Inside, an alcove glowed with electric candles. Three figures clustered near a faux campfire, two men and a woman.

"Alice fell down the rabbit hole. Come join us, Alice." The woman beckoned her over with a wave to reinforce her invitation.

Rachael made her way to the cluster and plopped down next to the woman. The woman wrapped her in a hug, startling Rachael. The woman held her until Rachael relaxed. Something about the woman's scent, patchouli, and something sweet, calmed her.

"You haven't really arrived yet, have you, baby? You're so tense."

"I'm working on it." Rachael muttered.

"Don't worry," the woman said with a wave. "You're among friends. I'm Dee Dee. That's Marco," she gestured to a shirtless man who nodded, "and that's Xav."

He raised a hand. "Hey."

They sat around a makeshift fire, coiled red lights threaded through stacked logs.

Rachael smiled. "Adorable."

"We're telling stories," Dee Dee said, eyes lingering expectantly.

Rachael blinked. "Oh, sorry. I'm super high. First time in years. I ate a brownie earlier and it just hit me like a truck. I'm Rachael."

"You go, Rachael." Dee Dee patted her thigh. "When'd you arrive?"

"Sunday." She paused. "Still trying to wrap my head around all this."

"Are you a virgin, girl?" Dee Dee asked.

"Excuse me?"

"First time at Burning Man?"

"Oh. Yes." She smiled self-consciously.

"Welcome home, baby." Dee Dee pulled her in again. This time, Rachael didn't resist.

"Thanks. I'm not totally sure I belong here."

"Give it time. It's a lot," Marco added.

Then Dee Dee tilted her head. "Hope I'm not overstepping, but are you trans?"

Rachael startled, her mind sharpening like a camera lens. "Uh, yeah."

Dee Dee beamed. "Fabulous. Me too, sista'."

Rachael laughed sheepishly. "Yeah, I think we clocked each other."

There was a beat of shared recognition. Dee Dee leaned in slowly. Rachael froze.

Her thoughts tumbled. *Is this safe? Do I want this?* And then, *I feel seen.*

The kiss was soft. Rachael hesitated. Then leaned in.

Dee Dee pulled back with a grin. "Come play with us."

"Huh?"

"We're off to find the next whiskey bar. Come take the night with us."

Dee Dee and the boys stood. Rachael followed them across the grassy sward, wobbling slightly as she put her boots back on.

Dee Dee grabbed her hands, spun around, pressed Rachael's palms over her breasts. "Hold these and follow me."

"Rachael! Hey, Rachael!" Nathan's voice cut through.

"Shit." She pulled her hands away. She'd forgotten entirely.

Nathan jogged up. "We're heading out. You coming?"

Rachael turned back to Dee Dee. "Sorry. I'm so high I forgot I had a crew."

Dee Dee smiled and hugged her. "Another time, baby. Happy burn."

"Happy burn." Rachael echoed as Dee Dee vanished into the crowd.

"You made friends," Nathan said. "Wanna go with them?"

Rachael considered it. "Honestly, I barely remember my name. And I think she had designs on me. You're a much safer choice."

Nathan clapped her shoulder. "I knew you were smart."

"Really, I'm just fucking high."

He grinned. "Let's go work it off while exploring Wonderland."

She chuckled, dazed and disarmed. "Just call me Alice."

1:30 and Inner Playa, BRC, 10:47 PM - Cypher

Cypher watched the big, thundering party bus move away from him, the fading cacophony eased his anxiety. It was incomprehensible to him that people willingly packed themselves like sardines in that unending noise. He aimed himself toward the quiet and the dark shape before him.

The tree loomed in the darkness, an inky relief rising up against the playa night. A distant flare offered a fleeting, wan illumination. In the tender light, the tree's surface gave off a subtle sheen, hinting that its strangely shaped trunk and branches were metallic. As Cypher approached, he saw it was uplit by a ring of low-intensity lights, just enough to tease out the details of the trunk and lowest branches.

In rapt fascination, he circled the sculpture, his eyes scanning every twist and crook. The tree beckoned music. Instruments; horns, woodwinds, strings, percussion, hung from its drooping branches, some whole, some seemingly grown into the limbs like fruit evolved for sound.

Other instruments were molded directly into the structure: a harp strung between curved branches, the necks of guitars and violins grafted into the grain, a keyboard spiraling like a twisted ribbon around the trunk. Embedded mouthpieces hinted at bespoke horns. One suggested a didgeridoo. Just as he thought he'd seen everything, Cypher found a hatch near the base. Inside glowed a built-in drum kit.

He stepped back, grinning, taking in the tree again. "Baby, you're something else," he whispered.

He moved to the harp, brushing his fingers across the strings. An ethereal cascade poured out, both acoustic and amplified through the trunk and branches. LEDs flared briefly, in lightening patterns across the trunk and branches, then faded. Guitar, bass, same deal. Each instrument awakened a different light signature. The tree was alive, wired for sound and spectacle.

Cypher wandered from mouthpiece to mouthpiece. He paused at the didgeridoo again and, without hesitation, formed his lips and jaw around the wooden tube. Closing his eyes, he blew with everything he had. A low, vibrating resonance rumbled through the tree, deep and slow. Earth-toned light began to glow from within the branches. He breathed through his nose, shaping subtle pressures from mouth and throat, coaxing the sound along. The tree brightened, pulse by pulse.

A flicker of disbelief crossed his face. Was he... making this happen?

As if called, silhouettes drifted in from the dark—singles and pairs drawn to the hum. The first was a thin, gray-haired man with long fingers and baggy clothes that hung like a stowed sail. He slid between trunk and branch, coaxing flamenco from a hidden guitar. Next came a young woman, braids cascading over her tribal garb, climbing into the crotch of the branches to bow a built-in violin. Her bow was a small branch at the end of a bungee cord.

A couple in desert camos tackled the keyboard. A solid woman in a black tank and jeans dropped into the drum kit. One by one, they joined until thirty people surrounded the trunk and perched in branches, each summoning sound from the strange symphony tree. The music was chaotic and lush, an unfiltered burst of playa jazz.

The music-driven LED capillaries tickled the trunk and branches.

Cypher stayed rooted to the trunk, the didgeridoo's deep call rising and falling in rhythm with his chest. This wasn't polished, wasn't planned, but it was his. For a moment, just a moment, he felt as if the music had made space for him, not just his sound, but his place among them.

He kept blowing, the vibration in his ribs steady, announcing to the city, not with words but with breath …*I'm here.*

04 Spins Until the Man Burns

11:45 and Deep Playa, 12:26 AM - Ruben

Ruben breathed in the cool night air, taking in a deep and deliberate breath. It was the quietest moment he could remember in years. A potent blend of restlessness and curiosity had pushed him to the outer playa; away from the now-bustling city, away from people, away from temptation. He had made it through the first day, more or less.

Idle hands are the devil's playground.

The playa crunched under his boots. He smiled at the sound: crisp, clean, untouched by the thrum of the inner city. The distant pulse of raves still reached him, but out here it was just a heartbeat on the wind. He moved by moonlight, content in the dark.

This was his first day without responsibility since landing. The build was over. The skeletal grid that the DPW had raised was now fully fleshed out. Pretty people flitted between camps like pollinators, scattering glitter and goodwill.It wasn't the chaos he'd expected. It was a kind of living system, organic, radiant, and utterly unpredictable.

Beautiful. Dangerous.

He knew enough about himself to treat it with caution. The pull of the sweet, casual party ethos was intoxicating. It would be so easy to surrender to it.

Fuck it.

Ataraxis Warrior was another pull, the angel on his other shoulder. The Warrior represented the pull of discipline. The pull of the straight and narrow.

Manage it.

But the art. The art was a different kind of pull, a horse of a different color, neither surrender nor discipline. It represented passion.

Embrace it.

Since the final bolts were set on Ataraxis Warrior, Ruben had become obsessed with the unfolding gallery around him. Installations bloomed in the hardpack void, strange and urgent. They slaked a thirst he hadn't known he carried. They spoke to the part of him buried under years of restraint and ruin.

Tonight was a pilgrimage. Tonight, while sitting in tension between surrender and discipline, he hunted for wonder.

A faint glow flickered in the distance, dim, violet, impossible to ignore. He veered toward it, the thrill of discovery quickening his steps.

As he approached, he saw a table and two chairs drenched in blacklight. The furniture glowed with fractal patterns, in violet, green, electric pink, buttery yellow, painted with the care of a jeweler, not a carpenter. On the table sat a full chess set, ready for play. Each piece was unique, hand-cast and painted in complementary palettes: one side cool, the other warm.

He eased into the purple chair and touched a pawn. The piece held fast, then gave with a satisfying *rip.* Velcro.

Of course.

He grinned.

"Each discovery here is like unwrapping a gift to find something unique and perfect, isn't it?"

Startled, Ruben looked up. A thin man with an extravagant beard stood at the edge of the glow.

"A gift I didn't know I wanted or needed," Ruben said.

The man stepped fully into the blacklight, silver ringmaster's coat trimmed in gold, cyberpunk top hat, hair in a waist-length braid. His beard was trained into a twisting lattice of wire, like bonsai for the face. Below the coat: hot pants, fishnets, and boots with heels so high they defied logic.

Ruben blinked, then nodded to himself. *Burning Man.*

"I'm Esteban," the man said, extending a hand.

"Ruben."

They shook.

"You know, Ruben," Esteban said, "we are the magic that makes those gifts come to life."

Ruben raised an eyebrow. "I'm not sure I follow."

"Well," Esteban began, "this whole city is built with incredible intention. DPW lays the bones. Artists provide flesh and fire. But none of it matters until we show up. Until we move through it. *We* animate the city."

"So... we're the blood?"

Esteban tilted his head. "More like... wild cards. We bring unpredictability. Tension. Surprise. And that's where the magic lives; not in the art, but in the reactions it sparks. We don't always get what we want out here. But we always get what we need." He paused. "The Rolling Stones got it right, man."

Ruben stared at the board.

"I've been trying to make sense of this place," he said. "You just helped."

Esteban smiled and gestured toward the empty chair. "Mind if I join you?"

"Be my guest," Ruben said, then added, "Want to play a game?"

Esteban sat and met Ruben's eyes with a twinkle. He moved his queen's pawn forward two spaces.

Ruben studied the board. His fingers hovered over a piece, then settled on the queen; not to move her, just to feel her weight. Discipline and magic were the victors of the moment. Sobriety had, at least for the moment, moved from consolation to ambition.

"Never played this sober," he murmured.

Esteban raised a brow. "Then it's time for your first win."

9:30 and Inner Playa, BRC, 7:25 AM - Emile

The chill that had clung stubbornly through sunrise was finally loosening its grip. Emile's workaday uniform; camouflage cargo pants, boots, and tank top, was becoming comfortable again as he walked. He had wandered without direction, taking the kind of aimless path that came more from a need to escape than to arrive.

A strained détente had settled between him and Liam, and between him and the crew. His interactions the night before had been polite, restrained, ... and exhausting. The crew had fallen far short of his vision for Magrathea's debut. That he'd avoided further scrapes was due only to his own effort not to critique what he saw as their sloppy preparations and hosting. They seemed more invested in partying than in delivering an exemplary experience. And Liam, like some permissive mother, enabled the worst of it. The discipline it took to stay composed had left Emile sleepless. He feared that a sloppy bar had been set that might haunt the rest of the week.

Early morning on the playa usually calmed him. It was a sacred window of softness, when the city hummed to a low pitch and the earth exhaled in slow motion. But this morning brought no peace. His mind remained clenched, agitated that the quiet refused to quiet him.

He approached a vaguely mushroom-like installation, maybe fifteen feet high, its 'stalk' about ten feet in diameter, the cap extending several feet beyond. Polished wood inlays spiraled up the base in dark and light whorls like a natural barber pole. It was beautiful, artful, and beguiling. Emile felt its quiet invitation. As he rounded it, he saw a wide entrance facing the sunrise.

He stepped closer. Inside, a low padded bench circled the interior wall, dotted with upholstered cushions, an invitation to stillness. Directly opposite the entrance sat a man, cross-legged, his linen clothing the color of dry bone and distant storms. A loose scarf covered his head and shoulders.

The man's dark skin intrigued Emile. It was even darker than his own. There were so few people of color at Burning Man. If this year was typical, there were fewer than five hundred Black folks on the playa. As their eyes met, the man spoke.

"Come sit with me, brother, and share this moment."

His accent was distinctly West African. Emile hesitated, reluctant to leave his own simmering thoughts. But curiosity overpowered his instinct to stew. He crossed the space and settled gently beside the man, acknowledging the solemnity of the invitation.

They sat in easy silence, both gazing out across the parched porcelain playa reaching toward the slate-gray ridge in the distance. After a while, the man pulled a steel bottle from the folds of his robe and offered it.

"It's water."

Emile took it, uncapped it, and let the cold sit in his mouth a moment before swallowing, cool, cleansing, grounding. It chased away the heat in his head.

"Thank you." He handed it back.

"Of course, my friend." The bottle disappeared again with a whisper of linen. The man then pulled out a bunch of grapes and placed them between them. He plucked one and popped it into his mouth. "Have all you want."

Emile smiled and took one. As he bit into the fruit, the sweet, tart, and sun-warmed juice filled his mouth . He tasted the season in it, the sun, rain, soil, nurture. His shoulders relaxed as he leaned into the cushion behind him.

The man stretched his legs out. "Nice way to start the week."

Emile glanced over. "I've been here for a couple of days. It's a good reset."

The man smiled back. "In need of a reset already?"

Emile sighed. "It's been a rocky start. My campmates haven't exactly locked in."

"Ethiopian?" the man asked.

"Eritrean," Emile replied. "You? Nigerian?"

The man grinned. "Ghanaian."

Emile nodded. "I'm Emile." He extended a hand.

"Owusu," the man replied, clasping Emile's hand with a relaxed overhand grip.

They sat in another stretch of silence. Then Owusu asked, "Is your family still in Eritrea?"

Emile shook his head without thinking. "No. They're in Texas. My dad's American. We moved when I was twelve."

"Is that where you live now?"

Emile gave a small smile. "No again. Nearly the opposite, really. I live in Seattle."

Owusu nodded slowly. "But you stay close to them, right?"

Emile side-eyed him, half amused. Close-knit families were a cultural norm across Africa. Beneath the question was a whole worldview, family as the constellation by which you understand a man.

"I'm afraid I'll disappoint you there. My dad's Southern Baptist. My mother is Kunama. She practices equal parts Christianity and indigenous divination. Me? I'm gay. So, nobody's thrilled. My mother believes I'm possessed and has employed healers to cast it out of me. Every conversation ends up there. So... there aren't many."

He stared back out at the playa, memories surfacing like bruises under skin. It was not a coincidence that Seattle looked nothing like Texas or Eritrea.

"Fuck, man," Owusu said softly. "That's tough. I won't even tell my family I came here, and we're close. I can't imagine what it's like for you, brother."

He reached out and squeezed Emile's shoulder.

Emile exhaled. "There's never enough I can do right to make up for it."

They sat again in stillness. Then Owusu stirred.

"My friend, I have to go make breakfast for my camp. You're welcome to join. We're small, eight of us from all over Africa. Want to be a ninth?"

He handed Emile a card:

Camp Afrodisiac
Where rhythm, heat, and chill beats collide.
4:30 & Fate

Emile smiled. "Thanks. I need to get back to my crew, but I'd love to host you sometime. You and your camp."

Owusu raised a brow. "And what camp is that?"

"I'm with Magrathea," Emile said.

Owusu didn't react.

"The big bus," Emile added.

Owusu's eyes widened. "Shit, man. That's your art car?"

"That's my baby. Come ride with us. Just tell the crew you're my guest, and they'll make space. Bring your whole camp if you want."

"I'll take you up on that." Owusu stood and turned to Emile. With a casual bow, he brought his palms together.

"Blessings, my friend. May your road ahead be filled with ease."

Emile nodded. "You too, brother."

Owusu disappeared through the arch, vanishing into the morning.

Emile sat a moment longer, watching the horizon. Then he sighed, stood, and reflexively scanned the bench for any left-behind belongings. The dust was starting to pick up in the distance. A wind was building.

He wanted to be ahead of the storm this time.

7:00 and Inspiration, BRC, 8:16 AM - Cypher

"Jesus, it's hot!" Cypher yelled to no one in particular. The pup tent that had been so warm and comforting the night before was now a hotbox. Not the good kind. He was lying in a pool of his own sweat. He flailed his arms and legs, trying to work his way out of the mummy bag. He was all motion and no progress. The sleeping bag was soaked and sticking to every inch of his bare skin. Working one arm out of the bag, he began to peel it down his torso bit by bit until his other arm was free. He felt like he was emerging from a cocoon. Finally, he kicked free and pushed himself through the flap, collapsing onto the earth.

He breathed in the dry playa air deeply for a few moments, thankful to escape the humid tent. But the reprieve was short-lived. The early morning chill had already dissipated, the rising sun unrelenting, heralding what would surely be one of the hotter days on the playa.

Cypher's camp could only be described as Spartan. His sole structure was the tent. He quickly inventoried his food supply. With provisions mainly consisting of protein bars, chips, crackers, and a salami, he needed only one paper grocery bag and a relatively small cooler. Captain Dusty had provided him with three apples as they parted company. Cypher stowed two in his cooler, along with a large bottle of juice and a single bag of ice. He kept all of it in his tent, alongside three large plastic water jugs.

He bit into the remaining apple with a satisfying crack that released a chunk of the tender flesh into his mouth along with a cool burst of succulent juice. He closed his eyes, enjoying the slow liquid drip down his throat as he chewed the pulp. Sitting across his tent flap, he put the apple down on the playa next to the tent, top-first to keep it from rolling. He stepped away to survey his camp. He had posted up about thirty feet from the road. The area around him was barren but for the spider cracks in the hardpan. Cypher liked the minimalism but could feel the sun already pressing down hard.

He saw that his neighbors had fashioned shade in various forms. To his right were two pop-ups lashed together, one over the tent and the other creating a vestibule in front of the flap-covered door. A single chair sat under the vestibule. The camp appeared to be unoccupied. To his left was a more ambitious setup, incorporating the back of a shell-enclosed truck bed used for sleeping and storage, and augmented with a long, lean-to constructed of shade cloth and upright stanchions. The structure rocked slightly in the morning breeze. On the far side of the lean-to was an upright cupboard that served as a makeshift kitchen, complete with a stove, cooking equipment, and dinnerware. The top was open-sided and held gear; the bottom, enclosed with a door, stored dry goods. The rig owner was making coffee from grounds pulled from the cupboard. He guided the cupboard door shut with his shoe, concentrating on the task at hand.

Cypher reached into his tent and dragged out the closest water jug. He uncapped it and took a long pull, letting out a satisfied gasp after he swallowed. Then he splashed some of the lukewarm liquid on his face and neck. He grabbed a protein bar from his stash and slid it into the front pocket of his pants for later. Pulling on his sandals, Cypher completed his playa uniform, calf-length, cut-off, cargo-esqe pants and sandals. A shirt would've been too encumbering. He was fully prepared for the day now.

"You want some coffee?" the man across the way called out. Cypher squinted in his direction. Then, without reply, he walked over to the shaded camp area. The man greeted him with a full cup extended via a tattooed arm. The sleeve was old, faded, with black-blue engravings, more shapes bleeding into one another than any recognizable iconography. He had a neatly trimmed goatee and steel wool hair tied into a long ponytail. The man had a no-nonsense air but wasn't unfriendly.

"Sugar's in the cupboard and half-and-half's in the fridge if you want it." He gestured toward a dorm-style refrigerator next to the cupboard.

Cypher saw that the refrigerator was plugged into a battery station. A cable snaked from the battery out to solar panels on an angled frame, catching full morning sun.

"Nice setup," Cypher observed.

"Yeah, it's just enough," the man replied. Then he extended a labor-roughened hand. "I'm Drummond."

Cypher took the hand. "Cypher."

Drummond nodded toward Cypher's camp. "You're barebones-ing it."

Cypher glanced over at his tent. "That's the way I like it. Fewer things, less to worry about."

Drummond chuckled. "I prefer some minor comforts in my old age. And I consider shade more of a necessity out here."

Cypher gazed thoughtfully at his bivouac. "I'm like the Comanches, travel light and adapt."

Drummond chuckled again as he settled into one of his two chairs. Gesturing at the empty twin, he said, "Even the Comanches went home after their raids. That is, unless you're preparing for a battle I don't know about."

Cypher dropped into the other chair, sipping his coffee. "Nah. I just like to stay frosty."

Drummond barked a laugh. "Frosty is the last thing you'll be out here, without shade."

Cypher grinned. "I'm used to tough weather. I welcome it. A brave man likes the feel of rain on his face."

"A wise man gets out of the rain," Drummond countered, sipping his coffee. "Where are you from, Cypher?"

"I'm staying in San Francisco," Cypher said.

"Oh? Which part?" Drummond asked.

"Wherever I can find a spot," Cypher replied.

"A nomad, eh?" said Drummond.

"Yeah. I'm perfecting my nomadic life, you might say," Cypher said, clearly pleased with himself.

"You're definitely field-testing it out here," Drummond replied, gesturing toward Cypher's camp.

"My life's about all the experiences, none of the encumbrances," Cypher declared.

"Well, you'll certainly test that theory this week. You'll have to share your findings at the end," Drummond said.

Cypher smiled. "Happy to." He stood and handed back the empty cup. "Thanks for the coffee."

Drummond nodded. "Feel free to stop by. Plenty more where that came from."

Cypher nodded and stepped into the sun. He paused briefly, squinting at the empty stretch of hardpan ahead of him. His shoulders straightened. Then he moved forward, still bare-backed, still certain, already scanning the horizon.

As he walked, he thought, *I'll strip this place bare and wear it as my crown.* Satisfaction oozed from his pores.

9:30 and Avatar, BRC, 12:26 PM - Harley

Harley stared at the legal pad and made a note with the nub of a worn pencil. He stared at the long list of maintenance tasks and fixes. He was excited about the whole day's effort in front of him. He was ready to give the Ataraxis Warrior well-deserved love before this evening's performance.

"Dust storm's coming! Batten down your camps!"

Harley looked up from the pad. An unkempt man with long, playa-fied hair shouted the warning as he wandered past on Avatar.

Harley stood from his camp chair, scanning the southwest. Beyond the tents and RVs, beneath the craggy ridge, a roiling beige cloud surged toward the city fast, pregnant with oppression.

He moved.

Though Harley ran a tight ship, he never assumed he was fully ready. Playa weather could lull you with calm, then strike like a sucker punch.

He slammed the camper shut, zipped the storage tent, and tensioned the guy lines on his shade. Everything cinched, battened, sealed.

The storm hit the outer blocks first, camps vanishing in the swirl. Two blocks back, already swallowed. Then came the wall of dust.

He pulled his kerchief over his mouth and pulled his goggles down over his eyes. Avatar, thirty feet away, vanished in a blink.

A rattle. A bump. His chair collapsed and nudged his leg like a spooked dog, trying to bolt for Avalon. He caught it, folded it, and lashed it to a shade post with a pocket bungee.

No hero moves now. The safest place was inside.

He opened the camper door, stepped backward into the din, and pulled it closed behind him. *Thumpsh.*

Inside now, the dusty wind was just a muffled roar outside.

He tugged down the kerchief and slid up his goggles. He grabbed a wet wipe, scrubbed his face, and patted himself down.

Only then did he unlace the boots he'd just tightened.

"Note to self," he muttered, reaching for another wipe. "Bring the air compressor out to Ataraxis. Gotta clean the nozzles before tonight's show."

4:00 and Inner Playa, BRC, 12:35 PM - Emile

Emile guided Magrathea between art installations, now between the Man and the Esplanade. In a fit of pique, he decided to take Magrathea out. She deserved to be shown off, given her due. And, he was the showman and host to do it. He did not invite any of his campmates. Nor did they offer to come. Their lack of commitment to perfection galled him.

He had not made any stops, so the bus was empty. He had just crossed the 3:00 artery to the Man when the vibration flared up again. It rattled loudly for a moment and then quieted, but did not go away.

As he reached the 4:00 intersection, the vibration screamed, followed by a grinding sound, and then a loud clunk. Emile slowed the bus, but hadn't yet stopped when a heavy thunk struck the floorboard. Magrathea came to a halt on its own. Emile pressed the accelerator, and the engine roared, but the bus didn't move. Magrathea was dead in the water. Emile shut down the engine, slamming his fists on the steering wheel in frustration. He rose, uncertain and tense.

"Fuck. Even Magrathea is betraying me." Frustration and a hint of self-pity laced his tone. Staring at the engine access plate, he caught motion out of the corner of his eye and looked up to see the Man swallowed by the roiling mass. "Goddamn it." He was nearly in tears, his frustration had peaked.

The world disappeared into an ochre haze, and the storm didn't discriminate. It swallowed art cars and installations, camps and wanderers, the prepared and the reckless alike. Some, like Emile, found themselves trapped in their own creations. Others, like Ruben, were about to discover that sometimes the playa provides exactly what you need, exactly when you need it.

1:30 and Deep Playa, BRC, 12:42 PM - Ruben

No installation left unseen.

The mantra had carried Ruben out of the DPW Ghetto shortly after sunrise, eventually leading him deep into the outer playa.

The broad, flattened orb, like a globe that had settled under its own weight, hovered no more than a hundred yards away. From this angle, it appeared dark and featureless. Ruben had been making his way toward it for twenty minutes, buffeted by winds sharp enough to sting his eyes. A single bicycle had been parked beside it since he first noticed it, but no human had appeared during his approach. That told him that either the interesting part of the orb was on the far side or inside it. Less likely, someone had abandoned their bike nearly a mile from the city.

As he closed the distance to the orb, he looked toward the western side of the city. A large dust cloud was in the process of engulfing the southwestern part of Black Rock City. As he watched the dust storm's rapid progress, the city's western flank disappeared.

"Shit. That's not good," he said aloud. The dust cloud was now rapidly closing the distance to him.

He picked up his pace, not quite running, but moving with haste and hoping like hell that the orb had an accessible interior. He broke into a trot for the last twenty yards and circumnavigated the orb, past the lone bicycle. For a moment, despair grew as the orb seemed unbroken. But, on its far side, he found a barely perceptible, low-profile door. It had no knob. He pressed on the door. It clicked, then popped open enough for him to push his fingers into the crevice and pull it open. He slid through the doorway just as the dust cloud engulfed the orb. He grabbed the latch on the inside of the door and pulled it shut with a satisfying click.

He was cast into inky darkness. He peered around the interior but could see nothing. He pulled his backpack off his shoulders, planning to pull his headlamp out of the side pocket.

"Give yourself a few minutes. Your eyes will adjust. You can pull your boots off in the meantime." A woman's voice came from the far side of the room. "Also, the ceiling is about five and a half feet high, so watch your head."

Ruben nodded reflexively, realizing afterward that she might not be able to see it. As he unlaced his boots, his eyes adjusted enough to see tiny stars twinkling and changing colors. As he stepped away from his boots, his feet were cushioned by a luxurious carpet. As his eyes further adjusted to the low light of the starlit room, he saw that the sweep of the room was bordered with a low bench of seats. The bowed-out walls were fitted with upholstered pads that served as comfortable backrests.

He now noticed ethereal, low-volume music playing from surround sound speakers hidden in the walls. This room was a stark contrast to the harsh playa outside, providing a soothing mood and an inviting space of comfort. The woman, whose voice had guided him, sat cross-legged at the far side of the room. Ruben found a seat halfway between her and the door and settled in.

"We may be here for a while. A dust storm just hit, and it seems to be raging." Ruben said.

The woman nodded, nonplused. She was patiently peeling an orange.

She was fit in a muscular fashion. She wore a vest that allowed her to show off the muscled lines of her shoulders and arms. Beneath her knee-length, cut-off shorts were equally muscled calves. Runner? Wrestler? Gymnast? Her honey-colored hair was shaved to a half-inch stubble, completing what he thought was a butchie visage. However, her manner and carriage were very light, feminine, and nurturing. For Ruben, it was an interesting juxtaposition. She was built for the DPW but perhaps too sweet for that crew.

"I'm Ruben," he offered.

She extended her hand with an orange slice. "I'm Val."

Ruben took the slice. " Thank you. Nice to meet you, Val."

Just then, the door opened, dousing them with light and dust, breaking the room's spell. A woman pushed her way through the door, followed closely by a man. He quickly shut the door behind them.

Val gave them the same gentle guidance. "Give your eyes a few minutes to adjust. And, watch the ceiling. It's low. In the meantime, you can take off your shoes."

They too complied and went through the motions of adjustment, eventually settling together on the far side of the room from Ruben. Val also offered them orange slices. They took them with appreciation, thanking her.

Ruben pulled peaches from his bag, compliments of Toucan Girl. He extracted a pocketknife and made quick work of slicing them into sections.

The walls shuddered as a gust broke furiously against the structure. The woman of the couple said, "Damn. I'm glad that we're in here."

Ruben took stock of his shelter companions. The man had short-cropped salt-and-pepper hair and a narrowly shaped, neatly trimmed beard and no mustache. He was good-looking and fit, with an easy, open smile. His grey houndstooth fedora was pushed back, sitting high above his forehead.

His partner was a beautiful, willowy woman who seemed to be smiling constantly. Her tight, athletic body complemented his, a feminine counterpoint to his frame. Auburn hair spilled in soft waves over her shoulders—too fresh, too clean. She had to be new to the playa; hair never stayed that perfect out here. Her most striking feature, however, was her eyes: playful, merry, impossible to ignore. Together, the couple was objectively beautiful.

He offered a peach slice first to Val and then to the couple. The woman took her slice. Biting into it she moaned with pleasure. "That peach tastes amazing. Thank you. I'm Chloe."

She looked at the man next to her. " He patted his chest. "Jasper. Just damn glad to be here."

Ruben and Val made their introductions in turn.

Chloe unzipped the large compartment of her backpack, unloading the contents. From the pile of items, she pulled out a quart plastic bag stuffed with watermelon slices. Breaking the seal, she looked up at her companions. "Watermelon, anyone?"

Jasper pulled out a bag of nuts and fruit trail mix. Chloe produced cheese slices. Val set out slices of barbecued chicken.

"I officially declare this lunch," said Jasper.

Val tossed out four, individually wrapped Bit-O-Honey bars. Jasper's eyebrows raised in amusement. "I haven't eaten one of those since I was a kid."

"Exactly the point." Val smiled.

The group was quiet for a moment as they enjoyed their jury-rigged potluck meal. Ruben meditated on the sudden shift of fortune. Moments ago, he had been on a solo walkabout and facing an oppressive dust storm. Now he was part of a gathering of comrades, enjoying a meal.

Jasper pulled a flask out. He unscrewed the cap and offered it to Ruben. Ruben blinked. He raised his hand, hesitated, then waved it away, shaking his head. They continued to eat quietly.

Val finally broke the silence. She asked no one in particular, "What's the coolest thing you've experienced today?"

Chloe went first. "We arrived on the playa in the wee hours this morning, fully expecting to have to pitch up our camp. Our campmates had set up our tent and laid out our sleeping bags, so all we had to do was slide in and take a nap."

Val went next. "I watched the first rays of morning light play off the Ataraxis Warrior. I meant to take pictures of it, but it was so beautiful I couldn't stop crying long enough to set up my camera." The retelling obviously moved her. Her eyes grew misty.

"My vote goes to the spontaneous potluck we're having," said Jasper. "I love that this sort of thing happens all the time out here."

They all looked at Ruben. He suddenly felt shy. He looked down at the floor, then back up to his companions. "Very early this morning, I played chess with a man somewhere out here in the middle of nowhere on a psychedelic chessboard. He told me that we burners create the chaos out here that brings Burning Man to life. I've only thought of chaos as a destructive force. But maybe... maybe it builds, too. This wasn't a plan for us. It was a storm. And somehow it turned into a little piece of grace."

A gust hit the structure again, shaking the walls around them.

Ruben looked around at these strange, beautiful people. Not a plan in sight.

Maybe this was the Burn. Not the fire. Not the noise. This.

He smiled. *Let it rage.*

The storm eventually passed, as all storms do. By the time Ruben emerged from the orb with his unexpected companions, the dust had settled into a thin haze, and the sky was already thinking about sunset. He walked back toward the DPW Ghetto with Val's orange slices still sweet on his tongue, feeling like he'd just witnessed something essential about this place... how chaos could birth grace if you let it. Across the city, in a very different camp, someone else was about to discover what happened when you fought the chaos instead.

Street Unknown, BRC, 12:51 PM - Rachael

Ambition Interruptus.

Rachael felt thwarted. She had wandered aimlessly and fruitlessly through the streets looking for someone, anyone with whom she resonated. And now this.

She had never felt claustrophobic in the open air... until now. The whiteout enveloped her like an oppressive cloud. She could barely see her outstretched hand. She knew she was on a street, but no longer knew which one or where she was on it. An imagined image of an art car looming from nowhere, to run her over, flashed a spike of anxiety through her.

She stepped carefully, each foot placed like she was testing a frozen lake. Veering left, she searched for the road's edge. A shape emerged. She touched a metal stake, one of the street delineator post. Relief pulsed through her, she had found the street's edge.

She wiped her goggles with her sleeve, barely improving her visibility. A few more steps brought her to a burn barrel, then a couch. Guy ropes brushed her leg, indicating a structure. A throw rug appeared underfoot. An entrance, maybe.

The idea of wandering into someone's camp uninvited made her hesitate. She preferred clear invitations. A reason to belong. But she was desperate now. The runner stretched ahead, a line of shoes beside it. A signal that this was a communal space. Two more steps, and canvas walls rose around her, a Moroccan tent. She pulled the flap open and entered.

Inside, dim light glowed. Music, laughter, the murmur of comfort. A bartender raised a hand. "Welcome, intrepid stranger. Take off your boots and join us in a libation."

He turned theatrically to the tent's occupants. "Friends, welcome another brave traveler!"

"Huzzah!" The crowd cheered in unison.

Clearly, she was not the first to arrive in this manner. She unlaced her boots, slid them outside, and shook the dust from her hat and goggles.

"I, uh... I don't have a cup," she said, stepping toward the bar.

"No worries." A woman stood and offered her a metal cup. "Come join us once you've got a drink."

Rachael blinked at the offer. She had expected suspicion, not welcome.

She accepted the cup, got her drink, and walked toward the group. The same woman patted a cushion beside her. "Please. Sit."

Rachael set her gear down and dropped cross-legged onto the cushion.

"I'm Aruna," the woman said, tapping her chest. "And these are my new best friends I just met: Catman, Liv, and Fakir." Each nodded or raised a cup in greeting.

Aruna handed her a packet of moist towelettes. "We're doing a little playa spa thing."

Gratefully, Rachael began cleaning the dust from her skin as they chatted.

"Still bad out there?" Aruna asked.

"I literally felt my way here," Rachael said. "Glad I found this place. It sucked out there."

"We're glad you did too." Aruna raised her drink. They clinked cups.

"Catman was just telling us about the origin of costumes out here," she added.

Catman nodded. "Back in the early days, people wore street clothes. It was more of an anarchist event. One year, a group of drag queens showed up in full regalia and changed the tone. We've never looked back."

"So drag queens are responsible for the costume madness?" Liv said, grinning. "I love that."

Catman sipped. "The event started with artists and oddballs. The oddballs aren't just tolerated, they're the point."

Fakir leaned forward. "But I've been struggling with a paradox. This place feels so white, burner culture, the people. I'm Arab, brown, and Muslim. I do feel like an outsider. But I've also never felt more... included. It's surreal. Like I'm suspended between worlds."

Aruna nodded. "I feel you." She held up her toffee-colored arm. "That threading-the-needle tension? Same here."

Liv chimed in. "I'm on the spectrum. This place is... a lot. But people have been kind. I'm used to being told to suck it up. That hasn't happened here."

Catman raised his cup. "As the straight, neurotypical white dude in the group,... sorry, and welcome."

They laughed.

Then Aruna looked at Rachael with gentle curiosity. Rachael hesitated, then surprised herself by answering.

"I don't have much figured out. It's my first year. I've spent the past three days wandering around with my mouth open. I mean... It's amazing. But disorienting. I feel the permission to just be. But letting my guard down? That's not easy."

She glanced around the circle. "I like to think that being trans isn't the most interesting thing about me. But... it flavors everything in my life. I'm seeing how much I brace. How I perform safety."

She trailed off. "No answers. Just questions."

"Maybe that's the point," Aruna said quietly. "And either way, you're with us now."

"Huzzah!" Liv said again. Their cups clinked.

Aruna reached out and touched Rachael's cheek. "You're so pretty. Can I braid your hair?"

Rachael rolled her eyes upward. "You can try. It's pretty playafied."

"I have wipes, oil, and a brush," Aruna declared triumphantly. She moved behind Rachael and got to work.

Rachael wasn't used to people fussing over her. The attention was unsettling and unexpectedly comforting.

"I'm glad you're here, Rachael," Aruna said as she smoothed the brush through her hair.

"I... I'm glad I'm here, too. Though this might be the first time I've actually said that. This week has been hard. I still don't know where to put it."

"Give it time," Aruna said. "In my first year, it took three months to understand what it meant for me. The immediacy of everything here makes processing a challenge. You need time to let it simmer."

She paused, her voice softening. "That sense of belonging, there are two parts to it. One is being welcomed in." She tapped Rachael's shoulder. "Like you were today."

Rachael nodded.

"The other is accepting the invitation. Choosing to step into the fold." She ran the brush again, gentle and sure. "I still have to remind myself to do that. Maybe you do too."

Rachael exhaled slowly. "I think you're giving me too much credit. I'm still stuck on accepting."

Aruna giggled and wrapped her arms around her. "I'm glad you're working on it."

She settled back and began the braids.

Rachael let her words settle inside her, warm and unsteady. Then she murmured, "Working on it seems to be my only job out here."

4:00 and Inner Playa, BRC, 1:19 PM - Emile

The deck plate had been removed, leaving a gaping hole in the floor. Tools sprawled across the floor like a battlefield with wrenches, screwdrivers, and wire ties scattered in a pattern of mounting frustration. Emile was waist-deep in the engine cavity, cursing. Dust enveloped him, rising through the opening like a punishment.

Every time he wiped his goggles clean, a fresh coat of grit settled before he could even resume. He swatted at them again, but it was pointless. His visibility, like his patience, was gone.

He slammed a socket wrench against the floor, the sharp clang lost in the wind. His frustration was eclipsed by anxiety, which was in turn drowned by a dull, aching misery.

His quest for perfection was rewarded with ash and dust.

1:00 and Deep Playa, BRC, 1:34 PM - Justine

Justine wiped the dust from her goggle lenses, making the world slightly less opaque. The immediately filmed over again. She sighed. Windshield wipers would have been handy. She studied the structure before her. The crooked sign over the door read, *Last Chance Cabaret and Fuel Depot*. She recoiled. Art and glibness did not mix.

Still, she wanted out of the dust.

"Beggars can't be choosers," she muttered into the scarf wrapped across her mouth.

A heavy curtain covered the entire side facing her. It hung weighted, swinging only with resistance. Down the center ran a slit from top to bottom. She pushed her fingers into the gap. A line of magnetic snaps popped apart under her touch. She slipped through and let the curtain fall behind her, magnets clicking shut, sealing the wind and grit outside.

"Crafty," she murmured.

She stood in place, waiting for her eyes to adjust. She pushed her goggles up to her forehead and lowered her scarf, breathing in the relative stillness. In front of her stood a neat formation of chairs, seating for maybe fifty. A dozen Burners milled about, chatting quietly. Beyond the rows stood a small stage. To her right, an unattended bar held only a five-gallon water cooler with a faucet near its base. A paper sign above it read: *Cocktail of the Day: Electrolyte Refresher*.

Justine crossed to the bar and topped off her water bottle. As she tightened the lid, a voice crackled over the sound system. It had the affected warmth of an AM radio DJ, and instantly confirmed her suspicion about the glibness.

"Attention, travelers and truth seekers. Our show will begin momentarily. Please take a seat if you are so moved."

The Burners settled. Justine found a spot in the back row. The air buzzed with that quiet anticipation that precedes something... good or bad.

She crossed her arms and prepared for a train wreck. Everything screamed amateur. Lights blinked on one by one, clumsily, as a stagehand worked a control panel. Justine thought about leaving, but the whiteout still raged beyond the curtain.

A man in a wheelchair was wheeled onto the stage. He had a scraggly beard and shook almost violently as he pulled deeply from a joint. A guitar lay across his lap, its neck resting on the armrest. With each inhale, his spasms softened. His assistant took the joint, placed the guitar gently into his hands, and jacked it into the sound system before slipping offstage.

The man began to strum, searching for melody. Sour notes clanged out.

Then came the woman. Heavy, disheveled, wheeling an oxygen tank behind her. *Skreet, skreet, skreet.* She stepped center stage and took several deep breaths through her mask.

A third figure emerged, a man whose right leg stayed stiff as a flagpole. His gait stuttered as he crossed to join the woman. She glanced at him, then to the man with the guitar. He gave a slight nod. She returned it and faced the audience.

The guitarist began the introduction to *Wicked Game*. Still rough, but with fewer missed notes. At the end of the riff, the woman took one last breath and began to sing.

Her voice was reedy and strained. She paused between lines to breathe. The man beside her began to dance, pivoting on his stiff leg in slow rotations.

It was objectively terrible. The notes wobbled. The melody frayed. The rhythm came and went.

And yet, it was beautiful.

The guitarist was completely present. He played not just with conviction, but with care, filling the space left by her gasps, adjusting as needed. The woman sang with her whole soul exposed. Every note cracked open something. The dancer was all in. His body moved like an incantation. He was in love... with the music, the stage, the audience, the world.

When the singer met Justine's eyes, something inside her caught. She felt seen in a way that cracked her armor. The moment stretched, soul to soul.

None of them were technically good. And it did not matter. The performance was a gift. Perfect in its imperfection.

A word surfaced from somewhere deep in her belly, rose like breath through her chest, and pushed its way out before she could stop it.

"Beautiful."

When the song ended, the room exploded. This was not polite applause. It was a mix of hoots, stomps, laughter, and tears. The three performers huddled together on stage, trembling with adrenaline. They had missed every cue. And they glowed like saints.

Justine clapped. Then she whistled, fingers between her lips. Her throat was tight. Around her, the room surged with emotion.

She was no longer watching as an expert. She was not evaluating. She was witnessing something true.

A fire welled up from her belly and ran through her chest. She suddenly wanted nothing more than to practice with passion. She bolted for the curtain.

4:00 and Inner Playa, BRC, 2:08 PM - Emile

Emile stared out at the dust that swallowed the bus. A brown haze in every direction. The wind turned the brightest part of the day into a world stuck in dusk. He checked the clock. "Fuck."

He kept cleaning, though there wasn't much left to do. The dopamine-flushed relief he'd felt finding the problem, a sheared linkage bolt, had long since faded. He'd made a temporary fix. Now, he was just pacing. Restless. Nothing left to tinker with.

He glanced again at the blur outside. The landscape hadn't changed. "Fuck. It's been an hour and a half."

The bus felt smaller by the minute. He crossed from end to end like a caged animal, boots echoing against the floor, sweat and grit clinging to his skin.

"Fuck it."

He climbed into the driver's seat, turned down the music, and pressed the start button. The engine rattled, then settled into a low, steady purr. Visibility had improved... barely. Maybe fifty feet. Dust still scraped across the windshield in gritty waves. But he'd had enough of waiting.

"I can grind this out at a few miles an hour."

4:00 and Inner Playa, BRC, 2:12 PM - Cypher

"Storms break men. I'm no man. I'm evolution's junkyard dog." Cypher screamed into the storm. Then he muttered, "I can't see shit." His diatribe was muffled by the scarf wrapped across his nose and mouth. The wall of dust was thick, impenetrable. His eyes stung, blinking against the bite of alkaline grit.

He rubbed at them uselessly, smearing more dust. A low rumble began to build in front of him, distant at first, then swelling, encompassing. Something massive. Something approaching.

Then, there it was. A bus. Towering. Barreling toward him out of nowhere. Cypher froze.

4:00 and Inner Playa, BRC, 2:13 PM - Emile

A figure emerged, right there in the windshield. Emile slammed the brakes. The wipers dragged a squeal across the glass, revealing the wide-eyed, dust-coated man inches away, unmoving except for his roaming gaze.

He looked like a sculpture, part playa, part man. Dreads, wrapped head, no shirt, no gear. Just a frozen statue studying the bus like it had been summoned.

Emile set the brake, steadied himself, then opened the door and called out, "Are you alright?"

"Yeah, I'm cool," came the muffled reply.

"Wanna come in?" Emile asked. No hesitation. The man moved forward, climbed aboard, and shook himself with a full-bodied whip, head to toe, like a dog. The dust cloud settled enough to reveal a young man. Late teens, maybe early twenties.

"You sure you're okay?" Emile repeated.

The man stood on the landing, scanning the space. "Wooooooooooah," he finally said aloud, still entranced.

"Do you have water?" Emile asked.

The man blinked. "Uh, I forgot it."

"You thirsty?"

A beat. Then, "Yeah."

Emile handed him a gallon jug. The kid collapsed onto a bench, turned up the jug, and chugged.

"You really need to carry water," Emile said gently. "That's survival 101 out here."

"Yeah, that makes sense."

"I'm Emile."

"Cypher," he replied, shaking the offered hand.

"Where were you headed?"

Cypher's brow furrowed, like the question hadn't occurred to him. "Nowhere in particular. Just looking for something new."

Emile smirked. "Here it is, I guess."

"Yeah. I guess so," Cypher said, taking in the space. "Can I check it out?"

"Sure. Might as well ride this storm out. We call her Magrathea..." Emile paused, studying Cypher's reaction. Something about this kid's timing bothered him. Who wanders into a dust storm without water, without destination, without fear? "Tell me, Cypher, how exactly did you end up wandering around in zero visibility with no supplies?"

Cypher's grin widened. "Things have a way of working out for me. Like right now."

Emile felt a familiar tightness in his chest. The kid's casual attitude toward survival protocols grated against everything he'd learned about playa safety. But there was something else, an odd synchronicity that made him wonder if this encounter was as random as it seemed.

7:30 and Enlighten, BRC, 2:22 PM - Cypher

Cypher followed Emile up to the second level. His eyes widened when he saw the DJ booth.

"I've always wanted to DJ," he said, already stepping into the booth.

"What's your genre?"

"Dancy shit," Cypher shrugged.

Emile smiled. "I might be able to hook you up."

Within minutes, Cypher was sampling tracks and layering sounds with a beginner's luck that felt freakishly intuitive. His hands moved across the controls like he'd been doing this for years, not minutes.

Emile watched, fascinated despite himself. The kid wasn't just pressing buttons randomly. He was building something, creating layers that shouldn't work together but somehow did.

A low rumble of bass began to vibrate through the bus floor. Then Cypher found the volume slider.

The music exploded outward, cutting through the howl of the dust storm. Even muffled by the weather, the sound would carry. In this visibility, audio was the only signal that traveled.

"Careful," Emile said, reaching for the controls. "We don't want to..."

But Cypher was already adjusting, bringing the levels down while maintaining the intricate mix. He looked up at Emile with a grin.

"Don't worry. I know exactly how loud we need to be."

Gordian Knot, 8:30 and Esplanade, BRC, 2:32 PM - Crawford

All hell was breaking loose outside. The RV rattled in the buffeting winds. Through the window, a wall of beige, coated in yellowed varnish, swallowed everything. A class-five dust storm. It didn't get worse than this. Nothing to do now but wait it out and assess the damage later.

Crawford had returned to the empty RV in the early hours. No sign that Vicky had been there. Asking around that morning yielded nothing. If anyone knew anything, they weren't sharing. He was sure Jimmy was behind it. The man had watched him for years, studied his moves. Now Jimmy was turning those strategies against him.

Maybe Penelope had been a setup. A wedge Jimmy drove between him and Vicky. That bastard.

He'd tried buttonholing a few campmates for intel, but the dust storm shut everything down. Now he sat stuck in the RV, drumming his fingers on the table. The irony wasn't lost on him, the storm outside, swallowing the horizon in a curtain of ochre, was a perfect mirror of the chaos in his mind. As the wind howled, so did suspicion. He sat motionless, stewing.

The RV door slammed open. A burst of dust surged in. Crawford heard a muffled curse just before Vicky stepped up into the rig and forced the door closed behind her. She tugged off her goggles and dropped them onto the dining table, then began patting herself down, starting with her hair and then her clothes.

Crawford stood, retrieved a packet of wet wipes, and pulled one halfway out of the slot, holding the pack out to her.

She stared at the offering long enough to make him uncomfortable. Just as he started to lower his hand, she took the whole packet without a word and went about wiping the dust from her skin. He slid back into the bench seat, watching. From experience, he knew not to speak. When Vicky was in a mood, his charm was a wasted effort.

She took her time, methodically wiping each exposed surface, then unlaced her boots and pulled them off. Crawford bit back the urge to comment on how long it was taking. In most situations, he'd already be complaining. This time, silence felt like the better play.

She slung off her backpack, gathered her goggles, and crossed to the nook. Dropping her gear on the table, she sat opposite him.

Crawford began, "I've been worried about you..."

"Nope," she cut in, pointing a finger at him. "You don't get to control this conversation."

He snapped his mouth shut. That tone. He'd never heard it from her before.

"Let's start easy," she said, fixing her gaze on him. "With you answering a question I already know the answer to."

"Okay. " His voice barely carried across the table. "Did you sleep with Penelope?"

The bluntness threw him off his game. He thought about finessing the answer, but something told him that would not play.

"Yes." Vicky looked down and sighed. "Thank you for being honest. That makes the rest of this easier."

She stood, fetched a cup from the cabinet, and poured grapefruit juice from the fridge. She drank slowly, deliberately, then returned to her seat.

"We talked about this open relationship thing while you were driving here. I told you I wasn't comfortable with it. You agreed to put it on hold."

"I agreed to talk about it when you got here," he corrected.

Her brow arched. "That's your position, counselor? Letter of the law?"

"I get that you're upset, but..."

"Stop. "She cut the air with one hand, not loud, not sharp, but final. "You don't get to play the 'now that I see you're upset' card. You knew what you were doing. You wanted what you wanted. You did what you did."

He pivoted. "Don't you see? Jimmy engineered this whole thing. He's trying to drive a wedge between us, make his play to take over the company."

She laughed. Once. Hard. "Only a narcissist like you could spin that fantasy. Jimmy? He's got no guile. Everything about him is right there on the surface."

"Are you kidding? You saw how he took over the camp meeting, it was a bald power grab."

"Crawford, stop." Her tone turned deadly calm. "Jimmy stepped up because there was a mutiny brewing. The crew was sick of you playing emperor while they hauled bricks. Then the news about you and Penelope got around. Half the camp wanted you gone."

"This is my camp," he snapped.

"That's the problem," she said. "You actually believe that. It's not your camp. It's our camp. Jimmy gets that. That's why he gave credit to the crew. That's why he led the meeting."

"Oh, Vicky," he said, patronizingly. "You're missing the big picture. Did you know he threatened to leave the company right before the IPO?"

"He didn't threaten," she said. "He told you straight up that he's resigning."

He stared at her. "Are you part of this?"

She rolled her eyes. "Fuck you, Crawford. No one has to plot against you. All we have to do is sit back and let your bad behavior do the work. Jimmy quitting, the crew's disgust, my departure, that's all you."

"I..." He started to argue, then froze as her words sank in. "Wait, what?"

"I'm leaving you, Crawford. Like Jimmy, I've hit my limit. I'm done waiting for you to figure out what an asshole you are. Penelope was the last straw. And by the way, she was mortified, apologetic, even. Turns out she values her friendship with me more than your little tryst."

She stood abruptly. "It's your lucky Burn, my friend. You get to do anything you want. Free pass. I won't be here. I'm taking time to make some decisions about my life. Enjoy the ride. Go crazy. Play jazz."

She turned and walked into the bedroom, shutting the door behind her. Crawford heard the sounds of packing, cabinets opening, zippers, and the scrape of gear being dragged across the floor.

"Vicky, come on. Let's talk. We can work through this. If I'd known you were serious about closing the relationship, I never would've..."

The bedroom door flew open. Vicky stormed past him, two satchels slung over her shoulders. She grabbed her pack off the table.

"Wait!" he said, rising. "Don't I get to tell my side?"

She stopped. Turned.

"This isn't your show, Crawford. That time is over."

Then she was out the door. She lingered for a moment, just long enough for the wind to fill the cabin with dust, then slammed it shut behind her.

Crawford stood in silence. The air inside the RV settled into a slow, smoky haze, curling along the surfaces like memory.

He stared down at the table.

"She forgot her goggles," he said.

7:30 and Enlighten, BRC, 3:36 PM - Emile

Magrathea was once again in motion, still at its slow crawl.

Emile was surprised at how quickly Cypher picked up sound mixing. They'd spent over an hour playing, Cypher grinning the whole time. Every so often, Emile would check the visibility, still beige walls on all sides.

Then, finally, the dust began to ease. Patches of open sight stretched a hundred feet or more. Emile decided to keep going as long as he could see and stop when he couldn't. Much to Cypher's disappointment, he shut the sound system down. Driving in this soup required full attention. One Cypher-related incident was plenty.

He was easing along when a new curtain of white-out swept across the road. His foot was lifting toward the brake...

BANG BANG BANG.

A pounding exploded from the right front.

Emile's heart leaped into his throat. He stomped both feet on the brake, killed the engine, and scrambled to the door, flinging it open in one motion.

He was about to bolt out when he spotted her: a small, dust-caked woman standing calmly at the bottom of the stairs.

"Can I come aboard?" she asked, not impolite, but with zero room for argument.

Emile's legs wobbled. He gripped the seatback. "Yes," he whispered, mostly so he could close the door.

She bounded up, shaking herself off as she climbed.

"Was that you?" he asked, still trying to coax his heart back into his chest.

"Yes," she said, sheepish but direct. "I shouted, but I don't think you heard me over the wind. So I knocked."

"Knocked?" he repeated. "I thought I'd hit an IED."

She blushed so hard it showed through the dust on her face. "I'm really sorry. You were headed my way, and I was kind of miserable out there. So I gambled to get out of the storm and get a ride."

Emile wiped sweat from his brow. "Only if you can restore the ten years I just lost."

She looked down, visibly contrite. "I'm really sorry."

Despite his frayed nerves, Emile smiled. "C'mon in. You're on the slow boat to the west side of the city. I'm Emile, and that's Cypher."

She looked over at Cypher, flaked out on the wall bench, then back at Emile. "I'm Justine."

"Where to, Justine?"

"My friend's camp is at 9:30 and Gnosis. If you get me to the grid, I can find it. I wouldn't be out in this garbage, but we've got performance practice."

"I can get you pretty damn close," Emile said. "What kind of performance?"

"Hoops and acrobatics," she replied. "Want a preview? Might earn back some of those lost years."

Emile laughed. "I could use it." He settled onto a bench along the wall.

Justine reached over her shoulder like she was drawing a sword, pulling out curved pieces of decorated PVC. In seconds, she had a hoop assembled.

"I only brought one, and the stilts would take a while. So this'll be the teaser. Rain check on the full monty."

"Fair trade," Emile said, as she stashed a bag beneath Cypher's bench. "We'll take what we can get."

"Need music?" Cypher called, already moving. He was up the stairs and back in the booth in less than a minute, music blasting.

Justine had already begun. She started with her left foot, not the waist, a bold move. She worked the hoop up to her thigh, let it drop, switched legs mid-skip, repeated.

Then she stepped in with both legs, letting the hoop rise smoothly over calves, knees, hips, and torso.

She dropped her hand to her side, letting the hoop ride up and out to her finger. She caught it with the other hand, spun it down her arm to her neck, then popped it to her forehead.

Emile whistled and clapped. "She's the real deal," he whispered to Cypher.

Cypher didn't respond, just leaned forward, hands clenched, mouth open.

Justine snapped her head again. The hoop flew toward the back, just skimming the ceiling. She dropped, rolled, flipped, cartwheeled into the catch, then flicked it forward again. This time, she stopped in a half-handstand, one leg catching the hoop on its way down.

She rose fluidly, the hoop now spinning at her chest. Arms lifted, hands nested like a diver's, she let it rise into her palms. She caught it and bowed.

For the first time in her life, she hadn't focused on precision. She freestyled. She felt it, expressed it. Gave herself fully to her audience of two.

Emile watched her, struck. Her movement was effortless, but something about it reached under his skin. She was not trying to impress. She was present and living *in* the moment. He clapped hard, standing, hooting.

Cypher stared, stunned. Then, barely audible over the music, he said, "That was the most beautiful thing I've ever seen."

"I second that," Emile said. Then to Cypher: "Mind turning the music off?"

Cypher bolted up the stairs.

When the sound cut, Emile turned to Justine.

"I don't know if you saw us last night..."

"I did," she cut in. "Heard you from deep playa. You were going off. Magrathea's the talk of the town. Nighttime place to be."

Emile grinned. "Anytime you want to perform, we'll host. Spotlight, sound, the works."

"You haven't even seen my good stuff."

"Great. Surprise me every night. You've got an open invite."

"You're on, Magrathea-man."

He headed for the driver's seat. As he passed, he saw Cypher still staring.

Uh-oh, Emile thought. *The boy's smitten. Hopefully, he'll talk more with her than he did with me.*

He fired up the engine. A window of visibility opened, and the bus crept forward. Longer gaps in the dust. Clearer sight lines.

They were headed home.

7:30 and Enlighten, BRC, 4:13 PM - Justine

Justine plopped into a seat within talking distance from Cypher. He gave off puppy energy, hopefully not the annoying kind. She pulled a towel from her backpack and wiped the sweat from her face, grateful for the excuse to regroup.

"Dust storm refugee too?" she said with a small smile.

"Yeah," he grinned. "Nearly got run over, but Emile made up for it with a ride and a DJ slot."

She nodded. "Good trade."

Cypher leaned back, exuding easy confidence. "Things come to me when I need them. That's how I live. I travel light, call for what I need, and it shows up."

Justine wasn't sure if she admired or pitied the certainty. "Impressive," she said, unsure if she meant it.

When she asked if it was his first time out here, he launched into a monologue about a gifted ticket, destiny, and avoiding "theme camp politics." His grin was wide, self-satisfied.

She noticed he hadn't asked a single thing about her. Sliding her backpack into place, she lay back and closed her eyes, not to sleep but to retreat. Some storms were made of dust. Others, of disconnection.

Across from her, Cypher blinked, sensing the shift but not understanding it.

7:30 and Enlighten, BRC, 5:06 PM - Emile

As Magrathea pulled into its parking spot, most of the encampment came out to greet Emile, relief softening the anxious tension that had shadowed his long absence. Dust was still in the air, but the storm was blowing itself out. They could see down most of 10:00.

Dobbs' voice boomed over the welcoming chatter. "Jesus, man. We thought you'd driven off a cliff."

Emile smiled. "Rumors of my demise have been greatly exaggerated." Then, more seriously, "Sorry, folks. First, the bus had a mechanical failure that I patched. But, it needs a real fix. Then that storm locked me down for hours. Visibility was zero. But..." he nodded toward the bus steps, "I found some friends along the way."

He gestured casually, but a flicker of pride tightened his chest. After hours alone in dust and silence, it felt good to return with something. *Someone*, worth sharing.

"This is Cypher, an up-and-coming DJ, and Justine, who puts on one hell of a hooping and acrobatic performance. Look for her to headline our gigs this week."

Both of Emile's storm companions offered quick, self-conscious waves. Justine's smile was polite but fleeting. Cypher blinked into the attention like someone unused to being seen.

Justine stepped forward. "Thanks for the ride, Emile. I need to boogie over to my friend's camp." True to his word, they'd stopped a few blocks from her destination.

Emile nodded. "You're always welcome aboard."

Cypher perked up, stepping closer. "I'll walk with you. My camp's that way too."

Justine gave him a side glance, not unfriendly, but measuring. After a beat, she nodded and hoisted her bag onto one shoulder. "Let's go, then."

She paused at the foot of the steps and looked back at Emile. "Thanks again for the ride. And the stage."

Emile dipped his head in a quiet bow. "Anytime."

He watched them head off, Cypher falling into step half a pace behind her, eyes scanning ahead and sideways like a curious stray.

A small smile tugged at Emile's mouth. "Let's see how that plays out," he muttered, before turning back to the grinning faces of his crew.

9:30 and Gnosis, BRC, 5:07 PM - Justine

Justine looked over her shoulder at him, "Okay." He seemed harmless enough, if a bit deluded. It was only two blocks away.

Emile hugged them both goodbye, reminding Justine to take him up on his invitation to perform. She promised she would. Then she made her way out of the crowd and onto 10:00 to navigate toward the rehearsal. Cypher was a step behind her but catching up. By the time they passed the tail of the bus, they were walking side by side. Justine realized, with the slightest twinge, that Cypher was smitten. His body language gave him away, eager, open, trying not to hover. He wasn't pushy, just quietly orbiting.

"Where are you camped?" she asked.

He was quiet for a moment, like someone searching through an overstuffed junk drawer.

Then, with triumph, "7:00 and Inspiration." She noted he was going a bit out of his way to walk with her.

"You seem like you were made for this place too," Cypher said, hopeful, like he was willing it into existence.

She gave a fleeting, wry smile. "I'm still figuring out how I feel about all this. I can't say I'm entirely comfortable with the freewheeling craziness."

"You looked comfortable on the bus," he offered.

"You mean my performance?" she asked. "That's my world. That's what hours and hours of practice get you. It's everything that isn't a performance that's harder."

"Well, yeah, that was amazing," he said. "But I meant when you chased us down and knocked. That was bold."

She shrugged. "The worst he could do was say no. And if he told me to fuck off, I'd still be standing in the dust, no worse off than I was."

He blinked, took that in, then nodded. "I guess that's true."

He was scanning the 10:00 strip and nearly missed it when Justine turned onto Gnosis. He shuffled quickly to draw even with her again. They were now wandering the deep back streets of Black Rock suburbia. The camps here were small, often personal, and many were in various states of nap-mode. Most structures were people's temporary living rooms, shaded, low-maintenance, dust-framed. Campers lounged in folding chairs and hammocks, letting the breeze do what it could.

The dust hadn't fully cleared, but it no longer strangled the city. Most passersby were friendly with waves, nods, and hellos. One man offered to hose them down with a Super Soaker. Justine declined. She wasn't eager to turn her outer layer into mud. Cypher, on the other hand, stepped forward with theatrical flair, arms open. He got a head-to-toe soaking, turned, and asked for the back.

Justine had kept walking. He jogged to catch up, water dripping from his hair. Then she stopped. He turned and found her smiling at him, something different in her expression now. Perhaps it was ease, maybe even affection. She looked relaxed, grounded. "This is me." She pointed her thumb over her shoulder at the camp behind her. "Thanks for walking with me, Cypher."

He blinked, surprised they'd arrived so soon. "Uh... okay." He hesitated, waved half-heartedly. "Goodbye."

She stepped forward and wrapped him in a warm, full-bodied hug. His arms floated for a second before settling around her, unsure where to land.

"Thank you for being my storm buddy," she said.

"Sure," he murmured. He touched his cheek where hers had brushed it. "Have a good practice."

"I will." She smiled, turned, and walked into the camp. She did not glance back.

Cypher stood still for a moment, feeling the imprint of her presence lingering like warmth in the air. The hug had short-circuited his usual internal chatter. He didn't know what to make of the feeling that crept in. It wasn't just awe or infatuation.

It felt a little like...belonging.

And he didn't know what to do with that.

7:00 and Inspiration, BRC, 5:22 PM - Cypher

Cypher was disappointed that she had left him. He felt like she was just starting to warm up to him. She was the first person he had truly felt comfortable talking with since he'd left San Francisco. As she disappeared into her camp, he turned away, a little hollow, and continued down Gnosis for several more blocks until he reached 7:00.

At 7:00, he turned right and followed it to Inspiration. Veering left, he began scanning for his camp. He spotted both of his neighbors' setups, slightly worse for wear from the wind. But his own plot looked... empty.

Closer inspection revealed that his water jugs were still where he'd left them. But his tent, sleeping bag, backpack, and food were gone.

After asking around, he finally tracked what remained of his backpack and sleeping bag to a camp across the street. According to eyewitnesses, a gust had turned his tent into a kite, launching it nearly to Hallowed before it tangled itself around a pop-up frame. The folks in that camp had salvaged what they could, weighing it down with water jugs to prevent further escape. The tent poles were cracked and broken.

He thanked them, gathered the limp remains, and trudged back across the street.

Another round of searching uncovered his cooler under a truck and his tent bag in someone's makeshift living room. The bag of food was gone. It looked like he'd be rationing for the rest of his stay.

His neighbor across the street wandered over. "Do you have any rebar?"

Cypher looked puzzled. "I don't know what rebar is."

"It's a heavy metal stake. You drive it into the playa to keep your tent from flying off. If I had an extra, I'd give it to you, but I'm out. For now, just stuff your water jugs inside your tent when you're not in it. That should keep it grounded."

Staring at the small, torn pile that used to be his camp, Cypher nodded. "Thanks. I'll do that."

The man hesitated, clearly sympathetic. "You want to join us for dinner?"

Cypher gazed at the mess in silence. His earlier certainty about calling in what he needed felt thinner now. He looked up. "Yeah, thanks. That would be great."

He sighed and followed the man back to his camp.

While Cypher was learning hard lessons about preparedness, other parts of the city were settling into their evening rhythms. The dust storm had reminded everyone that the playa gives and takes in equal measure. For some, that meant rebuilding. For others, it meant the day's real work was just beginning.

DPW Ghetto, BRC, 3:10 and Beatific, 7:02 PM - Ruben

"Look at these fucking hippies wandering around smiling as if someone had shoved sunshine up their collective asses," spouted Shakespeare, reminding Ruben where he was.

He was sunk deep into the middle of the couch at the center of the DPW living room and flanked by Thud and Shakespeare. If Ruben showed any inclination to succumb to the woo-woo side of Burning Man, Thud and Shakespeare were right there to bitch slap him back into reality.

Thud was being more productive about translating DPW animus into action. She was affixing an empty plastic bag to a weighted fishing line extended from a small rod and reel.

"What are you up to?" Ruben asked her, his curiosity real.

"My friend, to understand this game, you have to understand two terms. The first is MOOP – material out of place. One of the key Burning Man principles is about keeping this place tidy and clean. They call it — leave no trace. MOOP is anything that is not where it should be, trash being the worst of it. Burners live under the ethos that nothing but water hits the ground. If it does, it needs to be captured immediately. So if a burner sees trash on the ground, they feel obligated to pick it up."

She looked at Ruben to see if he was tracking. Ruben nodded. Satisfied, she continued.

"The next term is 'fucko'. Fucko is anything done to subvert or otherwise introduce dissonance into the love and light ethos that these motherfuckers bring to the desert. Today we're playing a little fucko game we like to call hippie fishing. Allow me to demonstrate."

She cast the line so that the plastic bag dropped into the center of the street. She turned to Ruben, smirking. "When fishing, you have to have a little patience."

After a few moments, a clean-shaven pony-tailed man in a tutu angled toward the ice bag. As he reached down to pick it up, Thud expertly popped the bag up so that it landed about two feet away from the man's hand. Wrinkling his forehead in consternation and not yet getting that he had been had, the man stepped forward to make a second grab. Whoosh. The bag popped back another three feet toward the DPW living room. This time, Thud needed to reel in some line, which finally gave away the gambit.

The man glared, which set Shakespeare to howling. "C'mon, you fucking hippie. Leave no trace. You're making my front yard look like shit." Shakespeare growled at the man. Guffaws and clapping resounded from the other DWPers watching the fun. Ruben knew that Thud would be at it for some time to come. This game was great entertainment for dyed-in-the-wool fuckos and would keep them busy for a while.

Ruben took the opportunity to quietly exit stage right. He wanted to watch the sunset. He made his way through the back of the camp and then up the 3:00 road to the Esplanade.

As he walked, he ruminated about the last few weeks. In prison, he wore a badass mask no one dared challenge. DPW gave him a new one... hardass, unfazed. But now, with the city alive, smiling, open... he felt something tugging at the edges. Something soft.

It was a version of 'him' that he thought was long gone, never to return. Now he saw the possibility of it. It both excited and frightened him. Fortunately, he did not have to make any sudden moves. For the time being, he could marinate in the mixture of emotions and watch the sunset.

Ruben made his way up to the Esplanade and slid onto a vacant bench that someone had put there seemingly for this very purpose – watching the world go by as the sun set. He was settling into quiet reverie when he was interrupted.

"Excuse me. Would you like a taco?" A redheaded woman, her hair twisted into pigtails, stood before him, plate in hand. She slid onto the bench next to him. "I was gifted three tacos, but I'm going to dinner at my friend's camp. I ate one and it was a really good taco. But, I need to leave room to eat dinner."

Ruben looked at the tacos, realizing his stomach was aching with hunger. They looked good, too. "Sure. Why not?"

He took the plate and hoisted a taco into his mouth, ripping a third of the taco with his first bite. Pleasure flowed through him as a mix of savory and fresh flavors hit his taste buds. "I think this is the best taco I've ever had."

"Right?" she brightened. He took another bite, closing his eyes to enjoy the sensation as the flavors burst into his mouth. This time, he allowed himself to feel the complete joy of it.

He opened his eyes to see the woman giving him a knowing smile. "The one I had was so good I had to share it with someone. I think I picked the right person."

"I really appreciate it," Ruben said.

She took a step, paused, and turned back with a smirk. "I'm Rachael, by the way. Don't forget the taco lady."

"Ruben," he replied.

"Have a good burn, Ruben." She eased into the moving throng on the Esplanade.

Ruben chewed slowly, savoring each bite as if it were his last. He relaxed, feeling himself slow down. The panorama before him was surreal, impossible. Costumed people, art cars, art installations, The Man, and the jagged peaks behind them.

The last rays of the sun were streaming above the ridge, the last hurrah before the sun extinguished itself into the golden red afterglow that heralded the coming evening. Hoots, howls, and screams exploded all over the playa, celebrating the ending of another glorious day.

Ruben smiled to himself, more content than he had been in years. The horizon glowed like embers waiting to catch. Somewhere inside him, the same spark flickered... quiet, but undeniable.

Gordian Knot, 8:30 and Esplanade, BRC, 7:40 PM - Crawford

Red and purple hues marked the dying day. The sun had dipped behind the jagged western ridge, the light fading into twilight. The dust storm had blown itself out. The living area was dusty but intact thanks to the crew's foresight in lashing everything down.

Still, the place was deserted. Crawford had expected to see dinner underway, people milling about. But not even the RVs stirred. Then a figure dropped from the gangplank above the crow's nest and climbed down the ladder. Millie. That was her name.

"Millie," he said, nodding. "Where is everybody?"

"Everyone except the shift crew is over at Ashram Galactica. Jimmy got an invite. He brought the whole crew for dinner."

Crawford blinked. It felt like a punch to the gut. He forced a neutral tone. "Oh. Okay."

"Any maze damage?" he asked.

"Looks solid. Good design." She patted his arm. "I need to refill my bladder and get back up top. We've got maze traffic."

She vanished between the RVs, leaving Crawford alone. The world had flipped. Jimmy was now the face of the Gordian Knot. The crew, once deferential, operated without him. And the cherry on top, dinner at BRC's five-star hotel camp, with him excluded.

He paced the empty common area. The idea of going out alone felt like defeat. He needed a retinue, a way to reclaim control. He considered a manufactured crisis, then sighed.

"Fuck, I'm hungry."

He retreated to his RV, reheated a frozen stew, and ate in distracted gulps. Normally, he'd rave about the wine reduction. Tonight, it tasted like... nothing.

Vicky's goggles stared at him from the counter.

"You're under Jimmy's spell," he muttered, though the words rang hollow. Then he emphatically vowed, "This is not my apocalypse, this is my armageddon." The sound of it barely penetrated the air. Even he could feel the hollowness.

He couldn't fathom that the very people he'd gathered had turned on him. Vicky's rejection had struck the deepest blow. Maybe this, too, was Jimmy's play.

Shaking it off, he dressed for the night in a fire-themed outfit: skin-tight lycra with flame graphics, a phoenix shirt, and a ridged cap meant to mimic a burning head. It matched the burn inside him.

Equipped with a CamelBak and a headlamp, he headed toward the Esplanade. He paused at the front of the camp, observing the maze. Tonight's barker, familiar but unknown to him, was charming passersby. Crawford smirked.

"Time me," he said, striding past the barker. "I'm setting the speed record."

He did not wait for an answer.

The first few turns were familiar. Then he dropped down a short ladder and froze. A long, straight corridor stretched ahead. He turned, another one behind. The ladder was gone, replaced by a smooth wall.

"What the fuck?"

The walls arched overhead, glowing faintly with a red-gold hue. Alien. Sealed. He picked a direction, running fingers along the fabric wall as he walked, needing to feel grounded. He walked what felt like forever before reaching a tee.

To the right: pillowed walls fading into darkness. Inviting. Vague movement.

Was that Penelope's silhouette?

He stepped forward, but then he heard a sound behind him.

He turned. A colder corridor stretched red-lit into stone and timber. Hellish.

"Really? Bit on the nose," he muttered. "Jimmy, you bastard. Are you fucking with me?"

A woman stepped into view. Vicky. Or someone who looked like her. She turned and vanished.

"Vicky!" he yelled, chasing her.

He ran around the curve, breathing hard. The path looped endlessly. He stopped, disoriented."

"What the fuck is going on?"

Did Vicky dose me?

Then, a shimmer down the hall, movement.

Is that a face? Jimmy?

He rushed toward it, another passage. How had he missed it?

This one twisted with sharp turns and tight squeezes. He clawed through the narrowing passage, stumbling into a room.

Every inch was covered in pink fur. Ceiling to floor. The lighting glowed low and blush. It was absurd. Disorienting.

He wandered deeper. A bisecting wall revealed a longer room with alcoves on either side. Human sounds... pleasure? Pain?

He peered into one. A red-furred nook. On silk sheets, three stunning women entwined, oblivious to him.

He stepped closer, smack! His forehead hit an invisible barrier. The women looked at him, laughed, and then resumed their pleasures.

Opposite, a man and woman moved in perfect sync, intimate, devoted.

More alcoves followed, each a surreal diorama. One revealed a conference room. Jimmy at the head of the table. Vicky beside him. Campmates attentive.

"Fuck this fever dream," Crawford growled.

In the next alcove, he found three lovers tangled together. To his horror, it was Vicky, Jimmy, and Penelope. Crawford recoiled.

He continued down the corridor, resolved not to look at the rest of the dioramas. Then he heard it.

"Crawford?"

He turned to see a young boy looking up at what was a teenage version of Crawford. Crawford's eyes widened. He slumped forward, putting his palms on the divider. "Randall?" he said aloud to the boy. The figures behind the divider ignored him.

"Don't leave me here alone with them," the young boy pleaded with the older boy.

"Dude, I've done my time here. I need to go live my life. I can't turn down a full scholarship to Princeton. And, I can't take them any longer."

"Neither can I," the young boy continued to plead.

"You'll be fine. A few more years and you can leave too," the older boy said. "I gotta go."

The older boy turned to leave. "Don't leave Randall, you asshole," Crawford screamed as his teenage doppelganger walked out the door.

He backed into another diorama with a thud. A chilling voice sent shivers up his spine. He turned and confronted her.

"Still playing dress-up in other people's success?" his mother asked without turning her head.

His father sighed, hands clasped behind his back. "There was a time we thought you'd outgrow this... need to impress."

"We always hoped you'd rise above your nature," his mother added, her gaze scanning him as one might assess a cracked vase.

"But in the end," his father murmured, "some people, namely the two of you, are simply not built for excellence."

Crawford flinched. He didn't remember taking a step back, but the ground found him anyway.

"Crawford, are you alright?" Millie was looking down at him. He realized he was on his back laying on hard playa. The woven maze wall curtains were familiar.

"What happened?" he asked stupidly.

"You seemed really confused and were having trouble walking. You screamed, fell backwards, and passed out." She let him take that in, then asked, "Are you on something?"

"Not that I know of." He said groggily. He pushed himself to a sitting position. "But I just had the weirdest fucking nightmare of my life, while I was walking."

"What do you need rignt now. Water?" She pulled his bite nozzle up to his mouth. He realized that he was parched and took in a few deep draughts. Millie let him have a few moments to recover, then asked, her tone anxious, concerned, "Do we need to get you over to Medical Services?"

"I don't think so." He honestly assessed. "I can walk. I feel clear-headed now." To prove his point, he stood up and took a deep breath. "I don't feel under the influence of anything. But, I have to admit that I was not in my right mind for the last... uh, what time is it?

Mille looked at her watch. "It's about 9:45."

"Okay,... I just spent the last two hours in a world other than this one. And, as far as I know, I am completely sober. I feel fine now."

Millie looked worried. "Alright, but I think you should take it easy and hang around camp. Since you have no idea what might have caused the episode, you might not want to press your luck."

"Fair enough." He said. He was uncharacteristically tractable and frankly a little scared. He stepped through the hidden exit and out behind the maze next to their camp. Millie walked him back to the RV. He collapsed into a folding chair and looked up at her. "I'm fine, Millie. I'll just hang out either out here or in the RV."

"OK. I'll head back to the tower. But I'm going to come back every so often and check on you."

He gave her a wan smile. "Thanks."

For the first time since she found him in the maze, she smiled. "Alright then." She turned and left.

The maze had different gifts for different people. For some, it was a revelation. For others, confusion. And for a few, it became a mirror that showed exactly what they'd been running from.

Crawford sat there for a long time after she departed. Had he been dosed? Did he have a brain tumor? Was that a psychotic break? It was as if every insecurity in his life had conspired to put on a show tonight. His own creation had turned against him. His Frankenstein was loose.

Sparkleville, 3:15 and Chakra, BRC, 8:35 PM - Rachael

Rachael paused at the edge of the Sparkleville common area. It looked like the whole camp had gathered. A flicker of joy at the sight gave way to hesitation. She stood there, caught in a quiet tug-of-war between wanting to slip away unnoticed and the longing to belong. Her surprise stumble into connection during the dust storm stood in stark relief to the gulf she now felt at the edge of this gathering.

The primitive setup she'd seen two days ago had transformed. Pop-up canopies lashed together into a sprawling communal hub. Camo-netting stretched between vans and tents, creating a sheltered hearth space. Tables sagged under food, and clusters of Sparklites laughed in loose circles. The air pulsed with warmth and camaraderie, and for Rachael, a rising sense of being out of place.

"Rachael! Yay!" Elise popped up from her chair and wrapped her in a bear hug, followed quickly by Leon with his own arms and smile. Their greetings triggered a ripple, heads turned, hands waved, more hugs followed. Rachael smiled through the swell of welcome, even as a familiar tightness grew in her chest. Too many eyes. Too much attention.

"Here." Elise thrust two bowls toward her. "Chili and salad. Jen scored fresh veggies. Sit, woman. Eat."

Rachael collapsed into the offered chair, Elise close by. "How's your burn going?" Elise asked gently.

Rachael chewed slowly, more for the sake of time than for digestion. "I've gotten out a bit," she said. "I'm just not sure this place is for me. I haven't had a moment of real comfort."

Elise watched her carefully, a weight in her gaze. "I know this place is intense. But knowing you, with what you've lived through? I think you're built for this."

Rachael looked down at the carpet beneath her boots, words just out of reach. "It's not the dust or the heat. It's..." She looked up, searching Elise's eyes for a foothold. "It's..."

"Bitch, why hast thou forsaken us?"

Bea's voice cut in, loud and pointed. Rachael turned, lips already tugging upward despite herself. "Hi, Bea. I'm right here, babe."

Bea plopped into the chair on her other side, arms crossed, expression tight with hurt veiled as bravado. "Yeah, but you're not here-here. You're supposed to be here camping with us. And you bailed on the kitchen stuff. We had to MacGyver it."

"I never committed to camping here," Rachael replied, even-toned. "I wasn't sure I was coming at all."

Bea leaned back, dissatisfied but holding her tongue. "Alright. It's a free country." She stood and stalked off into the dark.

Rachael exhaled hard. "She's not done," Elise murmured.

"No, she's not." Rachael managed a chuckle. "There'll be hell to pay and I'll be paying it."

Gordian Knot, 8:30 and Esplanade, BRC, 9:46 PM - Harley

"What the fuck was I thinking coming here?" Harley muttered aloud.

The dust storm had foiled his Warrior aspirations, and Ruben had tonight's shift. So his wasted day and unscheduled evening had brought him to the heart of this friggin' maze,

He stood alone in the enclosed room, trying to find the hidden egress. Mazes weren't his thing. Claustrophobia muddled his problem-solving. Centering himself, he took a few cleansing breaths and began scanning for clues.

The space mimicked a cozy living room; couch, recliner, end tables with flower-filled vases, a coffee table weighed down with permanently affixed books. The books wouldn't budge, but their pages turned.

One featured photos from previous Burns; dusty figures, lit sculptures, perambulating art cars. The other depicted different maze stations: a hall of mirrors, a fur-lined passage, a red silk tunnel, and a pie-wedge room in a central tower. Quirky and curious. None of it was helpful.

The walls were hung like a patchwork gallery, mismatched paintings and wall niches stuffed with small sculptures. The styles clashed: abstract beside realism, cubism pressed next to clumsy impressionism. Most of it looked like an undergrad art thesis exploded. It was as if someone had curated his personal hell.

But one painting stood apart, large, vivid, surreal. A twisted road receding into eternity, the winding path tiled with memories, loving moments, arguments, losses, victories. The ghosts of past lives are traveling toward the horizon of the cosmic landscapes and future possibilities. He felt an overwhelming urge to step into it.

He reached for the frame and tugged. Nothing. He tried the opposite side. Still nothing. Then squatted and lifted the bottom edge. It swung up, smooth and quiet. Garage door style.

"Bingo," he whispered, stepping through.

A dim, curving corridor led him to a set of canvas flaps. He passed through and emerged into a towering cone, a massive teepee. The floor was layered thick with skins: bear, buffalo, deer, rabbit. Around the perimeter, elders sat in silence. Some he recognized from Pine Ridge. Others, from memory, history... even dreams.

Sitting Bull. Wilma Mankiller. Atahualpa. Black Hawk. Cuauhtémoc. Bartolina Sisa. Montezuma, and so many others. The ancients filled the circle; from all of the Americas, all of time, all watching him.

At the fire's center, a medicine man tended the flames. He looked up, scowling.

"You're late."

Harley dropped cross-legged into the nearest patch of fur. Sweat rolled off him in rivulets. His eyes stung. He wiped at them, blinking.

The medicine man tossed something into the fire. It flared, then billowed smoke that filled the teepee. Harley coughed, hard. His chest seized. He gasped, chest on fire. He was suffocating.

Then silence. Darkness. Stillness. He was blind but could breathe again.

He saw nothing, but smelled everything: sweetgrass, pine, spruce, juniper. That unmistakable Black Hills perfume.

Home.

A white buffalo calf approached, bathed in moonlight — or was it radiating the light itself? As it drew near, it shimmered. Shifted. Became a woman in white.

"You're a mule, íŋyaŋska míla," she said, using his Lakota name.

"I've whispered in your ear, coaxed you onto your path. When you ignored me, I sang. Then I yelled during your vision quest. And what did you do? Shit out a metal tribute in the desert."

Her voice sharpened. "Do you really think *that* is your path?"

Harley's mouth opened, useless. "I'm... I'm trying. I'm sober. I—"

A bolt of pain struck the right side of his skull. He reeled, bracing himself on the ground. He looked up. She now held a drum mallet in one hand.

"If you won't listen to whispers, or songs, or screams; then it's time to beat that hollow drum you call a head."

She struck him again on the left side. He dropped to both hands.

When he looked up, he saw Clarence, his father, standing before a jury, fierce and eloquent. And there he was, young Harley, watching from the front row of the public gallery.

White Buffalo Woman's voice again: "This is the man you rejected, even as he fought for his people. For *you*."

He closed his eyes, then opened them.

The tribal police cars. The ditch. His mother's body, hidden in the weeds. His struggling form being held back by a tribal sheriff's deputy.

"This is how you avenged your mother, by destroying yourself."

Another blink. Claire. Cyan. His ex-wife, Arlene. His daughter. Staring at him, heartbroken.

"These are the ones who love you. You've given them only ashes."

He gasped. Another vision.

A wrecked gallery. His sculptures shattered, scattered like bones.

"You keep *doing*, hoping to rewrite your past. You need to start *being*. Your opportunities are running out."

"Stop!" he shouted.

Suddenly, he was outside the maze. Alone. Chill in the night air. Vision gone.

He spun slowly, disoriented. No goddess. No ancestors. Just himself and this barren desert, decorated for play.

He dropped his hands to his thighs, breathing hard.

He inhaled the silence, caressed by the chill. Touched by his memories. No more noise. No more escape. *Time to be.*

7:30 and Esplanade, BRC 9:50PM - Emile

"Jesus. The city's peacocking in full party regalia, and it's only Monday night." Liam's eyes sparkled, his grin wide with unfiltered awe. "The Esplanade is lit up like it's Friday. Every camp's out here flexing."

To Emile, the moment cracked open a window to Liam's inner six-year-old; wide-eyed, enchanted, free. On another night, that wonder would have melted him. But tonight, the mix was volatile. Affection laced with irritation. Liam was both muse and saboteur, lighting up Emile's heart even as he blocked his relentless push for perfection from the Magrathea crew.

Emile reached for bland charm. "Nighttime Black Rock City is a vivacious painted maiden full of allure and mystery."

"While I agree with the sentiment, ... dude, you don't have to perform right now. It's just us." Liam replied.

The Esplanade before them pulsed like a fire carnival. The more reserved camps displayed torches and burn barrels. The bold ones sported glaring marquees and flame cannons. The street throbbed with pedestrians and bicycles, parting for art cars, then clotting again in dense communal revelry.

They weaved through the crowds, dodging bikes and swaying bodies. Sometimes the flow yielded to them, other times it jostled them like flotsam in a restless tide. Emile's frustration mounted. "Let's get off the Esplanade before I strangle someone."

Given Emile's recent temperament, Liam took the warning literally. "We're close to Center Camp. Want to grab a drink?"

"No. That's just another crowd. Let's head out to the Serpent's Nest." Emile nodded toward the looming structure two hundred yards across the open playa. "I heard the Lotus Girls really went big this year."

"Then let's check it out," Liam said, veering away from the crowd without protest. Emile followed, feeling immediate relief as the noise faded.

They walked in silence. The overlapping music thinned, revealing the crunch of playa beneath their boots. As they neared the Serpent's Nest, Liam reached out and touched Emile's arm. Emile flinched. The tenderness of the gesture felt unbearable.

"I'm worried about you," Liam said quietly.

"I'm fine," Emile replied, too quickly.

Liam paused. "I've seen you fine. I love your fine. But you haven't been fine in a long time. This last year... and since we got to the playa, it's only gotten worse."

Emile said nothing. His first instinct was to push back and blame the crew. But Liam's words carried a truth Emile could not deny. The problem wasn't just out there. It was inside, and closer than he liked to admit. He had withdrawn, grown brittle. The 'why' still eluded him.

They stopped just short of the crowd gathered around the installation. Before them sprawled the Nest, a massive circular arena nearly a hundred feet wide, ringed by six coiled serpents forged from stainless steel and fire.

Each serpent was a spectacle. Sleek bodies rippled in linked spirals, the rear of one twining possessively around the next. Their heads rose twenty feet into the air. Half faced outward like sentries. The others glared inward, guarding something sacred or dangerous.

Beneath each skull yawned an opening wide enough for a person to walk through. From every joint along their steel spines, fire erupted in wild, unpredictable bursts, flooding the structure with heat and menace. The skulls gleamed with stainless-steel fangs, each one honed like a razor.

Without warning, a head would rise higher and spit fire into the night, roaring like a living creature. Each blast cracked the air with the ferocity of a war cry.

Emile stepped forward and entered the Nest through the nearest portal. Liam followed. Inside, a small crowd gathered at the center. The chill that usually slipped between layers out on the open playa was gone. Here, it was hot, easily eighty degrees.

Emile dropped his pack, slipped off his coat, folded it with precision, and placed it carefully on top of his gear. His tailored vest revealed his sculpted chest and arms.

A track by Massive Attack drifted into the air. Emile began to move. His body absorbed the beat. A nearby serpent exhaled a burst of flame, backlighting him in searing gold.

"You look like a god," Liam said.

Emile gave a crooked smile. "Gods control their worlds. I don't seem to be in control of anything."

"I'm not asking for a god," Liam said softly. "I'm asking for you."

Emile didn't respond. The silence thickened between them.

"I don't know if I deserve that kind of love," Emile said, voice tight. "I'm afraid I'll disappoint you."

Liam met his gaze. "Then let me show you that you deserve it."

Emile's face collapsed, his eyes hollow. "I... I don't know how."

He felt the mask slip. He was exposed. Raw. Like a wound. He took a step back without meaning to.

A sudden flash tore across the sky. A firework exploded above, a white bloom that turned night to day. The echo cracked like thunder, and for a moment, every face in the crowd was caught in perfect light, startled, open, transfixed.

As the fireworks dimmed and the final sparks rained down like stars, the crowd erupted in cheers. Wild and electric.

Emile didn't move. He scanned the faces, as if searching for a tether. Then something in him turned.

He didn't reach for Liam.

He turned inward.

And then he moved.

Gone were the elegant gestures and practiced grace. He launched himself into the frenzy with sharp edges and sudden angles. His body convulsed with each beat. Not dancing to seduce, but to exorcise.

The crowd surged. The air pulsed. Emile let himself go, swallowed by firelight, by noise, by motion. One frantic beat at a time.

Sparkleville, 3:15 and Chakra, BRC, 10:42 PM - Rachael

"Sure you don't want to come adventure with us?" asked a wavy-haired man in a silver cape.

"Thanks, Zorgon, but I'm toasted." She offered a wave as he joined the lighted bike posse.

Elise waved back as they pushed off. Rachael bundled up for the long walk across the city. "I should've taken my bike," she muttered.

She slipped between tents, aiming for the quiet back roads. Just as she reached the street, a sharp "Hey!" rang out behind her.

She turned. Bea.

They met, a body's length between them.

"I'm not okay with this," Bea said flatly.

"You're really not the simmering type," Rachael said, bracing. She sighed. "Alright. Let's do this."

"What the fuck, Rache? Why aren't you with us?"

"I'm camping with Nathan," she answered. "He's been solid. Had a plan. You all were... still figuring things out."

"But we're your family."

Rachael froze. The word slammed into her like a wave. Her face flushed.

"Family?" she repeated, voice rising. "What does that even mean?"

She turned, looking to the shadows as if they might offer better language. "Nathan and I have worked together for two years. I've known Elise for ten months. The rest of you? Less. Sure, we hang. And at every gathering, someone 'just wants to connect'. Which really means: explain yourself. Be trans 101. That's the price of entry."

Bea opened her mouth, but Rachael cut her off. Her breathing grew labored. "Look, I've appreciated the welcome. But family? I don't feel like family. I feel like your pet tranny."

Bea gasped. Her hand flew to her mouth. A sob slipped out, involuntary and raw. In the soft light, she looked almost childlike. Exposed.

"I made a choice, Bea. That doesn't make me a traitor. If you'd ever asked how I was doing instead of assuming, you'd have known where I was at."

Bea's face was wet now. And Rachael, instead of softening, felt the heat of rage still buzzing under her skin.

"I think we're done here." She turned and walked away, head high, fists clenched, not once looking back.

4:00 and Divinity, BRC, 10:54 PM - Justine

"Good night, kids. I have reached my stimulation quota for the evening. I need to build up my tolerance before I end up curled in a fetal position under the bad-idea-barbie art car," Justine said, slinging her backpack over one shoulder with theatrical weariness.

"You're leaving?" Susan pouted, not bothering to move. She was sprawled across the communal couch like a retired showgirl, head in Max's lap, legs over Zig, and her glittered feet resting in Daphne's lap.

"Mmhmm." Justine nodded. "Someone has to keep their liver unpickled for at least one night. You four seem fully committed to becoming tropical cocktails by dawn."

Susan lifted her mojito with royal flair. "When you find something that works, you honor it. These are practically medicinal. The Roca Negra lounge puts magic in these little green leaves."

"Yeah, mint and questionable decisions," Justine said, smirking. "Enjoy the steel drums and your journey of self-discovery at the bottom of a plastic cup. I will see you glitter zombies back at camp."

Daphne waved lazily. "We will light a glowstick in your honor."

Max called after her, "Do not get abducted by stilt walkers again."

"Not unless they have snacks," Justine tossed back.

She stepped into the soft chaos of 4:00, pleased with herself for plotting a route that passed the porta-potties, her small bladder having been assigned full navigational authority.

The block was dim, but the city's ambient glow kept things visible, and her headlamp painted a trail of halogen righteousness across the cracked playa beneath her boots. She moved quickly, focused on reaching those sacred blue boxes of basic human dignity.

She rounded the corner at Divinity and spotted the potties like a beacon. "Yes," she thought. "Relief, then sanctuary."

"Hey, love. Where are you off to?"

Justine glanced over her shoulder and immediately regretted it. A lean, middle-aged man with salt-and-pepper scruff and an overabundance of confidence had spotted his opening. She snapped her gaze forward again, but it was too late. He was already syncing his stride with hers, a smile dialed to maximum smarm.

"I'm Rance," he said with the relaxed grin of a man who definitely owned leather bracelets. "And you are...?"

Without slowing, Justine gave him a sideways look. "On the verge of becoming extremely impolite."

"Aww, I'm just being friendly," he chuckled, unfazed. "First year here at this crazy party. You?"

Justine picked up her pace. Engage creep-shaker mode. Her boots hit the playa with more force, but he floated alongside her like a sentient inconvenience.

"Look, I am not interested, and I need to get somewhere," she said, her voice clipped.

Then she felt his fingers on her arm.

She recoiled as if she had touched an electric fence. "Do not touch me."

He stepped in front of her with an easy glide, still smiling, as if this were a meet-cute and not a situation heading straight toward security.

"Sorry," he said, hands raised in mock surrender. "Didn't mean to offend you. I am really an Oookay guy."

Justine squared off, her whole body telegraphing back off now.

"Oh, you're an Oookay guy? Great. Is that the brand name? Do you come with a warranty? Or just the usual package of unwanted contact and stalker energy?"

Rance blinked, finally thrown.

Justine stepped around him without another word, her headlamp beam slicing the dust like a lighthouse of fury. She did not look back. She did not need to. If he followed, she would bury him under a verbal landslide so swift he would be coughing up syllables for days.

Behind her, the city shimmered and raged, oblivious. Ahead of her, blessed solitude, and a blue plastic box of semi-sanitary salvation.

I should have just stayed with the drunk glitter pile.

3:45 and Divinity, BRC, 11:04 PM - Rachael

Rachael's fast walk out of Sparkleville eventually slowed to her normal stride. She drew long breaths in and out, trying to bleed the heat from her veins. Anger was giving way to metastasizing regret. She had shocked herself. Not just the venom in her words, but that it was the word "family" that detonated her. Of course, it was Bea, being Bea, who found the detonator. Still, the vitriol of her own reaction unsettled her.

The quiet, unlit street was a comfort. She didn't want company. Not tonight.

She passed the bank of portolets and through the 3:30 and Divinity intersection, adjusting her route to hug the shadows. Up ahead, a small silhouette walked toward her. She angled closer to the camp structures to avoid being seen. But then another figure detached itself from the shadows, a much larger shape moving quickly toward the first.

Voices. Male. Female. An advance and clear refusal. The man grabbed at her. Blocked her. Rachael was even with them now.

She stepped from the darkness. "My friend, she's made it clear she's not interested. You should be on your way."

The man turned. He was tall and broad, loose-limbed but coiled. Drunk, she clocked it instantly. His eyes glittered with arrogance. "She's warming up to me. You're the one who should move along."

Rachael caught the sour stench of hard liquor and something acrid beneath it. She stepped between them. The smaller woman backed up.

A hand touched her shoulder. "We should go," the woman, young, light, with a dancer's body, said quietly.

Rachael didn't move. Her body was a tuning fork. Assessing. Sizing him up. She'd done this before.

The man's annoyance tipped toward rage.

"Don't," Rachael said firmly, lifting her hand. She stepped forward and shifted her weight, sending the small woman tumbling out of range.

"Bitch," the man muttered, drawing a large knife from behind his back.

Rachael closed the space between them before he could adjust. The knife came down.

The woman on the ground behind them screamed.

3:45 and Divinity, BRC, 11:49 PM - Rachael

Flashing cherries from the sheriff's SUV burned into Justine's eyes. Emergency lights flooded the scene, now circled by costumed burners rubbernecking.

A crumpled body lay on the ground, twitching occasionally, bone jutting through skin. Blood soaked into the playa. A paramedic crouched beside him.

A deputy approached her, surprisingly gentle. "Are you alright?"

"I think so," she said, her voice unsteady.

"Can you tell me what happened?"

Justine looked to the dust at her feet, still catching her breath, still replaying the snap of action she barely understood.

"I think he tripped," said a calm voice beside her. "He seems pretty drunk."

It was the tall, redheaded woman. Cool, precise. Her tone left no space for contradiction.

The deputy nodded. "Okay. Thanks." He turned toward the paramedics.

She tilted her head toward Justine. "Mind if we get going?"

"Sure," the deputy said, already onto the next thing.

"Can I walk with you a bit?" Rachael asked.

Justine gave a short nod. "Okay. But you have to answer several questions."

Rachael smiled. "That's fair."

They walked in silence, the thrum of adrenaline fading. Finally, Justine broke it.

"First, what's your name?"

Rachael chuckled. "Rachael. Nice to meet you."

"I'm Justine. I wouldn't exactly call that a nice meeting." She exhaled. "I mean, thanks for saving me, obviously. But also... what the fuck just happened?"

"That was Aikido." Rachael's tone suggested this was a Tuesday for her.

Justine blinked. "Like... kung fu shit?"

"Close enough." Rachael glanced sideways. "It's about redirecting force. Letting someone's aggression undo itself. Mostly, I just saw what he was going to do before he did it. Been in a lot of situations where reading people fast was the only way to stay safe."

Justine chewed on that. "So you saw the knife coming?"

"I saw the harness under his jacket and guessed. I set myself close enough that his only move would be overhead. He obliged."

"You make it sound like chess," Justine said. "With combat."

"Pretty much." Rachael offered a lopsided smile. "Lucky guess, well-timed footwork."

Justine fell quiet again. Her heart was still jackrabbiting under her ribs, not from danger anymore, but from the fragile fact of having *almost* been the kind of story no one wants to tell.

"I guess I've never had to think like that," she said, voice quieter. "I'm used to controlling what happens around me. On stage, you train for perfection. Out here? It's chaos. I hate chaos."

"That makes two of us," Rachael murmured.

Justine looked at her sideways. "So why did you lie to the cop?"

"Experience," Rachael said. "At best, we'd still be there filling out witness statements, with an inevitable court witness appearance. At worst... Well, I've had a few run-ins. And being trans usually means I'm not presumed innocent."

Justine winced but didn't argue. "I get it. I think."

Rachael shrugged. "Besides, he'll be medivaced out. He won't hurt anyone else out here this year."

"Yeah. Still..." Justine's brows pulled together. "You really meant to hurt him?"

Rachael hesitated. "I meant to stop him. The rest was the cost of that."

They walked another block. Justine finally stopped, nodding at a softly lit camp.

"This is me."

Rachael nodded. "I hope the rest of your burn is better than tonight."

Justine gave a small laugh. "Thanks. You were like... a pissed-off guardian angel."

Rachael chuckled. "I'll take that." Then added, "I saw you perform. Out of the Esplanade at 7:30. You're incredible."

Justine flushed. "Thanks. I'm still figuring it out."

"You're further along than I am. That's for sure."

Justine looked at her, uncertain. "Can I hug you?"

"Absolutely."

They embraced. Brief. Fierce.

"Stay safe," Rachael said.

"I promise."

Rachael turned back toward the road. As she passed the dim patch where the altercation had happened, she spotted the dark stain on the ground, blood. No pride. No catharsis.

Between her clash with Bea and this near-stabbing, she felt a pull back toward a darkness she'd tried hard to leave behind. The old her. The survivor-self is now back at full strength.

But the night had not ended there.

She had made a connection. It was unexpected, uninvited, and unearned. Justine had not needed her to explain or defend anything. She just... accepted her. Maybe not 'as family'. But not 'as spectacle' either.

And that, finally, felt like something new.

As she turned deeper into the winding streets of Black Rock City, Rachael felt like she had taken a step backward from whatever progress she had made here. She also felt a flicker of something she hadn't known she was missing.

Not joy. Not yet.

But maybe its shadow. Maybe its shape.

⓪③ Spins Until the Man Burns

7:00 and Inspiration, BRC, 7:06 AM - Cypher

Cypher woke up fully lucid. He was pretty sure his body had activated in self-defense to avoid reliving yesterday's sweaty misery. The air was still cool but rapidly warming. He worked his way out of the sleeping bag, then slid out of the over-bag that had once been his tent. Sitting up, blinking groggily, he realized he was still exhausted. Reaching into the tent bag, he pulled out his gallon water jug and took a long pull, hearing with satisfaction the glug, glug, glug.

He picked up a piece of rope he'd found while gathering his wind-scattered belongings. He fashioned a lanyard for the jug—freeing up a hand for the day's roaming. From his stash, he dug out a couple more power bars and the trail mix he'd thankfully stuffed into his cargo pockets before yesterday's dusty adventure. He slowly chewed one bar, masticating at length to trick himself into believing he was eating more. It was a trick he had taught himself on the streets of San Francisco.

He sat blinking for a few minutes, preparing himself for the day. A poor man's meditation. A moment to reset.

His reverie was interrupted by a familiar worn voice. "Jesus, son, you've barely got a pot to piss in here."

Cypher looked up to see Drummond ambling toward him. The man's dark, leathered skin testified to a life in the sun. His wiry, iron-grey hair was pulled back into a ponytail. He looked freshly shaved, his head shaded by a wide-brimmed straw hat. He chuckled as he closed on Cypher. "You make me feel like a rich man."

Cypher blinked up at him.

"Mind if I join you for a few minutes?" the man asked.

Cypher nodded. "Pull up a seat."

Drummond barked a laugh and dropped onto the bare playa cross-legged.

"I've been thinking about what I could do to make things a little easier on you." He paused, not waiting for a response, just catching his breath. "I don't have room to bunk you in, and I didn't bring a huge stash of food. But I do have a few things that might make the rest of your burn just a little better."

He handed Cypher two cans of blood-orange sparkling water. "Chill those in your cooler before you drink 'em." Cypher stared at the offering. Then Drummond placed a bag of beef jerky and a bag of chips beside them.

"Don't put those in a fly-away bag," he said with a wry grin.

The man looked him in the eye. "Do you like hallucinogens?"

Cypher's eyebrows rose. He nodded, surprised and intrigued.

"Good. Then your burn is about to get a whole lot better."

Drummond slid a calloused hand from his pocket. Pinched between his fingers was a small pill pouch, which he dropped into Cypher's lap. Cypher picked it up and examined it. Inside were tiny squares of toilet paper, each with a discolored, translucent blot at its center.

"What you have there are fifteen hits of some of the finest acid you'll ever travel with. I'll warn you now... start small. One at a time. Find what works for you. Got it?"

Cypher nodded again, slower this time.

"That's it," the old man said, rising with surprising agility. He patted Cypher on the shoulder. "Have a good burn."

He turned and began his slow amble back toward his truck.

Cypher cleared his throat. "Uhm... thanks."

Drummond glanced over his shoulder and spat, "You talk too much." Then cackled so hard he had to stop walking for a moment, wheezing all the way back to his rig.

Cypher looked down at the pouch in his lap, the sun beginning to warm his bare back. For the first time since landing on the playa and deep into the universe's test, he received a reward. The reward validated that he was going in the right direction. Now it was time to up the ante, like completing a level in a video game. Time to lean into his survivalist strategy. Today was the day to step into the unknown.

Temple of Serenity, 12:00 and Outer Playa, BRC, 7:09 AM - Ruben

Ruben felt the manila string tie envelope inside his shirt. Still there. Reassured, he returned to the evaporating morning chill. As the temple loomed, his emotions churned – relief, fear, sadness – so interwoven he couldn't tell them apart. Still, his gait remained steady.

This visit was long overdue. Since he had heard about the temple and its purpose, he knew a visit would be a critical part of his playa experience. Yet he had been reluctant to make the temple journey. Fear of what lay on the other side of the visit had a grip on him. It was terra incognita, a reckoning he'd resisted yet now needed. One thought cycled through his mind:

Stepping into the void is the necessary next step for me. Stay strong.

Even from a distance, the temple revealed itself as an architectural mashup, Arab spires, Asian arches, and European stairs, blending in unexpectedly elegant harmony.

The closer he got, the more beautiful it became. He reached a sweeping staircase arcing skyward and began to climb. Step by step, reverence grew within him. The temple demanded it. With every step, his bones seemed to vibrate: *Pay attention.*

Sharpie-scrawled messages blanketed the structure. *I love you, Dad. You're in my heart. You're in a better place than you were here. Peace has found you.* Some said simply: *Goodbye.* Others unspooled into multi-page letters, stapled to beams and railings. As he moved through the main chamber, tributes multiplied... photos, declarations, crowded altars filling every cranny. Ruben absorbed the collective grief, pain, and release.

Low, harmonic notes from Tibetan dungchen rolled across the space, punctuated by chimes. The soundscape wrapped around him, comforting, steadying him for what he came to do.

He thought of Esteban. The wild cards. The strange magic was born from sadness. Suddenly, Ruben felt unworthy, unsure he belonged among these intimate displays of grief. Surrounded by people, he felt alone. Or maybe, he wanted to be.

He closed his eyes, breathed in deep, then exhaled slowly. Unbuttoned his shirt. Pulled the envelope free. Unwinding the string, he opened the flap. Scanning the beams above, he found his spot.

Kneeling, he slid the sheets out and gently set his backpack down, pulling a heavy-duty stapler from the side pocket.

The first sheet: a sketch of a young man, maybe late teens or early twenties. Not quite Ruben, but similar enough to sting. The second sheet: densely filled with tiny, tear-stained block letters. A letter of sorrow.

At the bottom, a single line: *It should have been the other way around.*

Emotion welled. The memory excavated layers of regret, pain, and guilt. It reminded him why prison had been easy, and why it hadn't been enough.

He held the pages up and tacked each corner to the beam. The young man stared back at him. The confession behind him. Ruben stared for a long time, eyes misty. He did not cry. Not from bravery. Not from pride. He stayed composed because he was afraid that if he let go, he'd shatter beyond repair.

Outside, the wind stirred the dust. Inside, Ruben stood still, stapled to the past.

Center Camp, BRC, 8:02 AM - Justine

Hundreds of bicycles rested neatly in long rows around the large, dark circus tent-like structure curving away from its main entrance, which faced the Man. If Black Rock City had a parking lot, this was it. The sea of bikes hinted at the teeming crowd inside.

The "tent" was actually a canopy of industrial-grade mesh shade screen, covering most of the walls and all of the ceiling, save for a wide circular opening at the top. It wasn't exactly weatherproof, but it did a reasonable job of deflecting the worst of the sun, dust, and rain. A ring of colorful flags crowned the top, flickering and twisting on their poles as the breeze stirred.

Early morning Center Camp was the sweet spot on the playa clock. Those who had managed to rise and stumble to the city's central gathering space brought with them a quiet anticipation for the day ahead. The mood was gentle, optimistic, not yet frayed by heat or overstimulation. There were open spaces still, and the coffee lines were short. By late morning, it would be packed and buzzing, interesting in its own right, but less pure, less essential. This moment belonged to the early risers.

Justine entered from the Man-facing side. To her left, a woman lay supine on a yoga mat, surrounded by four kneeling figures sounding deep, resonant tones through didgeridoos aimed at different parts of her body. A dust-borne healing ritual, apparently.

To her right, a stage was flanked by battered couches and faded armchairs ten deep. A duo, one on percussion, the other shifting between wind instruments and vocal loops, was weaving African rhythms through the still air.

She had found the Center Camp contact improv dance schedule in the Who, What, Where, When Guide and curiosity had gotten the best of her. Susan had pressed her to get out of her comfort zone. Contact improv with qualified strangers. Barely.

She bypassed the installations and clustered seating, beelining for the movement area at the center of the ranging structure. A loose ring of contact improv dancers flowed around one another, improvising duets of momentum and resistance. Pairings seemed spontaneous; gesture, consent, alignment, flow.

She scanned the perimeter, hoping for a partner who looked both grounded and responsive. Several promising dancers were already paired. Then she caught sight of a tall, dark-haired man in earth-tone pants and a sleeveless vest. Lean, upright, composed. He had the posture of someone who danced or climbed for joy. He was watching her, too.

Justine started toward him, but a tap on her shoulder stopped her. "Excuse me." She turned to see a curly-haired man in his late thirties. "Would you like to work the session with me?"

He was fit enough, but something about his gaze set off an instinct. Too intent. Too eager. She hesitated only a beat. "I'm sorry," she said, gesturing subtly, "but my partner's right over there."

She circled the dance ring to approach the dark-haired man. He did not look surprised.

"Want to partner up?" she asked.

"Yeah, I think so," he said, measured but open. "Are you experienced?"

"Yep. I'm hoping we're working at about the same level." She smiled.

"My regular partner's showing up in about half an hour. Let's see what we can do till then. If we're in sync, maybe a trio?"

She liked his tone, clear, grounded, no fuss. "Sounds good."

"I'm Eric," he added as they moved toward the dancers.

"Justine," she called over her shoulder.

They found a pocket of space near the center. Palms lifted, almost touching, they began. Eric's hand floated upward past his shoulder; Justine mirrored the arc precisely, her other hand swooping low as she lifted a leg into extension. His movements matched hers, graceful, patient. Their bodies negotiated space, balance, and invitation.

She dove toward his hip; he caught her mid-fall and turned with her wrapped around his waist, spiraling them to the floor. She extended a foot past his face; he traced it with one hand. They rolled, rose, pulled, and released, working each other into a standing position and back again.

They met each other's eyes and smiled.

"This works," Justine said.

"Yep," Eric agreed. "Let's stay warm till my partner arrives. Then we'll take it up a notch."

And so they did.

Center Camp, BRC, 8:21 AM - Crawford

Crawford slumped against the plywood panel bordering the dance ring, arms looped around his knees. He had wandered the neighborhood without curiosity. Only hunger. He wanted hot girl attention. He wanted to be adored.

He watched the petite, athletic woman now lost in a trance-like duet with her contact improv partner. Part of him resented being brushed off. A quieter, sharper part knew she'd been right to say no.

He was an experienced dancer, but not that experienced. And he wasn't here to dance. He'd just wanted to be close to someone for a while.

Vicky was off somewhere, likely with someone else. He'd gotten the message from the Ashram Galactica dinner; he was persona non grata to the Gordian Knot crew. And with the maze up and running, he had little interest in daily operations. If they didn't appreciate his contribution, why keep contributing?

'Next year I'll build an art car,' he thought. 'Art cars come with attention baked in.'

Center Camp, BRC, 8:48 AM - Cypher

Cypher leaned against the half-wall encircling the movement area, eyes fixed on Justine. His journey into the unknown required a pitstop at Center Camp for a nap. He woke up to find Justine in close proximity.

She danced like no one he'd ever seen, fluid, precise, alive. She made him wish he had something to offer that could bring him into that orbit. Dance. Acrobatics. Anything.

He smiled, thinking of the hug she'd given him. That moment had lit up something inside him.

She was now dancing with the tall man and a statuesque, dreadlocked woman. Together they spun out something transcendent, intricate, mesmerizing, impossible to look away from. A private Cirque du Soleil moment, just for the lucky few who showed up and noticed.

Eventually, they broke apart for water. Justine took a long sip from her CamelBak and looked up, straight at him. She smiled. "Hi Cypher." Then she turned, already stepping back into the dance.

"She smiled at me," he whispered. "And she hugged me last night." He drifted away from the wall, heading toward the couches.

Time to catch up on sleep. Dreams might have something to show him.

Magrathea Base Camp, 10:00 and Divinity, BRC, 11:01 AM - Harley

Harley shuffled down the street, taking stock of the storm's wreckage. A mangled shade structure lay crumpled, defeated by the wind. Pale dust had piled into micro-dunes, like frozen waves mid-crest, swirling around his boots as he walked. Up ahead, a cyclist jerked sideways, nearly eating dirt after plunging into a dust-filled pothole disguised as solid ground.

And yet, it was a stunning day — clear, bright, almost deceptively gentle. A crisp breeze kept the heat in check, making it a perfect day for a stroll... or, apparently, for socializing. Curiosity had gotten the better of him. That's the only reason he'd accepted Emile's invitation. Still, with every step toward Magrathea's basecamp, a knot tightened in his gut. Until now, he'd managed to ration his people-time. At The Warrior, he could feign productivity by keeping his head down, hands busy, and interactions metered out on his terms. But this... this was different. He was stepping into someone else's world now, a world that happened to be a giant party bus packed with professional extroverts. It was, in every possible way, not his scene.

The moment he hit 10:00 street, the bus loomed into view, impossible to miss even from three blocks out. Taller than anything else on the block, it screamed for attention with its riot of colors. A walking billboard for cacophony. Instinctively, Harley drifted to the far side of the road, needing distance just to take it in. The thing was massive, eating up nearly a quarter of the block between Divinity and Enlightened.

As he neared the back end, he crossed the street, exhaled a slow, steady breath, and stepped behind the far side of the bus, straight into the belly of Magrathea's camp.

As soon as he passed behind the rear of the bus, he felt a calmness that deepened as he made his way along the length of the bus. The behemoth did an excellent job of isolating the Magrathea basecamp from the busy street. As he approached the large shade structure, he could see at least a dozen members of the Magrathea crew lounging on the couches and camp chairs that made up their living room. His stomach churned.

He recognized Liam standing behind a long folding table, scooping scrambled eggs onto a plate. As Harley approached, Liam looked up. Recognition flashed across his face. He smiled. "Harley. Welcome. Are you hungry?"

Harley stepped around the table, and they clasped in a brief but warm hug. "Nah, thanks. I ate before I walked over. But, if you have coffee, I'd be a happy man."

Liam laughed. "We have plenty. Liam picked a plastic cup from a dish rack and handed it to Harley. Pointing to another table. "There's the pot and fixings. Doctor it to your liking. This crew doesn't operate without strong brew. Once you're sorted I'll introduce you around."

Harley poured himself a full cup with a little room. Then he dolloped a bit of half and half into the cup. He sipped it, widening his eyes. "I'll be back every day. The coffee is strong and good."

Liam chuckled. "Just the way we like it. We are, after all, Seattle coffee snobs. Let me introduce you to the crew."

He escorted Harley to the rough center of the living room. "Crew, this is Harley."

He was greeted with raised hands and muttered hellos. "You're catching these night owls on the early side. They haven't yet built up steam. So you're safe. Let's do this clockwise."

Liam gestured toward a woman lounging on the couch in front of him. "This is DJ Bedlam."

She looked up from the book she was reading and smiled. "Welcome, Harley."

"This mountain sharing the couch is Dobbs." Dobbs nodded.

In quick succession, Liam introduced the rest as he rotated and gestured to each. "This is Sanjay, Gina, Kathy, Felicia, Stanton, Shimmer, Bart, Django, Misha, and Bryce." Each acknowledged Harley in their turn. If they were curious about him, they did not show it.

The crew seemed relaxed and content to chat amongst themselves, teasing each other in comfortable banter. Harley watched quietly, entertained, enjoying their exchanges, happy that none of it required his effort. He sipped the coffee, contented to have no socializing demands foisted on him.

"Harley." He turned to see Emile standing, smiling in the bus's door frame. He was shirtless, using a towel to wipe himself down. Harley felt a twinge of jealousy as he realized the man had just stepped fresh from a shower. "Are they taking good care of you?"

"Finest coffee on the playa." Harley raised his cup to Emile.

Emile stepped down out of the bus onto the playa and closed the distance quickly. He and Harley hugged. Harley wicked off a bit of Emile's dampness.

When they released each other, Emile turned toward Liam. "Have you told them who Harley is?"

Liam was neutral. He shook his head. "Didn't want to steal your thunder."

Emile nodded. Harley detected a strain between them, a stiffness. But as Emile turned toward the lounging sprawl of bodies scattered across couches and camp chairs, something shifted. A subtle recalibration, like watching a transmission slip into gear. Gone was the tension. In its place, poise, charm, a magnetic flare, as if a showman had quietly stepped in and taken the wheel.

Emile raised his hands in a loose, theatrical gesture, voice slipping into an easy cadence designed to carry just far enough.

"Alright, rise and shine, beautiful people, eyes open for just a second. I want you to meet someone." He let the pause hang, perfectly timed. "This fine creature here is Harley. The Harley. Sculptor of the Ataraxis Warrior. The hands behind the beast, the bones, the skin, the soul of it."

A few heads tilted up, curiosity flickering behind slow blinks and lopsided smiles. Someone raised a mug in lazy salute.

Emile's grin sharpened, eyes scanning his audience. "So now, when you're out there, lost, wandering, and you stumble on that hulking sentinel staring into the dust, you can say you've met the mind that made it real."

He dropped his hands, the performance landing with a gentle thud, not demanding applause but leaving the imprint of something quietly grand. The crew quietly cheered, a morning-time cheer with gentle applause, embarrassing Harley.

"We're taking Magrathea out to the Warrior. Harley's going to give us the artist's tour. You're all welcome to join us."

For a long moment, there was an awkward silence, campmates exchanging glances. Finally, Dobbs said, "I'm up for it, man." He looked at Harley, "Dude, I *so* want to get your take on the coolest thing on the playa."

After another moment, Gina said, "Kathy and I will come."

Stanton stood up. "I'm in."

Felicia and Gabe stood up simultaneously, grabbing their necessities. The rest of the crew begged off.

A peculiar stiffness permeated the crew dynamics. The same stiffness that Harley sensed between Emile and Liam. His spidey senses were tingling as they boarded the bus.

1:00 and Deep Playa, BRC, 11:24 AM - Harley

Harley leaned against the front rail of the roof deck, letting the breeze carry away the worst of the bass beat racket that the house music was to him. He glanced off to his left, taking in the emerging angle of the temple. By the time they arrive at Ataraxis Warrior, they will have almost circumnavigated the temple, allowing Harley to take it in almost all of its facets.

Closing his eyes, he took in a deep breath and exhaled, a bit closer to his happy place. He dropped his shoulders and let the tension release. Ataraxis Warrior loomed in the near distance. 'Not much longer,' he thought to himself.

"I see you found the sweetest spot on the bus." Emile interrupted his reverie.

"It's become my instantaneous favorite place," Harley replied.

"You're not completely digging the Magrathea scene, are you?" Emile's directness took Harley aback and simultaneously gave him a sense of relief.

"I'm mostly concerned about the work I need to do to clean up and prep Ataraxis. But, to be honest, no. Most of my life is spent in quiet, solitary places with busy hands. This is not exactly a quiet place, and my hands aren't busy so I'm way out of my comfort zone."

"I'm sorry about that, Harley. Making you uncomfortable was not my intention. I just wanted to share this thing I love with you, and have you share that beauty out there," Emile pointed at Ataraxis Warrior, "that you love so much, artist to artist. I think we both work toward perfection. That's our common ground."

"At that level, you're right. And you have built a masterpiece here. I just think your intended audience is not an introverted, curmudgeonly, middle-aged man from the Rez." Harley replied.

Emile chuckled. "You're right about that."

Harley turned toward Emile, concern wrinkling his forehead. "I couldn't help but notice ... a strain with your crew. It's none of my business. So feel free to tell me to fuck off. But, is everything okay?"

Darkness clouded Emile's face. He turned forward, leaning against the rail, letting the breeze soothe him. He let out a breath and turned back to Harley. "Yeah. I've been demanding perfection from the crew. They, in return, are demanding communally that I fuck off."

Harley nodded. "Perfection is a high standard. Very few are willing to sign up for perfect." Emile grimaced, clearly showing his feelings about those who do not strive for excellence.

"What happens if it isn't perfect?" Harley asked.

"Hmmmm..." Emile pondered. "I guess I am trying to make an immaculate impression with Magrathea. Something burners will talk about for years."

"I think you're there, my friend. This rig is a rave, an art car, a mobile stage, it's damn near a hotel on wheels. I'd say you've achieved noteworthy grandeur, even in Burning Man terms. How much grander do you want it to be?"

Emile stood quietly, hands gripping the rail before them. His gaze was fixed on a horizon that Harley could not see. He was quiet long enough that Harley assumed he would not respond.

But then he did. His voice started out muted, not so much quiet as it was far away. "Perfection has always been my bugaboo. My monster in the closet. My father thought that he could beat it into me. My mother thought she could throw enough spells to force me down the path to perfection, the perfect son."

His face scrunched up with despair. "But nothing they did resolved me into that perfect boy they wanted, a religiously compliant, straight boy."

He turned to Harley. "Do you ever feel like you're caught between worlds?"

Harley let out a coughing bark of a laugh that surprised both of them. "Between worlds is all I've known. My dad is full-blood Hunkpapa Sioux. My mom was Norwegian-German and hard as nails. I grew up on the Rez at ground zero for Native Americans 9/11, Wounded Knee."

Emile cocked his head. "I've read about that. There was a massacre there, right?"

"Right. In 1890, the Seventh Cavalry tracked down a ragtag band of ghost dancers led by Spotted Elk and, while attempting to disarm the band, managed to massacre about three hundred men, women, and children. Last of the free Indians, death of the first people's dream. The Native Americans' last hopes for freedom died there. Needless to say, being half white did me no favors."

"Jesus Christ, man. That's no joke." Emile said.

Harley raised one side of his mouth in a smirk. "Well, perhaps a cruel joke. It fucked me up. I'm obviously not white. Nor am I considered Sioux."

Confusion crept up on Emile's face. He gestured ahead of them at Ataraxis Warrior. "What's that about, then?"

Harley glanced at the installation, slowly nodding. "It's a peace offering of sorts."

"I'm sorry. I don't follow. Peace offering for a rough childhood?" Emile asked.

"No. My childhood was no piece of cake. But the real falling out happened when I was a teenager. I left the Rez in my rear view. Traded that in for being a miserable drunk, masquerading as an artist. Then just a miserable drunk. This...," he pointed at the Warrior, "is my grand gesture for making amends." He smiled self-consciously. "I work alone, so I'm not torturing a crew."

Emile winced. "Point taken."

They were quiet for a moment. Then Emile turned to Harley. "Wait. What happened when you were a teenager?"

Harley took in a long breath, expelling it slowly. "That's when the Rez murdered my mother."

Emile's head jerked to look at Harley.

"Well, at least that's the story I fed on to fuel my rage and self-hate. What actually happened was that AIM – the American Indian Movement – occupied Wounded Knee in protest for the treatment of Native Americans, when I was in high school. They did a lot of fucked up things while they were there, including running my mom down with a car. I never forgave the Rez or my dad for letting it happen."

"Are you serious, man?" Emile clutched Harley's shoulder.

Harley looked at him, his eyes soft, a faint smile on his lips. "I visited the Rez for the first time since I left last year after the burn. I did a sweat and had a vision. What I received in that vision birthed that baby." He nodded at the looming installation that was now close in front of them.

"It was time for me to put that burden down," Harley said, a declaration that signaled the end of Harley's willingness to chat.

The bus veered around under the head of the stallion and stopped so that Harley and Emile were staring up into its dark, flaring nostrils. They made their way down the stairs and out the door onto the playa. Once collected, the group made their way around the installation. After they had taken several steps, Harley grabbed Emile's upper arm and spun him round.

"That's a hell of a statement you've made there." He clapped Emile on the shoulder. "You should be proud."

He spun around, leaving Emile staring at the bus. Emile blinked. For once, the showman had no lines to deliver.

Harley had not planned to say that. But it felt right. Like closing a door without slamming it. His foray into the uncomfortable had resulted in an unlikely friendship. He looked up at the Warrior.

Time to get back into my comfort zone.

5:30 and Beatific, BRC, 1:07 PM - Cypher

Cypher's stomach growled loud enough to hear. He had a protein bar in one pocket and trail mix in the other. But three days of the same left him aching for something... anything else.

"Where's a garbage can when you need one?" he muttered. Burning Man's leave-no-trace policy had crushed his best scavenging strategies. His basic needs once again sidelined his big adventure into the unknown.

With a sigh, he surrendered to his hunger and began digging through his pocket. Protein bar coming up. His fingers brushed something else. It was the jerky. He'd forgotten all about it and was just pulling it free when:

"Sausage?"

Cypher looked up just in time to avoid walking into a woman holding a tray. On it were sausage bites, each pierced with a toothpick. He stared.

"Do you want one?" she asked.

He grabbed one and swallowed it nearly whole.

The woman's eyes widened.

"Thank you. Could I have another?" he asked.

She chuckled. "Take a few, love. You're clearly hungry."

He scooped six more off the tray.

"Thank you," he said again, mouth already moving. He wandered on, chewing slowly this time. By the time he reached the 5:00 intersection, the bites were gone, eaten with reverence, each toothpick carefully pocketed.

"You look like a man who could use a pancake," said a bearded man in a tutu... and nothing else.

"Pancake?" Cypher repeated, hopeful.

The man gestured behind him. A shaded camp bustled beneath a sign reading *Breakfast on Beatific*. People queued up at a long table while servers flung pancakes onto paper plates. Cypher slipped into the line and soon had three stacked high. He hit the syrup station and wandered off, munching blissfully.

By the time he hit the 2:00 end of the city, he'd been gifted orange juice, chorizo, cheese cubes, a margarita, and a sno-cone. He was beginning to feel full for the first time since landing on the playa. And he now had a new scavenging strategy: *follow the food.*

Intent on testing it, he left the city grid, planning to cross the inner playa toward 10:00 on the other side of the city. He wanted to see what could be scavenged there.

He didn't get far.

A chaotic wave of boisterous, costumed people swallowed him up, chanting. They wore floppy ears and held signs: *Bunny Power, Freedom to Shake Our Cottontails, Million Bunny March*. Some were in full fur suits. Others wore only headbands and enthusiasm.

Cypher froze, puzzled. His mind wrestled with the visuals. Literal as ever, he couldn't make sense of it.

A large bunny flopped a furry arm around his shoulder. "I hereby conscript you into the bunny army," the bunny declared, plopping ears on Cypher's head. "Join us in our noble leproid cause!"

"Leporid?" Cypher echoed, baffled by the bunny's rally cry.

"Rabbit. Hare. Coney. Bunny. We march for all!"

Cypher didn't fully understand, but the bunny's energy was magnetic. He followed, swept up in the bunny tide, chanting slogans he didn't grasp, propelled by motion and momentum.

Then came shouting from ahead, another crowd, advancing toward them. Orange costumes. Signs: *Million Carrot March, Freedom from Bunny Oppression*.

Cypher's eyes widened. The columns met, circling, jeering. One bunny mooned the carrots. The carrots booed and waved signs. Cypher tensed. This was going to be a fight.

Then, a silvery flash of foil. A bunny produced a shiny object and thrust it toward a carrot. Cypher held his breath.

"Don't mind if I do," the carrot said.

The carrot peeled the foil and bit into a chocolate bunny. Grinning, he offered candy-corn carrots in return.

More exchanges followed. Sweets changed hands. Laughter burst out. The standoff morphed into a street party.

Cypher watched, unsettled. The costumes. The slogans. The sudden turn from near-violence to celebration. It was all too... much. Comedic irony was lost on him. He slipped away, head down.

As he put distance between himself and the party, clarity returned. This food thing. He had figured something out. Easier than scrounging in trash cans. Here, people joyfully gave food away. All he had to do was be in the right place at the right time..

"I am the survivalist warrior," he declared.

He smiled. His belly was full. His pockets were crammed with sweets. He set a course for the western side of the city, ready for his next hunt.

Center Camp, BRC, 1:16 PM - Rachael

Rachael slid into what looked like the shortest barista line. She pulled out her crumpled bills, wiped her mug, and tried to focus on the promise of caffeine ahead. Once her hands were busy, her eyes lifted to the battered cardboard box beside the queue.

"Hope against hope," she muttered, rising on tiptoe to peek inside.

A quiet "Yes" escaped as she spotted a crisp, new *Black Rock Gazette*. She lunged a step forward with the moving line, snatched a copy, and unfolded the thin, two-page chronicle. Her eyes landed on the lead article—*At the Edge: Trash Fence Tales* by Poseidon Rex. Ironic, she thought. This felt like one of those edges.

She hadn't read a word past the byline. Despite her best efforts to stay invisible, the conversation ahead of her started to seep in.

"What's that about?" a woman asked.

"It's an experiment," came the reedy reply. "I've been thinking about surgery. My partner did this so I could see if I could live without it."

Rachael glanced up. The woman facing her direction was a curvy blonde in cornrows, decked in Woodstock-meets-harem chic. The woman answering the question had her back to Rachael. She was striking, over six feet, lean, and completely nude. From the curve of her breasts to the smoothness of her hips, she was unmistakably trans, early in her transition, no surgical changes.

Then, as the taller woman turned, Rachael's gaze dropped and caught the vertical gleam of surgical steel. A series of hoops created a crude simulacrum of labia. It was a bold, exposed, and deliberate statement.

"Everything's tucked inside and out of the way," the woman said.

"How does it feel?"

"Fine. I don't miss it. I'll probably schedule surgery when I get back."

"I'm so happy for you."

And just like that, they moved on. Rachael stood stunned. The emotional tangle rose fast and sharp. Admiration and revulsion churned in equal measure. That kind of audacity — pierced, sculpted, openly displayed. This was everything she had avoided. Her strategy had always been quiet conformity. Normalcy as safety. This woman wore her difference like a billboard and had just discussed her anatomy with the breeziness of a weather report.

The contradiction scraped raw. Rachael folded the paper in half without realizing. All she could do was toss her feelings on the emotional pile. But what gnawed at her more than the piercings, more than the conversation, was the way neither woman flinched. No weight. No judgment. Just casual presence.

Discomfort with addressing genitalia was foundational for her. This short, overheard conversation threw her into a deeply uncomfortable new world. One in which a trans person's genitalia carried no weight. Ironically, she had come to Center Camp and into the coffee line seeking the comfort of the known, only to be tossed into a new emotional adventure.

"Next in line."

She blinked. A barista was waving. She stepped up.

"What'll it be, my dear?"

"Latte, please." She slid the mug forward. Once she paid, she moved to the other side to wait, her mind still reeling. The sense of not belonging, already present all week, had fully cracked open. She felt unmoored, suspended over a chasm.

She needed stillness. A Center Camp bench. A latte. Maybe reading every word of the *Gazette* would bring some sense of order.

"I need to not think for a while," she said aloud.

"This is a good place to not think."

She turned. Leon smiled. "Hey." They exchanged a quick, sweaty hug.

Leon rested a hand on her shoulder. "We've been missing you. Want to come to dinner Saturday night? Watch the burn with us after?"

She hesitated. Either he had not spoken to Bea, or he was offering her a bridge back she was not sure she could cross. Or worse, did he just want to smooth over the discomfort, return her to the role she'd been assigned?

"Uh, sure," she said. "Dinner around eight?"

"Make it 7:30 so we can catch the fire spinners."

"7:30 it is. I'll be there with bells on."

He smiled again. "I'll leave you to your not-thinking."

She managed an embarrassed but grateful smile. As he walked off, she felt something twist inside her, uncertain if it was relief or doubt.

Rachael turned to scan the benches, hoping not just for a place to sit, but a place to land.

9:30 and Avatar, BRC, 4:06 PM - Harley

Harley held the gallon jug above his head, dribbling water into his hair. He massaged it into his scalp, then squeezed a line of soap into his palm and worked it into a gritty lather. With a practiced motion, he rinsed out the foam, letting the runoff splash into the plastic tub at his feet. A handful of water to the face, a scrub of baby wipes across his skin was no substitute for a real shower, but enough to feel halfway human again.

The afternoon heat still clung to the air, though the dry breeze promised some relief. By the time he'd finished his ritual, his hair was already drying. He moved through his camp, tightening guy lines that didn't need it, stowing gear that was already secured. He was burning nervous energy like kindling.

Then came the sound: a deep engine groan, a wheeze of protesting suspension. Harley turned. A beat-up, chalk-dusted '86 Ford F150 rattled to a stop in front of his camp. Behind the side window, Claire's grinning face burst into view.

"Hot diggety damn, it's good to be here!" she shouted.

Before Harley could respond, she exploded out of the cab and launched herself at him. Arms around his neck, legs around his waist, hitting him like joy in motion. He staggered, then steadied, pulling her close, inhaling the warmth of her skin, the scent of lavender and road trip.

For a long beat, the world shrank to just her. The weight of the playa, the years, the regret, lifted.

Then a voice cracked the spell.

"Hi, Dad."

Harley's eyes flew open. A few feet away stood his daughter, Cyan.

"Cyan?" The word rasped out of him like a half-formed prayer. Gently, he slid Claire to the ground and crossed to Cyan, folding her into his arms. The embrace was soft, cautious, like holding something fragile he'd long ago assumed was lost.

When he finally pulled back, he searched her face.

"How...? When...?"

"We started planning months ago," Cyan said, grinning. "You were so deep in Warrior mode, you didn't notice a thing."

Harley smiled, though something in her words stung. It was a familiar reminder of how often he had been elsewhere, even when he was physically present.

"But it wasn't easy keeping our *other* surprise quiet," she added, glancing back toward the truck.

From around its front end came a tall man, silver ponytail trailing, his walk stiff but purposeful. Harley's breath caught. Time stuttered.

The man stopped in front of him and extended a hand. Harley took it. Then he pulled the man into a full embrace.

"Dad," he said, the word cracking as it left his mouth. "You... you came."

"You think I'd miss this show?" the old man replied, Lakota cadence wrapping Harley like an old quilt. "Not a chance."

Harley stepped back, staring at the man who'd once haunted him. "This is the *last* place I thought I'd see you."

The old man shrugged, his smile crooked. "Even the most predictable people can surprise you."

Harley looked between the three of them – Claire, Cyan, and his father. Then he looked west, where the sunlight was softening into gold. Their arrival ushered in a new phase of Harley's playa experience. He had pushed the envelope of his discomfort since he had been on the playa – overextended in his solo ambition, taking on a partner, making new friends, and now this. Family in this strange place.

For most of his life, he'd carried his story like a scar: the Rez, the pain, the rage. But now, on this patch of dust that stripped people down to their core, his past had walked straight into his camp and offered him something else.

A different story.

And for the first time, he wasn't afraid to write it.

BRC Airport, BRC, 5:15 PM - Ruben

"Perfect timing." Elise smiled. She turned to her campmates. "Ruben, this is Lupita, Margo, Geo, and Jules."

Ruben had never been to the airport. He was surprised by how substantial it was. A trailer office served as the tower and check-in. Behind the fence were more than twenty prop planes, guy-wired into the hardpack against the wind. As the Sparklites and Ruben locked up their bikes, Jim stepped out of the office.

"Excellent!" he grinned. "Let's go for a ride." The group followed him out to the plane. The guy wire had already been removed. Jim circled the craft, inspecting it. When satisfied, he opened the hatch and showed them where to step on the wing to enter. Ruben was last.

"Hi, I'm Jim."

"Ruben."

"Looks like you're my copilot. Wait till I'm in, then we'll get you set." Once Jim was seated, Ruben followed and buckled in. Jim handed him a headset.

"Put this on. When you need to talk, press this." He pointed to the mic button. Ruben looked back. The Sparklites were already geared up.

Without ceremony, Jim fired the engine and taxied out. After a quick chat with air traffic control, they lined up and took off.

Jim banked them into a clockwise arc around the city and tipped the starboard wing, revealing a breathtaking view. The entirety of Black Rock City unfolded before them. Seeing the literal landscape below had the effect on Ruben of widening his emotional camera lens to view his emotional landscape. While he had not been seeking discovery today, his emotional panorama was not entirely unwelcome. The broad perspective was eye-opening. His introspection was interrupted.

"There's our camp," Jules said. Ruben spotted the 3:00 plaza and the white peaked tent at Sparkleville. Behind it, he thought he saw the DPW ghetto. Until now, he'd only seen the city in fragments, camps, installations, and venues. But from above, it was a whole organism, pulsing with life. Tiny people clustered around The Man, the Temple, and scattered art like ants at a picnic.

Center Camp slid beneath them, its flags fluttering, bikes strewn in every direction. No line at Camp Arctica. It must be closed. They continued past the city's southwestern edge. Thousands of people, all having wildly different, deeply personal experiences, at the same time.

"So this is what a forty-thousand-person city looks like," said Lupita.

"Yeah, if you put it in the middle of nowhere and build it to disappear after a week," a man replied.

It hit Ruben then. *I did this. Or at least helped make it possible. I'm part of this city.* One of many layers.

They passed the 9:00 plaza. "Check out the Chinese dragon art car," said Margo. Below, a fifty-foot dragon snaked along Chakra. Rumor had it they launched firecrackers when no one was looking.

The plaza gave way to the final blocks and the massive sound camps on the perimeter.

"This part of the playa's going to shake tonight," said one of the men.

"Good," said Lupita. "I'll be getting my dance on. Who's with me?" Cheers and hoots followed.

They flew past open playa. Ahead, Ataraxis Warrior gleamed in the sun. A crowd had already gathered.

"That is one gorgeous sculpture," said Margo.

"Have you seen it at night?"

"It's breathtaking," Elise replied.

"I've been helping run the Warrior," Ruben added.

"Really?" came multiple voices.

"Yeah. I met the artist last week and helped install it. We take turns babysitting it at night. There's a lot of flamage. It can't be left alone."

"We'll come visit," said Lupita.

"Please do," Ruben smiled.

The plane reached the 12:00 position. Below, the Temple of Serenity rose in quiet majesty.

"That is the most beautiful temple I've ever seen," one of the men said. The others murmured in agreement.

The Temple slipped away behind them as they curved toward the eastern edge. From here, Ruben saw the Man in full, an iconic center in the pulsing circle. So much to take in.

Jim angled the plane and dropped toward the runway. After confirming with the tower, they landed and taxied to the lot. He shut the engine down.

Ruben opened the hatch, stepped out on the wing, helped Jim slide the seat forward, then hopped down. The Sparklites followed.

"Need help tying down?" Ruben asked.

"No thanks. Got another crew waiting," Jim said. "One more tour today."

"Well, thanks for taking me along."

Jim clapped him on the back. "How'd you like it?"

Ruben smiled. "It's a hell of a view. Thank you."

"Come back later this week. We'll go again."

As they walked back to the gate, Elise sidled up.

"How was it?"

"Almost overwhelming," Ruben admitted. "The city's beautiful in a completely different way from up there."

"That it is, Ruben. That it is."

The Sparklites mounted their bikes and headed back toward the city. Ruben hung back, slowly unlocking the borrowed bike. He liked them, but he needed time to process.

Seeing the city in its full majesty had rocked him. For the first time in his life, he felt like part of something bigger than himself. For years, maybe always, he'd seen himself as a waste of space. But something had shifted.

He leaned against the bike, stunned. *Maybe I actually have something to offer. To myself. To the people around me. Maybe even the world.*

Then a stark realization hit him. He had not planned to live this long. He had been living as if he were already dead.

If I'm going to contribute, if I'm going to have a life well lived, I need a fucking plan.

Gordian Knot, 8:30 and Esplanade, BRC, 6:35 PM - Crawford

Crawford's eyes were pointed into the maze, but his gaze was a million miles away, searching for any way to shift the narrative. He was used to navigating challenges, playing politics, and lining up support. But he had never racked up so many failures so quickly. He was not out of moves. He just wasn't sure what any of them were.

His stomach rumbled. Without looking at the man beside him, he said, "Monty, I'm gonna grab a bite. I'll be back in a few."

"Take your time," Monty replied. "I'm not going anywhere."

At least not everyone hated him. Monty and he had managed a conversation, however perfunctory, while they shared the crow's nest.

Crawford shimmied down the ladder, dropping onto the hardpack with a slight bounce, enjoying the brief charge of physicality. Burning Man was good for burning calories. Just being here demanded nearly constant motion.

As he passed between RVs into the common area, he spotted the main cabin light glowing through his kitchen window.

Vicky's home.

His heart leaped. Then he reeled it in. Why was she here? To talk? To collect a forgotten item? Regardless, a window had opened. He just needed to stay composed.

He drew a few slow, steady breaths, calming himself. He walked casually across the compound, unlacing his shoes before stepping inside. He wanted his entrance to feel smooth, natural.

He opened the door and stepped up into the RV, sliding out of his boots without looking up. When he turned toward the main cabin, his face relaxed into a performative nonchalance.

But she wasn't there.

The bedroom door was ajar. It was closed enough to obscure the view, open enough to catch the sound of rummaging. He slid into the edge of the bench seat, legs out in the aisle, instinctively readying himself for anything.

The door slid open. Vicky eased out sideways, her shoulders burdened with what looked like the last of her belongings. She turned fully into the cabin and saw him.

She froze.

"Can I help you carry those out?" Crawford offered.

She looked at him for a moment, assessing. "No. I got this."

She was civil. He could work with civil.

"Before you go, can we talk?" he asked, quiet but clear.

"Everything that needed saying was said." Resignation laced her voice. Her anger had burned off.

"Vicky, our blood was up last time. Can't we just talk like people?"

She let out a long sigh, staring at the floor, then shook her head.

Looking up, she said, "Crawford, your life spun off the rails in every direction this week. And instead of a moment's introspection, you went on a boogeyman hunt."

She blinked hard. A tear slid down her cheek.

"You have a lot to sort out. But I won't be sorting it out with you."

There was no anger in her tone, just something colder, quieter. The finality of despair.

He knew what to do with hope. He had no idea what to do with despair.

"I need to go." She moved to the door, nudged the handle down, and pushed it open with her shoulder. At the top of the steps, she paused, turning her head toward him.

"For god's sake, get help. You're the only one who can save yourself."

The door shut softly with finality.

Crawford stared at the handle, willing it to turn. He heard her car start and idle. Then the soft sound of gears shifting, the slow roll away. Still, he watched the handle, holding his breath.

Long after the engine sound had faded, he exhaled.

He stood, put on his hat, slung the Camelbak over his shoulder, and stepped out into the fading light.

He crossed the dust-coated compound and reached the ladder. One hand on the rung, he hesitated. The crow's nest had always given him a sense of control, of altitude. Tonight, it felt like climbing into someone else's story.

He climbed anyway. But the air felt thinner now. And colder. And he was no longer hungry.

3:30 and Inner Playa, BRC, 7:21 PM - Justine

A wide, overhang-shaded porch embellished the front of the building on either side of the entry stairs and then wrapped around the building's sides. A bench swing was suspended from the overhang on the west side porch. Justine reclined across the swing like a cat in temporary respite from a world of chaos. As Susan glided up and perched on the opposite end, Justine gave her a lazy smile.

"I'm indulging myself in a playa sunset," she drawled, hand flopping dramatically toward the horizon like she was narrating a vacation in paradise commercial. The western clouds had massed in drama over the serrated peaks, the sun was throwing theatrical golds and reds across the sky like it had a flair for production design.

"It's the kind of majestic that makes you momentarily forget the smell of playa funk," she declared.

"Mind if I join you, ma'am?" Susan said, affecting a syrupy Southern drawl.

"I'd be *crushed* if you didn't," Justine replied in her best Scarlett O'Hara.

The city hall building standing before her looked like it was plucked out of a 1940s Midwestern town, then fed massive amounts of hallucinogens before it was plopped down on the playa. Walls were bent, and the clock tower was twisted ninety degrees from bottom to top, so the clock faced west instead of toward the south-facing front entrance. The clock hands moved backward, tracing a path across an odd assortment of letters, Greek symbols, dates, equations, and pictures. The wall and trim colors were psychedelic.

The paintings of past mayors lining the walls of the rotunda included Buddy Hollie, Ritchie Valens, Jimi Hendrix, Jerry Garcia, Jim Morrison, Janice Joplin, Kurt Cobain, Otis Redding, Aaliya, Tupak Shakur, and Sid Vicious. The current mayor's painting hung at the top of the grand staircase. Amy Winehouse was resplendent standing on the mayoral desk.

They swung in silence for a time, breathing in the colors and weird serenity. Eventually, Susan leaned in, voice gentle, "You seem pretty relaxed. How are you doing with all this craziness?"

Justine expected the question. It was so Susan to give her space, only to ask just when she needed someone to. She exhaled, staring out into the fading light. She remained quiet for a moment, mulling her yet unformed response.

"Honestly, my answer varies moment to moment out here." Again, she took a moment to sift through the gumbo of her thoughts and emotions. In the quiet chambers of her mind, a delicate scale hung suspended, not of brass or steel, but something far more ancient and uncertain. Its arms swung wildly with each new experience here in this alien place.

"At the moment, it's like someone took the contents of my subconscious, hit shuffle, then set the dial to 'full sensory overwhelm.' I mean, I've been lifted by joy, desire, hope. But also dragged face-first through dread and shadow. Heavy portions of both, with no idea when the next turn is coming or what it's going to look like."

She gave Susan a sideways look. "If this were just a normal festival, I'd have my game face on, do my gigs, flirt a little, collect stories, and peace out back to my tidy life with my meal preps and calendared schedule. But this place?" She shook her head, a crooked smile playing on her lips. "This place wants my soul."

Justine sat up straighter, more animated now. "And it's not like I'm not getting my performance fix. The gigs? They're practically throwing themselves at me. I walk down the street and get offered a stage, a practice partner, or a mango-passionfruit smoothie that somehow unearths my deepest childhood wound. *What is this place?*"

Then her smile faded. "But yeah... the indulgence here? It's a bit like offering chaos your couch for a night and waking up to find it's unpacked its bags, rewritten your story, and made itself at home in the part of you that used to feel safe."

"The creep factor's real. I've been collecting unsolicited male energy like it's a Burning Man punch card. Ten sleazy encounters and I get a free trauma!" Her voice dropped. "And of course, there was that almost-incident. If Rachael hadn't been there... let's just say the playa would have a body count. Predators are going to predate, but this permissive environment out here grants license to predatory instincts like it's an entitlement."

She glanced at Susan, and her voice softened. "But it's not all disaster. I've met these... unexpected people. Like the Magrathea guy who just handed me a stage like it was no big deal. And the weirdly charming anti-social artist, father of Ataraxis Warrior. And the lost puppy boy with too much enthusiasm and not enough self-esteem. These men feel safe in their gentle generosity. It's as if, in this theater of all possibilities, you get both the best and worst of humanity."

She chuckled. "And, I gotta say, our camp? Y'all are kind of the dream team. The way you guys show up for me... It's messing with my ability to maintain emotional distance. Rude."

She shrugged. "It's all like... my life, but in fast-forward and surround sound. Every part of me; good, bad, pretentious, tired, is getting shoved under a magnifying glass and slapped by the wind. I'm really glad that I'm here. This is a powerful experience. But I'm way out of my comfort zone."

Susan listened without interrupting, just nodding and letting Justine talk it out. When she finally spoke, it was soft, "You don't have to make sense of it yet. Let it marinate. BRC brews slow epiphanies."

Justine smirked. "Wow, you really *have* been out here too long. You're starting to sound like a philosopher who gives away grilled cheese at 3 a.m."

Susan laughed and squeezed her shoulder. "I'm just glad we finally get to share this madness together. I love you, woman. I've been waiting years to grant you honorary Black Rock citizenship."

Justine swallowed the automatic sarcasm that tried to leap up and fill the silence. Instead, she smiled; soft, sincere, and rare.

"Thanks," she said, voice light but real. "You didn't tell me the initiation would involve joy, trauma, and spontaneous crying in public, but I'm honored."

Susan's eyes sparkled. "Regardless of what you do or don't do, I'm still planning on having a grand old time with you while we're out here."

Without warning, she smacked Justine on the ass and leaped from the swing, just out of range of Justine's retaliatory kick.

"Bitch! How *dare* you?" Justine gasped, mock-scandalized. "I'm gonna beat your ass with a glow stick!"

"You'll have to catch me first!" Susan called over her shoulder as she mounted her bike and sped off.

Justine jumped up and launched herself onto her own bike, already standing on the pedals. There would come a time to thank Susan properly, for her love, her timing, her ability to pull her out of spirals with a mojito and a slap.

But right now? Right now, Justine had a chase to win and a revenge to deliver.

7:00 and Inner Playa, BRC, 8:20 PM - Emile

Howls rang out across the city, heralding sunset. The sun fully disappeared behind the western crags. Deep reds, oranges, and purples offered a dazzling send-off as the playa around Magrathea was cast into shadow. A small knot of crew members gathered at the railing on the northeastern-facing side of the bus. The Man stood watch on them in the distance. Their attention was, however, on the gathering crowd in a makeshift playa dance floor below. The ethereal, Middle Eastern-flavored music was throbbing through the bus at a volume that still allowed for socializing.

"It's basically dinner time, right?" Bewilderment laced Shimmer's tone.

"Let's not forget that it's only Wednesday night." Said Bart, equally perplexed.

"Not to mention that Bedlam is basically playing dinner music," Misha noted.

In the fading light, they could see burners on bikes and on foot, in ones, twos, and small packs beelining toward them.

"Houston, we're achieving critical mass." Django declared.

These early-arrivers were ambitious. Costumes abounded with every conceivable artistic flourish. Some were sexy, others were blinking, still others were animatronic, wire creatures. Revelers were out to party tonight.

"The customer is always right. If this lot wants a party, we'll give them a party to remember. Let's crank it up to eleven." Emile proclaimed, arms raised, slipping into his master of ceremonies persona. Liam and Kathy exchanged glances, rolling their eyes.

Liam muttered. "Here we go."

But something felt different tonight, as Emile worked the crowd like Hugh Hefner at his Penthouse parties. Charming them, flirting, spreading cheer, his smile seemed stretched too tight, his movements just a fraction too aggressive. He moved through the crowd, schmoozing his way to the stairs, but Liam caught the edge in his voice when someone bumped into him.

Liam watched the performance, disgust gripping him. Dobbs slid up next to him, smiling and shaking his head. Liam glanced at Dobbs.

"Who is that guy?" Liam asked, a hint of exasperation in his voice.

Dobbs affected a Scottish brogue. "A piece of work, he is. A great piece of work." It was Liam's turn to shake his head.

Emile had smoothly disengaged a reveler and made his way down the circular stairs.

DJ Bedlam was subtly cranking up the energy, manipulating the dancers into inspired writhing. Liam and Dobbs followed in close pursuit. They needed to witness the train wreck.

By the time Emile stepped onto the second-level dance floor, Bedlam was a woman possessed. The rhythm tightened, coiled, then snapped loose in a pulse that shot through the floor and into the bones. The crowd caught it instantly: spines straightening, limbs loosening, heads tilting back in anticipation. The drop hit. Bodies ignited.

She didn't just play music. She bent time, and the crowd moved in its new gravity.

Not even Emile could find fault in her magic. He shifted his trajectory away from the DJ booth and continued to work the crowd. But Liam noticed how his hands clenched when someone didn't respond to his charm quickly enough, how his jaw tightened when laughter didn't come on cue. Liam and Dobbs halted near the spiral stairs, watching Emile from a distance. He made a full round of the dance floor and through the chill space and the front of the bus, eventually making his way back to the stairs, dancing his way down them. Liam and Dobbs exchanged glances and followed.

The first level was thick with celebrants. The human mass muted the dancing to shuffling movements. Those lucky enough to find seats were in animated conversation. Emile slowly made his way through the crowd, heading for the door, intent on imposing his charm on the crowd outside.

Liam and Dobbs found Sanjay and Gina leaning against the articulation joint between the front and back modules.

"How's it going, kids?" Liam asked.

Sanjay smiled. "We have quite a party here."

Gina nodded toward the front of the bus. "The natives are getting restless."

Three men pushed through the crowd, faces flush, bringing their frenetic energy into a space too tight to contain it.

"Fucking yahoos," Sanjay muttered.

The first of the trio grabbed a vertical handrail, lifted his body nearly perpendicular, and spun himself around the pole. Another pushed through the throng to claim an adjacent pole. He cleared the path for his spin by shouldering and kicking several bystanders out of the way.

The third leaped onto the bench behind the poles and began to jump up and down, hollering and egging on his companions to keep up their spinning. The jumper lost balance at the apex of his jump and came down hard on the bench backrest. His boot caught fabric, ripping a ragged tear. He turned and surveyed the damage through wild eyes, then turned back to his buddies, starting to say something.

"Hey!" Emile's voice cut through the music, sharp as broken glass. The man turned, still grinning with chemical euphoria. "You just ripped my fucking upholstery."

"Chill, man, it's just..."

Emile hammered the man's chest with both hands, sending the man's upper body backward. His shoulder blades and head crashed into the window behind with a loud thump. Emile had the man by his shirt collar and was staring into the man's crazed and confused eyes.

"This is my house, motherfucker. You don't disrespect my house." Before the man could respond, Emile dragged him down off the bench onto the floor, dragging him by his collar across the floor, then rolled him down the stairs onto the playa.

By the time Emile turned around, the other two of the trio had collected themselves and were moving toward Emile, girding for a fight, blood in their eyes. Suddenly, one tripped, crashing to the floor. The other fell over his splayed body. Emile looked up to see Dobbs wink and smile as he pulled back his size fourteen boot from the aisle.

Emile reached down and grabbed a collar in each hand and dragged the two sprawled men out of the bus. As they collected themselves, he glowered at them, shouting, "You're not welcome here again." Liam reached the door in time to see a spittle fling from Emile's lips. He seemed almost beastlike.

The three men reluctantly stumbled away, newfound caution overriding their drug-induced belligerence. Emile stood hulking, shoulders raised, arms out, chest heaving in ragged breaths. Once they disappeared into the dusk, Emile drew himself upright, straightened his clothes, and returned to the bus. His campmates had gathered at the front of the bus. Their faces reflected both concern for and fear of him. "Are you okay?" Gina asked.

He breathed out a long, slow breath. "Yeah. I'm fine." The Magrathean cabal dispersed, leaving Emile and Liam alone at the door. Liam slid his hand into Emile's. Emile looked at him. "Can we go out on the backside of the bus, where we can talk?" Emile's eyes darkened. He nodded stiffly.

They exited the bus and skirted around the speaker wing, making their way into the dark playa in silence. When the noise diminished ever so slightly on the far side of the bus, Emile stopped and turned to Liam. "What's up?" He asked in a defiant tone that indicated that he really did not want to know.

Liam looked down at the cracked earth for a moment, then up into Emile's eyes. "Those guys needed to go. I'm pissed that they ripped the upholstery. So thank you for getting rid of them."

Emile smiled, "Sure. It was nothing."

"No... it was really something!" Liam's voice cracked. "It was terrifying, Emile. The way you looked at that guy, the way you moved, like you wanted to hurt him. Really hurt him."

"I did what I had to do," Emile said defensively.

"You wanted to keep going." Liam's words came faster now, desperate. "I saw it in your face. If Dobbs hadn't tripped those other guys, if I hadn't been there, what would you have done?"

"Those guys were out of their minds. They couldn't be reasoned with, " Emile said, his tone matter-of-fact.

"You didn't even try!" Liam's voice broke completely. "The Emile I fell in love with would have tried. He would have found a way that didn't involve violence. He would have protected people, not terrorized them."

They were both quiet for a moment, but the silence felt explosive now.

"The gentle spirit and charming man that I love so much isn't just taking a break, Emile. He's disappearing. And you're letting him go." Liam's voice was barely above a whisper. "I'm watching the person I love most in this world become someone I don't recognize. Someone who scares me."

Emile stared at him, something dangerous flickering behind his eyes. When he finally spoke, his voice was cold and deliberate. "Maybe you should be scared. Maybe you should run while you still can."

The words hit Liam like a physical blow. Emile turned and tramped back toward Magrathea, leaving Liam standing there in the dust, shattered.

4:30 and Inner Playa, BRC 10:42 PM - Cypher

The cityscape blazed through the still night with iridescent reds, blues, greens, golds, purples, and oranges flashing like beacons. Some blinked. Some pulsed to unseen beats. Some traced the outlines of animals, faces, and creatures. It was a swirl of color, rhythm, and motion, with thousands of moving lights in a synchronized, yet chaotic, dance. A living, breathing art piece. Cypher stared in awe. He had been out here for days without really *seeing* this. And now, it hit him all at once.

This place is beautiful.

The acid tab he'd taken two hours ago was stretching his consciousness, but in the best way. He was truly deep into a new adventure. Everything shimmered. Everything moved. And it all made sense. This trip was strong but clean, like the world had finally snapped into proper focus. After the first wave, he'd taken two more hits. Now, he was tripping balls. And he was in love... with the sky, with the ground, with the miracle of being.

Not in a touchy-feely, cuddle puddle kind of way. This was raw, electric joy. A wide-eyed awe at every flicker and breath of the world. He loved himself. He loved the force, whatever it was, that had allowed him to witness all this. "I am the prophet of collapse practicing the discipline of dust!" he bellowed to the open night.

He thought nothing could top this feeling. That was, until he turned around.

Out of the dark, a vehicle rumbled forward. It looked like a cyberpunk pirate ship crossed with a tank, built by the Death Guild, industrial and mythical all at once. As it rolled up, a cannon on the cab exploded into a giant arc of fire. Cypher let out a whoop, jumping and fist-pumping the air. The ship squealed to a halt beside him.

The grinning man on the cannon called down, "Wanna be a gunner?"

"Hell yeah!" Cypher shouted.

"Then find an open turret and make yourself at home."

There were three. One turret near the cab, one midship, and one in the rear. The front was taken. Cypher beelined for the rear. He climbed the short ladder and dropped into a padded seat inside the turret.

But there was no trigger. No handle. No button. Just what looked like an industrial drum kit. He blinked. Stared. His tripping brain couldn't make sense of it.

The front gunner shouted something, but Cypher lost track halfway through. His attention span had vaporized.

"What?" he called.

"Put on your headset!"

He found it hanging behind him and slipped it on, adjusting the mic. "Hello? Hello?"

No response. Just silence. He was about to bail when, "HEY REAR GUNNER. YOU ON?" The voice blasted through his headset. Cypher yelped, leaping up, banging his head on the ceiling.

"Ahh, ow... yeah, I'm here."

Pause. Then: "You gotta key the mic, rookie. Press the button on your mic to talk."

He did. "Yeah, I'm here."

"What's your name, gunner?"

"Cypher."

"Well, Cypher. Here's the deal. Your cannon only fires when I flip the switch. We don't shoot when we're moving or near anything flammable. But this? This is prime fire-play territory, so... you got juice." Cheers rang out across the headsets.

The voice continued, "Your cannon is vibration-triggered. Look up. See those drumsticks? Pull 'em out. That's how you fire, lay down a beat."

Cypher grinned and went to work. He had no rhythm. But what he lacked in skill he made up for in sheer enthusiasm. Every strike blasted a flame. The faster he played, the farther it stretched. The cannon roared like a beast, spewing fire fifteen feet across the playa. He was ecstatic. A part of the machine. A fire god in a drum seat.

They stopped three times, each time a mini inferno. For the final stop, they parked near the Serpent's Nest. Cypher played with abandon, coaxing twenty-foot bursts from the turret. He was weightless. Glowing. Transformed.

When the ship finally pulled away, Cypher clambered down, waving at the crew. The front gunner sent him off with one last glorious blast from the main cannon.

Cypher turned toward the Serpent's Nest and sprinted, high on fire, light, and the first real sense of *power* he had felt in a long time. He was ready to continue his adventure playing in the fields of fire.

Gordian Knot, 8:30 and Esplanade, BRC, 10:45 PM - Justine

The churn that had plagued Justine earlier had quieted, like a background process still humming, but out of view. She might have relocated to Black Rock City, but her default mode remained unchanged; train, perform, sarcasm on tap.

Still, something was shifting. Earlier, she'd playfully chased Susan through camp, and it had turned into actual play. She couldn't remember the last time she'd let herself just play.

Now, solo and curious, she wandered into the Gordian Knot. Normally, she'd dismiss something like this as a burner gimmick, but tonight she let her curiosity steer. She dove into the maze, breezing through the early puzzles and sinking deeper in.

The passageway twisted and branched, surprising her with its layered complexity, taking her up stairs, down a slide, through crawlspaces, and over cargo nets. She wasn't lost, exactly, but she definitely wasn't confident. At least she hadn't doubled back.

A faint white glow edged the next doorway, subtle and dreamlike. She stepped through and took a sharp left, then flinched.

A burly man in an orange tee and khakis stared back at her. She froze. That was, until she realized it was a mirror.

She spun, checking for the real man, but the hall was empty. She stepped closer. The man mirrored her confusion perfectly.

She smirked. *At least he looks as baffled as I feel.*

Turning away, she slid between two mirrors and kept going.

Gordian Knot, 8:30 and Esplanade, BRC, 11:03 PM - Ruben

Ruben had let the momentum of his fly-around escapade carry him. He wandered the city trying new things. Unfortunately, he had been casually offered alcohol so many times during his wander that he was not sure he could withstand the temptation of another offer. The greatest appeal of this maze was that no alcohol was to be had here.

He welcomed the glow ahead. Finally, a lit section. But the unexpected face in the mirror startled him. A woman. Young. Wryly amused. And then she was gone.

He blinked. "Well, that was strange," he muttered, stepping forward. There she was again, multiplied in every direction.

"What the hell?" he said aloud.

"This is pretty fucking weird, isn't it?" her voice replied, echoing in the strange acoustics.

He laughed, startled and intrigued. "You must be in here somewhere."

"Oh no," she teased. "I'm just a figment of your imagination. But a very chatty one."

He grinned. "Touché. Shall we keep moving forward? Maybe we'll meet in the middle."

"On it." She slipped away.

He entered the next turn, and there she was again.

"How the hell did they build this?" She scanned their infinite reflections.

"No idea." He stepped forward again.

"Well met, once again."

"Weirdly met," she smirked. "Next section, before we start finishing each other's sentences?"

They advanced.

"You'd think we would've actually collided by now," he said.

She looked up. "Clearly the playa gods love a slow burn."

They both laughed. Then he emerged into a new corridor. Behind him, she was still framed in the final mirror.

"You on the other side of this magic trick?" she asked.

"Looks like it."

"How did we miss each other?"

"Blame the laws of physics. Or mirror gnomes."

"Nice nearly meeting you," he said.

"If we ever *do* meet," she replied, "I expect at least this level of mystique."

She gave a wave, not quite a goodbye, and vanished into the maze.

They moved on, still slightly off balance, not entirely sure what had just happened, yet not in a hurry to explain it either.

02 Spins Until the Man Burns

Gordian Knot, 8:30 and Esplanade, BRC, 1:15 AM - Crawford

The night was mild. Even in the wee hours, the ambient temperature held in the mid-60s. Crawford sat hunched in a camp chair outside his RV, lacing his boots. Since Vicky left, the RV had started to feel airless. That claustrophobia had grown until it settled into his chest like a weight, dull and insistent. He didn't know where he was going. He just knew he could not stay here.

"Crawford?"

He looked up. Millie stood a few paces away, watching him.

"Whoa." Her eyes widened. "Are you alright? You're pale and sweating."

He looked down, tugging at a bootlace. "I'm good."

"Are you sure? You don't look okay."

He sighed. "I just need to get out of here."

She stepped closer, placing a hand gently on his shoulder. "I came over to invite you out with us."

He glanced past her. Three campmates lingered by the dining area, watching. He recognized them but didn't know their names. He had never spoken to them.

"We're heading down to 10:00 to find some music that suits our groove. A mini adventure."

He blinked, trying to process what she'd just said. No one had spoken to him voluntarily in days, let alone invited him anywhere. He drew in a breath, slow and deliberate.

"Sure," he said. "Why not?"

He stood, slung his CamelBak over his shoulder, and fell into step beside her. The invitation felt surreal. His acceptance is even more so. It was the first time in memory that he had not decided what the group would do, had not even considered trying... yet.

As they reached the waiting trio, he paused and gave a slight nod.

"Hi. I'm Crawford," he said.

The words tasted unfamiliar. Not a leader's declaration. Just a name. Still, he could use this as an opportunity to rebuild his power position, starting with these four people.

9:30 and Avatar, BRC, 6:14 AM - Harley

The Black Rock Desert was not stingy with heat or dust. But rain? Summertime rain was damn near a myth. July and August were particularly brutal: bone-dry, airless months when even a passing cloud was a rumor. But every now and then, the desert broke its own rules.

This was one of those times.

Storm clouds had been gathering in tense anticipation, like a hoard secreted behind the western ridge, until suddenly they weren't. By the early hours, the clouds had rolled in like a military invasion, cresting over the escarpment and spilling onto the playa with no preamble. The sky cracked open, and the heavens unzipped their fury.

Harley had smelled it before he heard it. That wild petrichor, the sharp, primal tang of water touching parched earth, ripped him from sleep. It wasn't logical. His trenches were dug, his camp secure. Still, some old animal instinct flared in his gut and pulled him up by the spine.

He sat up, the blanket falling away. Rubbed the crust of sleep from his eyes. Tipped back a lukewarm bottle of water and drank until his pulse stopped racing. The silence outside wasn't quite silence. It was more like a held breath. The kind that comes before something big.

And then it began.

First, soft, just a whisper: a few scattered tics on distant tarps, like the first kernels in a popcorn bag. Then more. And more. Until the desert roared, the downpour arrived like an ambush, washing the camp in a curtain of silver.

Harley grabbed the flannel shirt from the floor and stepped into the storm's soft jaws. The shade structure did its best to shelter him, but beyond its edges the world was being rinsed clean. He stood there, barefoot on wet carpet, absorbing the moment. In all his years out here, he'd never seen the playa like this, drenched and otherwise still.

The camper door creaked, a long, drawn-out complaint of rust and metal. Cyan stood framed in the door. She said nothing, just met his eyes. He pressed a finger to his lips and extended his hand. She stepped into it, light and sure.

"Want to watch the rain with me?" he asked.

She nodded and slid into one of the chairs. He draped a throw around her shoulders and handed over his water bottle. She drank, then exhaled with a contented sigh. For a long moment, they sat in silence, listening to the soft roar that muffled the city's noise. Just the two of them, sealed off from everything by a ring of falling water.

"In a weird way, this is a gift," Harley said, still watching the storm. "We never get rain like this during the burn."

"I like it," Cyan replied. "It smells... honest."

Harley glanced sideways, surprised by the word. Honest. That's what this was. No artifice. No noise. Just two people, connected by blood and scar tissue, sharing space.

He hesitated before asking, "Do you drink coffee?"

Cyan turned to him, something soft flickering behind her eyes. Not amusement. Not sarcasm. Something warmer. Forgiveness, maybe.

"Yeah, Dad. I like coffee."

She reached for his hand and held it gently.

Harley let the moment settle into him. "Good. I'll make some when the rain lets up."

They sat like that until the storm passed. They made the coffee together in silence, each movement deliberate. The rhythm of grinding, boiling, and pouring felt almost sacred, like a quiet tea ceremony. When Claire and Clarence finally emerged from the camper, the four of them stood together at the edge of a transformed world, ankle-deep in the desert's rarest element.

Mud.

7:30 and Enlighten, BRC, 6:18 AM - Rachael

Rachael woke to a smell she knew well—that water-heavy scent that rose from the ground just before rain. Then she heard it. Tac... tac, tac... tac, tac, tac... tac...

"Yep. Rain," she mumbled.

And then the heavens let loose, pounding her tent-fly in a steady roar.

"Wow. It really comes down out here," she said aloud, relieved she'd trenched the tent. She wasn't sure what kind of mess she'd find outside, but the sound of rain brought a strange comfort. She always slept better when it rained.

Still, the thought came unbidden: *Would I rather be here, or back at home?* She rolled the question in her mind like a smooth stone, worn by time but still undecided.

Here, everything was intensity and chaos and strangers. There, everything was history. Familiar. Easier to disappear into. Maybe.

The tent rattled under the storm. She pulled the blanket up to her chin and let the drumming sky drown her thoughts.

She didn't have an answer. But for the moment, she didn't need one.

The rain kept falling. And she slept.

DPW Ghetto, 3:10 and Beatific, BRC, 6:22 AM - Ruben

Some DPW fucko was throwing marbles on his roof. At least that is what a cranky Ruben thought as the racket roused him from a deep slumber.

"Knock it the fuck off!" he shouted. But the unabated racket increased. "Mother fucker!" He sat up, exasperated, and looked groggily around the small room, seeing nothing that might explain the noise. Then he noticed that the room was cool, almost cold. It had not felt cold in this room since he moved in. Ruben dropped his feet onto the linoleum floor, stood, and padded over to the curtained window. He held up the material and saw the veritable wall of water obscuring the view.

"Rain!?" He asked aloud, his tone tinged with disbelief, as he wandered back to his bed. He sat down hard on the stiff mattress and combed his fingers across the sides of his balding head. "Rain." He said again, this time a soft declaration.

He was awake now, no longer confused. He realized that the foreignness of the sound had thrown him off. It had been over four years since he had heard rainfall. Now this reintroduction offered a patter amplified by the sheet metal roof above him, as if he were listening to the heart of the storm through a stethoscope. The ceiling remained still, passive, showing no signs of strain. But Ruben knew better. This shelter was temporary. The concrete and steel walls of his prison cell had kept him safe from more than weather... they'd kept karma at bay. The routine had protected him from the natural chaos that would surely deliver his righteously deserved punishment for a life badly lived. Prison had been both refuge and penance.

His prison cell had been far removed from nature's interventions. Even the greatest of storms carried little more than distant, muted rumbles to his cell. That was what made prison life bearable, even in some ways appealing. The looming concrete and steel walls held back the karma he knew was waiting for him outside.

Now, for the first time since he had been released, he contemplated the implications of his freedom. Destiny had lost its patience and now lay claim to his soul. It was no accident that he was here in the most chaotic, harshest environment he had ever known. He had arrived on the playa believing it to be a respite while figuring out his next steps. In truth, it was the crucible in which his sins would be measured. He shuddered. He had been avoiding this reckoning for over twenty years.

That avoidance had underwritten the half-life he had lived until now. Perhaps it was time to surrender, let the reckoning commence, let fate wash over him without resistance. Perhaps it was time to quit hiding and come out into the light. He let out a sigh, and his shoulders relaxed. He let his head slump so that his chin rested on his chest. A quote floated into his consciousness, *'There is no more dangerous man than one that has nothing to lose.'*

The only thing that Ruben had to lose was the man he had been until now. That, in his mind, was not much to give up. He was a danger, all right, but only to his psyche. He looked down at his palms, just making them out in the weak pre-dawn light. He released another great sigh and felt, maybe for the first time in his life, relaxed.

"Rain!" he said one last time, this time his tone satisfied, almost happy. With that, he lay down, pulled the ratty quilt up over his shoulders, and nestled into the fetal position, sighed, and closed his eyes, falling almost instantly into the most peaceful slumber he had had for years.

The rain had been chaotic in its distribution, touching every camp, every street, and every carefully laid plan. Some woke to disaster. Some inconvenience. And some, like Cypher, are to the discomfort of familiar sounds in an unfamiliar place.

7:00 and Inspiration, 6:29 AM - Cypher

The playa surface had been an unyielding mattress for three days. Cypher's body ached from head to toe. An hour earlier, he'd crawled into the sleeping bag and drawn the pup tent lining up to his chin. Exhausted but still buzzing from the LSD, he hadn't really slept, just lay there, eyes closed, watching the fading flickers of a psychedelic movie play across his eyelids.

But the movie was over now. All that remained was the ache, the chill, and a hollow, post-euphoric emptiness. Last night, he had loved the world, felt like a prophet of beauty. Now, all he could feel was the punishing weight of his bones against the cold, indifferent earth.

Then the rain came.

It started with five fat raindrops slapping his exposed face like warning shots. He flinched and ducked beneath the tent fabric, but the tarp was no match for the storm. The drops turned to a barrage. It felt like a massage with metal chopsticks.

Then came the deluge, so heavy it felt like an elephant sitting on his chest. He threw his arms over his face and cinched the tent bag closed in his fists, trying to shield himself from the hydraulic beating.

"This fucking sucks," Cypher muttered.

Then came the cold, sharp, and invasive. Cold water seeped through his clothes, soaking his back, legs, and everything pressed against the ground. When he reached down, his hand plunged into a shallow pool. Not dampness. A puddle. A wide one.

He scrambled out of the sleeping bag just as the downpour eased to a light sprinkle. It hardly mattered. He was drenched to the bone. Stepping away from his failed shelter, his bare foot sank into an inch of ooze. He jerked it back, but it was too late. Mud clung between his toes. He shook it off, unsuccessfully, then planted his foot on the tent, sinking to his ankle in water.

He yanked his sandals free and managed to slide one onto his clean foot. Then he tried using the puddle to rinse the other. It was only now, ankle-deep in muck, that he realized his camp sat in one of the playa's rare hollows. Every drop of the storm had gathered here, turning his tent into a soup pot.

He waded in and pulled everything out; shirt, two water jugs, both sandals. Food was gone. Spare clothes were floating debris. He stood over the wreckage, shivering, cold slicing through his acid hangover and into his bones.

Cypher tied the soaked shirt around his waist, grabbed a jug, and trudged into the street. Mud caked his sandals. He shook so hard that the slosh of water in the jug was the only sound he could hear. He did not know where he was going, only that he was *away from this hell*. Dry. That was the goal.

He had gone a short distance when a voice called from a nearby camp. "Are you alright?"

He turned his whole body, muscles stiff, teeth rattling too hard to answer. The woman stepped under her awning, a look of concern on her face.

"Do you have any dry clothing?"

He shook his head. Barely.

"Come over here. I'll get you something warm to put on."

He slogged toward her. She threw a bulky fake fur coat around his shoulders and handed him a pair of furry pants. "While you're putting those on, I'll make you some hot tea."

Cypher stared at the pants. Then, his gaze lowered from his soaked trousers to the unholy globs of mud clinging to his feet.

He looked back at her and said, "This is going to take a while."

3:00 and Divinity BRC, 6:31 AM - Justine

The deluge pounded the porta-potty. The plastic walls amplified the racket, turning the chamber into a drum. Justine squatted on the closed commode lid, trying to touch nothing at all. She'd just been doing her business when the rain hit. Staying put had been the lesser of two evils. She loathed porta-potties as the dirty, foul, hell-box disease vectors they were. But when she cracked the door, a wall of water greeted her. Getting soaked in the chill morning air seemed worse.

She held her breath in short bursts, trying to inhale as little as possible. Thank God it was cool out, muting the waste off-gassing. She listened to the storm, perched and breathing shallowly. Why hadn't she brought her dust mask?

Then, as suddenly as it began, the storm stopped.

Justine hopped off the commode and cracked the door again. A world of mud stared back. She gingerly stepped down from the port-o-let into the muck, thankful for her flats. Her boot sank with a soft *skwit*. She grimaced. Mud oozed over the toe of her black pleather boot.

She sighed and stepped away, the door slamming shut behind her. *Skwit, skwit, skwit.* The mud was both greasy and thick. One wrong step and she'd wear it all the way to her neck.

Her camp was two city blocks away. Normally, a five-minute walk. Today, she'd be lucky to get back in fifteen. *Skwit, skwit, skwit.* She looked east. Dawn was blooming. The city shimmered in patchwork gold as morning rays spilled through gaps in the cloud cover. It was shaping up to be a beautiful day. With any luck, the muck would be hard playa by afternoon.

She smiled and trudged on. *Shloop.* Her foot broke free with a sucking sound. She stepped forward, heavy with mud. Another *shloop*, and she repeated the motion. Each step was like walking through glue.

At last, she reached camp. Susan was emerging from her tent, stretching. She spotted Justine's awkward gait and smirked. "I see you got yourself a pair of playa-platforms."

Justine looked down. Nearly three inches of mud clung to her soles. "Not the best-engineered platforms. They weigh a ton," she laughed, clomping toward her.

"Want some tea?" Susan asked as Justine pulled a chair under the pop-up canopy to scrape off her boots.

"God, yes. I need to wash the porta-potty stench out of my soul." She got to work, watching the muck flake off. One of a thousand small tasks today, she would not even think about at home.

Out here, everything was basic: stay hydrated, keep your shade intact, eat something sustaining, navigate the bathroom situation. Each small thing demanded attention. Her health, sanity, and happiness hinged on it.

It was a kind of playa-zen. She smiled to herself, then looked back at Susan.

"At least we won't have a dust storm this morning."

She glanced again at the golden light warming the city and let the smile linger. For the first time all week, it felt like things might just even out and hold together. What else could possibly go wrong?

Magrathea Base Camp, 10:00 and Divinity, BRC, 7:28 AM - Emile

The sound of a door slamming and urgent steps down the spiral staircase abruptly truncated Emile's alcohol-infused sleep. He lay vaguely awake, eyes shut, attempting to piece together the evening's trajectory that landed him in this state. He remembered the argument with Liam. He remembered holding an extended court at the Magrathea bar. He remembered an extremely difficult climb up the stairs. He remembered having trouble sliding his key into the door lock for his suite. He remembered Dobbs taking the key from him and doing the honors. He remembered face-planting in the bed.

A quick assessment of his current state told him two things. He was still in that faceplant position. He had not moved. The other thing he realized was that he was deeply hungover. "Fuck me!" he mumbled.

He considered a return to slumber. Then he recalled the reason he was now awake. The roof deck hatch is slamming, and urgent footsteps. Something was going on. Something not good. He rolled over onto his back and listened. Urgent footsteps on the roof deck, directions being shouted, and the sound of equipment being moved. He opened his eyes, screamed, and immediately snapped them shut. The morning light greeted him with searing pain.

As he pushed himself up to a sitting position, the room lurched, forcing him to lean forward and grab the edge of the bed. The nausea hit hard. He reached for the wastebasket just in time. The voluminous disgorgement racked his abdomen and ribs. Once his stomach was empty, he continued dry heaving for several minutes before collapsing, chest against his thighs, breathing raggedly.

After a time, his breathing returned to normal. A dull ache pressed against the back of his eyes. His tongue felt like it was wearing a coat, tasting as if it was pulled out of the bottom of a garbage bin. He tied the plastic bag closed with shaking hands, his nerve endings were fried.

Eventually, he felt strong enough to sit upright. He pulled a water bottle from the shelf and sipped carefully, letting the water slowly trickle down his throat. When his stomach didn't revolt, he continued until the bottle was empty. He was now lucid enough to feel dread about the sounds of the crew.

Gripping the shelf, Emile pulled himself to standing. Getting shitfaced in his mid-thirties was leagues worse than when he was younger. Despite his condition, he was needed. The shouts and footsteps had continued unabated. He sensed something serious was afoot, and as captain of the ship, he needed to man the helm. He rallied.

Emile opened the suite door and stepped into the main bay of the bus's second level. A large puddle lay on the dancefloor tiles around the stairwell. The windows were so splotchy and streaked that he could not see out of them.

He was about to make his way up the stairs when Gina came flying down, clenched hands sliding down the rails, using her feet to kick against the stair faces to accelerate. She nearly bowled Emile over as she hit the landing. He flung himself out of the way as she squeaked to a stop.

"What the hell is going on?" he demanded.

Her initial wide-eyed look of concern from the near collision was replaced by fleeting annoyance. She clearly did not want to spend time explaining herself or bringing a latecomer up to speed.

"We have a lot of wet electronic equipment out there. We won't have a show tonight if we don't dry it out and test it." She said it over her shoulder as she disappeared down the stairs before Emile could respond.

No show tonight. The words hit him like a slap. Magrathea's reputation, their entire reason for being here, hung in the balance because he'd been too drunk to do his job.

Deciding that height would give him the best vantage to assess the situation, he lumbered up the stairs, feeling as if someone had fastened weights to his limbs. It felt like an eternity before his eyes rose above the hatch comb, squinting at the unfiltered morning light. With a burst of effort, he heaved himself onto the deck.

He slowly turned around, surveying the activities, trying to get a bead on what was going on. The deck was wet, very wet. He stepped to the rail and looked down onto the 10:00 street. It was a mud wallow.

"Rain," he said quietly to himself. They had not set up these top speakers to be watertight. Emile had covered them post-performance every night. However, last night he had instead passed out drunk. So it was likely that all of Magrathea's outside speakers were compromised.

The speakers mounted on the top deck were getting due attention. Stanton, Shimmer, and Bart were each at their own speaker station, disconnecting cables and accessing housings. Emile knew that once they were open and toweled out, the hot, arid playa air would dry them to a hopefully usable state.

He walked to the back of the bus and looked down at the aft speaker trailer. Several crew members had gathered around the large bass speakers, disassembling their components. He walked to the front of the deck and looked down at the forward speaker trailer. Another gathering of Magratheans was at work there as well. Other than him, the entire camp was galvanized to address the crisis. He realized that they had things well in hand without any prompting from him.

He suddenly felt useless and sad. Then he felt sick. He lurched to the rail and heaved. The water that he had drunk washed up his throat with vigorous expulsion, followed by several minutes of dry heaving. He realized that even if he wanted to, he was in no shape to help. He held onto the rail, clinging for dear life.

"Jesus, Emile."

He looked up to see Stanton standing nearby, speaker cable coiled in his hands, staring at him with a mixture of disgust and concern.

"You look like death warmed over." Judgment rather than empathy laced Stanton's tone.

"I'm fine." Emile wiped his mouth with the back of his hand.

"Yeah, you look fine." Stanton's voice carried an edge Emile had never heard before. "Real fucking fine. While you were sleeping off your bender, we've been up since it started raining trying to save our asses."

Other crew members had stopped their work and were now looking in their direction. Shimmer shook her head and turned back to her speaker. Bart muttered something under his breath.

"We've got twelve hours to get this shit working," Stanton continued, his voice carrying across the deck. "Twelve hours to save Magrathea's reputation. And our fearless leader can't even stand up straight."

The words hung in the morning air like a challenge. Emile wanted to respond, to assert his authority, to do something, anything, that would reclaim his moral high ground. Instead, another wave of nausea hit him.

He gripped the rail tighter and watched his crew work around him, their movements sharp with efficiency and barely contained anger.

No one was looking at him anymore. They were too busy cleaning up the mess he had made by not doing his job.

Gordian Knot, 8:30 and Esplanade, BRC, 7:45 AM - Crawford

The knock wasn't particularly aggressive, more patiently persistent. It demanded attention, not through force but by refusing to go away. At first, Crawford ignored it, assuming the knocker would give up. Then he shoved a pillow over his head, but still it came. Finally, admitting defeat, he sat up and swung his legs over the side of the bed, muttering to himself. His body ached from the previous night's carousing; he was running on maybe two hours of sleep. He strained to remember what had happened.

His tenacious campaign to commandeer Millie's crew had failed spectacularly. He had envisioned himself as a phoenix rising into a dragon. He would be charismatic, commanding, and inevitable. In reality, he had come off more like a fruit fly, irritating the shit out of everyone without affecting anything, except maybe their commitment to ignore him. He'd become a tagalong, tolerated at best, drifting behind Millie's crew until dawn, when he stumbled back into camp just as the eastern sky brightened and dark clouds rolled in from the west.

Now he stumbled to the door in a pair of gym shorts, grumbling with each step. He cracked the RV door, already interrogating. "What?!"

Millie stood there, fresh as a daisy and smiling like the sunrise. How did she look so put-together? She was tent camping. And she got less sleep than he did.

"The rain made a mess of the maze," she reported. "We're clearing out the handful of folks still wandering around so we can get an early start on repairs. Thought you might want to have a gander."

Crawford's irritation loosened at her tone. She was not commanding. She was not pitying. She was just... inviting.

"Okay," he said. "I'll get dressed and be right out."

He turned back to the bedroom and paused, staring at the tangled bedclothes. Just days ago, he wouldn't have given someone like Millie the time of day. He'd only engaged with power players, those with leverage, with capital, with networks worth exploiting. Millie had none of those things.

And yet, she was here. Offering him a role. A purpose. Acknowledging him as leader. He was already moving to accept.

It was a disorienting place to be. No power. No leverage. No obvious win. Not since childhood had he felt so untethered. He was off the map now, outside the carefully guarded territory he'd spent decades mastering. *And thar lie dragons.*

Normally, he would be scanning for his angle, but Vicky's last words still echoed in him, quiet and absolute. He couldn't summon the rage, not yet. And maybe that was a kind of mercy.

But he could go to the maze. That, at least, was something he might still understand.

He quickly dressed.

Gordian Knot/Deep Playa, BRC 8:21 AM - Crawford

Crawford stared at the strip of yellow caution tape fluttering in the morning breeze. The damp ground lent the air a clammy chill that settled into his clothes and clung to his skin. Behind him, he heard Millie approaching in a graceless slog, each step a struggle against the clinging mud gripping her boots like a reluctant lover.

She stopped beside him, breathing heavily. "Jimmy flagged all of the damaged and swampy places so the crew could find and fix them more easily."

He sighed. "Of course he did."

They moved into the maze. Crawford passed crew members working in silent pairs, tending to repairs with quiet efficiency. His instinct was to interject, offer direction, and reclaim ownership. Remind them whose maze this was. But they clearly did not need him. They had rhythm, competence, a shared cadence for which he was no longer a member. Any assertion he made would be so obviously fabricated that it would render the effort pointless.

His silence tightened around him as they wove deeper into the structure. His frustration grew with each purposeful hammer swing and knowing nod he witnessed, each one rendering him more obsolete.

They found Jimmy near the hub, pulling back a cloth curtain to let the sun pour onto a particularly sodden passage. He looked up at their approach and gave a quick nod before returning to work.

"Hey, Jimmy," Crawford said.

"Morning," Jimmy replied without looking up.

"Any serious damage?" Crawford asked, trying to sound helpful.

"Nothing major," Jimmy said. "Minor wear and tear. We'll get it sorted."

"Which area needs the most supervision?" Crawford pressed, searching for a foothold.

Jimmy paused for the briefest moment, then kept working. "No area needs supervision. The crew knows what they're doing. If you want to be useful, grab a tagged section and apply some elbow grease."

The words landed without malice but with absolute finality. Crawford stood there a beat too long, absorbing the weight of being unnecessary.

Millie glanced at him sidelong but said nothing.

He turned and walked away, the sound of hammers and laughter echoing behind him like a party that had passed him by.

The Man, BRC 1:41 PM - Ruben

"Burning Man ground zero," said the man ahead of Ruben to the woman climbing just in front of him. Ruben smiled to himself as he trudged up the stairs. He had not thought of it that way, but it fit. They were on the third of seven flights, and he was already panting. He would be full-blown dieseling by the top.

At the next landing, he paused to catch his breath and looked out across the playa. The city shimmered in the sun. The couple ahead kept moving. As he started up again, Ruben turned sideways to pass a descending couple. They crab-walked by with mutual nods.

Ahead, the man mused loudly, "Funny how we flex more out here. Back home, we expect everything to accommodate us, wide stairs, clear signage. Out here, you expect inconvenience, so you adapt."

Again, Ruben thought the man had a point. He also wondered whether philosophizing on the width of the stairway was worth the reflection. He slowed his pace to let them pull ahead.

At the fifth flight, Ruben leaned over the inner railing, peering upward. The Man loomed above. Last night, someone had rigged a flashing neon cock-and-balls in its crotch. It was gone now, the wood pristine again. Ruben smirked at the memory. Adolescent low humor played hand-in-hand with the highbrow art out here, lest citizens take themselves too seriously. He kept climbing.

At the top, he veered to the far side of the platform to avoid further exposure to the ongoing monologue. From his vantage, the 6:00 spoke stretched straight to Center Camp, flanked by fluttering flags. Oil lamps hung from lampposts, and the playa sparkled, returned to pristine condition, compliments of the rain. Art installations dotted the expanse: some towering and kinetic, others subtle and low to the ground.

The inner playa was abuzz with burners exploring the installations and engaging in daytime adventures. The rain had washed away the dust, making the view sharper and clearer than Ruben had experienced since he arrived out here. The arid conditions and hot sun had done their work over the last several hours. The playa around the man had baked hard again, except for the occasional, stubborn damp low spot. By tomorrow, the foot and wheeled traffic would be well on the way to grinding playa cake back into dust.

Ruben let his eyes wander, catching sight of a woman beside him. She was lean and sun-kissed, wearing a breezy sundress and sandals. Her curly hair was tucked under a straw hat pushed back far enough to reveal smiling gray eyes. No makeup. A few gray streaks. She looked vital, grounded, radiant in her ease.

Homosapien granolis, he thought. *Native habitat: Pacific Northwest.*

"It really is a great view," she said, still gazing outward.

"Yes," he replied, "on a gloriously beautiful day."

She suddenly pointed skyward. "Hey, check that out."

Ruben followed her finger. Six parachutes twisted through the air above the Man, three veering off toward 12:00, the others dancing in slow spirals before them. With a burst of color, each lit a flare – green, orange, purple – leaving trails like sky ribbons. The three landed inside the light perimeter ringing the Man, hit the ground at a run, and packed up quickly before the breeze could claim their chutes.

"Seems like we're at the right place at the right time," Ruben said as the parachutists climbed into a waiting art car.

"Things move so fast out here. Blink and you miss something incredible," she said, eyes still on the sky.

Ruben nodded."You never know what's going to show up out here."

"That's what I love about it." She smiled. "The constant surprise."

"Yeah." He found himself smiling back. "Stay awake, and something cool finds you."

She laughed. "I'm stealing that philosophy."

"Let's make a pact to witness all the 'cool' we can find the week."

She grinned. "Let's check in at the end of the week and see if it stuck."

"Deal." He thrust out his hand.

She slid past it and wrapped him in a full-bodied hug. He stiffened at first, caught off guard, then slowly melted into it. She was warm, real, and familiar in a way he had not felt in years. It was deeper than Sunshine's hug. Intimate, without expectation.

"My name's Ruben," he said hoarsely near her ear.

"Bridgette," she whispered back.

She stepped away, smiled, and placed her hands on either side of his face, locking eyes. "Now we have to exchange contact info so we can keep each other honest."

Ruben froze. He had no phone, no address, no working email. Just this moment, his memories, and maybe, for the first time, something to hope for.

Gordian Knot, BRC 4:21 PM - Crawford

Crawford pounded a nail into the loose board with a bit too much enthusiasm, anger, and frustration simmering just under the surface. Even the wettest spots had dried and hardened under the relentless glare of the afternoon sun. The maze was reasonably refurbished and ready for use.

He was done.

He picked up his tool pouch, slung it over his shoulder, and made his way out of the maze. Sliding through a hidden exit adjacent to the common area, he nearly collided with Millie.

She smiled. "Looking good in there, eh?"

"Fucking fantastic," he grunted, glaring at her.

She met his glare, unruffled. Her eyes were patient, slightly weary, as if waiting for a tantrum to pass. Her brows arched. Slowly, her lips curled into a wry grin.

"You really can't stand it when you're not the center of attention, can you?"

It landed like a slap. He blinked, the anger blown out of him like a candle in a draft. His mouth opened, but nothing came out. He shut it. Then narrowed his eyes.

"Why the fuck are you being so accommodating? What are you getting out of this... schadenfreude? You enjoying my fall from grace?"

She chuckled. "Of course, that's where you'd go."

Shaking her head slowly, she added, "You're just like my daddy. Your lens is so twisted you're mistaking a lifeline for a snake."

He cocked his head. "You feel sorry for me?" His tone was stung, almost incredulous.

She guffawed. "Fuck no." She kept laughing. "Why would I feel sorry for the wealthiest, most accomplished, and well-known man in the camp, who's also shown every sign of being a greedy, narcissistic child?"

Astonished, he paused. Then, "Don't hold back. Tell me how you really feel."

"You're in a tough moment. I see you're in pain. You did this to yourself, but you're still a human being. While I can't relate to a lot of who you are, I *can* relate to being human. And there's a million things you could do with this moment. Stewing in your own juices alone isn't your best option."

He had no comeback.

"Look," she continued. "You spent the day being a real contribution, part of a team. But instead of letting that nourish you, you chose misery. So, let me give you some unsolicited advice: get the fuck out of camp. Go somewhere out on the playa and actually *feel* what you're feeling. Pay attention to that hurt."

He stared at her for a long moment. Then, quietly: "Yeah. Good idea."

He turned and walked away, brushing a smear of dust from his forearm like it might reveal something beneath.

Deep Playa, BRC 4:49 PM - Crawford

The steady northeastern breeze pushed Crawford deep into the outer playa. When he reached a point furthest from people in every direction, he clenched his brakes and rolled to a slow stop. He dropped his bike to the ground and sat down hard, suddenly exhausted.

He closed his eyes and leaned his head back, letting the wind press against his face.

He felt empty. Of all the stories he could tell himself about his situation, one truth refused to be spun: Vicky was gone. He had heard it in her voice. She wasn't coming back. Not to the camp, not to the playa, not to him... ever. He had been so sure he had everything under control. But now he knew that he had lost. Irrevocably.

Then it stirred. A dark, bilious feeling, rising from somewhere deep in his gut and bubbling up into his chest. He was sure he would vomit, but the nausea was shoved aside by something heavier, something that made him want to crawl out of his own skin and disappear – terror, hopelessness, despair. It rose through him like a black hand, gripping from the inside, trying to drag him under. He resisted. He knew this thing. It had always lurked just beneath the surface, this darkness that kept him ever moving, ever conquering, ever in control.

He fought it. Fought it until it overwhelmed him. And then... he let go.

He waited.

He had always assumed that if he surrendered to it, he would die. But he remained, here, whole. The fear and despair just... moved through him, catching the wind like dust and fading into the desert air. It kept flowing through, and then... it was gone. Not vanquished. Just... dissipated.

He was drained, but alive.

He opened his eyes and gasped in shallow breaths until the tension finally eased. Eventually, he looked up, empty. He wavered in a moment of consequence.

His reverie was interrupted. Five men were crossing the horizon on foot, about fifty yards out, chatting animatedly. All were dressed in Jedi garb. As they passed directly in front of him, a lone bicyclist overtook them, madly pedaling a small black children's bike. His long black cloak streamed behind him, hood drawn up to hide his face.

The Jedis sprang into action.

"Lord Sith!" shouted one.

"Darth Maul!" called another.

"Black Rider!" added a third.

"Ride your mighty steed!" urged the fourth.

The rider, summoned by the chorus, turned and made a wide circle around them. Sure enough, he wore a Darth Maul mask.

With a dramatic over-the-shoulder draw, he pulled a red lightsaber from his back and raised it high. The Jedis hooted and jeered.

Then, as he rounded behind them, a sudden crosswind caught his cloak. The fabric twisted around him and the bike, slipping into the gears and spokes, locking up the tires. Darth Maul, frozen upright in a cocoon of his own cloak, tipped and crashed sideways with a heavy thump on the playa.

"Darth Maul falls prey to a Jedi mind trick!" one Jedi shouted triumphantly.

From the heap came a muffled groan, "Mmmphth."

The Jedis, slowed by laughter, trudged over to the cloaked wreckage. The Sith was hopelessly tangled, immobilized in a swirl of fabric and spokes. The Jedis tried to free him, but the cloak had woven itself tightly into the machinery.

Eventually, they had to cut him out. When freed, he sat holding his cracked mask like a broken relic. Then, after examining his bruises and scratches, he gathered up the shredded cloak, bent bike, and mask. He hoisted the whole mess onto his shoulders and stumbled-limped back the way he came.

Crawford watched the scene, still seated on the hardpan.

He shook his head. "Fucking Burning Man."

2:45 and Enlightenment, BRC 8:05 PM - Justine

The heat radiating from the burn barrel suggested a healthy blaze within. The flames danced behind the makeshift grill, provided by the filigreed vine cutouts, which were blow-torched into the side of the steel drum. The fire danced high enough to lick the barrel's rim.

"I bet that's how the signs in hell look... flames behind the letters." The chunky, young man with a wispy mustache chuckled to himself. He was stuffed into a ragged easy chair with his legs tossed carelessly over the chair's arm, staring at the fire through glassy, bloodshot eyes. Justine gave him a sideways glance. "I'm pretty sure your default state is baked, Brandon."

Brandon laughed as if it were the funniest thing he had ever heard, proving her point without saying so.

Max flopped down on the couch next to her, "What up my sista' from another mista'... and my brotha' from anotha' motha'?" He asked, not really expecting an answer. From the smug look on his face, he just liked saying the words.

Brandon answered anyway. "Just watchin' TV here and thinkin' about how much better this would be with munchies."

"We share precious little in common, Brandon, but our mutual desire for continuous grazing is one of those rare overlaps," observed Justine.

"The reasons are different," Max piped in. "You come by yours honestly, Justine. What with your high metabolism and grueling workout schedule, you can't help it."

"Whereas, Brandon," he pointed a damning finger at the pudgy man, "has constant munchies from being just high as shit all the time."

Brandon stared at the finger through glazed eyes. "Your honor, guilty as charged."

They all chuckled. It was hard to stay annoyed with Brandon. His wit and honesty combined to make him vaguely charming and occasionally adorable.

"I'm feeling a bit peckish myself," she said. Then continued, "I just haven't gotten up the juice to go make myself something."

"If you do, make me something too." Brandon chuckled. Justine rolled her eyes.

"You're lucky your affability offsets your truly annoying personality," Justine said.

"What she's saying is that you are lazier than shit, sir," Max interpreted.

"But, I give great gratitude. It's my superpower," Brandon bragged.

Justine and Max exchanged glances and shrugged. Brandon had a point.

"What we need here is some good old-fashioned playa manifestation," Max declared.

Justine roused from her reflection and looked at him dubiously. "You mean we just sit here and expect food to show up?" she asked.

"Well, not exactly 'expect,'" Max said. "More like 'intend.' You see..." he said, stretching out the 'e' sound, he adopted his professorial explanation nerd voice,

He continued, "We know that our fellow Black Rock citizens are prone to acts of generosity. Since there are forty thousand of us out here, you have to figure that at any one moment, hundreds, if not thousands, of magnanimous gestures are happening all around us. We just invite it in our direction."

He smiled triumphantly as if he had just explained the general theory of relativity.

"Thank you, doctor pseudo-science. That's all, huh? Just will it to us. Simple as that?" she said skeptically.

"I prefer to think of it as 'inviting' it to us," said Max, smiling coyly.

"Invite in one hand, shit in the other. See which one fills fastest," she countered cynically. "I'm a big believer in doing for myself. I don't sit around and wait for things to show up."

"Ah, grasshopper. Then it is time for your playa manifestation lesson. Once learned, you will be able to snatch the burning pebble from my palm." Max winked at her. The two of them argued like siblings as a matter of sport.

"I'll snatch the pebble from your palm because you're a slow assed motherfucker and I am Sporty Spice!" She tried to sound as street as possible, but street is a stretch for a white girl from the suburbs. He chuckled and made a fake gang sign at her.

"The bravado is strong in this one," Max said, using his Yoda voice.

"What are you two arguing about now?" Susan sauntered into the light cast by the burn barrel.

"Your boy is comparing his magic to my practical reality, as usual." Justine shot back.

"My boy is magic," Susan laughed as she put her arms around Max from behind. He slid his hands over her arms and tipped his head back to kiss her.

"Whatever," Justine said, her nonchalance tinged with a hint of bitterness. Although there was certainty in her tone, her time on the playa had begun to gnaw at her confidence in cynicism.

"Y'all are grasshoppers living for the moment, with the mystical expectation that things will just show up when you need them. What happens when your luck runs out?" Justine asked rhetorically, asserting the assumption that their fundamental adherence to abundance thinking would fail them.

"Oh my dear sweet fool..." Max started.

"Oh, lord, woman. You just put a dime in him." Susan rolled her eyes.

Max continued. "Your slavish adherence to the theology of the practical and tangible is limiting your possibilities and causing you to suffer. While you craft your life by your own will and effort, you do not avail yourself of the lubrication available from communal generosity."

Max was teasing her, trying to get her goat. But the words stung. There was a subtle wisdom in his words that she had not yet touched. They all seemed to move through life with relative ease, things appearing as they were needed. In the meantime, her way was all work and little joy. Regardless, she hated that the certainty she arrived with was now under siege. She would not go quietly into the night.

"My way has always worked for me," she declared, although her tone was wavering.

Her ego was wrapped up in being a concretely self-determined person. Yet she was feeling the tectonic plates of her psyche shifting. She knew that Susan was acutely aware of her unmooring. Although Susan had not brought it up, Justine felt her gently observing, watching her go through it, quietly offering a lifeline should she choose to take it. Now she suspected Max noticed it too. Then he confirmed it.

"My sweet friend, you are one stubborn mofo. I think you came out here committed to leaving unscathed, proving that Burning Man is, in fact, not for your hard ass. How is that going?"

She cocked an eyebrow. "What? Are you jockeying to be my on-playa therapist now?"

Susan came to her aid in the most Susan way. She bent in and gave Max a deep kiss.

When the lingering smooch ended, Susan looked over at Justine. "What are you up to tonight, Sporty Spice?" Justine blushed. She did not think that Susan had overheard her bluster.

"Shocker. I don't have concrete plans. No performing tonight.'

"Reeeeally?" Susan stretched the word out. Theatrically, Susan rubbed her hands together. Clearly, she was hatching an evil plan. "Perhaps I can entice you to come with me tonight and have a uniquely Burning Man experience."

Justine warily asked, punctuating each word, "And what might that unique be?"

Susan smiled. "I'm doing a greeter's shift tonight. Wanna join me?" She batted her eyes at Justine.

"Greeters shift? What's that? I'm not a, 'Hellooooo, my name is Tammy. Here's your name tag, sorta gal.'"

Susan cocked her head, blinking. Then her eyes widened. "Oooooh, you flew in. You didn't get a greeter station experience."

"Greeter's station?" Justine felt like she was speaking another language.

"We non-VIP plebeians get greeted when we drive in. There's a whole station for it with guidebooks, hugs, virgin bell-ringing, the works." Susan explained.

"Uh, that sounds horrible. Do I impress you as huggy-feely?" Justine's face was a mask of repulsion.

"Girl, you don't have to hug people if you don't want to. But, I promise you, there is magic happening at the greeter's station. Connection will happen in most unexpected ways. You've been pushing your envelope this week. Trust me and push it just a bit further. Be the anti-Nancy Reagan. Just say 'yes.'"

Brandon guffawed.

"I'll join you, babe." Max volunteered.

"You're my sugar plum." Susan kissed Max's forehead.

"Not me. Too far to bike for headlights." Brandon waved a hand of dismissal.

Justine waivered. "I... uh. Fuck it. Okay. I'll go."

Susan squealed. She bound over to Justine and wrapped her in a hug, shaking her.

Justine gently pushed her away. "Easy girl, you break it, you buy it."

She braced herself to push up off the couch. "I guess that adds some urgency to the eating and getting ready chores."

Before she could push herself up, a woman came into the firelight from the street carrying two heavily laden plates. "Hi, neighbors. We made too much lasagna for dinner. Would you like some?"

By then, the savory aroma had wafted into the campers' olfactory senses, setting off a wave of salivation reaction that would have made Pavlov proud. Justine and Max exchanged glances. Justine's eyes widened in surprise. Max's were crinkled in amusement. They both laughed. Then Max quickly regained himself so as not to be rude or inadvertently chase off this gift-bearer.

He looked the woman in the eye and said in utter sincerity, "We'd absolutely love your lasagna. In fact, we were just talking about how much we would like for you to show up. You are our playa angel tonight with perfect timing. Thank you so much. Can we offer you a group hug as an expression of our appreciation?"

The woman laughed, and then so did the campmates. She put the plates down on the wooden boxes they had been using as footrests. The group gathered around her, wrapping her in a long, grateful hug. Even Justine, usually quick with a sarcastic comment, joined in quietly, impressed by how well Max's manifestation ideas had worked.

The crew quickly divided the food among them and began eating. As Justine shoveled her first bite into her mouth, she looked up to see Max grinning at her. She shook her head. "Fuck you, Max."

Everyone but Justine laughed. She hated being wrong. But, more to the point, she was not yet ready for Max to be right. Connection was already happening.

9:30 and Avatar to Ataraxis Warrior, 11:00 and Outer Playa, BRC 8:23 PM - Harley

"Go on, you two. Get outta here. Clarence and I will be out there once you have the warrior fired up." Claire dismissed them with a grin and a flick of her wrist.

Harley looked at Cyan with a shrug and half-smile, as if to say, *What are you gonna do?*

They fell into step next to each other. Harley was surprised at how naturally her stride matched his. "The last time we walked together, you couldn't keep up. I had to carry you." His voice held a note of humor, laced with quiet regret.

She smirked up at him. "More likely I'll be carrying you this time, old man."

He chuckled. "That's probably true."

They walked in silence for a while, boots crunching softly on the dry playa. As they crossed the Esplanade and slipped free of the city's buzz, Harley adjusted their heading slightly, steering them in a line that gradually peeled away from the revelry, angling toward the hulking silhouette of Ataraxis Warrior.

Harley broke the silence. "How does your mom feel about you being out here?"

"She came out here about ten years ago," Cyan said. "Said it was pretty nuts back then. But she's heard it's mellowed some. And with you being sober, and Grandpa here, she figures you'll keep me on the straight and narrow." She grinned. "She made Claire promise my experience would be rated PG."

Harley chuckled again. "Sounds like your mom, alright."

They walked on. This time, Cyan was the one to break the silence.

"She doesn't hate you, you know."

Harley glanced at her. "She's got plenty of reasons to. You too." He exhaled sharply through his nose. "But I've been doing enough self-hating for all of us."

Cyan nodded. "We had a heart-to-heart before I left. She said she never would've bet on you straightening up. That you've been sober this long... that you run your own business... it shocks her."

"Yeah," Harley said. "I was a mess. She's not wrong to be cautious."

"You won big points when you brought me back from Sonora," Cyan added, her voice lower. "That was ballsy. Showing up at a meth dealer's house with no weapon?"

"I didn't want to raise the temperature," Harley said. "That asshole was playing house with my *minor* daughter."

"Did you really tell him to have me in your truck in five minutes or your next stop would be the Tuolumne County Sheriff?"

A wry smile crept across Harley's face. "I was appealing to his sense of self-preservation. Jail time and losing his meth biz didn't strike me as a good deal for him."

"He was unstable and violent," she said. "You could've ended up dead."

He turned to her, gaze steady. "You're my daughter. There was no way I was leaving you there."

She walked quietly for a beat, her expression unreadable. Then: "Thanks, Dad."

He squeezed her shoulder. "My recollection is you weren't exactly grateful at the time. You cursed me out for the whole drive back."

"I had a lot of rage. And I was high. Sobriety's better for both of us."

"Yeah," Harley sighed. "Sorry, you got both my addiction and my anger. Shit deal."

"Dad," she said, voice cracking ever so slightly, "we're here. We survived. And we've got something better in front of us."

He nodded. "You're right. We do."

They walked in silence, the city falling further behind them, the glow receding until it was just them and the open expanse. The outer playa held a stillness the inner city never could. It felt sacred.

Ahead, the Warrior loomed. Even inert, it demanded reverence.

Cyan broke the spell. "Mom thinks Claire is really good for you."

Harley barked a short laugh. "Claire is crazy."

"She's loud, uninhibited... and sane. You and I are quiet and crazy."

Harley looked over at her, his expression softening into something warmer. "Who made you so wise?"

She shrugged, her smile small and knowing.

Now the Warrior towered before them, hulking and dark, its limbs rigid in silhouette. After these days on the playa, it no longer felt like he was alone. It had taken on a life of its own, grown wise in its stillness, distant in its purpose. Like Cyan, it had outgrown the shadow of its maker.

Harley turned to her, a gleam in his eye. "Wanna fire it up?"

She grinned widely. "Yeah!"

They moved as a team, checking valves, clearing lines, and aligning regulators. Harley showed her each step, trusting her hands, letting her lead.

Then came the final switch.

A breath. A click. And then — *whoompf* — a blossom of flame erupted from the base, climbing the steel in waves of gold and red. The Warrior lit up, alive again. Fire traced its veins, poured from its tears. The warrior and iron beast wept flame into the desert night.

They stood alone, father and daughter, haloed in firelight and silence. And for that moment, they belonged to each other, to the desert, to the burn.

Harley looked at her, face aglow. "You know," he said quietly, "Our bond has endured despite my bad behavior. I think we're both still figuring out how to carry each other."

She nodded, her eyes reflecting fire. "One flame at a time."

3:30 and Inner Playa, BRC 9:27 PM - Cypher

"What's this thing called?" a woman sitting on the steps above and to the right of Cypher asked.

"The 'Temple of Destruction and Resurrection,'" responded the man standing just above her on the stairs.

Cypher chose a route that avoided the stairs entirely. He was ascending a steeply angled ramp toward the first ledge. If he lost his grip, nothing would ease his fall to the playa other than plywood splinters or maybe a stray nail. He kept his weight evenly distributed, pressing flat palms and sandaled toes into the wood as he worked his way upward.

"Maya pyramids inspire its design," the man continued. "Those gargoyle-looking things on the corners of the third level are Maya gods. That one above and to the left is Ah-Puch, the god of death. Over there's Ixchel, goddess of birth and creation, and the only woman among the top-tier gods. Around the other side are Voltan, god of war, and Kinich-Ahau, sun god. Altogether, they're a badass quartet."

Cypher pulled himself onto the first ledge.

"Who's on top?" the woman asked, pointing toward the apex.

"That's Chac, god of rain and lightning. Pretty benevolent, actually, the go-to god for agriculture and fertility."

Cypher started up the incline to the second level.

"How do you know all that shit?" the woman asked.

The man laughed. "I read the installation blurb online when I was checking out the Burning Man art proposals. I'd already seen real Maya pyramids in the Yucatán, so I was curious how this one would stack up."

Cypher worked his way onto the second level and immediately started his ascent again.

"Apparently," the man added, "they're gonna burn this one after the Man burns."

By the time Cypher reached the third plateau, their voices had faded. He could no longer make out the conversation between the couple now far below.

All those facts were constipating his experience.

He moved down the ledge to the closest gargoyle and hunched next to Ah-Puch. From this corner, he had a great view of the eastern city.

Cypher wondered what it would be like to be a gargoyle god. He reset his hunched form into an upright squat to better emulate Ah-Puch. There was a mocking grin in the gargoyle's expression, but Cypher didn't let it dissuade him.

He looked at the god out of the corner of his eye. "Don't make fun of me, asshole. I'm new to this. You've had lots of practice." With that, he proceeded to disregard the deity and focus on his own deification practice.

He surveyed his domain, or at least what his domain would be if he were a playa-god. He heard footsteps coming from the other side of Ah-Puch. Soon, a small painted face emerged around the corner.

"Hello. Whatchya doing?" The face belonged to a girl of maybe ten or eleven. She was decked out in a miniature version of night playa wear: dance pants, leggings, a lycra top, and a furry vest. Her face was painted light blue with white, gyred feathers curling from her temples down her cheeks. Her bright eyes were wide with earnest curiosity.

"Being a god," he said, matter-of-factly.

"What kind of god?"

He looked up, thoughtful. "I've been thinking about that. I'm the god of random, weird-ass occurrences."

She giggled. "Then you'll have plenty to do out here."

She looked at the gargoyle between them. "You know, this guy, Ah-Puch, was sort of a nasty customer. Ruled the lowest level of the underworld. He liked to team up with Voltan and Kinich-Ahau to mess with Chac's good deeds. Ixchel and Kinich-Ahau could go either way depending on their moods. These gods had a whole lot of drama going on."

"Are you related to that guy down on the stairs?" he asked.

She giggled again. "That's my dad."

"Figures," he said. "No drama for me. Unless you call 'weird-ass shit' drama."

"Not me." She shrugged. "Weird stuff is pretty normal out here." She climbed around the gargoyle and skirted past him.

"Have fun being a god," she said over her shoulder as she moved toward the steps. Oddly, he felt more in common with this little girl than anyone he had met out here.

He did have fun. Willing his transformation into a deity, he stared out into the dark playa, summoning weird-ass shit. He knew he wouldn't have to wait long for something to show up.

11:30 and Inner Playa, BRC 10:18 PM - Ruben

"Goddamn. I am motherfucking hungover," Bunny Boy groaned.

"Hold on," said Snag, digging into his jeans pocket.

Bunny Boy perked up. "Vitamin B?"

Snag pulled out his middle finger. "Just this, pussy. Man up. You want sympathy? Look between 'shit' and 'syphilis' in the dictionary."

The truck bed erupted in laughter. The DPW crew loved a sharp fuck-you, as long as it was aimed at someone else. Bunny Boy dropped back onto his cushion with a groan, hat sliding over his eyes.

The vehicle bounced over potholes and playa scars, each jolt rattling its passengers. Bunny Boy howled. Those with instruments clutched them tight.

Ruben felt more kinship with this rough crew than he had with any group in his life. He perched where a tailgate should have been, watched the city unravel behind them. The streets gave way to Esplanade, then to the open playa. The further they drove, the less it felt like civilization and more like a myth.

Most of the crew was deep in their cups. Only Ruben, and maybe Squeaker, tonight's driver, seemed sober. Maybe. If Ruben had committed to ride the whole night, they'd have switched places hours ago.

The DPWers were tough. Armor-plated with jokes and grit. Sensitivities were hidden like contraband. But Ruben had started to see the soft centers, especially when music poured out of them.

Sunshine held a fiddle under her chin and played with a frenetic energy that had Ruben checking the instrument for smoke. Lenny strummed along on guitar. Shakespeare thumped out rhythms on his doumbek, fingers impossibly precise. And Thud, voice rich and raw, belted out bawdy verses with operatic swagger.

Ruben kept a low profile. DPW saw him as a man of few words, and he liked it that way. Snag, especially, was someone to avoid showing weakness around. Hilarious until you were the punchline.

Squeaker steered them wide of the thumpy-thumpy art cars, which Ruben appreciated. Booze and bass rarely mixed well for this crew.

They arced around the Man, heading for darker reaches. Good. That meant Ruben could peel off near the Ataraxis Warrior later. Also meant the jam session would echo undisturbed in the night.

A hand gripped his shoulder.

He turned as Stitch landed beside him with a thump, lean and wiry, her bare arms ropy with strength. She had the wild, rangy presence of someone who could fight, fuck, or fix a carburetor... possibly all at once. Her eyes were bleary, but steady.

"S'up, Cheshire?"

"Hey Stitch." He hesitated. "How'd you get your playa name?"

"'Stitch'? First year, I was a disaster magnet. I needed more sutures than gear. I earned my name. You, my friend, just smiled and shut the fuck up to get yours."

He chuckled. She'd always struck him as hard-edged and private, much like him. Tonight, though, there was a flicker of softness behind the sarcasm. She leaned in close, warm and loose-limbed.

"Just watching the playa pass by," he said. "Sometimes that's enough."

"You're a man of few requirements," she said. "Rare bird around here."

"It's easy to be satisfied when you don't expect much."

Then he caught himself. "Actually... I'm calling bullshit on that. I'm not sure if I'm satisfied. I just got used to living with little. Sometimes that's enough. Sometimes it's a cage."

She nodded, gaze serious. "Needing less isn't a flaw."

"It's not... unless it's hiding." He looked at her. "After years in a grey, concrete world, this..." he gestured to the chaos, the lights, the music "... makes me happy. Maybe that's something."

She looked toward the crew, then back at him. "You're not the average DPW bear, are you?"

He smiled. "Pretty average. No profession, no plan. Just this crew, for now. This is home. Until it isn't."

"There are worse things."

"Four weeks ago, I was in federal prison. This is light-years better."

She raised her beer. "Amen, brother."

He tapped his scuffed Nalgene bottle against it. "Cheers, sister."

She slipped an arm around his shoulders and pointed into the night. "Look."

Ruben followed her finger.

At first, nothing. Then, motion. Dozens of LED-lit figures shimmered into view like bioluminescent fireflies sweeping across the darkness. Bike riders in glowing suits, wheels, and frames, trailing pixelated ribbons of light. A silent ballet. It was like watching choreographed lightning bugs dancing.

They spun apart in every direction, scattered stars across the horizon, then slowly regrouped in the center. Like atoms reforming. From stillness, movement again, pairs circling, joining a swirl that became a single spinning shape.

A glowing propeller of light.

Faster. Brighter.

And then, dissolution. Riders peeled away, disappearing one by one into the night, until only darkness remained.

Stitch exhaled. "Cooler than shit."

Ruben didn't answer.

He stared into the empty dark, throat tight, overwhelmed. Of all the wonders he'd seen this week, this moved him most. Something in its fleeting beauty cracked him wide open.

Stitch didn't say a word. Her arm stayed around him, her head resting gently on his shoulder. The truck rumbled on. The music played. The others joked and laughed.

Ruben sat quietly, tears slipping down his face, unseen. Not hiding. Not quite exposed. But finally beginning to feel.

Gordian Knot, 8:30 and Esplanade, BRC, 10:23 PM - Rachael

Rachael sauntered along the Esplanade in an unhurried meander. She was beginning to feel the effect of the edible that Nathan had offered her. She had no intention to have a conversation with anyone, so being high fit her evening plans, or more accurately, her lack of plans. There would be no desperate attempt to connect tonight.

The burgeoning high lay a filmy, colorful gauze over Esplanade frontages and decked-out revelers. Enjoying the warm, fuzzy sensation, she approached the gaudy, circus-like entrance to the Gordian Knot. She had passed it a number of times during the past few days but had not wanted to invest the time exploring its innards. Her distinct lack of agenda now made it appealing. "Tonight's your night, Gordian Knot." She walked through the maze's grand entrance and was quickly swallowed up in its labyrinth.

The maze turned out to be far more complex than she imagined, a maze and a puzzle squished together. She briefly considered retreating, but she could not remember the path back. So she gave herself to the maze, accepting that she may spend most of her evening lost. In this case, 'lost' might not only be acceptable, it might be desirable.

The passage before her was punctuated by sliding doors that continuously opened and shut in an asynchronous cadence. Moving through them required timing. Step through. Stop. Step through. Stop. It wasn't difficult, but she had to stay on her toes. Each section offered two doors. More than once, she arrived at a dead end marked with a taunting sign, 'Nope. Try Again. There's no cheese in this tunnel.' Each time, she had to retrace her steps. Normally, agility was not a problem for her. But, at this moment, she was not operating at her usual level of nimbleness.

The next series involved secret doors with hidden latches. Several times she experienced the victory of unlocking one, only to find herself again in a dead end. This maze was a lot of work. Normally, she loved a good puzzle, the harder the better. But she preferred to have her wits about her. Tonight, her wits had left the building. She expelled a long breath, releasing her mental effort and allowing the cannabis body rush to shiver through her.

The door before her was a rotating portal like those used in darkrooms. Rachael stepped in, rotating the cylinder to face the opposite side. It revealed more dim corridors framed by canvas curtains. She sighed, reluctant to move forward. She spun the cylinder back around to the passage she'd come from. Equally unappealing.

Alone and unhurried, she decided to make the rotating cylinder her womb. She spun it a quarter turn so the portal faced the chamber wall. Now literally in the dark, she relaxed. No puzzles here. No noise. Just a pocket of stillness where she could enjoy the high and the intimacy of the confined space.

She yearned to find a place that was soft, fuzzy, and pleasing to the eye. She leaned her back against the cylinder wall and raised a booted foot to brace against the opposite wall, only to find no wall there. Confused, she reached out. Her palms found the slick PVC, and soon her fingers traced a lip at waist height. A hidden crawlspace.

She confirmed the flooring and walls were carpeted. Encouraged, she smiled to herself and slid into the space, squatting to protect her thigh-highs. The crawlspace turned gracefully, the walls covered in silk cloth. The tactile pleasure of sliding her hands along the surface grounded her in her body, soothed something raw in her.

The passage straightened and revealed dim golden-red light at the end. She emerged into a fully enclosed room, warmly backlit and womb-like in every way. Carpeted floors and walls, futon beds with silky throws, gauzy canopies suspended like a dream. Silky tendrils brushed her skin as she moved. Heaven.

The far end narrowed into another passage. Dropping her tote and jacket, she followed it in a spirit of reconnaissance. The corridor narrowed until she had to turn sideways. At the tightest point, she stopped. That's when she felt the caress. A soft brush across her calf.

She froze. Then another, higher on her thigh.

Historically, this would have terrified her. But these touches were different, gentle, and curious. Not a demand, but an invitation. She let herself feel it.

Another touch graced her arm. She turned her head. A delicate hand emerged through a lycra-clad hole in the wall. It withdrew, vanishing into the tight fabric. Then more: on her neck, her shoulder, her hips.

These were playful, feminine hands. Exploring. Teasing. Not taking. Just... asking.

She smiled and responded, brushing her fingers over the pulse point of a wrist. More hands emerged from both sides. She was surrounded. Obviously not alone.

And for once, that felt like safety.

The sensuality deepened, hands cupping her breasts, teasing the backs of her knees, pinching nipples until shocks of pleasure crackled through her. Her knees buckled, and she let out a shaky moan.

From the womb room, footsteps. A woman entered, tall, stunning, radiant. Black bustier, red filigree, heels like knives. She kissed Rachael deeply, arms wrapping her in warmth.

"Welcome to our little pleasure den," the woman whispered. "Come, lie back. Let us take care of you."

Rachael followed her to the futons, where two more gorgeous women joined them. Boots and tops disappeared. Names were shared. And for the first time all week, Rachael didn't feel like someone's curiosity project. Not a pet. Not a puzzle. Not an outsider.

Just Rachael.

They shared water. Then, they shared a lot more.

Gordian Knot, 8:30 and Esplanade, BRC, 10:35 PM - Emile

Emile quickly strode the length of the short catwalk that bridged the tall divider wall and stopped to survey the section of the maze ahead. "A sea of friggin' maze," he said aloud to himself.

Open-topped fabric walls stretched out before him. He studied the pathways, then murmured quietly, "Fuck!" He had hoped, from this vantage point, to figure out the right path to escape. Instead, he was vexed with the sheer complexity of the possible routes. There was no obvious express path out of the maze. Part of him wanted to conquer the maze. Part of him was bored and frustrated.

He had entered the maze to distract himself. He thought that presenting himself with a puzzle would keep him occupied. Instead of shoving away his churning, it simply added a level of dynamic mental struggle. The rational part of his brain engaged in logic and evaluation. The emotional part of his brain was off balance, swinging between anger, sadness, exasperation, wistfulness, and despair. He couldn't seem to settle on a single feeling.

Now he stared at the maze before him with no clear path presenting itself. It was as if the maze was mocking his emotional struggle. Mirroring it. He was lost in the maze as much as he was lost in himself.

He eased himself down the ladder into the new section. He took the left passage for no particular reason. None of his options seemed particularly better than another. More than once, since he had entered the maze, he had found that appearances can be deceiving.

He traversed several hairpin turns to find himself in a place he had not seen from the catwalk. He emerged into a wide space, which was the confluence of several paths. In front of the wide space was an equally wide opening, bounded by a bona fide glittery metallic-gold arch. The arch was outlined with small bright carnival lamps that flashed on and off in sequence so that it looked like the lights were racing circles around the sign. Large red letters outlined in metallic blue glitter ran across the top section of the arch, boldly announcing 'THEATRE OF ALL POSSIBILITIES'.

He passed through the arch into a large, empty lobby. The concession stand was unmanned. On the far side of the lobby, an usher stood in front of the theater doors. He was bored, cleaning his nails with a pen knife, and did not look up at Emile.

Emile cocked his head, muttering, "This is fucking weird. A working theater with a bored usher in the middle of a maze."

He approached the usher. The usher did not look up from his task at hand. "Ticket please."

"I don't have a ticket." Emile responded.

"Then you can't..." The usher looked up. When he saw Emile, he cut himself off. "Ooooh, of course. Guest star and all."

He opened the door and held it, gesturing for Emile to enter. Emile stepped through the door, and it shut behind him with a quiet, yet secure seal, as if vacuumed shut. Emile's eyes slowly accustomed themselves to the dark. The stage was well lit but empty. He could not make out the audience but sensed that the theater was packed.

A man in a tuxedo, giving master of ceremonies vibes, walked purposefully from the side to the center of the stage and up to the mic. "Ladies and gentlemen, I have the esteemed honor of bringing to the stage Emile Baptiste."

He gestured directly at Emile as spotlights snapped on. Blades of white light cut down from above, clean and merciless, carving Emile from shadow like a statue summoned from stone. Emile threw his hand up to shade his eyes. Dozens of men in gold lamé long-tailed tuxedos and top hats flooded the stage in synchronous dance, singing "Let's Get It Started" by the Black Eyed Peas.

Someone clapped Emile on the shoulder from behind. "Go, man. This is your show."

Reluctantly, Emile stepped toward the stage as the audience rose to their feet, cheering and giving him a full ovation. He could not make out any of their faces as he moved down the aisle. He made his way up the stairs onto the stage. As he walked to the center, the chorus slipped offstage, leaving him alone under the bright lights, unable to see the audience.

He stood in awkward silence. He had no idea what to do or say. He felt like he had just shown up late for an exam in his underwear. Someone deep in the audience coughed. Emile stepped to the mic and opened his mouth. The orchestra in the pit just in front of him burst into Copland's, "Fanfare for the Common Man." He had not realized that there was an orchestral pit.

A couple entered the stage. Both were objectively beautiful and stunningly arrayed. The man carried a black box. The woman held a card in front of her. They confidently took their places on both sides of him. The woman moved to the mic. "The Hyatt Foundation is pleased to present the Pritzker Architecture Prize for Emile's accomplishment and contributions to the Seattle skyline."

The man opened the box, flashing a bronze medallion. "The Pritzker honors living architects whose built work demonstrates talent, vision, and commitment, and who have produced consistent and significant contributions to humanity and the built environment."

They handed him the envelope and box, gave him perfunctory handshakes and hugs, and then efficiently departed the stage, before Emile could react. He stared at the medallion. "Firmitas, Utilitas, Venustas" was etched across its face. But as he held it, the bronze felt cold, lifeless in his palm.

"See You Again" by Wiz Khalifa began to play. Hip hop dancers filled the stage, executing an immaculately choreographed, energetic routine. As they wound up, two dancers peeled off and moved toward Emile. The man held a statuette of a slender, gold dancer. The woman stepped to the microphone with a thick French accent. "France is pleased to present the Juste Debout Ultimate award to Emile for his flawless dance choreography and execution."

The man handed Emile the statuette. They each kissed him on both cheeks and departed, leaving Emile staring, his hands full of hollow tokens.

The beat dropped into "Adagio for Strings (Deadmau5 Remix)", filling the theater with deep bass. A man in a tan shirt and a grey stetson entered from the wings, smoking luxuriously. Behind him, a man in a chicken costume rode a battered tricycle, wheels squealing in anguished complaint.

The stetson-topped man shuffled directly up to Emile, letting out a massive expulsion of smoke in his face, sending him into a fit of coughs. As Emile recovered, eyes watering, the man clapped his shoulder. "You did it, my boy. You created the pinnacle of Burning Man achievements. No one will ever be able to top that art car."

The chicken-costumed man stood, reached into a crumpled paper bag, and slowly extracted two long, yellow balloons shaped into The Man, a balloon diamond shaping its head. A banner stretched diagonally from hand to foot. It read 'Magrathea's Final Answer' in nearly illegible marker.

He pushed it into Emile's chest. Emile wrapped his arms around it, his hands already occupied. Without adieu, the pair shuffled off to the wings.

Emile shook his head. All these awards, all this recognition, and he felt... nothing. Empty. He looked back toward the audience. He took a deep breath. Then he stepped up to the microphone and... the lights went out. It was dark. Dark-dark. Emile was afraid to move lest he run into something or fall off the stage. He suddenly felt very alone.

A tiny light appeared at a distance, in front of him. It swung back and forth as it moved slowly toward him. The dim flickering indicated that it was a lamp of some sort. As it finally closed on him he realized that it was held by a tiny woman, in a thin, bony arm held high. When she was a few feet away, Emile could see that the woman was ancient, stabilizing her gate with her weight braced on a wooden cane.

She wore a red Luwyet embossed with orange geometric patterns, marking her as someone from the Eritrean lowlands, Emile's ancestral home. A chill ran up his spine.

That small woman embodied the cultural moral authority that condemned his lifestyle and sexual orientation. She represented the mindset that would send him back to Eritrea for "spiritual healing," to purge the so-called demon within.

Sweat gathered on his forehead as her rheumy eyes lingered on him, studying him, taking his measure. Then she smiled and said, in a thick Eritrean accent, "You look lost, boy."

"I... ah, I... guess I am." He said cautiously.

"Come walk with me, boy. Make an old woman feel good. Here. Take my lamp."

He scrambled to shift the items in his hands, but realized they were gone. He took the lamp and held it up. The terrain was an arid and uneven desert with low bramble. It was not the playa. Rather it had an older familiarity, the desert of his childhood. The old woman pointed forward into the dark. "That way, boy."

They walked in silence for a few minutes. Then the old woman asked, "Was it everything you hoped for?"

He glanced at her, confused. "Was what everything I hoped for?"

"Don't be daft, boy." She slapped his arm. "The pomp. The accolades. The acknowledgement. Did it fill that hole in you?"

He walked in silence for a moment, considering. Recalling how he felt. "I didn't feel anything."

Her laugh was a sound akin to the noise of metal grinding against metal. "But, isn't that everything you wanted? Isn't that the eventuality of all of your work?"

He thought for a moment. "I'm not sure it's that easy. I don't know that there is an end to this, just a discipline. Isn't life supposed to be about the journey, not the destination?"

"That, my child, is the truth." Said the woman. "That is, if you are living life."

He glanced at her. "That's exactly what I'm doing."

Again, her coughing laugh filled the space. "My child, you're living a life. But you're not living your life. There's a big difference between going through the motions of life and surrendering to who you are."

He stopped and looked at her. "Auntie, I think you know that I am gay."

"And, I am old, child. Facts are facts. Deal with it."

"I am dealing with it. I have a partner and a community," he retorted.

"Do you? Is that what they would say if you asked them? Your path requires an authentic connection. How much connection are you feeling right now?" Her face was stern, gaze searing. He relented, understanding that his bluff and bluster would not work here. He had had enough auntie ass kickings in his youth to know better than to try.

"The boy who left home," she continued, "he ran so far from shame he forgot how to feel joy. He built walls so high to keep judgment out, he locked love out, too. Now he feels happiness instead of living it. He gives audiences instead of intimacy. He controls everything except what matters most."

The words hit him like physical blows, each truth a sharp recognition of what he'd been running from.

She gestured, "Move, boy. I don't have all night."

He turned and began to walk, feeling the difference immediately. The ground was flat, barren, and filled with spider cracks. The parched air had lost its fragrance. But her words followed him, echoing in his chest.

"You can't outrun who you are, child. You can only choose whether to embrace it or let it starve."

He turned to her, "I..." She was gone. Deep darkness and nothing more. He reached back to shine the lamp in that direction, but nothing was in his hand. The lamp was gone. He pivoted back in the direction they had been walking.

He found himself outside the maze a hundred feet from the Esplanade. Revelers wandered past, going down the street on foot and bicycle, coming from or going to their next party stop. Emile looked at the maze wall next to him. It was solid and unbroken. He shook his head, but couldn't shake her words.

"Fuck." His voice was barely a whisper. The awards, the accolades, the perfect performance, all of it was meaningless if he was just going through the motions. If he were performing his life instead of living it.

He looked toward Magrathea moving across the playa in the distance, its lights pulsing with music and laughter. Liam was there, probably worried, probably hurt. His crew was there, working around his failures. His life was there, the real one, not the fantasy version he'd just been awarded for.

Auntie is right. I'm not connecting with anyone. Maybe unable to connect.

But walking back meant facing what he had become. What he had done. What he might lose.

Emile stood frozen between the maze and the playa, between the performance and the truth, unable to move in either direction.

01 Spins Until the Man Burns

9:15 and Esplanade to Center Camp, BRC, 5:04 AM - Cypher

"Hey... I'm sorry, but you're going to have to get up. We're closing the chill space to clean it."

Cypher felt a hand on his shoulder, gentle but insistent. He had been sleeping deeply and did not want to leave slumber's warm cocoon. But the hand drew him up, dragging him through the fog of semi-consciousness. He blinked up into a kind, resolute face, her eyes were not without sympathy, but with no sign she was going away.

With a sigh, he pushed himself upright and took in the orange-themed dome: pillows, futons, and fuzzy blankets piled across the space like a crash pad for spent souls. He wasn't the only one rousing from oblivion. Others sat groggily or shuffled toward the exit.

He had found this place hours ago, just as the city-wide bacchanal began to fade. It was stuffed with exhausted burners, and he'd burrowed under a pile of plush like a desert animal. It had been the best sleep he'd had since arriving.

Now, peeled from comfort, he shook off the furry blanket, stood, and gathered his things. As he reached the door, the woman murmured, "Sorry." She sounded like she meant it. Cypher stepped out into the dark.

The chill morning air slapped his cheeks and tweaked his ears. His thin clothing offered none of the insulation the dome had lent him. But the cold snapped him alert. He turned toward the street just as a man fell in step beside him.

"Time to head back to camp, eh?" the man said.

"The rain killed my camp. I'm... homeless," Cypher replied. "SNAFU. Situation normal, all fucked up." He couldn't help but appreciate the irony. Once again, his Burn mirrored his outside life.

"That sucks, man."

"Not really. It's all part of my test," Cypher said.

"Test?"

"I'm a survivalist warrior. Always being tested. Losing my camp? Just another phase." He was matter-of-fact. "I lost my food in the dust storm. So now I do food runs and have found a Who, What, When, Where guide. Half the listings are wrong, but that's enough. Way better than living on jerky and protein bars."

The man gave him a sideways look, half amused, half skeptical.

"For sleep, I've found a circuit of chill spaces and open couches. Getting tossed out's an inconvenience, but manageable. Not ideal, but it works." He nodded as if validating his own report card. "I've been tested and I'm showing my metal."

"This is me." The man peeled off toward the 8:30 street. "Good luck with your... uh, quest."

Now alone, Cypher walked southeast down the Esplanade. The city had gone quiet, the night's revelry spent, the new day not yet begun. He passed the last of the guttering lanterns. The wide street felt strangely suburban.

Here and there, burned-out partiers shuffled like zombies. A group huddled around a dying fire barrel, warming fingers. He considered stopping but kept moving. Sleep was still calling.

Across the inner playa, a small art car crept slowly, muffled beats pulsing faintly: *unce, unce, unce.* Then silence.

A roadside chill space came into view, bodies curled together like toys abandoned across the floor. Either more people were homeless than he realized, or a lot of burners didn't care where they slept.

As he turned the corner bordering the wide 6:00 promenade, the air grew even colder. The final hour before dawn always cuts the deepest. He pulled his thin jacket tighter, missing the blanket he'd been forced to abandon. Even the drowned sleeping bag felt like a luxury now.

At last, the latticework of Center Camp came into view. The space was dim and mostly hushed. A lone barista served a drink in the distance. A couple whispered on a bench. The rest were prone, scattered like driftwood.

He scanned the perimeter couches. Amazingly, one was empty, with all its cushions still in place. Even better, the nearby stage was blessedly silent. He collapsed into the seat, pulled two cushions over him as makeshift blankets, and let go.

As sleep took him, he thought, *Test passed for now.*

Greeter Station, BRC, 5:38 AM - Justine

The orange hue rising behind the eastern ridge had brightened enough to render the floodlights irrelevant. Justine could now see the row of greeter stations clearly. Each was an artful pyramid of fabric, open on the city side to offer storage and a modest break from the wind. There were enough booths to process ten vehicles at once, though just five were staffed this morning. Flags fluttered in the breeze above the structures. The traffic was steady but light, stragglers arriving at the last possible moment, buzzing with excitement.

They had greeted a steady stream of cars, RVs, and box trucks. People arrived in ones and twos, trios, and small groups.

"Have a great Burn." Susan patted the car's window as it rolled forward. Hoots and cheers erupted from inside the vehicle and trailed off as it headed toward Black Rock City.

Susan turned to Justine. "It never ceases to amaze me, the excitement people feel driving into the city. They've been traveling all night, and still they're lit up."

Justine gave her a crooked smile. She had been swept up in the childlike joy of the incoming Burners, their open-hearted energy infectious.

"Greeting these people may or may not have made me... feel," she admitted.

Susan raised an eyebrow. "Feel what?"

Justine exhaled. Then, barely audible, "Happy."

Susan opened her mouth to reply, but a bus rumbled up to their station.

The bus was covered in wild neon paint, with swirling galaxies, flames, and glittering symbols that shimmered under the desert sun. Its doors burst open, releasing a surge of energy as sixteen dancers and misfits spilled out, their laughter echoing across the greeting area. They looked like desert elves, leaping from the steps and twirling through the dust. Half were first-timers.

Justine led the newbies to the bell. As Susan had shown her, she guided them one by one to ring it, marking their entry into a strange, temporary world. The kind of world too delicate to last. Still, this moment was real. The bus pulled away, its passengers waving madly from the windows.

"You were saying?" Susan prompted.

"I was trying not to say…" Justine began, then gave in with a sigh. "I thought this would be a pain in the ass job. But greeting these people… it made me feel like I was part of something bigger. Bigger than anything I've been part of in my life."

She looked out at the desert, searching for the right words. "It's like I'm… a midwife. Helping people cross over from individual to Black Rock citizen."

"Damn girl. That's beautiful," Susan said, visibly moved. "Despite yourself, you might just be bonding with … strangers."

In the soft light of dawn, bone-tired and dust-coated, Justine felt affected. Inspired. Exposed. A little foolish.

"Is this all volunteer?" she asked.

"Yep. All volunteers," Susan said simply.

"That's incredible," Justine murmured, gazing back toward the glowing sprawl of Black Rock City.

"How are you doing?" Susan asked.

Justine turned back to look at the approach road. She could now see the full length from the gate in the far distance, lined with pickets. In the dim morning light, the headlights looked less harsh. She turned from the traffic and met Susan's eyes.

"I'm good, actually. Tired. But good. I gotta admit, this has been pretty cool. I've never been around this much genuine joy."

Susan smiled softly to herself. Her eyes drifted. "Yeah. As much as I'd love to say I do this for others, the truth is, I do it for me. My faith in humanity only needs thirty minutes out here for a full reset."

She looked out at the desert, then back to Justine. "Does performing restore you?"

Justine smirked. "Not my faith in humanity."

Susan gave a half-laugh, then tilted her head. "That's not what I meant. Does it give you juice, or take it away?"

Justine sighed. "It's complicated. I'm good at it. It's my path to perfection. I'd be a frazzled mess if I didn't power-train every day. Performing lets me get paid for pushing myself as hard as I need to."

"Makes sense," Susan said. "It's a healthy outlet. Could be worse. And yeah, you're brilliant on stage. I just wondered if it makes you happy."

"Happy is slippery for me," Justine admitted. Her voice carried a weight she rarely allowed. "I mostly go for... 'not.'"

"Not?"

"Not pissed. Not frantic. Not shut down. Not crazy. Pushing myself physically helps keep me hovering in the 'not' zone."

Susan nodded slowly. "I think there's something beyond 'not' for you."

Justine gave a sidelong glance. "What's the secret, Yoda?"

Susan laughed. "It's different for everyone. You have to find what satisfies you. But I do recommend loving yourself exactly as you are. You have ways of managing anxiety. That's good. But I think you deserve more than just 'managing.'"

"Easy to say." Justine rubbed her face. "Hard to do."

"It doesn't have to be dramatic. Look at this moment. If you'd gone out partying or stayed in bed, would you feel this grounded, this good?"

Justine thought about it. "Probably not."

"Then let it start small. Build on that. If you pay attention, your body will tell you. I just want you to be kind to my dear friend. She deserves your kindness."

Susan pointed toward a small group of Burners approaching on bikes. "Our reliefs are here."

Center Camp, BRC, 9:07 AM - Emile

"Crane position. Bakasana." The yogini's voice cut through the circle's center. Emile moved smoothly into position, knees braced against upper arms, feet tucked against his backside. *Liam's resolute, disappointed face flashed through his mind.* He breathed steadily and held firm. Around him, others shook, panted, or collapsed in sweaty defeat. This yogini did not mess around.

"Side crane. Parsva bakasana." Legs and knees shifted to the right. Most around him wobbled or faltered through the transition. Emile focused, *pushing aside flashes of the chicken man and the absurd armload of trophies.* His balance held. Sweat slicked his dark skin. He was in the zone.

The toxins from the past days, alcohol, processed food, rooftop uselessness, coursed through him. He was paying for the comforts he had clung to. His body stayed steady, but his stomach churned. The nausea only strengthened his resolve. Today, he would sweat it out. Return to form.

"Prasarita padottanasana." The group unwound into a wide A-frame pose. Emile dropped into it, letting the dull ache seep through joints and muscles. *A warm face, the Afrodisiac man, flickered in his memory.* Sweat beaded and dripped from him in fat splatters onto the mat. A small grunt escaped as he pushed deeper into the stretch.

"Pincha mayurasana." He folded to his forearms and lifted his legs into a controlled handstand. Muscles across his back, shoulders, core, and legs lit up. He drew breath and focus. *A stoic Harley on the prow of Magrathea flashed through him.* Sweat rivulets traced his spine. The moment absorbed him. All other concerns dissolved.

"Vrischikasana," she said softly now, working through it herself. Emile bent his knees, dropped his calves until his toes pointed toward his head. As he settled in, *the Eritrean auntie's harsh laughter rang through his mind.* And then something inside him shifted. Not snapped or broken, just gave. An emotional dam gave way. Tears welled, unfamiliar and clean, mixing with the sweat. He didn't feel grief, or rage, or sorrow. Just peace. The tears marked not a breakdown, but release.

I don't know how to take off my armor and authentically connect, Auntie.

"Adho mukha svanasana, downward dog." A communal sigh rolled through the circle as they transitioned. Emile dropped his feet and raised his hips, pushing up from his forearms to his hands. Muscles stretched and released. Tears continued to fall, wringing something deeper from him with each breath.

Music reentered his awareness. *Happiness* by Riceboy Sleeps played, a feather across his ears.

"Balasana, child's pose." He folded forward, arms back, forehead resting against the mat. He imagined gravity increasing, pulling him downward, deeper. The last tears slipped out. His breath slowed. *His mind thankfully emptied.*

"Savasana, corpse pose." It was over. He rolled to his back, limbs outstretched. The world dimmed. No thoughts. No worries. No weight. He missed the close of the session, the shuffle of mats and gear. Contact dancers were already moving in. Still, he lay there, long past stillness. *It was the first peace he'd felt in months.*

A voice called him back. "Good morning, sunshine. You are going to be trounced if you keep lying there."

A gentle palm tapped his shoulder. He resisted, not ready to leave the peace. The tapping persisted.

Emile opened his eyes slowly, shapes swimming into focus. And then her face appeared above him. Justine. Smiling, possibly smirking, though her eyes brimmed with compassion.

"Hello, Justine," he said, smiling through his daze. Not sheepish, content.

"Yoga's done, I take it?" he asked, taking in the dance crowd filling the arena.

"Yep. It's dance time."

"Shame. I was in my happy place."

"Your next happy place might demand some motion. Want to be my contact improv partner?"

His brows lifted. "Sure. But I doubt my prowess matches yours."

"I'm not looking for prowess. Just not-creepy."

He laughed. "Practice, I can provide. And I'm only sporadically creepy."

"That'll do." She laughed too. Without ceremony, they began, moving into and around each other. Shoulders, hips, backs pressed, twisted, followed. Justine smiled at Emile's intuitive movement. He was no expert, but he held his own at contact improv. They built energy like a rising tide, sustained it, rode it. For forty-five minutes, they danced.

They collapsed together at the arena wall, panting.

"Not bad for a civilian," Justine said, elbowing him.

"I do like to move."

After a beat, "When are you performing on Magrathea?"

"I have a gig at ten tonight. Then I can hoof it to your party by midnight. That work?"

"Perfect." He rose, slapped her knee, and offered his hand. "We'll roll out the red carpet." He pulled her to her feet and hugged her warmly.

"Thanks for the dance."

"Thank you, Emile. Great workout." She held the hug longer than expected, surprised by how comfortable she felt.

As they pulled apart, he held her hand. "Justine, I think this is the beginning of a beautiful friendship."

She laughed. "Okay, Rick. Maybe I'll start calling myself Louis Renault." Sliding on her sunglasses, she shouldered her pack. "I'm out of this gin joint." She vanished into the crowd.

Emile watched her go, then murmured, in his best Bogart, "Here's looking at you, kid."

He gathered his things and drifted toward the coffee lines. Center Camp buzzed. Burners milled around. The barista queues were twenty deep. Emile picked a line and settled in.

He relaxed his muscles and took stock of his peace. The crowd's costumes dazzled. Some queued in chatty clumps, others silent in caffeine-deficient stasis. A gap in the line opened ahead of him. No one had rushed him forward. Time slowed for those who had acclimated to this place.

He stepped forward, then stopped. Something glinted in the dust. A folded bill. He bent, brushed it off. A twenty. He glanced ahead at the man in front of him.

Stocky, compact, balding blonde, inked from wrist to shoulder in intensely stylized tattoos. Not a biker's. Not a hipster's. Emile's guess was that the man was an artist.

He stepped to the man's side and touched his shoulder lightly. "Is this yours?"

The man blinked at the bill, then searched his pocket. Nothing. "Yeah. Looks really familiar. Thanks." He took it and stowed it carefully.

"Really. Thanks. I would have been bummed if I hit the barista station without it."

"No problem." Emile smiled.

"I'm Ruben. Campmates call me Cheshire."

They shook hands, then Emile hugged him. "Well met, Ruben Cheshire."

"Those sleeves are something else."

Ruben shrugged. "Labor of love."

The tattoos were intricate. Emile studied them. "In some cultures, tattoos mark victories. Triumphs."

"These mark failures. Betrayals. The beauty that came from a badly lived life." Ruben acknowledged.

"That awareness is its own victory," Emile declared.

A pause stretched.

The barista called, "May I assist you, sir, with a caffeinated beverage?"

Ruben stepped forward. "Coffee. And..." he turned to Emile. "What would you like?"

"A latte, please." Emile reached for his wallet.

"I've got this." Ruben held up a hand.

"Thank you, Ruben. Blessings." Emile bowed slightly, palms pressed.

"I wouldn't be having coffee if you hadn't returned that twenty. Please enjoy."

"That I will."

They stepped aside. Ruben collected his drink and change. "Nice meeting you." They shook again.

"Be well, Ruben." He nodded and disappeared into the crowd.

Emile watched him go. "There goes a man with an interesting story." He turned inward, feeling his own story start to string itself together and unravel at the same time.

7:30 and Enlighten, BRC, 10:22 AM - Rachael

Rachael sat in front of her tent and stared at her car. It was coated with a thick layer of hardened mud and a light dusting of playa silt, like an unfired clay sculpture of her vehicle. Around her, campmates moved sluggishly through their morning rituals. Some were mid-ablutions, quiet chatting, prepping for the day's playa adventures. People were everywhere. And still, she felt utterly alone.

Her gaze returned to the car. Tents and vehicles boxed it in, but if she really wanted to, she could extract it. She could make a run for the nearest road, vanish from the city, and all these happy, shiny people whose joy only highlighted her own disconnect. Their smiles made her ache.

She stepped toward the car. Then another step. Her hand hovered over the door latch. And stopped.

She stood there, suspended. Then, slowly, she dropped to her knees and leaned forward on her hands, reaching underneath. Her fingers closed around something round and textured. She pulled it free and blinked in surprise. A cantaloupe. Mostly intact. She was shocked that it was still in edible condition. She reached again. Another. Again. Again. Until a dozen cantaloupes sat in front of her like an absurd offering from the earth itself.

She stared at them in silence.

Then, a long, slow sigh. "Okay, okay, okay," she said to the playa, to the city, to the quiet ache inside her. "I give up."

She ducked into her tent, retrieved her only sharp knife and a large plastic bag. Cross-legged in front of the cantaloupes, she began slicing them into bite-sized pieces. The rinds and seeds were set aside carefully, and the playa kept clean. When the bag was full, she rose, slung it over her shoulder, and headed to the road.

The first person she encountered, a bare-torsoed man, looked at the bag skeptically.

"What's in it?"

"Cantaloupe. Just cantaloupe."

He grinned, scooped out several bites, and walked away. Rachael turned toward the next passerby.

3:45 and Esplanade, BRC, 11:03 AM - Rachael

The bag was more than half depleted when she reached the raucous knot of Black Rock citizens. From the other side came cheers and taunts, but she couldn't make out the words. She nudged through the crowd, offering a cantaloupe to anyone who glanced her way, most too enthralled by whatever lay ahead.

She broke through to the front and saw it. A kissing booth just off the Esplanade, rainbow letters overhead. Seven people, men and women, jammed shoulder-to-shoulder inside, heckling the crowd with flirtatious charm. One by one, people peeled off and leaned in for pecks and smooches.

Rachael watched, amused and skeptical. Then she walked to one corner of the booth and stood in front of the man there.

"Cantaloupe?"

The man blinked, took a piece. "Thanks."

She continued down the line, offering fruit to each of the kissers until she reached the last, a beautiful young woman. The woman accepted the cantaloupe, savored it, and smiled.

"That's so sweet. Would you like a kiss?"

Rachael's cheeks flushed. Her impulse was to decline, to disappear. But something softer, steadier moved her forward.

"Sure," she said.

They leaned in. The kiss was lingering, tender, almost reverent. When they pulled apart, the woman looked at her, surprised.

"That was a nice kiss. You should be in here."

Rachael wobbled a smile. "I don't think so. No thanks." She turned away, walking down the Esplanade, offering the last of her cantaloupe.

But the invitation stuck with her. What would it be like to *be* in the booth? The idea unnerved her. And intrigued her.

"I'm already out of my comfort zone," she murmured. "Why not go all the way?"

After giving away the last of her canteloupe, she turned back, rethinking her strategy as she walked. Perhaps she could stand wedged behind others, reducing her exposure and choosing her kisses.

Then she was struck with a horrific thought. *What if no one wants to kiss me?*

And then, there it was. The booth. Empty. The crowd was gone. The moment had passed. The spontaneous gathering gathering had dispersed.

"Fuck," she breathed. Her heart thudded painfully. The impulse to flee nearly overtook her.

But under the panic was something else. Something solid. A quiet echo of the vow she had made in the dust beside her car.

"I brought myself back here for a reason," she whispered. "Time to see it through."

She stepped into the booth, dropped her belongings, and didn't hide. She leaned into the rail, elbows resting forward, waiting. Not posturing. Not pleading.

Waiting.

A young Asian woman strolled by, paused under the sign.

"Is this a kissing booth?"

"Yes, it is." Rachael's voice came out hoarse.

"Can anyone kiss you?"

"Yes."

"Can I kiss you?"

Rachael nodded.

The kiss was sweet, brief. The woman smiled. "Thanks."

"You're welcome."

Something in Rachael's shoulders unknotted. And then the tide came in. Dozens, then more. She lost count at fifty. Some kisses were lovely.

Some were weird. A few were downright awful. All were fleeting, like waves lapping a shore.

A lull. She exhaled.

A young couple approached, the woman stepping forward.

"I've never kissed a girl before," she said. "Should I start with you?"

Rachael smiled. "I think that would be a good idea."

The kiss bloomed slowly, playful, tentative, curious. Five minutes passed before they pulled apart, like a sigh.

"I liked that," the woman whispered. "I'd do it again."

They walked away, and the world seemed sharper, quieter.

Rachael looked around the booth and touched the edge of the rail.

"Whatever I needed to get from this," she said, "has been received."

She gathered her things and walked back toward camp, lighter.

Not just kissed. *Seen.* And, if only for a moment, *wanted without question.*

Temple of Serenity, 12:00 and Outer Playa, BRC, 11:45 AM - Harley

"Are you sure you don't want to come into the temple with me, Dad?" Harley looked across the truck cab at Clarence. The older man sat preternaturally upright in the passenger seat.

"No, son. Go make your peace. I made mine a long time ago." The older man's words carried quiet fanality.

Harley nodded, pushed open the driver's door against the gust, and stepped into the wind. The steady, insistent breeze cut across his path, nudging him to veer right. Pressing against it, he stayed straight. Though the playa was once again dry, the effect of yesterday's rain could still be seen. No ambient dust faded the structures or people. The wind tugged at gritty particles too heavy to lift, so they scuttled low across the earth in shimmering rivulets. Above them, the view remained sharp and bright.

The Temple of Serenity loomed ahead, dominating both his view and his thoughts. Today, Harley was not approaching as a tourist. He was here on business.

Against the wind, his arm lifted protectively to his chest. His hand moved instinctively to the envelope tucked beneath his shirt. Feeling its shape, he exhaled and lowered his arm.

The whisper of wind chimes faded in and out beneath the wind's steady roar. At first, he thought he had imagined it. But as he got closer, the tinkling notes grew stronger. Then, a single horn let out a deep, mournful bellow. A crooked smile flickered across his face. The temple was welcoming him. It was ready.

He circled the exterior until he found the entrance. Stepping beneath the tall, sweeping lancet archway, Harley entered the meditation chamber. Despite the arched portals on every wall, the temple's design scattered the wind into a gentle hush. The chaos outside softened into stillness within.

He settled cross-legged near one of the hexagonal perimeter walls. Closing his eyes, he drew a slow breath and exhaled. The music of wind chimes and bells drifted through him. His tension melted. Then, with a steady hand, he untucked his shirt and slid the large envelope onto his lap.

Staring at the blank face of it, he knew he would never be more ready than now.

He flipped it over, pinched the metal clasp open, and slowly withdrew the contents. He placed two items side by side on the envelope: a black-and-white photograph and a charcoal drawing. The photo was of his mother, Florence, in front of their house. Clarence had taken it on Harley's tenth birthday. She looked relaxed, smiling, and young. Younger than he was now. The charcoal etching was one Harley had drawn when he was eighteen, four months before she died.

He touched the photo. His breath hitched.

"Mom..." he said softly. "It's been thirty-six years, and I don't miss you any less. I think of you every day. I still want to talk to you, to ask your advice, to hear you laugh." He drew in another breath. "I need you to know that it's not from lack of love that I'm here to let you go."

His voice rose, steady but pained. "I thought I was honoring you all this time. I hated Dad for moving on. I hated him for working with those mother fuckers who killed you. I believed I was the only one keeping your memory alive."

He paused, then gave a dry, bitter laugh. "What a load of shit that was."

A long silence stretched between him and the two images.

"Really, I just stopped living when you died. I've been walking around ever since, an empty husk, a bitter ghost. Denying my past. Denying myself a future."

He shook his head.

"I've spent the last year waking up. And now I'm here, Mom. I'm putting this down. I'm letting you go, not to forget you, but to live while I'm still breathing."

His voice cracked. "I forgive you... for dying. I forgive your killers. I forgive Clarence. And most of all, I forgive myself for not saving you. For not being enough. For everything."

He looked up. "If you can hear me, please give me your blessing because I'm getting on with my life. Hell, maybe I'm just starting it. Just starting to be truly there for those I love."

He fell silent, bowed forward. Still. Breathing deeply.

Eventually, he sat upright. Pushing to his feet, he winced at the tightness in his joints. He dusted off his pants, gathered the photos, and scanned the wall. Finding an open space, he pulled an industrial stapler from his pocket and fixed the images to the wall with eight deliberate clicks. Then he unfolded a handwritten note and tacked that up too:

Florence Long Knife, beloved wife and mother, 1934–1973.

Harley stepped back, took it in. Kissed his fingertips and touched the photograph.

"Go in peace, Mom. I will too."

He turned, and for the first time since he arrived, looked around at the others in the temple. No one had watched him. They all had their own ghosts to tend.

He inhaled as if tasting air for the first time.

Then, smiling softly, he walked into the wind, lighter by a thousand invisible pounds.

Clarence stood waiting under the archway. Their eyes met, and Clarence held a quiet smile.

He clapped Harley on the shoulder, and together, they walked back toward the truck, Harley steadying Clarence with a hand on his arm.

As they walked, Harley glanced up at the thinning clouds and wondered, *What now, Mom? What will I build with this life I'm just beginning?*

Gordian Knot, 8:30 and Esplanade, BRC, 2:00 PM - Crawford

"Can I talk to you, Crawford?"

Crawford looked up from the fruit plate, popping a strawberry into his mouth. Ganesh stood there, holding a satellite phone at his side, as if it weighed more than it should. The man looked stricken.

"Sure," Crawford said around his chewing.

"It's probably best if we talk in your RV."

Crawford raised an eyebrow, cocking his head slightly. "Okay. Let's go."

They made their way to the RV. Both men unlaced their boots, leaving them on the doormat before climbing the stairs. Crawford slid into the nook bench.

He motioned to the other end of the curved bench. "Have a seat."

Ganesh slid in, looking like he would rather be anywhere else.

"What's up?" Crawford asked.

Ganesh stared down at the table, the phone now resting between his hands. After a long beat, he looked up.

"Crawford, there's no easy way to say this. The board voted this morning to remove you as CEO."

Crawford blinked, the words settling like sand in water. Before the past few days, he would have exploded. Driven off the playa. Burned it all down. Fought it tooth and nail.

Now? It just felt inevitable.

"No one called for my vote," he breathed, voice tight

"They didn't need it," Ganesh replied. "They had the numbers without you or me."

Crawford let out a dry laugh. "No shit." He leaned back. "Jimmy?"

"He voted no. Said he didn't want the job. But with you out, he agreed to stay on. That's what the board wanted. It was Vicky's vote that tipped the scales."

Crawford inhaled slowly and exhaled even slower, his chest rising with the breath. He let out a quiet tone of resignation, "Well. Fuck."

It hit like a gut punch. He stared past Ganesh, gaze unfocused, as if watching something collapse far away.

After a moment, Ganesh cleared his throat. "Well. I'm gonna leave you to it."

He slid out of the booth and made his way to the door, quiet as fog. The latch clicked shut with a soft finality.

Crawford didn't move. He had never heard a sound that landed with such quiet, brutal weight.

11:00 and Outer Playa, BRC, 3:04 PM - Ruben

The stairway spiraled around the metal tree trunk, each step ringing out a metallic clang that vibrated through the railings. Ruben paused midway, palm buzzing from the contact. He looked down. The base of the tree, twenty feet wide, was a tangle of twisted roots. The trunk rose forty feet before forking into massive branches. The bark shifted in style – redwood plates, baobab smoothness, acacia warts – like a patchwork of global trees.

Branches spread in broad, horizontal arcs, supporting platforms connected by steel cable bridges with grated deck slats. Each platform held a small, one-room structure with peaked roofs made of metal palm fronds, like a punk-industrial Tarzan compound.

As Ruben moved from room to room, memories stirred. He'd adored the Tarzan treehouse at Disneyland. As a kid, it was an exotic escape. But here, the dream had corroded. Syringes, beer cans, and ashtrays replaced fantasy. It felt like rediscovering a long-forgotten childhood memory.

Midway across a bridge, he spotted a ladder leading higher. He climbed to a final bamboo-and-palm-frond platform, more natural than the others. Flowers and greenery spilled across the canopy in a lush, unexpected bloom.

Peeking into the hexagonal room through rope-netted windows, Ruben was stunned. It was immaculate. Books on science and classic literature lined the shelves. A sextant and compass sat on a desk. Maps adorned the walls. It was the dream intact, a preserved pocket of wonder. He felt a flicker of hope.

Rounding the platform, he found a young man sitting cross-legged against the wall. The view was stunning: the city, the far-off ridgelines, the vastness of the playa. Ruben asked, "Mind if I join you?"

The young man looked up, then slid over. Ruben sat beside him. They watched the desert in silence. The young man's eyes were closed, fingers twitching like he was typing in a dream.

Ruben's stomach growled. He pulled out a sandwich, took a bite, and noticed the man eyeing it.

"Hungry?" Ruben asked.

The man nodded. "Yeah..."

Ruben handed over his spare sandwich. The young man devoured it, followed by a handful of cookies and a deep pull from a water jug.

"When was the last time you ate?"

"Last night, I think. Rain trashed my food cache."

"I'm Ruben."

"Cypher."

"Nice spot you've got here," Ruben said, scanning the view. "Last bit of paradise on this ruin."

"Hopeful, isn't it?" Cypher said.

"Yeah. Hopeful."

They sat together in the hush. The wind whispered through the canopy. Below, the playa bustled. Ruben let the moment settle.

He offered an orange. Cypher peeled it in seconds and devoured the fruit.

"You want, we can head back to my camp later. I'll set you up with a real meal."

Cypher smiled, almost to himself. "I knew it."

"Knew what?"

"Burning Man's been testing me," Cypher said. "So I tested it back."

Ruben blinked. "I'm lost."

"It's a test. To see if I can survive with nothing. So I scrounged. And I manifest."

"Manifest?"

"The world's dying. Civilization's a trap. People build, but it's pointless. I don't play that game. I live free. I scrounge what I need. And when that fails... " he gestured at Ruben, "... I manifest it."

"So... you're homeless."

"I'm prepared. I have a tent. I couch surf. I stay off the grid. I'm training for collapse."

"And I'm part of your manifestation?"

"Exactly. The machine builds. The awake scrounge, manifesting what they need."

Ruben shook his head, amused. "Interesting philosophy."

Nothing about this kid's philosophy made any sense to him. Just weeks ago, he would have walked away and left the young man to his delusion. But, time on the playa had, like the Grinch, made his heart grow three sizes. He liked this kid.

He stood and offered Cypher a hand. "C'mon. Let's go manifest you some food, Lord of the Dust."

1:30 and Inner Playa, BRC 6:17 PM - Rachael

"Hold up. I want to get a picture of it," Nathan called.

Rachael swung her bike in a lazy arc and rolled to a stop behind him. Nathan had wedged his water pack between his belly and the bike seat and was already elbow-deep in its outer pockets.

Rachael was obsessively organized. She could list the contents of every pocket, bin, drawer, and stuff sack she owned. For her, retrieving something was a surgical operation. For Nathan, it was an archaeological dig. The moment a physical object left his hand, it ceased to exist in his mental inventory.

She took a deep breath, already familiar with this ritual. But to her surprise, Nathan pulled out his camera before she'd finished exhaling.

"Got it," he said, pumping the pouch into the air like a prize.

"Bravo, sir. Well played," she offered with mock reverence.

"Get your ass over there," he said, pointing at the distant installation. "I need a hot woman in the foreground."

Rachael chuckled and slung her pack onto her handlebars. She strode thirty feet ahead, pivoted sharply, then struck a pose, hip popped, one hand on it, the other flung upward like a game show model unveiling a prize.

"Perfect," Nathan laughed, snapping a burst of photos.

She hustled back and remounted her pack while he began the reburial of his gear. As he did, Rachael studied the distant installation.

"It's even more amazing than the descriptions," she said.

Nathan followed her gaze. A massive steel tripod rose from the playa, supporting a rotating mobile made of three immense granite slabs. Yet they hung from steel cables, each tilted slightly upward at the far end, like cosmic levers of stone.

Crowds had swarmed the slabs, standing room only.

And yet, a single, not especially large man grasped a short chain attached to one slab and began to rotate the entire structure—slabs, people, all of it, as if it weighed nothing.

"I'm amazed and boggled at the same time," Nathan said, awed.

"I can tell you why it works, and I'm still amazed," Rachael laughed. They mounted their bikes and pedaled toward the installation.

Within minutes, they'd arrived and dismounted for a closer look. As they approached, one of the slabs rotated slowly toward them, crowded with people lounging and laughing. A lanky, shirtless young man was climbing up the tilted face, weaving between standing bodies and stepping over seated ones. Near the apex, as he reached for a cable, someone shifted back without looking.

The collision was minor, but enough. The climber was pitched sideways, just missing the edge of the moving slab as he flailed and fell. A woman screamed. Heads turned. But all anyone could do was watch as he dropped to the playa and landed hard, crumpling.

Rachael didn't hesitate. She ducked under the slowly swinging slab and ran to him.

The young man was on all fours, coughing, breathless.

"Before you move, let's make sure you're okay," she said, calm and focused.

She looked up and saw the next slab rotating toward them. "Nathan! Tell them to stop the mobile!" she shouted. Nathan was already sprinting around the base.

Back with the injured man, she crouched beside him.

"Did the fall knock the wind out of you?"

He nodded.

"Good. Stay there. Just breathe."

He dropped his head to the ground, catching his breath.

When his breathing evened out, he looked up at her.

"My name's Rachael," she said. "I want to make sure you're alright. What's your name?"

He rasped, "Cypher."

"Nice to meet you, Cypher. Let's check your back and neck. Any sharp pains?"

He gently moved. "No."

"Any bleeding?"

He slowly inspected his limbs. "I don't think so."

"Great. How about breaks or sprains? Mind if I touch you?"

"Naw... go ahead," he said.

She ran through his arms, shoulders, and ribs. All clear.

"Now your legs. Any pain?"

He moved to kneel, then rose... almost. When he shifted weight to one foot, he crumpled again, gasping.

"Where does it hurt?"

"My ankle."

"Mind if I take a closer look?"

"Huh uh," he muttered, shielding it. She gently moved his hands and rotated the foot. He cried out, grabbing it again.

"Yeah, that's a king-sized sprain," she said, picturing the torn ligaments beneath the skin.. "You're gonna need it wrapped, iced, and you'll need crutches.."

"Shit," he whispered.

"I do energy work. I might be able to help. Is it okay if I try?"

He hesitated, then nodded.

"Just relax. It won't hurt."

Rachael closed her eyes, hands around his ankle. She drew energy up through her body and into him. It flowed fast and full, more than usual. It was as if he were hollow, waiting for it. She directed the warmth deep into the damaged tissue.

"Jesus. My ankle just got hot," he whispered.

She didn't respond, letting the current run until it ebbed.

Finally, she opened her eyes. "Let's get you up and see if it helped."

Nathan had returned. A small crowd had gathered, quiet and curious. Rachael ignored them and focused on Cypher.

"Try it."

With her support, Cypher stood. He tentatively pressed his weight onto the ankle. His expression shifted from concern to disbelief to joy. He stepped forward, limping slightly, but walking.

"Whatever you did... It works. Still sore, but it works."

Rachael smiled. "You should still wrap it and ice it. Go to one of the medical tents."

He took her hands. "Thank you."

She nodded, turning to move away. A wave of dizziness hit her. Nathan slid an arm around her waist.

"C'mon. Let's find a place to sit, get some water, and have a snack."

"Good idea. Energy work takes it out of me."

They leaned against the front wheel of a parked art car. Rachael ate apple slices, recovering in silence.

"You've mentioned how difficult it is to feel connected out here," Nathan started. "Yet the minute someone needs you, you're all in."

Rachael sighed. "Well, providing services is my M.O. I don't really have to connect with other people to do my thing. But, honestly, things have started to shift for me. I'm... experimenting with participation."

Her wry smile signaled her embarrassment at admitting it. Nathan squeezed her shoulder, saying nothing.

After a moment, Cypher passed by, walking gingerly but steadily. He gave them a shy wave.

Rachael raised her hand and smiled. "Something odd about that kid," she spoke softly to Nathan. "He's like an empty vessel. I've never felt anything like it before."

5:30 and Gnosis, BRC 10:08 PM - Justine

"You're up in two." Justine roused from adjusting her costume and looked at the master of ceremonies. He doubled as the stage manager, as well. His quiet, almost gentle, demeanor when talking with her was at odds with his stage persona. He was adorned as a circus ringmaster, his bright red jacket trimmed in gold piping. His top hat sat squarely on his head. Knee boots finished the look. Costume and personality imbued him with authority.

As he talked with Justine, he was calm and reassuring. Justine felt oddly safe, in good hands. As the last act exited the stage, the ringmaster, who had strided confidently on the stage, unfurling a persona in stark contrast to one on one containment. "Give it up for 'Tumble and Sass'!" He gestured expansively for the exciting act. The crowd erupted again.

As the cheers surged, Justine closed her eyes for half a second, steadying herself. One breath, one beat, and then it would be her turn to meet the roar.

5:30 and Gnosis, BRC 10:12 PM - Rachael

"That's one goddamn magical sign!" Nathan stared up at the throbbing mass of changing yet perfectly balanced colors. It arched high over the 30-foot-wide entrance into the camp victoriously claiming, 'The Last Circus Waltz.'

"It's a piece of art!" Rachael breathed, managing to sound both bright and wistful at the same time.

"You know what they say out here, the more magical the sign..." He finished the sentence with a wry smile and arched eyebrow wiggle full of innuendo."

"The bigger the camp?" she made the obvious finish.

"No, silly. The more magical." Nathan beamed.

"We'll see, I'm reserving judgment on that one. I've seen plenty of camps out here with signage that was all hat and no cattle." Rachael said suspiciously.

"Huh?" Nathan looked puzzled.

"All marketing and no product," she responded.

Nathan laughed. "Sometimes camps invest so much into their sign that they forget to build the rest of the stuff."

"Shall we find out which way these folks went?" Rachael gestured through the gate into the camp behind it.

They wove their way through the crowd, glimpsing snapshots of the act on stage, as they navigated ever-tightening clumps of people enthralled with the performance. The couple on the stage was finishing what looked like a combination of contact improv and acroyoga. It was the sort of act that Rachael expected to see at a Pilobolus or Cirque Du Soleil performance. The couple completed their final pose and moved smoothly into bows, trotting off stage right as Nathan and Rachael arrived center stage, at the front of the audience.

An ornately decorated ring master strode confidently onto the stage from the right, bellowing, "Give it up for Pipedream Tango."

The crowd erupted into thunder, and Rachael felt the vibration in her ribs, something electric was about to happen.

5:30 and Gnosis, BRC 10:14 PM - Rachael

"We here at Last Circus Waltz are committed to bringing you the very best talent and bringing out the best performance in all of us," he went on. The crowd screamed with enthusiasm. "Our next act exemplifies perfection of craft. This artist, and I use that term in capital letters," He adopted the cadence of a charismatic preacher, "has made her hoop performance masterpieces." He paused for effect, and the crowd responded raucously.

"Her acro-dance is transcendent." He paused again expectantly. The crowd let out another cheer..

"My lovely burners, I am honored to introduce you to our own tiny hoop dancer, Juuuuuuuustiiiiiiiiiiiiine!!!!" The crowd exploded in screams, whistles, and applause as Justine crossed the stage in a run.

"Holy shit. That's the woman who was attacked the other night." Rachael said.

"Really? The one you told me about?"

"Yeah. Small world," Rachael mused.

On the stage before them, the petite woman moved with supreme confidence, executing deft movements that built an increasingly complex choreography into a tempest, each transition more demanding, more impossible, more breathtaking. She finished up by spinning out five hoops that she had been juggling in a high arc across the stage. Bursting into a triple cartwheel and a round off, she smoothly caught each of the hoops and gathered them at her side. She curtseyed as the crowd went wild.

Looking down, she caught Rachael's gaze and pointed at her. She mouthed, "Stay there."

Gathering up her equipment, she tossed a small hoop to Rachael. She walked off stage to a cacophony that ballooned and lingered long after she exited the stage.

Rachael looked at the ring. "I guess that she was making sure I didn't go anywhere."

She looked at Nathan. "I saw her perform a few days ago. She looks completely different tonight, as if she were in love with what she was doing. I wonder what changed?"

"Burners, friends, and Black Rock Citizens, that concludes the first half of our show. Enjoy the dance intermission accompanied by 'The Last Circus Waltz' house band.

The audience politely cheered as the band dropped the beat. Rachael recognized the tune. It was 'Carousel' by Circus Contraption, a haunting waltz. For all she knew, that was Circus Contraption on the stage.

"Interesting way to start a dance intermission," Rachael noted.

The band transitioned from that short piece into Gregory Page's 'Magic Carousel'. Some of the audience members paired off and started waltzing.

"Waltzing at Burning Man. Who would have thought," Rachael mused.

"You can find anything out here," Nathan responded.

Justine appeared from the dancing crowd.

"Wow. Justine, I'm at a loss for words. Your performance was mind-blowing. You're an amazing performer and athlete." Rachael was not used to stretching for words, handing Justine her hoop.

"Thanks," Justine responded.

"Justine, this is my friend Nathan. I'm camping with him." Rachael gestured at him.

The two greeted each other with a brief, perfunctory hug.

Then Justine turned to Rachael, taking her hand. "I'm glad you're here. I've been thinking about you the past few days. I don't think I thanked you properly. I was pretty shell-shocked."

"You don't owe me anything." Rachael dismissed.

"Rachael, if you hadn't been there, I shudder to think what might have happened," Justine retorted. "You have no choice but to deal with my gratitude."

Rachael chuckled, sheepishly looking down and then back to Justine. She sighed. "Fine," she resigned.

"As a gesture of appreciation, if you two don't have plans, I'm headed to Magrathea to perform. Want to be my guest?"

Rachael glanced at Nathan. He was rapidly nodding in the affirmative. She turned back to Justine. "We've been pining for a Magrathea experience. Adding another one of your performances to the mix... how can we turn you down?"

"Tonight's different," Justine added quietly, a strange light in her eyes. "I want you to see it."

5:30 and Gnosis, BRC 10:14 PM - Emile

Magrathea rocked slightly as Dobbs corrected course. His stoic calm at the wheel stood in stark contrast to the chaos unfolding behind him. Emile turned away from the steadfast driver to glare at the crowd.

"These fucking people have no respect for what we've built," he muttered to Liam.

Liam looked over sharply. Emile's hostility toward their fellow burners had been growing more obvious by the hour.

"They're just having fun. That's why we built this thing," Liam said gently.

Just then, a piercing ululation rose from the crowd. They turned. A woman perched on the shoulders of a large man had her hand across her mouth in a dancer's gesture as she let out the cry. But as she finished, she slumped sideways, her full weight unbalancing her partner. He stumbled, slamming both of them against the window. It bowed but held. They collapsed laughing onto the padded bench. The woman cradled her elbow. It would bruise badly. Neither of them seemed to notice how lucky they were that the glass had not shattered.

"Yeah... just having fun," Emile spat. His disgust clung to every word.

Liam glanced at him. Emile's shoulders were clenched. His face drawn, eyes sharp. Liam had never seen him this way. Possessive. Bitter. On edge. And getting worse.

"I'm heading up top. Justine's about to do her thing."

He didn't wait for a response. He took the spiral stairs two at a time. The night air hit his face, cold and bracing, washing away some of the claustrophobia from below. But the irritation still pulsed under his skin, darker now, more insistent.

Justine stood by the roof deck pole, towering over the revelers, her stilts making her regal and imposing. She was laughing with a woman and a man. Emile pushed aside the anger and put on his host smile. When she looked down at him, he raised his hands in welcome.

"Greetings. Welcome to Magrathea-on-the-move." His smile widened. His voice was warm, practiced. He made eye contact with each of them. "I'm Emile. And you are?"

Justine looked to her companions. "This is Rachael and Nathan."

Emile kissed the back of Rachael's hand and embraced Nathan. "Welcome to our humble home on the playa," he said, stepping back.

He turned to Justine. "Are you ready to perform?"

Justine eyed the pole. "How well anchored is this thing?"

"If you take the pole down, the bus comes with it," Emile replied.

"Then I'm ready." Justine smiled.

Emile pulled a two-way radio from his pocket and keyed the mic. "DJ Bedlam. Bring down the house music and drop Justine's track right after my intro."

"Copy that," Bedlam replied. The music faded.

Emile slipped the radio away and took the microphone from its mount. "Ladies and gentlemen," he announced. "Welcome to Magrathea!"

The crowd erupted. Cheers. Whistles. Hands raised.

"Tonight we have a special treat. Please clear space around the center deck. Make way for the incredible stylings of Justine!"

The crowd parted. Rachael and Nathan followed Emile to the rail.

The music swelled. Justine stepped forward, graceful and sure. A single hoop spun around her waist. Another, smaller, spun atop her head. She raised her right leg and spun up three hoops in quick succession. The leg extended straight up, a perfect vertical. Then, bouncing on the stilt below, she spun three more hoops onto that leg.

With a sharp bounce, she launched two-thirds up the pole, catching it with both hands. Her torso turned out, horizontal, one leg down, the other up. All eight hoops continued spinning.

The crowd howled.

Then, with one explosive move, she brought her legs together and flung the hoops skyward. She tucked, flipped twice in the air, and landed clean on her stilts. Using the bounce, she flipped again, back toward the pole, and stuck the landing.

She raised her arms. Seven hoops dropped around her, clattering in a loose ring. The eighth, the smallest, slipped neatly down around the pole.

She bowed low. The crowd went wild.

Emile, Rachael, and Nathan rushed in to embrace her. Others swarmed, showering her with praise. Bedlam dropped another beat. The rooftop pulsed with music and dancing.

For a moment, watching Justine accept the crowd's adoration, Emile felt the familiar hollow ache. All this applause, all this energy, and none of it was really for him. He was just the host, the facilitator, the one who made it possible for others to shine.

They chatted as the bus continued its crawl around the inner playa. More burners climbed aboard. It became packed and hard to move. Emile's chest tightened again. The crowd pressed closer, their voices louder, their movements more careless. He muttered an excuse and pressed through the crush toward the front of the bus.

He squeezed in between a man dressed as a goat and a tall, bearded guy in a thick coat.

"Ease up, hard case. Everyone's taking turns up here," the tall man warned.

Emile did not respond. The rage was building now, hot and unstoppable.

"Back off. You'll get your turn." The man leaned down. His breath hit Emile's face, hot, stale, and sour with alcohol.

A hand landed on Emile's shoulder.

"I'm not a kid..."

Emile spun. He grabbed the man's coat and lifted him clean off the ground, fast and brutal. The man's face twisted from anger to shock to panic as Emile shoved him forward over the rail. He flailed, bracing himself as he looked down at the moving night, the playa rushing by below.

"Fuck man! Ease up!" His voice cracked, full of fear.

Emile stared. Breathing hard. Jaw clenched. For a moment, he looked ready to let go. The power felt intoxicating. Finally, someone who understood exactly who was in charge.

"Emile! Stop!" Liam's voice came from behind, low and urgent. His hand clamped down on Emile's arm, nails biting into skin. "Don't do this."

The man clung to the rail now, rigid with terror. "Please," he said. "Let me up."

Emile held him there a beat longer. Then he yanked him back.

The man stumbled away, pale and speechless. The crowd around them had gone quiet, staring at Emile with a mixture of fear and disgust.

Emile turned to leave. Liam grabbed his arm again.

"Whatever this is," Liam said, his voice tight, "it ends now. If you want me around."

Emile met his gaze. Something in his face shifted, part rage, part confusion, part shame. But underneath it all, something darker. Something that whispered this was just the beginning.

"Maybe I don't."

The words hung in the air like a threat. Liam's face went white.

Then Emile pulled free. Without another word, he pushed through the stunned crowd, past the women near the stairs, down to the lower deck.

He opened the rear doors and stepped off the moving bus into the night, leaving behind a trail of shocked silence and the man he'd almost thrown to his death.

Behind him, Magrathea rolled on without its captain, carrying his crew and his partner toward an uncertain future.

Gordian Knot, 8:30 and Esplanade, BRC, 10:39 PM - Cypher

Cypher walked with the weight of dusk on his back, turning endlessly through corridors that bent like time and memory. His feet pressed shallow prints into the powdered dust. Somewhere along the way, the noise of the city had faded into a quiet breath, as if the maze had swallowed the world whole.

He felt uneasy about the connections he had made that day. On one hand, their help proved his ability to manifest what he needed, to shape his circumstances. But both had given something up for him; one shared his food, the other gave her life energy, and that troubled him. He was meant to draw from those who had abundance, not from those who lacked. He didn't know how to accept sacrifice. It didn't make sense to him

He came to a crossing. Two paths: one gleamed with unnatural light, the glow of oracles and machines. Screens pulsed in silent language. The other fell away into shadow, where a sagging tent slouched beneath a broken arch. A single flame flickered within.

Drawn by something older than reason, Cypher turned toward the fire.

A man sat beneath the tent, stirring a small iron pot. His hair was wild, his clothes draped like offerings scavenged from forgotten times.

"You've come far," the man said, voice coarse as windblown rock. "And yet you've made no progress at all."

Cypher watched the man in silence.

"You aspire to transformation," the old man went on. "But you carry only tactics. Tricks. Survival stories. You feed on scarcity like it's a birthright."

Cypher shook his head. "I'm doing what I have to to get by."

"Are you?" The man turned, eyes bright and ancient. "Or have you mistaken exile for freedom?"

Cypher tried to answer, but the words stuck. He settled for, "Who are you?"

The man's stare pierced Cypher's soul. "I am your inevitability."

Behind him, a shimmer of silver split the dark. A figure approached, robed in wind and moonlight, a staff etched with signs from forgotten dreams. This warrior monk's footsteps sang softly across the dust.

"Do not listen to him," the newcomer said. "He speaks of comfort. You were not made for comfort. You are made to endure."

The old man growled, "Endurance without joy is not strength. It is rot."

"He is forging a path through hardship," the tall one said, firm. "He has begun the sacred shedding."

"He's hiding," the elder countered, rising. "He's starving his soul and calling it strength."

Their voices cracked the stillness, echoes clashing like distant thunder. Cypher stood between them, heart pounding.

"You are close to greatness," the robed one said, "but only if you leave the need for others behind."

"You are close to healing," the old man said, "but only if you remember that love is not a weakness."

They circled each other now, fire and wind, the staff striking the earth, dust spiraling in rising fury. Cypher stepped back, shielding his eyes.

The moment cracked open. A burst of light, dream-light, or dawn.

And then... stillness.

Cypher lay on his back in the dust, blinking up at nothing. His chest was tight. His limbs ached. The tent was gone. The corridor returned. The fire extinguished. A strange silence pressed in.

"I've been tracking you from up there," the man said, pointing to the elevated walkway. "Bet you're hungry."

Cypher checked in with his stomach. Desperate. "Yeah."

The man led him toward a circle of RVs and a well-appointed kitchen area. He handed Cypher a plate. "Quesadillas. Have all you want. Just made 'em."

The aroma made his mouth water. "Thanks," he said, already chewing.

"If you want a drink, there's a selection in the cooler."

Cypher scarfed the food, then grabbed a lemonade.

"You probably need water too," the man added, handing him a sealed jug. "Keep it."

"Thanks," Cypher said again, softer.

"You're not much for words, huh?" The man smiled.

"Sorry. Got knocked for a loop in there."

"I'm Crawford." He extended a hand.

"Cypher." They shook. Cypher balanced food and water in his arm.

"Were you just gonna spend the night there?"

Cypher considered. "I guess. I thought I was somewhere else."

That amused Crawford. He laughed. "Pretty fucked up, eh? You're not the first. Won't be the last. The maze has been tripping people out."

He handed Cypher another hot quesadilla. "There's a recliner over there. You're welcome to crash."

"Thanks." Cypher took the food, nodded, and Crawford clapped him on the shoulder.

"Good burn, man. I'm headed back up to the crow's nest. There might be others like you."

Cypher watched him go. Then he made his way to the recliner, blanket in hand.

It was a damn fine place to sleep, even for someone not made for comfort.

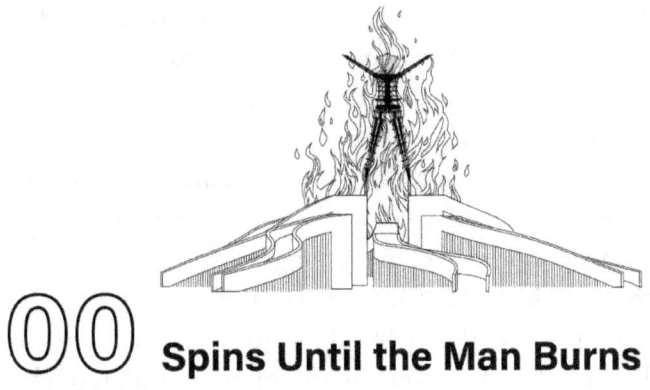

⓪⓪ **Spins Until the Man Burns**

Trash Fence, Outer Playa, BRC, 12:40 AM - Harley

Harley walked at an uncharacteristically slow pace. It was a saunter. Harley didn't do saunters. Then again, he had never walked arm in arm with Claire before. Her arm was tucked loosely into his, grounding them together.

"Cyan adores Clarence," Claire chirped.

Harley smiled. "She didn't have to deal with him as a father."

Claire laughed, a light, bubbly giggle. She was more relaxed than he could remember. They walked for a moment in silence, footfalls muffled by the hard-packed playa. City sounds were distant, subdued.

"I'm glad you brought them," he said, giving her arm a squeeze. For once, she didn't fill the silence. She waited.

Harley let the quiet stretch, then spoke. "I realized over the last few weeks that I miss them." He hesitated. "I missed you."

She pressed her head into his shoulder.

"I've been angry for so long," he said, exhaling. "Angry at Clarence. At the tribe. At my ex Arlene. At Cyan. At you. At the whole damn world." His breath caught. "Mostly, I've just been angry at myself."

His words came ragged now. "I spent years convincing myself I didn't deserve a happy life. And I made damn sure I didn't have one."

They walked on, his voice soft but steady. "I think... I think I'm ready for happiness."

Claire glanced at him out of the corner of her eyes.

They slowed as they approached the trash fence. They now stood at the far edge of Black Rock City, stopping close enough to the orange plastic webbing that they could reach out and touch it. They stared out into the inky, star-speckled night. As dark as it was, the mountain ranges to the east and west of the playa stood out as darker patches. Away from the city lights, the stars sparkled brilliantly.

Harley drew in a deep breath of cool evening air and turned to face Claire. "Thank you for hanging in with me." He attempted a wan smile.

Claire smiled and stepped in, burying her face in his shoulder, crushing Harley with a tight hug. "I... you're so worth it!"

He held her close and kissed her head above her ear. "I love you."

She shuddered, choking out an exclamation. And, though she tried to stifle it, she cried. She sobbed quietly, holding herself tightly against Harley's chest. Usually, he withdrew from her display of emotion. But not tonight. This time, he held her, physically and emotionally. He held her.

They stood like that for a long time. They stood through years of release, for both of them. They held each other as they shed their hurts, their resentments, their pain, their defenses. They shed until there was nothing left to shed, until they were breathing slowly, deeply into each other.

In that emotional silence, that unprotected moment, Claire tilted her head up to look at Harley's face. He smiled at her, leaned in, and for the first time kissed her gently. He was tempted to leave it there, almost pulling away. But then he didn't.

The kiss became more heated and passionate. Their hands roamed, navigating over clothes to find warm skin and soft bits. Claire maneuvered them until her back was against the closest fence post. The kisses had released her from her demure, space-holding trance. Claire-out-loud was back. She pulled away from his mouth and took him in with an impish grin.

"This is happening!" she declared, deftly unbuckling his belt and unbuttoning his pants. He made no effort to resist. Rather, he slid his hands up her fishnet-clad thighs to her panties. No panties to be found. Shifting tactics, he slid his hands between her thighs and ripped the fishnets at their crotch.

"Fuck yeah!" was all she could get out before his fingers found her moistening lips. He slid his fingers along them. They were immediately soaked. "Move those fingers or lose them," she gasped as she pulled him, by his cock, to her. She wrapped her legs around his waist and guided him into her without preamble. He groaned. She hissed, "Yes!"

They kissed deeply as he thrust into her. She began to moan. Entwining her fingers into the fence mesh, she lifted her hips and jackhammered herself onto him. Seconds later, she exploded into a massive, body-shaking orgasm.

Harley continued to thrust through several waves as Claire gripped the mesh, screaming her pleasure. Coming into consciousness from her last peak, Claire opened her eyes and stared hungrily into Harley's. "Let it go, baby! Give it to me!" He needed no further persuasion. He increased the rhythm of his thrusts, feeling his orgasm welling up. He clutched her ass cheeks, pushed himself into her, and came so hard that he expelled a loud, earthy groan.

They stayed in that position for a few more minutes, kissing. Neither wanted the moment to end. Slowly, his erection faded, eventually slipping out of her. Only then did Harley let her legs drop to the ground. He held onto her, and she stood unsteadily on her feet. "Holy shit! It may be a few minutes before I can walk."

Harley laughed. "Take your time. We're in no hurry." Pulling her into him, he kissed her again. As they separated, he smiled at her. "That was a hell of a stunt you pulled there. Do your orgasms always require circus tricks?"

She laughed. "Not always. Sometimes I use bronco breaking moves."

Harley laughed again. "I have zero doubt about that."

They stood close for a while longer, the stars indifferent witnesses. Then Harley asked, "You ready to go back?"

Claire's grin softened. "No," she said. "I'm never going back." She touched his chest. "You said you're ready for happiness, right?"

He nodded.

"Well, I'm ready too. And happy's forward. So let's go forward... together." She paused, then added, "But I'm happy to walk with you to camp."

They turned together, arms around each other's waists, and made their way toward the city lights, toward something new.

Gordian Knot, 8:30 and Esplanade, BRC, 2:34 AM - Cypher

"You need to go home!" The voice was not angry, but it was insistent. Cypher felt a persistent hand shaking his shoulder. The shake perfectly matched the voice, firm in its demand for his attention. He kept his eyes shut, hoping it would go away. It didn't.

"C'mon now. I see you're tired, but this isn't your camp. You need to go home." The shake grew more determined. Cypher opened his eyes to see a not-unfriendly woman looming over him.

"Here!..." She thrust a Gatorade bottle into the crook of his folded arm. "Stay hydrated... Now off with you."

Cypher sat up, bleary-eyed. He slowly sloughed off the blanket Crawford had given him. The Gatorade rested in his lap as he rubbed his face. The rubbing only served to redistribute the smeared dust and sleep crust.

It felt like porcupines had been inserted into his nostrils. He pinched the bridge of his nose and blew through his nostrils, trying to dislodge the grit. It shifted but didn't release. He dug into one, then the other nostril with his thumb, extracting large, black, crusty mucus balls.

The woman laughed. "Playa boogers. They grow 'em big out here."

Cypher flicked his hand to whip the unwelcome masses to the ground. He stood, gathering his belongings. He looked around at the highly organized RV camp, sighed, and drifted out toward the Esplanade, still adrift in the test. He was starting to think it wasn't the righteous quest he'd embraced. He was still searching for a place to land.

9:30 and Gnosis, BRC, 2:37 AM - Emile

The throbbing house beat rose as the neon art car approached. It was a tall Conestoga wagon affair, garish neon trim lending it an otherworldly tackiness. Emile's irritation spiked when it turned onto his street, disturbing the dark calm. The pounding bass felt like fists against his skull as it passed, the same mindless rhythm that had been driving him crazy all week.

As it faded behind him, the dark enveloped him like a comforting blanket. The muscles around his shoulders and neck released slightly. But the relief was temporary. The anger was still there, coiled tight in his chest, waiting.

He had been walking ever since he stepped off Magrathea. Ever since he'd seen the look in Liam's eyes, it was not just hurt, but something worse. Fear. Of him. The memory made his hands clench into fists. The tacit bridge between him and Liam, him and the Magrathea crew, felt like a chasm. Impossible to cross.

He found more solace in the dark parts of the city where people were peacefully sleeping in their camps. He had worked his way to the outer streets where it was quietest, but even here he couldn't escape the images replaying in his mind. The man's face when he'd dangled him over the rail. The crowd's stunned silence. Liam's voice: *"If you want me around."*

Maybe I don't, he'd said. The words had come out of him like venom, and he'd meant them in that moment. But now, alone in the dark, they felt like a confession he wasn't ready to make.

Emile quickened his pace, breathing hard. As he came up to the intersection, he turned right onto 9:30. The street stretched ahead of him, lined with dark, sleeping camps and the occasional glow of a late-night fire. He could keep walking. Past Inspiration, past Karma, past the outer edge of the city altogether. Walk until the lights of Black Rock City disappeared behind him, and there was nothing but empty desert and stars.

The thought should have terrified him. Instead, it felt like the first honest impulse he'd had in months.

A figure emerged from the shadows ahead, a woman sitting in a camp chair beside a dying fire, nursing what looked like a cup of tea. She looked up as he approached, her face illuminated by the orange glow.

"Rough night?" she asked quietly.

Emile stopped. He should keep walking. He should maintain his privacy, his control. But something in her voice... no judgment, just simple recognition, made him pause.

"Yeah," he said, surprised by how raw his voice sounded. "Something like that."

She gestured to an empty chair beside her. "I've got more tea if you want to sit for a minute. Sometimes the walking helps, sometimes it doesn't."

Emile stared at the chair. Such a simple choice. Sit down and maybe talk to a stranger about whatever was eating him alive. Or keep walking into the darkness until he found whatever he was really looking for out there.

The fire crackled between them, waiting for his answer.

Rod's Road Near Center Camp, BRC, 3:22 AM - Ruben

Ruben stopped mid-step, caught by a swirl of rich colors and shiny meandering lines. The air was chill. His surroundings still. The few sounds emanating from the sleepy city were far away, muted. This moment felt intimate.

Nestled between two diverging streets, half-swallowed by the surrounding camps, was a sculpture quietly commanding its own gravity. Its gleam reflecting the upturned floodlight, gold and silver filigree catching and throwing tiny flashes of light like a mirrored flame.

Ruben took a step closer. The piece was intricate, delicate, clearly handcrafted, and entirely intentional. At its center: a globe, maybe seven feet across, held aloft on the raised arms of a ring of human figures. The earth's surface was inlaid with colored ceramic, deep forest green, ochre, lapis, and ivory-white, rendered without borders, only topography.

The edges of each landmass extended outward into shadowed reliefs of human silhouettes. People of every shape, ethnicity, and age, reaching across oceans toward one another, as if gravity had shifted sideways and togetherness was now the only true north.

Ruben circled the piece slowly. The base figures, Atlases of every gender, race, and form, braced the world with arms locked at the elbows. Their ceramic skin tones contrasted and complemented in a careful mosaic, bound with gold and silver solder. The figures leaned in, shouldering the weight of something far greater than themselves.

He swallowed hard. His chest tightened. He wasn't sure if the stirring emotion was joy or grief.

"You found her."

The voice was warm, edged in fatigue but clear. A woman stepped into the light, not costumed but layered in working gear – dusty pants, boots, a knit scarf, a fleece vest zipped up against the night chill. Her hair was messy, tied back without affectation.

Ruben turned. "Yours?"

She nodded. "I call it *Gaia Unboundried.*"

He looked back at the piece. "It's... astonishing. I've seen so much beauty this week, but this feels different. It feels like an aspiration."

She stepped beside him, placing a hand lightly on his shoulder. Her touch was firm, grounding. "It's hope," she said simply.

Ruben nodded slowly. "For dark times."

She tilted her head. "We're always in dark times. And light ones. This is a world that could exist if we choose it. No borders. No fear. Just people leaning in."

He repeated her phrase, tasting it. "Leaning in."

She smiled. "We're tribal creatures. Built to seek safety in sameness. It helped us survive when the world was simply predator and prey. But now? That instinct that once protected us now divides us. We draw hard lines for skin, nation, creed. We assume difference is dangerous."

She gestured to the sculpture. "But connection is just as natural. We've just forgotten how to choose it. *Gaia* is a reminder. A map, if you will, of what it could look like if we rewired our reflexes."

Ruben took that in. "I felt that, but couldn't put it into words. It makes me ache a little. For how far we are from it."

She nodded. "But it's not fiction. Not entirely. Look around. Here, in this dusty, impossible place, we gift. We collaborate. We reach out to strangers with no need to trade. The scarcity mindset loosens its grip, and something else can breathe."

Ruben let out a long exhale, staring into the glimmering glass continents. "You've turned yearning into something beautiful."

She studied him for a moment, then opened her arms. "Hug?"

He didn't hesitate. "Yeah. I'd like that."

They embraced. It wasn't performative or fleeting. They held each other quietly, her body solid against his, the warmth of her breath soft on his neck.

Ruben let go of the week's whirlwind for a moment and simply stood, held.

Behind her, the globe stood as a possibility. The city, in its exhaustion, breathed and continued to pulse, albeit gently. Here in the quiet center of things, he felt the ache ease.

Just people leaning in.

Temple of Serenity, 12:00 and Outer Playa, BRC, 6:10 AM - Justine

She relished the stillness of early morning on the playa. No music. No distant beat. No droning art cars. No echoing laughter or yelps from party stragglers. Just the hush of breeze across hard-packed earth, brushing her skin like a welcome. There was nothing to do but take in the slow climb of the sun as it broke free from the mountains.

A low hum from the Dungchen horns began to thread into the quiet. Justine smiled. "Not a bad way to greet the day," she murmured, though no one was near enough to hear her.

She leaned back against an elegant column fronting the looming structure behind her. It was said to be a place of mourning and closure. But she had no clear grief, no known loss. She felt like an imposter making the pilgrimage. Still, something had pulled her here.

My friends are incredibly loving, deeply bonded, and incredibly open. I know that I'm not. But I feel so close, yet so far.

The pull had started in the pre-dawn hours. She had woken in the dark needing to pee, and her trip to the porta-potty turned into something else entirely. Afterward, instead of returning to camp, she drifted through the hush of early morning until she found herself at the temple. Not ready to go in, she settled against the column to watch the sunrise.

She now cupped her hands over her brows, squinting into the morning light as it breached the jagged eastern ridge.

The breeze gathered and rose in a playful gust that sent a shiver down her spine. It was no longer the comfortable wrap of a sunrise sit. She needed to move, to warm up. She exhaled and pushed herself to her feet.

Turning away from the sunrise, she stepped past the buttress into the shadowed interior of the temple. A scattering of burners occupied the main cloister. A few meditated. One read the memorials etched onto the wooden wall. To her right, a sleeping couple curled together like a pile of discarded clothing.

She hesitated at the threshold, scanning the space until her eyes landed on a small apse across the cloister. She moved quickly toward it, grateful for the possibility of privacy. Once inside, she sat cross-legged, her back to the room. Whatever was going to happen here, she would face it alone.

She took in the space around her. Memorials covered every surface: walls, shelves, cubbies, layered with pictures, letters, drawings, beads, feathers, and trinkets. In front of her, someone had arranged a small altar on an embroidered scarf, studded with figurines and crystals. Incense cones burned at each end, their smoke curling upward and dispersing quickly in the open air. The scent was familiar but nameless.

She was overwhelmed by the care behind it all. Each tribute seemed to echo with longing and presence. And she, in contrast, felt unprepared. The person she was mourning lived inside her. Or rather, used to.

She was not suicidal. Suicide took too much energy. She simply felt emptied out. Numb. As if the lights were on but no one was home. She was an automaton, grateful for the awareness of that deadness. But the awareness offered no path forward.

Susan's words echoed from the greeter's station: *Start small and build on it.* Maybe showing up here was her start.

Normally, she would move to get out of her head. Grinding out practice routines. Dance drills. Rides across the playa. Long hikes. Motion was her escape hatch. But now, stillness wrapped around her like a cocoon, and her thoughts pressed inward.

She began to read the memorials.

"I miss you every day, Mom," scrawled beneath a photo of an elderly woman.

A cluster of snapshots showed a young man in his thirties, mugging for the camera. Below them, a multi-page letter began, "Too soon! Too soon! Too soon..." The letter was an untamed outpouring for a man claimed by glioblastoma, written in looping cursive and uneven ink.

"I don't know who the fuck I am or what THE FUCK I'm doing," someone had scratched down a beam in thick black Sharpie.

Justine inhaled deeply. She was not the only one in the throes of an identity crisis.

She read dozens more. Some were a single, raw sentence. Others, intricate arrangements of pain and memory. When she had taken in all that was near her, she leaned back on her arms and exhaled.

Her hands touched something behind her. It shifted.

She turned and found a leather-bound portfolio. In her lap, its gold-embossed title read: *David Spears, Friend, Husband, Father.* The album walked her through his life, from childhood joy to the fragile grace of old age. She flipped through scenes of college romance, a wedding, and then the arrival of children... a daughter, then twin boys.

She slowed on the family photos. The couch dogpile. The camping trip. Faces aglow around a firepit. Each image shimmered with affection.

Her chest hitched. Something deep inside cracked open. She had been lamenting her numbness, and now... Now she was flooded.

An involuntary sob ripped out of her. Her cheeks were already wet with tears.

She doubled over as another sob broke free, this one deeper, rounder, shoving air from her lungs. It was the kind of crying that took control of your body. There was snot. She did not care. Her limbs trembled.

When she finally tried to stand, nausea swept through her. She dropped to her knees and vomited.

Then it started again.

It went on and on. She sobbed until her throat was raw and her ribs ached. When the tide of grief finally began to subside, what rose in its place surprised her.

It was small. Indistinct. But growing. Irritation, then anger, flamed in her chest.

"So that's it? My big problem is that I have goddamn daddy issues? I'm dead inside because I didn't get some suburban slice of birthday cake childhood? What a joke. What a spoiled, shallow joke I am."

She stood up fast, indignant, wiping at the mess on her face to no effect. Looking down, she saw the mess she had created. She reached into the grit in an ineffectual attempt to gather the muck.

Then a hand touched her arm. Light. Steady.

She looked up.

A woman stood before her in a flowing robe. Her hair was loose under a scarf. She held out an outstretched hand, offering a wet wipe and a plastic bag.

Justine stared, then took them. "Thank you."

The woman smiled and walked away.

Justine wiped her face clean, then set about cleaning the space she had defiled. When that was done, she stood still in the quiet apse, staring into the hollow space where love should have lived.

Gordian Knot, 8:30 and Esplanade, BRC, 6:13 AM - Crawford

Crawford slid into the maze through the secret door adjacent to the common area. From his earlier crow's nest reconnaissance, he believed the maze was empty. It seemed like a good time to check how things were holding up. Just one more day of operation. The maze was the worse for wear, but still standing. In a world where he had lost all control, it remained the one thing he could still claim.

At least for now.

He welcomed the solitude. Word of his ouster had spread. He had not been told, but he could feel it. His campmates had become awkward.

Conversations turned tight. Their glances now held something he couldn't stand, pity.

Normally, that pity would have sparked a fight. This morning, it just felt static, unpleasant, but not worth chasing.

He'd thought about leaving. But he had nowhere to go. Running would be worse. The least-worst option was to stay and face the music.

He moved quickly through the maze, inspecting previous repair sites. Satisfied, he stepped into a wider run that opened toward the hub tower. He took a slow turn, scanning the structure.

"Bruised but holding together," he murmured aloud. It wasn't clear if he meant the maze or himself.

He patted the upright next to him, then paused. Jimmy emerged from the hub.

Crawford blinked, startled. "Doing a walk-through?"

Jimmy nodded. "Things have held up better than expected. Heavy traffic, wind, rain, we stress-tested this beast. Could probably take it on a world tour."

Crawford snorted. "Not sure my life could handle a world tour. I'd have a stroke. Or catch cancer."

Jimmy nodded again, unreadable. He started to turn away.

"Jimmy," Crawford called out. Jimmy turned.

Crawford exhaled. "You did a hell of a job with the maze. It's been a great experience for everyone who has come through. And our camp loves you. Congratulations."

Jimmy studied him for a beat too long. "Thanks. You too. It's been a great project."

"Congratulations on taking on the CEO position," Crawford added.

"I don't want it," Jimmy said, stiff. "Told them it's temporary until they find someone."

"Regardless. They made a good choice." Crawford's voice softened. "If you need help... I promise I won't be a dick."

For the first time, Jimmy smiled. It flickered across his face like a sunbeam breaking through clouds... there and gone. But it was real.

"Thanks. I'll probably take you up on that."

Crawford nodded. "Good." He stepped past Jimmy, patting his shoulder as he went.

He didn't look back. But for the first time in days, the silence behind him didn't feel like judgment. It just felt quiet.

9:30 and Avatar, BRC. 7:08 AM - Harley

"Here you go, Dad." Harley handed Clarence the thermos cup filled with dark, bitter brew, just the way his father liked it.

Clarence held the cup to his nose, inhaling the rich steam. He looked up and smiled. "Smells good."

Harley chuckled. "It should. It's your recipe, old man."

He considered asking Clarence to take a walk. The man was spry for nearly eighty, still vital, still sharp. He'd even walked out to Ataraxis. But Harley couldn't help feeling protective. Instead, he grabbed two camp chairs and set them up on the corner of their camp, facing the intersection.

"Watch the world go by?" he asked.

Clarence grinned and followed. They sat.

For a while, they said nothing. The quiet took Harley back, those long silences on the front porch of Clarence's house, gazing out over the pine-covered hills of the Rez.

Clarence broke the stillness. "You done good here, boy."

Harley's eyes widened. He glanced at Clarence, but didn't turn his head. "Thanks, Dad," he muttered, almost not trusting the words. Compliments from Clarence were rare. The ground beneath this relationship was shifting.

Silence settled again. A few burners wandered past, most on their way to or from the porta-potties. Biology didn't pause for the magic of the playa.

Then Clarence asked, "What you gonna do with it?"

Harley's thoughts spun. "Do with what, Dad?"

"That big-ass statue of yours," Clarence said with a crooked grin.

Harley looked at him, then back out to the street. This time, his silence was not easy. He knew the answer. He just wasn't ready to say it, not even to himself. But he didn't feel rushed. Clarence never pressed.

A voice interrupted them. "Want some bacon?"

Their neighbor stood over them, a broad-shouldered, tutu-clad drag queen with a full, groomed beard, Sisters-of-Perpetual-Indulgence makeup, a navy Cal Bears sweatshirt with gold lettering, and a rainbow cowboy hat.

Of all the unique souls Harley had met on the playa, this man held the most contradictions with the most flair.

He extended a wooden tray, piled high with hot, crispy bacon. It was Black Rock gold.

"Thanks, man," Harley said, peeling off two pieces and biting in. Clarence grabbed three.

"Enjoy, gentlemen." Their glittering benefactor drifted off, offering bacon to all in his path.

As the man disappeared down the street, silence returned. Harley finished his bacon quickly. Clarence chewed slowly, savoring each bite.

Harley sipped his coffee, then cleared his throat. "I'm giving it to the Rez."

Clarence raised his eyebrows, the only sign of emotion.

He chewed, thoughtful. Then, after a long pause, he said, "Seems about right."

They sat and sipped their coffee, watching disheveled burners shuffle by, the silence between them now full and earned.

7:15 and Esplanade, Pink Heart, BRC, 7:23AM - Emile

Emile drifted into consciousness, hearing the sounds of busyness around him. He breathed in deeply, his lungs filling with stale dust, forcing a rattling cough. He blinked his eyes open, taking in his surroundings as his vision shaped into focus. He was sprawled on a couch. Scattered about the near vicinity were couches and chairs. Many held burners in various states of recline. Some had, like himself, made use of the furniture as opportunistic lodging for the night. A large shade structure covered the chill space. Everything in the room, from the furniture to the walls, curtains, and carpet, was pink and strangely inviting.

The light chill in the air told him it was early morning. He pushed himself up on one elbow and squinted into the distant east. The sun had crested the ridge but was still low on the horizon. Another day at Burning Man. Another day of pretending everything was fine while his world fell apart.

His mouth felt like it was full of cotton, and his throat scraped like sandpaper.

Water! He needed water. Then panic and adrenaline coursed through him as he realized he'd lost track of his CamelBak. He sat up and looked around frantically. Nothing on the couch or on the carpet in front of him. He slid his hand under the pillow he had been using as a headrest. Contact. He grasped and pulled on a strap. The attached CamelBak emerged. Relief flowed through him, prompting a sudden sweat dampening his forehead and temples.

Remembering his thirst, he pulled the camelback nipple loose from its clasp. Shoving the nipple into his mouth, he sucked greedily. Water dribbled down his throat into his uneasy belly, flooding him with relief. So when the water stopped, his disappointment was profound. He shook the camelback, light in his hand. Empty.

Emile stood up shakily and spotted a large water jug about fifty feet away, roughly marking the center of the chill space, resting on a makeshift bar. As he approached, a woman stepped from the back and sidled up to greet him. "Happy day, my friend." She chirped, way too happy and awake for the early hour.

"Hey." Emile forced out the return greeting. "Do you mind if I fill my CamelBak?"

"Feel free. That's what it's there for." She smiled. "It's iced and has lemons in it."

As he filled the bag, she studied his face with the kind of gentle concern that made him want to run. "Rough night, love?"

He looked up sharply. Something about her tone reminded him of the woman from last night, the one by the fire. The one whose offer of tea he had declined. He had walked away from her just like he'd walked away from everything else.

"Something like that," he managed, sealing the cap and drinking half the bag.

"Well, you're welcome here as long as you need. Pink Hearts's always open." She gestured around the space. "Sometimes we all need a soft place to land."

The kindness in her voice made his chest tighten. He quickly topped off the CamelBak, shouldered it, and tipped his hat. "Thanks."

He stepped onto the Esplanade, squinting at the rising sun. "Now what?" he asked out loud, to no one in particular.

He was not ready to go back to camp and could not yet face Liam. But the thought of another day of running, another day of avoiding the wreckage he'd made, felt suddenly exhausting. He turned his head to the right and surveyed the Esplanade venues. Most were quiet with little activity. He turned left, reconnoitering all the way down to the big sound camp at the corner of 2:00. Nothing appealing that way either.

Then his eyes veered off into the distance, toward the temple. He had been avoiding it all week. The temple was where people went to confront their demons, to lay down their burdens, to mourn their losses, to find some kind of peace. Everything he'd been running from.

A weary smile shaped his face, but this time it held something different. Not resignation, but a kind of grim determination.

"The temple it is."

With that declaration, he stepped off the Esplanade onto the hardpack. For the first time in days, he wasn't running away from something. He was walking toward it.

Setting a steady pace, he headed out onto the playa, ready or not to face whatever waited for him there.

Temple of Serenity, 12:00 and Outer Playa, BRC, 7:37AM - Rachael

Rachael marveled at the graceful arches that swept up to meet at the top of the temple's main chamber. It was as majestic, in its own way, as any cathedral she had visited. She took in the artful details of the structure around her; the arched ribs of the hall, the silent dungchens built into the walls, the ornate alcoves filled with writings, pictures, and tributes, memorials of every kind.

She made her way to the center of the chamber, gently seating herself on the hardpack. She immediately felt herself surrounded by a velvet hush. It was a place that inspired reverence with no allegiance. She felt a shift in her; not gravity, but weight, as if the space itself was exhaling around her and expecting nothing but presence in return. It invited, not demanded, her grief.

Rachael's mourning was purely metaphorical, vague, and difficult to touch. The mirror held up to her during the past days had revealed one urgent cruelty pressing hardest: her unwillingness to embrace and love herself. All the barely remembered losses, indiscretions, lost moments, missed opportunities, banal cruelties, failures of presence when it was most needed, they all circled back to this central wound.

As if someone had opened a relief valve in her soul, she felt a chronically buried grief release. She did not attempt to suppress it. Nor did she press herself into it. Rather, she relaxed and let it flow through her, letting it seep through her skin, sullenly dispersing into the space like acrid smoke. She had no tears for the deep grief that flowed through her. It felt like she was excising a festering abscess, relieving its putrid, hateful toxicity.

As the pain became more acute, her martial arts training muscle memory kicked in. Accept the pain. Love the pain. In that pain lies progress. She sank deeper, letting everything she suppressed flow through her. The suspicions and judgments of others. The insecure fears that they might be right about her. She let it all fill her without resistance, every monster, every ghost, until that vault of horror inside her was empty.

In the end, she felt hollow. But at the bottom of that hollow place was something she had not experienced before. There lay a seed, a weakly glowing ember. Even as she noticed it, the ember grew, light flooding her being. She felt love. Unfettered, grateful love.

She let out a long, slow breath and opened her eyes. The cathedral around her had become twice as exquisite. Her fellow mourners were gorgeous, beautiful, so incredibly human.

She smiled, an unselfconscious act without pretense. A great weight had lifted from her. She felt, for the first time in years, as if she saw new colors, smelled new aromas, and tasted new flavors. Speaking of which, she was suddenly aware of a deep yearning pang. "Jesus," she muttered, "I need to eat."

Temple of Serenity, 12:00 and Outer Playa, BRC, 8:09 AM – Emile

Emile circumnavigated the temple. He was not ready to enter it yet. He wanted to give himself a moment before he passed into that sanctuary, and he wanted that moment to be in the morning sun. He circled to the eastern-facing entrance, where he saw a woman sitting on the entryway bench. As he approached, he noticed various packages between her and her backpack. She extracted a handful of mixed nuts from one of the bags and popped them in her mouth.

She was thoughtfully chewing when he asked, "Mind if I join you?"

Her mouth full, she gestured toward the bench with her hand open in offer. He sat down, removing his backpack. He took a long pull from the nipple while the woman hastened to swallow. "Emile?"

He took her in for the first time. "I know you. You're..." He snapped his fingers, trying to reach for her name.

"Rachael," she said with a smile.

"Yeah," he said. "Good to see you." It was a perfunctory response, but not quite a lie.

She nodded. "You hungry?" She gestured at the food next to her: orange slices, mixed nuts, apple slices, grapes, and cheese bites.

He smiled. "I could eat."

She pulled her backpack to the other side of her and said, "Help yourself."

He slid over and took some grapes, biting into one and letting the juice trickle down his throat.

"Could I have some of your water?" she asked. "I'm out." She gestured toward an empty plastic bottle.

He handed her his CamelBak. She opened the nipple and took a long pull. Closing the valve, she gave it to him. "Damn, it's iced with lemon. What a treat."

He waved it off. "Make sure you hydrate yourself before you head back."

"Thanks." She said and placed the CamelBak on her backpack. "Eat all you like. We're having our own stone soup experience."

He chuckled, tossing an orange slice into his mouth. When he swallowed the pulp, he asked, "Coming or going?" He gestured toward the temple.

She smiled. "Going. I had my moment there. Left my emotional baggage in the middle of the temple. Don't trip over it."

He grinned knowingly. "I'd like to add mine to your pile."

She turned her head, gazing directly at him. "Are you okay? You got a bit tense last night."

His face clouded. Dropping back, he let his shoulders and the back of his head rest against the temple wall. He let his eyes wander across the slate, broken ridges along the horizon.

He breathed out hard through his nose. "Seems that I brought rage as my guest this year."

He was quiet for a long time. Then, he said softly, "I want to blame my crew for slacking, for missing the mark. I want to blame the guests for being careless and disrespectful. I want to blame the world for not making room for someone like me. But the truth is... Liam's right. Whatever this is, it's not coming from out there. It's coming from inside."

He exhaled, jaw tight. "I've had a handful of blowups since I got here. Flashpoint moments. And I realized something that scared the hell out of me: I'd have a lot more of them off playa if I didn't keep myself locked down so damn tight. I'm constantly bracing. Containing. Choking it back."

He looked down, voice low. "But bottling it up does its own kind of damage. It cost me real connection, closeness. I'm so focused on not blowing up that I've built walls around the people I love. And the worst part? I know I'm doing it. I see it. But I don't know how to move forward or back. I'm just... stuck."

The silence that followed wasn't uncomfortable, just heavy. The kind that asked to be held, not filled.

After a beat, he sighed. "I'm sorry. I shouldn't have dumped all that on you."

She gave him a small smile, warm and knowing. "You didn't dump anything. I asked. You answered. And honestly? I'm honored you trusted me with it."

She looked out toward the dust, letting the moment breathe, then turned back to him. "Since we're being honest... I've had a pretty shitty time out here, too. Lonely. Off. I almost left a couple of days ago. Yesterday was the first day I stopped spiraling and actually reached out. Did something for someone else. Just little things. But it cracked something open. For the first time, I didn't feel like a ghost out here."

Emile let her words settle. Then, slowly, he nodded. "That's the kicker, isn't it? I've done so much out here, run events, built things, hosted the chaos. On paper, I've 'contributed.'" He made air quotes with a small, rueful grin. "But the whole time, I've kept a shield up. No vulnerability, no risk. Just execution. And anything that threatens that perfect little plan? Gets the fire."

They both sat with honesty, not fixing it, not rushing to soothe it. Just letting it be tender, messy, human.

She turned and looked at him. "I don't know about you, but I'm sick of hating myself for being what and who I am. I think that for the next leg of my journey, I'm just going to let me... be me. I don't know what will happen. But I do know that I won't feel so goddamn alone."

He stared at the ridge, saying nothing. She continued, "You have a partner that clearly loves you,, and you've assembled a talented, caring crew. I recommend that you don't fuck that up."

He coughed a laugh. "That's probably a good idea."

She began to put her food back into her backpack.

"I... I'm not sure how to do it," he admitted.

She took another long pull from his CamelBak and handed it back to him. He took it and held it close to him.

"I'm obviously short of wisdom. I haven't sorted my own shit. But," she nodded toward the temple interior, "spending some time there 'being real' might be a good start."

She stood up and did a quick scan of the area to ensure that she hadn't forgotten anything. She looked at him. "Can I get a hug?"

Emile stood up and wrapped her in a deep hug. Her usual reticence around men evaporated. They leaned into each other for a long moment. They leaned back, looking at each other.

"Thank you, Rachael. I won't forget your name again." He said.

"Thank you, Emile. I'm in your corner." She replied.

He nodded toward the temple interior. "Time to meet my reckoning."

She smiled. "Enjoy the pain. It helps."

She turned and walked along the vestibule, turning the corner of the temple's outer wall and back toward the city. Emile shouldered his CamelBak and turned toward the temple portal.

Time to get to work.

Camp Stella, BRC, 10:20 AM - Ruben

"Uh... I'm not sure that I'm up for this." Harley looked over his shoulder at Ruben and shot him a lopsided, knowing smile. He reached back, clapped Ruben on the shoulder, and held on. Lifting the tent flap with his other hand, he ushered Ruben through the threshold in one smooth motion. Despite Ruben's misgivings, he did not resist Harley. He was flying blind, trusting this man whom he did not really know well, but understood completely.

Inside, rows of chairs were set up auditorium-style, enough to seat thirty. About half were filled with burners; some were chatting, while others were silent. A few others lingered at a makeshift wet bar with a coffee pot and a water jug. Spotting the coffee, Ruben grunted in gratitude. Unclipping the mug from his backpack, he made his way over. Harley joined him but opted for the water.

Before Ruben could take his first sip, a woman at the front used her outside voice. "Welcome, everyone. Let's get started." The scattered crowd filed quickly into their seats. Harley and Ruben took chairs in the back. Ruben was surprised by how swiftly this unruly-looking group fell into quiet order.

The woman began as he settled in. "Thank you all for being here and taking care of yourselves this morning. Burning Man is a place of infinite distractions. You could be anywhere right now, lured by a million ways to hurt yourself. But you're here. Give yourself a round of applause." The crowd complied politely.

"Is anyone here for their first, second, or third AA meeting?" Ruben reluctantly raised his hand. She smiled warmly at him. "Welcome. We're here to support you in your sobriety." She clapped, and the group joined in. Ruben felt exposed. "You're welcome to share or just listen. Whatever supports you."

Then, "Anyone moved to share?" Harley rose and walked to the front.

"I'm Harley, and I'm an alcoholic."

"Hi, Harley," the group replied.

"I'll make this short and sweet." He paused. "Not a day goes by that I don't want a drink. I wake up hungry for it." His throat parched, he sipped from his jug. He held up his bottle.

"Water!" Chuckles bubbled up.

"When I drank, it was all that mattered. More than work, family, and friends. So I lost them all. My wife left, my daughter hated me, and my career crumbled. When I sobered up, there was nothing left. Not even me."

He took a breath. "This morning, I watched the sunrise with my dad. I kissed my girlfriend and daughter goodbye before walking here. I've built something I'm proud of. The one constant in it all is that I'm sober."

He turned and walked straight back to his seat. The applause followed him.

Beside him, a man with a serious expression had his long hair in a ponytail. He was dressed in a tank top, a rugged utilikilt with functional pockets, and sturdy Doc Martens. Ruben recognized him from the DPW. "Hi, I'm Scott, and I'm an alcoholic."

"Hi Scott," the group chorused.

And so it went. One after another shared. Eventually, the facilitator stood again. "We've got time for one more. Anyone have a burning desire?"

The room stilled. Harley leaned in and gripped Ruben's forearm. "It's why you're here, man."

Ruben shifted, uncomfortable. He blinked slowly, exhaled deeply, then stood. The short walk to the front stretched like forever.

He faced the group. "I'm Ruben, and I'm an alcoholic and drug addict."

"Hi, Ruben!" the group responded with warmth.

He stared at his shoes, silent. Then he looked up. "This is the first time I've said that out loud. That I fucked up my life by keeping myself fucked up." He paused. "I just got out of prison a few weeks ago. DNA evidence exonerated me. I didn't do the crime, but I deserved the sentence."

He swallowed. "Could I get some water?"

Harley stood and tossed his water bottle in a perfect spiral. Ruben caught it, surprising himself. He drank.

"A lifetime ago, I had a booming business, a girlfriend, and a decent life. But the partying outweighed everything. My girlfriend was at her limit, yet she threw me a birthday party. I got wrecked... drunk, high, wired on meth and coke. That night, I insisted on driving my brother home. She tried to stop me. I peeled out, flipping her off."

He took a breath. "We were having a great time. We always laughed. He was so damn funny. Especially when we were high.

It was raining, always raining in Portland. I didn't know how fast I was going when I hit the bridge. Then it didn't matter. We hydroplaned. I lost control. The rail gave way. We flew. Then came the river. Cold, hard, wet.

I woke up underwater, blood in my eyes. I somehow managed to get free and reached for my brother. His head was through the windshield. Water was pouring around him. I pulled and pulled, but the glass shredded him. The harder I tried, the more I tore him apart. And then... the air was gone.

I got the door open. I swam, then drifted. Eventually, the current let me go.

I lay by the river until I sobered up enough to feel it. He was gone. I had killed him."

Ruben paused, trembling.

"I went on the run. Hitchhiked south. Got lost in drugs. I didn't care. I just kept numbing myself. Drifted like trash.

Eventually, I borrowed a car. It had been used in a bank robbery. I got pulled over. They pinned it on me. I didn't fight it. Prison felt right.

Then I got out. Early. DNA cleared me. But not from what I did.

So here I am. No idea what's next. But I can admit this, I'm a fucking addict. I've ruined lives. And for my sins, I'm at Burning Man."

He stood, silent. "I've been sober since I got locked up. But this is the first time I've said it aloud."

He walked back to Harley, who threw an arm around his shoulder and pulled him in. The group applauded.

The leader stood. "Let's recite the Serenity Prayer."

"God grant me the serenity to accept the things I cannot change..."

When it ended, the group dispersed. Ruben rushed for the tent flap, Harley trailing. They walked two blocks in silence before Ruben spoke.

"I don't feel better. I feel worse."

Harley waited, then replied. "It's not about feeling better. It's about climbing out of the hole. You made a heroic start."

"Fuck heroes," Ruben muttered. "I'll settle for human. And human still feels like a high bar. I've had no purpose for years. I've been flotsam. I still am."

Harley said nothing. Ruben walked on, heavy with what he'd released. Neither man had any idea that the purpose Ruben was searching for would dick punch him before the next sunrise.

5:30 and Inner Playa, BRC, 2:23 PM - Cypher

Cypher watched the dust puff out from under his ratty sandals as he walked. Most of the playa was hard-packed and wind-swept, stingy with dust. But here, a rare patch of soft, powdery ground clung to his feet. Bicyclists veered around it to avoid bogging down, but Cypher shuffled straight through, undeterred, eyes still on his feet. He pressed on with no particular destination, each step slow and deliberate. A clod of dust tumbled ahead of him onto firmer ground as he emerged from the soft stretch.

He considered looking up. But nothing above his feet felt urgent. His shoes lifting and falling had become his whole world. He let himself drift, lost in thoughts of the maze and the strange visions he couldn't quite shake.

He didn't notice the crowd lined loosely across the playa. By sheer luck, he passed through it without collision, their voices dim echoes on the edge of his awareness.

But he *did* hear the scream.

It was shrill, sudden, a victory cry whipped by wind. A woman on a bike soared past him, missing his face by inches. She was topless, both arms raised in triumphant salute as she tore down a corridor formed by the gathered crowd.

Cypher looked up, startled. The scene snapped into focus.

He stood dead center in a gauntlet. On both sides of him, unbroken lines of burners stretched across the playa, cheering. And now, bicycles barreled toward him.

He blinked. The confusion came with urgency.

Still, instead of fleeing, he simply adjusted his posture. He turned slightly, drew in his elbows, trying to make himself smaller. The first wave of bicycles whooshed past him. He stood frozen.

Fast-moving, laughing, bare-chested women surrounded him.

"Critical Tits! Wooooo!" one rider shouted, pumping both fists as she passed.

Cypher slowly raised his arms in response, an improvised gesture of tribute. He closed his eyes and let the cyclists flow around him. Wind, laughter, heat, dust. The smell of sun-warmed skin and sunblock. The sound of joy in motion.

Again, a creeping sense of belonging to something larger began to emerge, echoing that feeling he got from the bunny march, but louder. He didn't know what that *something* was. Did not know how he'd joined it. But at that moment, it didn't matter.

The feeling was rushing toward him at speed. He surrendered to it. Floated in it. Determined to hold on for as long as it would let him.

Gordian Knot, 8:30 and Esplanade, BRC, 6:23PM - Crawford

Crawford checked his watch – 6:23.

Just over an hour to eat, get ready, and catch the art car.

He moved through the common area, headed to the RV to replenish his water bladder. The space buzzed with energy. The volunteer dinner crew was in its final prep stages. Campmates clustered around tables in various states of getting ready for the night. Excitement crackled in the air. The Man would burn tonight.

"Want me to embroider your face?"

Crawford stopped mid-stride, reflexively checking his just checked watch. He scanned for the voice. The words sounded like a threat, but the tone was warm. A theatrically adorned woman sat in a camp chair beside a folding table covered in glow-in-the-dark fluorescent body paints.

"How could I turn down being one of your pieces of art, Tallulah?"

He dropped into the nearest camp chair, leaning back and letting her work.

"Are you closing the maze for the burn?" she asked as she began.

"I was going to, but it was empty when I checked. Doubt we'll get any traffic during the burn. No real reason to close her. And, really, this is the last night. The maze only has a few more hours to go before she is no more." He exhaled. Her brushstrokes were precise and cool on his skin.

"This is my first burn, everyone seems excited. What should I expect?" Tallulah asked, the slightest angst in her tone.

"The week has been all foreplay. Tonight is the big metaphorical orgasm," Crawford replied with a slight grin. It was not the first time he had trotted out the trope. "If you haven't found a catharsis out here yet, tonight's your best shot."

"Are you doing any drugs tonight?" she asked.

"Nah. Drugs are for the good times. I'll take my tragedy sober." He thought he sounded noble, stoic.

They sat in companionable silence while she filled in more delicate filigree.

"What time do you start the takedown tomorrow?" she asked.

"Around one. We need to let everyone recover from tonight's fun." He was not thinking of the camp. He was thinking about himself.

"Done!" she said brightly.

He looked into the mirror she held out. The delicate lines danced across his cheekbones like neon lace.

"Nice," he said, meaning it.

"Dinner?" Millie appeared in front of him, holding out a plate and a fork.

"Thank you." He accepted the meal, surprised by the small kindness. For a moment, he imagined a life where this sort of treatment was a given. He ate quickly, the food passing through him without much notice. He felt the pull of the night building.

He looked once again at his watch - 7:15.

Fifteen minutes. Got to get my shit together. I have an art car to catch, and I'm not about to be late.

He stood up and aimed for his RV. "Brownie?" Millie asked, holding out a large cake.

He smiled. "Don't mind if I do."

Sparkleville, 3:15 and Chakra, BRC, 7:27 PM - Rachael

The brakes squealed as Rachael brought her bicycle to a halt. The bike's brakes had grown increasingly stiff and cranky over the week. *Much like my joints,* she thought wryly.

She stumbled off the frame, buzzed just enough to make balance elusive. The kickstand groaned beneath her boot. Bicycle maintenance was in her future. The week had been its own version of a fitness program... movement, effort, sweat, repeat.

She slung her tote bag over one shoulder and threaded through a ragged gap in the thicket of tents and vehicles. The path had been all but swallowed. As she emerged from the narrow passage, she had to sidestep quickly to avoid a collision. She caught the figure by instinct, arms outstretched, stabilizing them both.

A flustered Elise looked up at her from the impromptu embrace. "Hi."

"Nice running into you. Literally," Rachael smiled.

"Leon said you might come by tonight," Elise said.

"Might? The man hedged his bets. I told him I'd be here for dinner and the burn." Rachael's tone was half-playful, half-chiding with a note of defensiveness mixed in.

"Uh-huh," Elise replied. "Thou doth protest too much."

Rachael smirked but let the moment pass. She had a hunch Elise had talked to Bea. But this was as confrontational as Elise got. "What've you been up to today?" Elise asked with her trademark segue.

"Take me to the common area and I'll tell you on the way."

They walked side by side, navigating the cluttered terrain. "I woke up saying 'yes' to everything. Rode out after breakfast and stopped at every camp offering something. I met more people and drank more booze than the rest of the week total. I got a foot massage, witnessed a slave auction, don't ask, and had a flower painted on my boob." She tugged her top aside to reveal petals radiating from her nipple.

"That's so pretty," Elise said.

"Thanks. I can't take credit... I just said yes."

"That seems like a leap from where you were earlier in the week."

Rachael paused. "Maybe," she said, softer now. It wasn't just the experiences. It was that she'd allowed herself to be seen, put herself out there.

In the common area, half the camp was gathered for dinner made from leftovers. Bea was notably absent. As Rachael rinsed her borrowed plate, Leon approached.

"Hey, can you come with me to my van for a sec?"

Curious, Rachael followed him to his "throne area."

"A few of us are going to roll tonight," he said.

"Roll?"

"MDMA. Ecstasy. You in?"

"I've never done it. What should I expect?"

"It comes on slow, maybe forty minutes. Then you'll feel good. Connected. Just stay hydrated and you'll be fine."

"That actually sounds... nice."

Leon handed her a small pill. "We're timing it to hit perfectly as the burn starts – around 9:30. Take it in twenty minutes. They don't fuck around. That Man goes up hard."

She fingered the tiny pressed pill, her hand shaking slightly as a thrill rushed through her body.

Am I really ready to let go like this? For the first time in my life.

She felt her heart race. Was it excitement or fear? Were those just two different words for the same feeling?

Her watch said 8:30.

An hour from now, I'll be flying in the cosmos. Who knows who I will be on the other side?

3:00 and Beatific, BRC, 8:13 PM - Justine

"We're less than ninety minutes out from the Burn," Susan noted. Then she added, "Fifteen minutes away from fire spinning. Better keep those little legs of yours in motion."

Susan leaned into Justine, looping her arm through Justine's elbow. Their height difference made it awkward. Susan's statuesque frame was made even more dramatic by her platform boots, putting nearly a foot and a half between them. They switched around, Justine linking her arm through Susan's instead. Both giggled.

Brandon and Max walked ahead of them, just far enough that Justine could not make out their conversation. They too were giggling, though Justine knew the mushrooms had a hand in that. As she watched the men, more people joined their slow-moving procession toward the Man.

"The boys are having a good time," Justine noted.

Susan chuckled. "They are enjoying the pretty, pretty lights."

"When we get out to the Man, I'm going to have to leave you to it. I'm running late and Sasha is going to be pissed," Justine said.

"So you are saying that Sasha will be Sasha then," Susan replied.

Justine snorted. "You could say that."

As they passed the Esplanade, they saw people and art cars pouring toward the Man from every direction. It was as if the entire city had tipped, sending everyone out toward the burn.

"I went to the temple this morning," Justine said, almost casually. No emotion in her voice.

"Oh yeah?" Susan asked. "Did you have something to mourn?"

"I didn't think I did. I just went for the experience." A beat. "Turns out I was wrong."

Susan looked at her, but Justine kept her eyes forward. They walked in silence for a moment. Susan waited, not pushing.

"Turns out I'm mourning the lack of a normal, loving childhood. Specifically, not knowing my dad," Justine said flatly. "I have daddy issues." She turned to Susan. "And no, I won't be bringing home older men."

Susan laughed.

"I had no idea that was a thing for me. It's not like I ever think about it. Apparently, Burning Man has moved around my emotional furniture and found a hole in one of my mental walls," Justine said. "And now I feel embarrassed and disgusted with myself for being wrapped around a pole with high-class white girl problems."

Susan exhaled a long, steady breath. "Dude, judging the stuff that comes up does not make it go away. It just layers judgment on top of pain. If that is what you are facing, then that is the work in front of you."

They walked another few steps.

"I think this is the first time I have seen you not fully scheduled and locked in. I am not surprised something would come up when you finally have a breather. I am, however, surprised it has to do with your dad. I don't think I have ever heard you mention him."

"Not much to say. I never knew him. He died before I was born," Justine replied, like she was reading it off a newswire.

"Really? What happened?" Susan asked.

"Apparently, he drove off a bridge and drowned. I think he had been drinking. His brother died too."

"Jesus. That is horrible."

"It's not real for me. It's the story my mom told me. Kind of a pre-origin story. He was never part of my life. Not even as a hole. My stepfather held the title of shit-dad like it was a family heirloom."

Susan smiled. "Okay. I forgive you, then."

Justine offered a wan smile. "At least one of us has. I don't even know what to do with this. How do I get closure on something that was never in my life to begin with?"

The question hung in the air between them like an uninvited guest.

They had reached the outer ring of art cars. Susan raised her head and squinted. "Girl, I see spinners flaming up. You'd better get your ass in gear. You are going to have to crowd-surf your way into the fire circle. Go."

Justine stopped, pulled Susan in toward her. "Love you, babes." She hugged her and kissed her cheek. Then she broke into a trot, running past the boys and into the mass ahead. She pushed through the crowd, instantly claustrophobic; the press of bodies, the heat already building, bass lines colliding. It was like cutting her way through a human jungle. Even with a forced progress bordering on rude, her progress was glacial. Her anxiety, building sweat, and anticipatory adrenaline took hold.

3:30 and Chakra, BRC, 8:17 PM - Cypher

Large clots of ebullient people streamed past Cyper heading toward the Man. The city is emptying itself onto the playa for the big event. Cypher padded down the street, heading the wrong way on a mission to find a porta-potty. He wanted to make sure he was unburdened before making his way out to the big celebration. Uncharacteristically, he was lost in thought. The battle between the old man and the warrior monk had been circling in his mind all day, surfacing into consciousness, then drifting back into the depths. He felt like they were still fighting. For him. For his soul. And he was grasping for some solid ground to stand on. But it kept slipping away in the noise around him.

"My friend, could you use a meal?"

Cypher turned to see a man holding out a plate of food. "We had extra from dinner," the man said by way of explanation. "If you like, we can sit over here, chat, and you can eat."

Cypher looked past the man to where he gestured. A couch was positioned behind a burn barrel.

"Yeah, I could eat, for sure," Cypher said, taking the plate. The pair walked to the couch. The man pulled a dinnerware set wrapped in a napkin from his pocket with a flourish. Cypher took it, and the man flopped onto the couch with a self-satisfied grin.

"My campmates call me Tater Trash," he said.

"Cypher," Cypher mumbled through a mouthful.

"Happily met, my friend. How's your burn?" Tater asked.

Cypher chewed thoughtfully. "I was just thinking about that. Highs and lows, man. Highs and lows."

Tater Trash laughed. "Ain't that just Burning Man?" It didn't need an answer.

Revelers whooped and rang bicycle bells as they passed by. Art cars blaring every genre of music rumbled by, leaving the smell of fuel and stale exhaust in the air. It seemed like the city was purging itself.

"Most of the week, I felt like I was making this place my bitch. Now I feel road-worn. Like maybe I got it all wrong."

"There's no right way to burn, my man. But things sneak up on you. It's like standing in front of a giant parabolic mirror. You can't get away from yourself."

Cypher nodded slowly. "Before I came out here, I thought I had life figured out. Now I feel like I'm at a crossroads. Do I choose the path that I know... or do I choose..."

He paused, searching for something vague and heavy.

"...people."

Tater Trash's tone shifted, softened. "Yeah, man. This place can restore your hope in humanity. But what you do with that hope,... that's on you."

Cypher nodded again, chewing in silence. He was shoveling the rest of the food into his mouth now. He needed to get moving.

Seeing him finish, Tater held out his hand for the plate. Cypher handed it over, swallowed, and wiped his mouth with the napkin. He rewrapped the silverware and passed it off, too. Then he stood, stretching. Tater rose and gave him a one-armed embrace.

"Have a good burn, man. And good luck with that crossroad."

"Thanks," Cypher said, already turning.

He resumed his walk toward the portos. As he approached the blue-green wall of toilets, he reached into his pocket, pulled out the little pill pouch he had carried for days. It was his only possession that had survived unscathed.

He dropped the toilet paper strips into his palm, almost weightless. He stared at them, pausing as if on a precipice. The old man and the warrior tugged at him in opposite directions, so that he could not reconcile. He needed a guide who could break the tie.

He popped one of the strips into his mouth... one. He tasted the lightly bitter chemical taste immediately.

Then he popped a second one into his mouth... two. He took a step forward, sliding in another... three. Each step added yet another four, five, six, seven, eight. He looked up at the approaching porta-potties, then continued – nine, ten, eleven. He stared at the lone strip in his hand. He smiled and tossed it in after the rest. Twelve.

Challenge accepted. Time to choose a path. When the Man burned, dissolving back into the dust, so would he.

The Man and 10:00, BRC, 8:34 PM - Emile

Dobbs eased the bus into its position, maneuvering smoothly as usual. The music was joyful, inspiring, and dance-worthy. Shimmer had the helm as DJ.

Magrathea had a full load of revelers. Liam stood alone, leaning against the rail of the top deck. He looked toward the Man. The fire spinners had not started yet.

Emile made his way through the crowd and leaned against the rail, looking at Liam. The swell and roar of forty thousand Black Rock City citizens swept up in the inevitability of the impending shared moment. Magrathea's sound system had competition firing from all directions a fusillade of dissonant beats and melodies, meeting in a cacophony that trumped any of the week's earlier offerings.

"Hey." The music drowned out his greeting. Liam was impassive, anger and caution glinted in his eyes.

Emile raised his voice to just below the yelling threshold. "Can we step off the bus and get away from the noise. I'd like to talk, if you're willing to listen."

Liam glanced at Emile again, this time skeptically. He held his position for a moment, then nodded. The two of them made their way down the spiral stairs and out the open doors.

They walked in silence, letting the distorted thump of overlapping art car sound systems fade behind them as they moved away from the gathering. A hundred yards out from the ring, near the city side of Magrathea, they stopped beside the giant eagle sculpture, wings outstretched in mid-attack, every feather made of tarnished pennies. It loomed over them like a witness.

Liam crossed his arms, guarded.

"I know I've been an ass this week," Emile admitted.

Liam blinked, surprised. His arms fell to his sides. "*This* week?"

Emile gave a short, self-aware smile. "Fine. My assholery is not a limited-time offer. But this week... this week's been the peak. The full deluxe edition."

Liam exhaled hard, rubbing his hands down his face. "Well, at least you're not trying to turn yourself into a victim."

"I'm not," Emile said. "I see it. I see what I've done to you. To the crew. The more I let go, the more they rise. They're killing it out there with Magrathea. They don't need my perfectionism. They just needed space."

Liam nodded slowly, still silent.

Emile took a breath, searching for something real to hold onto. "I don't have all the language for it yet. But I've been thinking hard about what's been driving me. The anger. The control. The performance. I hide behind a persona because I'm scared that if people really see me, they'll leave. I never figured out how to be fully myself and be safe."

He hesitated, then pressed on. "There's still so much in me that's unresolved. My parents. My upbringing. The part of me that thinks I have to earn love by outshining everyone else in the room."

Liam shook his head. "You focus so hard on what's broken, you miss what's beautiful."

Emile's throat tightened. He nodded. "I know."

The irony of the moment did not pass him by. All around them, the city was gathering to watch something burn. He was trying to save something instead.

He stepped closer, lifted his hands gently to Liam's face, holding him like something both fragile and essential. His voice dropped, raw and clear.

"I don't know how to love you the way you deserve, not yet. I'm still learning how to love myself without conditions. But I do know one thing, Liam... I don't want to keep figuring this out without you. I don't want to keep building a life that you're not in."

Liam didn't answer with words. He simply reached up and laid his hands over Emile's. Held him there. The contact said everything.

And Emile finally did not pull away. For the first time in a long while, perhaps ever, he was completely present to Liam.

They stood in silence, eyes locked, as the wind carried the bass lines away and the playa softened the edges of the world.

But, even there, the boisterous moment took them. The gathering let out a cheer.

"That would be the fire spinners," Liam smiled. "Let's go watch them together."

The Man and 8:30, BRC, 8:36 PM - Justine

Justine stepped past the fire watch into the pressure cooker. Seven hundred spinners. One massive pyre. Mere minutes until ignition.

"You are late, bitch!" Sasha bellowed, arms crossed, chin raised with theatrical disdain. "We have just over forty minutes before combustion. Time to put on a show."

Justine did not flinch. "Yeah. Sorry. Where do you want me?" she asked, already scanning the circle.

Sasha jabbed a finger at a gap in the fire spinner line. "Introduce yourself to your team. You will be trading out when your fuel is exhausted. Figure out your rotation."

Classic Sasha. Bossy, belligerent, absolutely predictable. Justine found the familiarity oddly comforting. She looked up at the Man, dark, waiting.

Soon. Very soon.

She jogged to her spot and gave quick introductions to the spinners and fire watches around her. The energy was palpable, so many performers, so much heat and skill in one vast, breathing ring. It stirred something in her. Relief, maybe. Relief that her mind would be busy, that there was no space for introspection when the air itself would be humming with flame.

She crouched to prep her gear, dipping the wicks into the thick, dark fuel. The kerosene odor curled into her nose. She sneezed, hard.

"Guess that batch is potent," she muttered, half to herself, half to anyone listening. Someone chuckled nearby.

She conferred with the woman beside her. She was tall and sinewy, with a staff in hand. They worked out the order. Justine would go first.

She lit the soaked wicks with a torch. The flames roared to life, eager. Everything was ready. Everyone was waiting. The crowd in front of her cheered.

The heat brushed her face. She gripped the hoop on both sides, launched it into a spin, and caught it on her hip in one clean motion.

Game on.

She stepped into the circle, one of more than seven hundred dancers of flame, feeling the rush of fire and focus push the rest of the world away.

The Man and 8:00, BRC, 9:25 PM - Crawford

The Arabic chill music soaked the air around Crawford, muting the competing sounds from the other art cars in the distance. The brownie had done its work. His brain was muddy, slow, numb. He had chosen his seat deliberately — dead center in the passenger area, surrounded by velvet pillows and bathed in the low ambient glow of lantern light. The art car was arranged like a harem tent, a belled spire overhead, sheer sashes tied to uprights at each corner, everything swaying softly in the desert breeze.

On any other night, he might have leaned into the fantasy. Most of the passengers were women, and the setup practically begged for indulgence. But

Crawford was not feeling indulgent. Not tonight. His fall from grace still hung on him like smoke, visible, clinging, inescapable.

He barely registered the fire spinners taking their positions. The blur of torchlight and movement couldn't penetrate the weight in his chest. He was tipsy, just enough to notice, not enough to forget. He nursed the warm haze from a shared wineskin of Don Roberto Extra Añejo. The tequila dulled the edge, but the ache remained. His hypocrisy, in the face of his earlier resolve to sobriety, passed him by.

"Want an orange slice?" Millie offered him a dense little square.

He took it. "Thank you." Popping it into his mouth, he bit into it, chewing slowly, more out of habit than hunger.

Caleb leaned in close, grinning. "She would totally fuck you."

Crawford smirked and nodded like they were old conspirators. Then he turned and murmured back, "Too close for comfort. It'd turn into a mess."

The mighty had fallen. But no matter how far the fall, appearances still mattered.

Caleb chuckled, drifting back and pulling from the hookah between them. Crawford shifted his gaze to the fire spinners, bodies now blurring in arcs of flame. A long whoop escaped his throat, surprising even him.

"Burn the Man!" he shouted.

As if summoned, the Man erupted in fireworks. The fireworks didn't just sound, they punched the air. His chest cavity vibrated. The crowd's roar was a physical force. The entire playa lit up in bloom and thunder.

Crawford sat in the middle of it all, beautiful women, velvet pillows, sweet smoke, and tequila, feeling for a moment, completely untethered. This was too much. Way too much. But there was no stopping it now. "The Man was fully engulfed. Crawford watched from inside his velvet prison, beautiful and untouchable and completely alone.

The Man and 3:20, BRC, 9:38 PM - Rachael

The drug had been creeping up for twenty minutes. Now it slammed into Rachael all at once. She squeezed her eyes shut as the wave of pleasure filled her and took her away. Drums pounded like thunder as fire spinners blurred before her. Behind her, art cars blasted incongruent music into the sky. The Sparkleville crew had worked their way near the fireline, close enough to feel the heat when it came. The Man loomed tall and stoic, arms raised in celebration or surrender.

The buzz in her chest felt like carbonation. She slowed her breathing to let the swell come without panic. She wasn't sure if it was the drug or something deeper uncoiling inside her. Soaring, she was made of light. The fire wasn't outside her; it was inside her, always had been, finally free. She loved everyone. She loved herself, completely, warts and all.

Leon, Galetta, Zorgon, Paloma, a friendly new guy named Jaxon, and Rachael stood together, eyes wide, smiles warm, pulsing with chemical joy.

Fireworks exploded in starbursts. Flames licked the man's base, oily smoke curling upward. A hand slipped around her waist. Galetta. "How are you feeling?"

"So good," Rachael replied, sliding her arm around Galetta's back, surprised herself with how true it felt.

She leaned into Galetta, the warmth of her body unfamiliar but welcome. The fire rose, and so did she, waves of euphoria bursting through her chest, a blaze of light ripping through old trauma, fear, and doubt. She surrendered fully, finally. Just as the Man ignited, so too did she shed the parts of herself she had carried too long.

Her mouth felt strange. Dry.

When did that happen? What's going on?

Her tongue was thick. The music sounded far away. Why was everything tilting?

Then it hit her like a brick. "Fuck," she muttered. She was desperately thirsty.

No bag. No water. She'd forgotten it. Eyes wide, she turned. "I need water."

Leon handed her a bottle. She drained it in seconds. Then another from Galetta. Still not enough. Dehydration, from a day of drinking and little water, betrayed the moment. She had broken the most basic rule of both the playa and MDMA. Her vision blurred, and sounds muffled. The ground tilted.

The ground rushed up. The fire spun. Everything went sideways. She started to fall, and then, Leon's face was there, his voice cutting through the grey.

"Stay with me, Rachael. I've got you. Stay with me."

For a moment, she couldn't remember where she was. Who she was. There was only thirst and grey and the terrible feeling of slipping away. Then she caught the lifeline of his gentle, competent voice.

His calm gaze became her anchor, pulling her back from the grey. She clung to his voice, to the light he offered, inching her way toward clarity. Her body trembled. "I'm so thirsty," she whispered.

More water came. She drank. Slowly, the world settled. Leon's arm looped under hers, Galetta's joined on the other side. They guided her out of the firelight and into the dark.

The Man and 10:00, BRC, 9:52 PM - Harley

The Man's leg had fallen. The body was coming down any moment now. Harley felt blessed. But he also felt the week ending, the dissolution coming. This fleeting moment couldn't last. In this surreal world of flame and dust, he stood surrounded by those he loved most.

Clarence, Claire, and Cyan crowded in close. Around them, a raucous sea of burners pressed forward, art cars blaring their contribution to the moment. A wild wave rippled through the crowd of barely contained chaos. A woman kissed a stranger next to her. A loud wail broke out, reminding Harley that not everyone was having a transcendent experience.

They'd carved out a small pocket of stillness near the edge of the crowd. Harley knew Clarence did not want to push deeper into the crowd, both out of politeness and overwhelm, so they stayed back. Claire and Cyan flanked him, arms wrapped around his waist. Cyan's hand was clasped with Clarence's, a quiet bridge across generations.

In front of them, the Man blazed. Flames clawed upward, hungrily devouring the figure. It burned fast, hot, and alive.

Harley watched his little constellation of people more than he watched the fire. He felt impossibly wealthy. Not because of what he'd made. But because they were here with him, now.

"Thank you all," he said softly, "for sharing this moment with me."

Claire and Cyan both squeezed him tight. Clarence offered a small, private smile. The kind Harley rarely saw. Then Harley smiled to himself. The Man was not yet consumed. The night was just beginning. But he felt like he'd already given everything.

"I'm not used to giving speeches," he said. "Now I'm exhausted."

They all laughed, laughter lit by firelight, carried off by the wind.

The Man kept burning.

The Man and 4:00, BRC, 9:58 PM - Ruben

The DPW crew was generally a stoic crowd. So that they were relatively quiet while the crowd around them frothed was not a huge surprise to Ruben. Since he was a virgin, Thud, Sunshine, and Lenny had brought him out to the burn in a DPW truck. They had wedged their truck between two art cars so they could stand in the bed and watch the burn. His campmates were all smiling. They enjoyed watching things burn. "The Man ain't fuckin' around this year. He's burning to the ground." Thud growled. One of the legs cracked and fell into flames beneath the Man, prompting a sustained cheer from the crowd. The remains of the Man hung suspended in the air.

"This Man's not long for the world." Harnessed excitement punctuated Sunshine's declaration. "What are you doing tonight?" Lenny asked Ruben.

"I'll head back out to Ataraxis."

"That thing has you by the balls." Lenny needled Ruben. It was good fun, Lenny did not have a mean bone in his body.

Both men swiveled to the loud crack from the Man. The crack was enormous. The body teetered, suspended for one impossible moment, then crashed into the flames below. The crowd went feral, screaming in prolonged ebullience. The man was down.

Ruben had been building for weeks. Now he watched it all come down. Perfect. Necessary

"Another burn faithfully executed. Now let's get the fuck out of here before it's impossible to drive." Thud was done.

Ruben vaulted out of the bed over the side of the truck. He landed on the hard pack, spinning on his heel, and headed into the dark. He didn't say goodbye. Didn't wait for their response. He was already gone, already moving away from the light, the people, into the dark night, alone.

The Man and 6:00, BRC, 10:06 PM - Cypher

Cypher was no longer entirely human. He was energy and light and the beat of 40,000 hearts. The Man had collapsed, and the crowd was pressing in.

Cypher was over the moon. The world breathed. The fire had consciousness. Every face in the crowd was a work of art rendered from stardust.

He had taken the remaining twelve hits, not on a whim, but as a sacred ritual, a walkabout. The playa would show him which path to choose.

Now, with his ego dissolved, his body was electric with energy, and he floated on the ecstasy and excitement of the crowd, fire, and the rest of the elements.

As the mass began to shift forward, Cypher surged with it, weaving through the bodies. Ahead, the fire watch still held the line, holding back the wave as sparks and flames danced against the night. The crowd pressed with growing anticipation, momentum building like a wave.

Finally, the fire line dissolved, and the flood broke. Order became chaos. The wave broke, and Cypher broke with it, laughing, running, flying toward the heat.

People ran. Laughing, yelling, sobbing.

They streamed toward the pyre.

Cypher ran with them.

When the crowd reached the smoldering wreckage, it veered into motion, circling the remains. A wide loop of ecstatic reverence. Sparks traced geometric patterns in the air. The embers spoke in colors that didn't have names. His feet barely touched the ground.

This was a perfect moment for Cypher. He sprinted, legs flying, arms loose, breath wild.

He was circling the Man. Or at least, what was left of him.

Ash, ember, and the echo of fire. And maybe, if he let it, an answer.

He ran circles around the burning ruins, around and around, trying to outrun the question or run straight into the answer. He no longer could tell, nor did he want to.

Outer Playa and 12:30, BRC, 11:05 AM - Ruben

The music was a distant pulse now. Out here, darkness swallowed sound. Ruben was done running. Done hiding.

If grief wants me, it can fucking have me.

He drifted aimlessly at first, hoping the vast emptiness would swallow him. Eventually, he recalibrated to find a respite where solitude could hold him. Eventually, his meander led him toward the glow of soft, multicolored ground lights deep in the outer playa. From a distance, the low-profile shadows revealed little.

He wasn't sure what he needed, only that he needed to be alone. Since his confession at Camp Stella, he'd felt like a walking wound… raw, exposed, unsure what to do with the pain now that he'd stopped running from it. He was ripped open.

He hadn't enjoyed the Man burning. The thundering music and forced revelry grated on him. It all felt wrong. His grief had cracked wide open, regret pouring through like floodwater. He couldn't bottle it anymore, and for once, he wasn't trying to. So he wandered.

As he neared the installation, a faint sound began to emerge. A soft, rhythmic heartbeat beckoned. Solar lights outlined a wide fenced circle with a single opening. Inside was a meandering path, a peace-maze lit by dim LEDs that cast an otherworldly glow.

The maze's path was traced with old shoes. The shoes on the path looked like ghosts. All the people who'd walked this before him. All their pain, worn into the soles. Shoes worn with experience. Shoes that showed the way. At this moment, he needed them to guide him.

Ruben stepped into the maze and walked slowly, syncing breath to footfall. In and out. In and out. As the heartbeat grew louder, so did his awareness of the weight he carried. The path twisted gently. With each step, he imagined letting go. At the halfway mark, tears streaked his face. He didn't stop them. The dam had broken. He kept walking.

At the maze's center stood a low heart-shaped bench, carpeted and pulsing with the beat. Ruben lay down, the vibration rising through his back. The sobs came from a deep, primal place. His chest heaved. Snot and tears and no dignity left. He didn't care. He wept harder… deep, ugly sobs. He let it come, eyes clenched, throat raw.

For the first time, he saw his past with clarity. A question bloomed in the ache at his center, insistent, unresolved.

He whispered, "Now what?" He asked it three times. The heartbeat answered with nothing. Just rhythm. Just presence.

Sparkleville, 3:15 and Chakra, BRC, 11:44 PM - Rachael

She was sprawled in a camp chair, mortified. The shame sat thick in her throat. She had been sitting for thirty minutes. The shame was exhausting. Heavier than the dehydration.

Leon crouched in front of her, meeting her gaze.

"We're heading out. We're going to find music and enjoy the night. We'd love for you to join us."

She waved him off. "I fucked up. I ruined your burn. I didn't take care of myself."

Leon's gaze didn't flinch. "You do what you need. But if you want to come, we'd love to have you. You can come or stay. But you're not ruining anything by existing, Rachael."

She wasn't used to this. She'd spent her whole life proud of never needing anyone. Look where that got her. Alone in a camp chair, mortified, while people who barely knew her kept showing up. She had never leaned on anyone. But Leon had leaned in and had gently made himself her rock, without hesitation. He continued to extend an invitation to her. Something clicked. She nodded. What if she just trusted his good intentions and leaned in? "Okay. I'll come."

She stood, wobbly but determined. Her crew gathered, offering quiet squeezes of support.

"One sec," she said, and stepped away.

She doubled over, heaving. Liquid poured out of her, convulsion after convulsion. She purged everything. The shame. The fear. The story she'd been telling herself about having to be strong alone. It poured out of her onto the playa dust.

She wiped her mouth. Looked at their faces; warm, patient, waiting. 'Okay,' she said. 'I'm ready.' And for the first time all week, she meant it.

For once, she didn't feel like she had to explain.

She nodded, mostly to herself. Then again, she said, "I'm ready."

01 Spin After the Man Burns

Ataraxis Warrior, 11:00 and Outer Playa, BRC, 12:09 AM – Emile

Emile stood at the rail, taking in Ataraxis Warrior in its full fiery glory. People were streaming in from every direction. The last big party would be here. As if the sentient playa had transmitted it via dusty neurons, everyone knew this was the place to be.

Dobbs had placed Magrathea, positioning the bus to create a large 'dance space' between them and Ataraxis Warrior. For many of the burners gathering here tonight, this would be their last hurrah. Most camps would be breaking down on Sunday. Sunday night, the temple burns. Tonight was the last big night to cut loose, for those inclined. Emile wanted Magrathea to accommodate the city's last gasp of partying.

The bus was packed with revelers, so they arrived with a party starter pack. The crew moved like a single organism. Finally, after all the chaos of the week, they'd become something whole. They all drifted to their set-up positions without conversation. A few of the repeat bus partiers also pitched in, so the setup was completed in minutes. Sanjay took the DJ helm, immediately working his magic to ramp up the feisty crowd to a higher pitch of frenzy.

Owusu and his crew stumbled out of the bus to dance on the playa, giving Emile a chance to introduce him to Liam.

Emile and Liam walked around the bus, looking at the external setup. The crew was rock solid. They had everything covered. Satisfied that everything was as it should be, they wandered over to the Ataraxis Warrior control station to check in with Harley.

Harley smiled and waved as they approached. Harley looked *different*. Peaceful. Like he'd finally set something down. It took Emile's breath away. He yearned for that and admired Harley for finding it. It inspired Emile to find his own.

They hugged, and then Harley hugged Liam. "Quite the setup." Harley nodded toward Magrathea.

"That ol' thing." Demurred Emile with a sly smile. "Distance okay?"

Harley nodded in affirmation. "We're all good."

"Liam and I are going for a walkabout. We're in deep need of a playa honeymoon. After almost fucking things up with Liam, I'm not wasting another minute."

Emile's transparency made Liam's eyebrows raise. Emile could still surprise him.

"We'll be back in a bit." Emile said. "The crew will keep it tight."

Harley nodded. "I understand completely. I had a honeymoon myself yesterday." He hugged them both again.

As they walked out of the glow, Emile looked at Liam and said, "The playa relaxed the shit out of that man."

The crowd was building behind them. But out here, it was just the two of them and the stars.

Ataraxis Warrior, 11:00 and Outer Playa, BRC, 12:33 AM – Rachael

Rachael clung to Jaxon like a life preserver. She could not let go. Every time she tried, the ground tilted and she was falling again, drowning in grey.

Ataraxis Warrior loomed as they approached it. Leon and Galetta led the way just far enough ahead that Rachael could not hear their conversation. Zorgon and Paloma lingered behind, deep in their own conversation. Rachael had tucked her arm around Jaxon's elbow. She felt fine as long as she was touching someone. When she let go, she felt unmoored, out of control. Jaxon accommodated her as her grounding rod.

As they circled around the installation, the horse reared up to full height. The beast let out a rageful neigh. Fire shot a hundred and fifty feet into the air. The heat wave hit her face, and for a split second, she was back at the Man, collapsing, dying.

The crowd cheered. Leon put his fingers to his lips, letting out a piercing whistle. They merged into the dancing crowd midway between Ataraxis Warrior and Magrathea, working their way to the center of the dance area. Dropping their gear into a neat pile, they began dancing. With some trepidation, Rachael let go of Jaxon and peeled off her jacket, tossing it onto the pile.

This is insane. I'm barely holding it together. I can't just stand here touching Jaxon all night like a child.

She began to dance. At first, she felt awkward, out of sync with the beat, as if her brain was not fully connected to her body. Then, as she continued to move, she relaxed, surrendering to the music, letting her mind go. She felt the music flow through her, lifting her onto the melody. She gave up all pretense of control and let her body move through the crowd, letting her emotions express themselves through her movements. She felt a drop roll down one cheek, surprising her. Then another down her other cheek.

She felt a tremor in her chest rising, vibrating into her throat, her breath catching as it rose, then releasing slowly. She felt her emotional dam cracking, hairline fractures running across all her well-laid protections.

Then the dam exploded. The flood came unbidden, unstoppable. The fear, rage, and sadness rushed out of her all at once and into the night. Everything she'd been holding came pouring out.

Her movements became frenzied as she unburdened years of keeping it together. Then the howl came, primal, desperate, aching. It was an unfiltered roar of agony, lifetimes of empty, rageful pain.

She was sobbing and dancing and utterly exposed. And somewhere in the chaos, she didn't care.

Ataraxis Warrior, 11:00 and Outer Playa, BRC, 12:36 AM – Justine

Justine heard the howl. That sound. Raw. Desperate. The kind of sound you make when you can't hold it in anymore. She turned to see Rachael's frenzied movements. She turned back to the circle of her dancing crew and leaned into Susan. "I'll be back. I see the woman who saved me from that shitbird." She abandoned her crew mid-dance.

She made her way through the crowd, half dancing, half walking, making her way toward the manic dancer. She had to adjust her trajectory as

Rachael changed hers continuously. By the time she caught up to Rachael, they were close enough to feel the heat from the flames shooting up from Magrathea's flame garden basin.

Rachael's frenzy calmed as she danced, gazing at the flames and the stallion and warrior above. Justine approached from behind, reaching out and touching the woman's forearm. Surprised, Rachael looked first at the hand. Then she looked at Justine. Her face relaxed into a broad smile. She whipped around and embraced Justine, lifting her off the ground. No one had picked Justine up in joy since she was a kid. The spontaneity of it, the sweetness of it

Then, as if realizing what she had done, Rachael gently placed Justine back onto the playa and backed away sheepishly. "Sorry."

"Don't be sorry. I'm glad to see you, too." Justine responded. They moved into each other, Rachael wrapping Justine in a gentle bear hug. When Rachael eventually let her go, she slid back, holding Justine's hands. "How are you?"

Justine met Rachael's eyes. "I'm good. I'm performing on Magrathea for a bit."

"That's awesome. I can't wait to watch." Rachael said.

Justine cocked her head, looking at Rachael's broad smile and saucer-like pupils. "Are you rolling?"

Rachael nodded sheepishly. "Yeah. My first time." Christ. Of course it was.

"It kinda sucked earlier," Rachael continued. "But I'm feeling good now."

"Well, I'm glad I found you. Do you mind if I dance with you for a while until I need to go get ready to perform?" Justine asked.

"I'd love that," Rachael responded. The pair continued to dance, backlit by the flames.

They danced. Rachael had saved Justine. Now, Justine was returning the favor in her own way. This was not an act of reciprocity. It was an act of love.

Ataraxis Warrior, 11:00 and Outer Playa, BRC, 12:37 AM – Crawford

So much for being noble and stoic.

Crawford sat cushioned in the belly of an art car, watching it all from behind a pharmaceutical haze. He was numb from his mounting cocktail of shame–tequila, weed, and cocaine.

He gathered himself and slid off the harem art car. Caleb, Davey, and Millie, the intrepid remnants of the Gordian Knot campers, slid off the car, as well. The chill music from the harem art car was completely drowned out by the heavy beats from the Magrathea sound system.

The Gordian crew quickly made their way into the dancing crowd and set up a waist high gear pile, a mound of camelbacks, backpacks, coats, and sundry items. The crew set up a loose phalanx around the pile allowing them to keep an eye on their belongings while they danced. Trust knew bounds even with this crowd.

Crawford danced with Millie, not on purpose but because she was there. That was enough. He didn't have to pretend to care. He liked attention that required no effort on his part. Crawford surveyed the crowd as he danced, hoping to find a young hottie to distract him. Somewhere in this crowd was a pretty face that would help him forget the kid in the maze, forget Vicky, forget that he'd fallen so fucking far.

Ataraxis Warrior, 11:00 and Outer Playa, BRC, 12:39 AM – Ruben

Ruben circumnavigated the gathering to avoid the maddening crowd. He'd had enough of people. But this place, this *thing* he'd helped build, he could not stay away. He needed to be there as he needed to breathe.

As he approached, he studied Harley. The man was animated, hugging people as they approached him, smiling. The man who had been wound so tight all week was now... loose.

He slid quietly up to Harley's side. Not that he had to be quiet. The music was loud as hell. He was there for a few minutes before Harley noticed him.

"Hey, man! We've been missing you." Harley turned and clapped his shoulders, then wrapped his arm around Ruben's shoulders. He was surprised but appreciated the gesture.

"I'm happy that you're here," Harley said.

Ruben had not experienced this man emoting like this during the previous week. "I could do without the noise, but I can't imagine being anywhere else."

Harley chuckled and clapped Ruben's shoulders again. "Me too, brother," he said. "Me too."

Ruben watched Cyan work the controls. He leaned into Harley. "She's kicking ass."

Harley smiled and nodded. "That she is my friend." They stood quietly together for a while. Their mutual silence was a condition that brought both men comfort.

Ruben took in a long breath and leaned into Harley again. He had not intended to say it, but the words seemed to flow out of him of their own volition.

"Thank you for today," Ruben's voice cracked. "That was years in the making. I'm pretty sure that I wouldn't have made it through all that had you not been there."

Harley looked at Ruben and put his hand on his shoulder. The hand felt like an anchor. "I'll be there for you anytime, brother. Anytime." Ruben believed him.

They both looked out at the crowd. The two men who had spent the week hiding were now standing together in comfortable silence while the party raged.

Ataraxis Warrior, 11:00 and Outer Playa, BRC, 12:43 AM – Emile

Emile and Liam glided into the dancing crowd holding hands. They worked their way through the crowd and stopped not far from the flame garden under the warrior. Liam's hand in his. That was all that mattered. The rest of the week; the fights, the control, the performance, felt like someone else's life.

"Hey there." A hand on his arm, the touch electric. He turned to see Rachael. She was glowing. Whatever she was on, it was working. She looked free.

"Hey!" Emile exclaimed and enveloped her in a hug. When he finally released her, she pointed at Justine.

"I think you already know this one." She jerked her thumb toward Justine.

He gave the diminutive woman a warm hug. "Are you up for performing?"

"That's why I'm here." She smiled.

He grabbed both of them by their hands and pulled her over to Liam. "Liam, this is Justine, our tiny dancer. And this is Rachael. Rachael is the angel of my salvation, at the temple today."

Emile's gaze moved slowly from person to person. These people. Rachael, who'd saved him at the temple. Justine, who'd trusted him with her body and fire. Liam, who'd somehow stuck around through all his shit.

As they hugged, Liam whispered in her ear, "Thank you."

She whispered back, "My pleasure, really." When they released each other, she took them both by the hands and ushered them to her friends.

They formed a ring, hands linked. For a moment, they were a constellation. Emile's grin increased until he felt like it would swallow his face. This was what he'd been chasing all week. Not perfection. This. Connection. Presence. Being fully here with people who showed up.

Ataraxis Warrior, 11:00 and Outer Playa, BRC, 12:46 AM – Harley

Harley noted Cyan's exhaustion. She had been running the controls since they had made their way out there from the Burn. As he reached out to touch her shoulder, she craned around from the control panel. "Dad? I'm getting tired. Can you take over?"

"I'll do it." Ruben stepped forward. Cyan looked at her dad.

Harley nodded. "He'll do," he winked, a wry smile on his face. "He helped me erect the Warrior. He's my new best friend." He meant it.

She stepped out of the way. Ruben moved forward without hesitation. The man who'd been falling apart all week. Now stepping up. He stepped up to the control station and went to work.

"I'm heading back to camp with Claire." Cyan almost yelled in Harley's ear. "Don't have too much fun."

Harley shook his head, smiling at her. "I don't think you have to worry about that. I'll be happy for the silence when it comes."

She kissed his cheek. "Love you, Dad." Harley's eyebrows raised. When had she last said that?

"I love you, Jellybean." He resurrected the pet name for her that he had abandoned when she was young.

She smiled at him, her eyes soft.

As Cyan moved away from them, Harley let out a breath. His daughter was safe. His installation was running. A broken man at the controls, finding his way back to light, to life. Maybe he'd done something right after all.

Ataraxis Warrior, 11:00 and Outer Playa, BRC, 12:52 AM — Cypher

Cypher came into the light, all kinetic activation, pure emanation, a stellar wellspring of energy. He walked less into the party fray as much as floated. He had been drawn to this magical gathering from the ethers of the outer playa, as if drawn in by magnetism. He stopped briefly, vibrating as he surveyed the scene. "So beautiful!" The colors. The people. The love. It was all real. It was all true. He'd found the answer.

A passing dancer, clearly cued into Cypher's condition, placed a pair of cardboard diffraction glasses on the bridge of his nose and wrapped the earpieces over his ears. The world splintered into infinite beauty. Every light is a galaxy. Every face is a universe. Cypher beamed. He was home for the first time.

Movement retook his body, unleashing him to, for the first time in his life, dance. He shifted about in arrhythmic, almost spastic movements, arms waving akimbo, legs hopping about.

"We are all one!" he shouted. He convulsed into the crowd almost aggressively, working his way inadvertently toward the Ataraxis Warrior end of the festivities. Every few moments his new mantra erupted, geyser like. "We are all one."

His movements became increasingly erratic, almost violent, projecting indiscriminately without focus, as if he was being electrocuted. His body had become a vessel, at the mercy of a cosmic fountain, like a tube man writhing in perpetual ecstasy, a prophet of manufactured joy dancing his seizure-sermon, all gesture and no substance.

At a particularly lurching spin, the diffraction glasses went flying. In front of him was Ruben at the Warrior controls. "We are in love!" he screamed, loud enough for Ruben and Harley to look at him. They smiled and waved.

"Woo!" he let out an excited yell which erupted from his toes, as he careened back into the crowd, now with the benefit of unimpaired vision.

He continued thrashing through the crowd. Some dancers were annoyed, others took his slam dance stylings in stride. Everyone got out of his way. He was a force of nature at the moment, and like a tornado or hurricane, he just needed to exhaust himself.

He stumbled forward and caught himself on the lapels of the dancer in front of him. He looked up into Crawford's face.

Dude, you are tripping balls," Crawford observed.

Cypher looked up at the man, eyes filled with wonder. "The maze." Cypher responded exuberantly, clutching Crawford in an awkward embrace. Crawford patted his back. Cypher pushed off from the man on a new trajectory, continuing his zigzag through the dancers. He bound into an open space, realizing as he looked around that he was in the center of a dance circle. He got his bearings by looking around at the dancers. He was surrounded by most of the meaningful connections he had made this week – Rachael, Emile, Justine.

In the span of a few moments he had reencountered all of his Burning Man angels. Silhouettes of his community surrounded him. They were beautiful. *They are me and I am them.*

"We are all in love. Woo!", he shouted, accosting each of them like a deranged golden retriever. He lingered at the center for a few minutes, dancing with each person individually. Finally, he careened out of the dance circle and into the crowd. His heart was bursting with joy.

The music shifted to darker chords as "Combustion" by Dark Soho slowly cranked up.

As he moved into an open space, he looked up at Ataraxis Warrior. His erratic convulsions instantly stilling as he, body and soul, locked in communion with its majestic countenance.

The great horse bucked and reared. The warrior held on gracefully. Then both looked down at Cypher, flaming tears rolling down their faces. The flames seemed to pulse with urgency as the warrior, the beast, the fire itself became a chorus of voices thundering a single word command: "NOW!"

Cypher's hands began to shake. He looked down across the flame pond to see the old man, palms out, frantically signaling for Cypher to stay. Then he saw the warrior monk stride through the flame pond and step up to him, his form blazing with desperate intensity. "Come with me! Time is running out!" The monk's voice was commanding, almost threatening.

The old man shouted, "No! Don't listen!" He stepped forward first, firelight, from the flame pond, casting shadows across his weathered face. His voice softened, almost tender.

"Boy, you think survival is the same as living. You've learned to take what you need, to move through the world like smoke; untouchable, unaccountable. But look at what happened today. The people, these angels, gave to you freely. Not because you were clever enough to extract it from them, but because they *saw* you."

"It terrified you, didn't it? Because if they can give, then you must be capable of receiving. And if you can receive, then you're not the island you've convinced yourself you are. You're starving yourself on purpose, calling it discipline. You think needing nothing makes you strong. It doesn't. It makes you hollow. There's no transformation in a vacuum, child. Only echo."

The warrior monk struck his staff against a flame pond nozzle with a metallic scrape, like a blade being drawn.

"He offers you chains disguised as embrace. Dependence dressed as connection. You didn't come to this place to remain what you were; soft, compromised, bound by obligation. You came to shed that skin. Yes, they gave to you, and it unsettled you because you recognized the trap. Debt. Expectation. The slow erosion of self that comes from needing others. You feel the pull toward comfort, toward their warmth, and you mistake it for wisdom."

"But comfort is the enemy of greatness. Every master, every sage, every one who transcended, they walked alone first. The sacred shedding requires isolation. It requires hunger. Not because suffering is holy, but because it burns away everything that isn't essential. What remains is pure will. Pure self. The old man wants you tethered. I offer you wings."

The old man laughed, bitter and sad. "Wings to fly nowhere. Freedom without destination is just falling with style."

"And roots without sky," the warrior countered, "are just a prettier cage."

They both turned to Cypher, waiting.

The triumvirate chorus of voices from the Warrior thundered as if they were the Fates – Clotho, Lachesis, and Atrops – intervening.

"Choose your destiny NOW or become the dust you endure!"

With destiny in the balance, he despaired. His hands shook. His chest heaved. The choice was crushing him. He was sobbing. Both paths were real. Both paths were right. How could he choose?

The warrior's and the stallion's eyes bore into him, demanding an answer.

Then in a desperate hiss he exclaimed, "I'm coming." With that, he bounded into the flame garden.

The first step felt like victory. The second step felt like burning. The third step felt like dying. Searing pain shot through his extremities like lightning. The acrid smell of his own burning hair filled his nostrils. Suddenly, the wind was knocked out of him as he shot sideways. He landed on the hardpack well outside of the flame garden and rolled onto his back. Agony coursed through every part of his body.

Ataraxis Warrior, 11:00 and Outer Playa, BRC, 12:59 AM – Crawford

Every molecule in Crawford's body screamed STAY. The smell. The heat. The smoke. Then he saw the kid's face. Randall's face. And, almost against his will, he moved. Within three paces, he was at a full run. As he reached the flame basin he leapt, tucking his arms and legs as he hurdled into the flames.

The heat seared his forearms. The smell of burning flesh. He crashed into Cypher's lower back like a bowling ball mowing down a bowling pin. Both men hit the baked earth hard, Crawford tumbled, Cypher limp and unmoving.

Crawford rolled up onto his knees and looked down at Cypher, patting his smoking leggings. His hands were shaking. From adrenaline. From pain. From something else.

For a split second, self-preservation screamed at him to stay back. The smell of burning flesh made his stomach lurch. Then he saw the kid's face and instinct took over. Crawford felt the heat searing his forearms as he'd wrapped around Cypher's waist to drag him clear, but he pushed through the pain.

The young man was badly burned everywhere. His hair and pants smoked. Crawford patted down the smoking from his own singed pant legs, his hands shaking from adrenaline.

The flame columns in the flame garden sputtered and disappeared. Then the horse and warrior came to a rest, flame tears guttered and extinguished. Crawford looked over at the control panel. Harley was working furiously to shut down the operation. The music dropped off shortly after leaving the gathering in grim silence.

Rachael dropped down. Then Emile. Then Justine. Then Ruben. Their circle reformed around the gravely injured boy. Their faces pale with shock. Cypher stared at them, surprise in his eyes. Rachael patted down his smoking pants to make sure the fire was out, fighting back nausea at the smell.

The sound of Cypher's labored, rattling breathing filled the sudden silence. He was attempting to talk, but the only thing that came out were gargling, strangled sounds.

"Take it easy, buddy." Crawford said quietly, his voice steadier than he felt. Cypher lifted his head and craned around at the people who surrounded him. He dropped his head to the ground and smiled through his pain.

"My family." He smiled through agony. Those were his last conscious words.

The word echoed in the sudden silence. Family. He'd spent the week alone, scrounging, manifesting. And in his final conscious moment, surrounded by near-strangers, he'd found what he'd been missing all along

Shock and horror had forced sobriety on Crawford. He'd saved Randall, er the boy. He had pulled him out. And it wasn't enough. It was never going to be enough.

Ataraxis Warrior, 11:00 and Outer Playa, BRC, 1:12 AM – Justine

Red and blue lights strobed across their faces. Everyone looked like ghosts. The accompanying siren and honking drove the crowd out of the way. The party was over. The stricken Burners were dispersing. Magrathea had been silenced. Its crew gathered near its door, watching from afar. Ataraxis Warrior was dark, inert.

"Please step away from him." The deputy said loudly but calmly as he approached.

"He's unconscious." Rachael said as they backed away, her voice shaky.

"Does anyone know if he was on anything?" asked the deputy.

"Not sure what it was, but he was definitely tripping." Crawford said.

"Thanks." Said the deputy as he started checking vitals. Other emergency vehicles pulled into the area.

Two paramedics dropped their kits and went into assessment mode as the deputy stepped back. "He's got a weak pulse and labored breath."

The paramedics cut away his pants and lifted Cypher onto a stretcher. They hurried him into the ambulance. One of the paramedics keyed his radio. "We're going to need an air ambulance. We have a patient in critical condition with burns over eighty percent of his body."

The grim reality rippled through the group. The odds of Cypher surviving were slim, perhaps nonexistent.

The paramedic slid into the ambulance driver's seat, closed the door, and put the ambulance into gear. The ambulance pulled away. Cypher was now in professional hands, leaving this strange collection of people to their own collective company. They sat together, each lost in their own thoughts.

The deputy approached the group. "I'm going to need to interview you. Stick around for the time being." He pointed at Crawford. "You saved him, right?"

Crawford nodded numbly, his gaze unfocused. "I'll start with you. Come with me."

Crawford pushed himself up and followed the deputy. The rest continued to mill together. Conversation was limited to checking in with each other. One by one, they were called over to the deputy's cruiser. Crawford disappeared after his interview. The rest returned to the shellshocked group, each seeking quiet solace in their shared grief. Dobbs, after checking in with Emile and Liam, drove Magrathea and crew back to base camp.

The other crews also left after checking in. Interviews took over an hour. The emergency vehicles peeled off one-by-one. Eventually, Harley, the last of them to be interviewed, returned to the group as the deputy pulled away. The group looked up as he approached. His face was aged with sadness.

They stared at each other in the dim ambient glow given off by Harley's installation marker lights. Justine started to turn away, overwhelmed by the night's trauma, when recognition hit her. She stopped and looked back at the burly man.

"Weren't you the guy I passed in the maze?" she asked.

"Yeah, I'm Ruben," he said.

She nodded. "Justine."

Justine, suddenly feeling exhausted, rubbed her face, leaving dust smudges across her cheeks.

"You smeared dirt across your face," Ruben said, offering her a wet wipe.

She took it and looked up at him. "Thank..."

Something caught her eye. A flash of blue at his throat. She stopped, looking closer.

No. It couldn't be...

Her hand moved to her own necklace without conscious thought.

Confusion creased Ruben's face as she froze in disbelief. Then his face fell as he reached for his own pendant. They stood in silent understanding. Neither spoke. Neither needed to.

The two halves. Together. After twenty-three years.

"Shit," he muttered. They were both quiet for a moment, looking at each other.

His knees buckled slightly, and his hand reached instinctively toward her. After a long frozen moment, she finally breathed out in only a whisper, "Dad?..."

The word felt foreign in her mouth. The siren faded. The world tilted. Everything had changed.

Gordian Knot, 8:30 and Esplanade, 6:17 AM - Crawford

Crawford leaned back against the RV bench, staring at the ceiling. He had been staring at the ceiling since he returned from Ataraxis Warrior. Had not moved. Did not want to.

A tentative knock at the door irritated him. He ignored it. But the rap came again, louder this time.

"Come in," the frustration in his tone made clear the visit was not welcome.

Millie stepped inside but stopped on the steps. "Bad night?"

He looked at her briefly, then back to the ceiling. "Yeah. Bad night."

"You want company?" she asked, her voice soft, cautious.

He drew a long breath and let it out slowly, eyes still closed. "No. I'm not in good company right now."

"You're marginal company at your best," she said as she kicked off her boots and slid into the nook at the far end.

She wasn't leaving. Of course, she wasn't leaving. Nobody ever left when you needed them to. People only left when you needed them.

"You're really hurting about that kid. Did you know him?" she asked.

"Isn't serious injury and likely death enough?" he retorted evasively, sarcasm dripping off the response.

Silence hung in the space between them. He did not want to be prodded. He felt flayed open.

As usual, Millie was not cowed. She stared at him, waiting. She had smelled the rat.

With an exasperated sigh, he relented. "I barely knew him. I pulled him out of the maze the night before last and gave him some food. He seemed... lost. On multiple levels."

"Got ya," she said. Then, gently, "Why's it hitting you so hard? And why did you risk your life?"

He rubbed his face with both hands, smearing what was left of the face paint.

"He reminds me of my little brother, Randall."

Millie paused. "I didn't know you had a brother."

"He's dead." The words came out flat, final.

She said nothing, just waited.

Eventually, the silence became too loud.

"Randall killed himself as a teenager. My parents were... overbearing. Awful really. Continuously disappointed in us. I left. I made my own way. Fuck them. But, he was weak... ill-equipped. He couldn't deal with them. Spiralled. And, I wasn't there for him." Crawford's voice dropped. "Even though he begged me to be."

He sighed, "This kid tonight was a lot like him, underequipped, even looked a bit like him. I couldn't save him either."

"Fuck, Crawford. That's horrible." She reached across the table and gently squeezed his hand.

"This hasn't been my best week," he muttered.

"No shit. I'm surprised you're still standing. Says something about you."

A faint, wry smile tugged at his lips. "Still standing. That's all I do. Stand and watch people fall."

They sat in silence for a long time. The RV creaked softly in the wind. Eventually, Millie stood and gathered herself.

"Get some sleep, Crawford."

She shut the door behind her with a soft click. Crawford kept staring at the wall, unmoving.

Sleep did not come. Only memories and ghosts. Randall's face. And, Cypher's burning.

DPW Ghetto, 3:10 and Avatar, 8:06 AM - Justine

Dawn found them still walking. Ruben and Justine had circled the entire city, saying everything and nothing... Their circuitous route passed the city's highlights. Neither noticed. They spent their walkabout awkwardly revealing themselves to one another.

Both came to the conversation unprepared and unarmed. Two introverts. Two damaged people. Trying to build something from wreckage. Ruben, for his part, struggled with an atrophied capacity to share himself vulnerably, each confession an exhausting, Sisyphian struggle. The evening's events and unexpected introduction had robbed Justine of her trademark sarcasm. Honesty, without her standard joust and parry approach, left her off balance, graceless in her delivery. The conversation was clunky, filled with long pauses, and the most real thing either had experienced in a very long time.

As they passed the Opulent Temple sound camp, Ruben said, "When I drove off that bridge. Both my brother and I died that day."

As they passed under the branches of the music tree, Justine observed, "My stepdad was shit. But at least he was there." Ruben winced involuntarily, shot through by the implication.

At the penny-eagle, Justine kept shaking her head in disbelief and awe as Ruben traced his aimless nomadic wanderings, taking on pickup work from construction to ranchhand to death-cleaning.

While they rested on the bench swing at the hallucinogenic city hall installation, Justine admitted, "I keep myself so busy to avoid introspection. I don't like what I see when I look at myself. I'm not even sure that I enjoy performing."

While Ruben showed Justine Gaia Unboundried, he admitted, in a shame-laced tone, "While I'd like to think I would have done things differently had I known about you, in reality I've been barely human until a few weeks ago."

When Justine showed Ruben the spot where Rance, but for Rachael's intervention, had nearly had his way with her, she squeezed her eyes shut in vivid memory, saying, "It was so close, razor thin that I walked away." Ruben's chest spasmed as he choked back tears. When he could talk, he let out a strained utterance. "It's all so fragile. We might have never met."

As they passed by a now gutted Xaraland, Ruben let out an anxious, exasperated, "I have absolutely no idea what comes next."

Ruben had shared his life with her, including his shame, his regret. She in turn, had shared her life of emptiness and joyless focus with him. Now, as they approached the DPW Ghetto, they were physically, mentally, and emotionally, spent. Fatigue cloaked them both.

"Do you want to come in, hang out in our living room?" Ruben asked her as they approached the plywood structure.

"Thanks. But I'm pretty done. And, I think I can finally sleep," she said.

He nodded, then cast his eyes down at the playa. After a moment, he brought his gaze back up to meet hers. "No words are going to make up for what I did, my absence, my failings. No words can articulate my regret for not knowing... "

"Stop." She held up a hand, cutting him off. "Just... stop." She stared at him, her eyes burning. "Neither one of us has whatever it will take to deal with an apology or what it means right now."

She let out a sigh. "We have the rest of our lives to deal with that." She paused, then said, "That is, if you plan on dealing with it."

Ruben felt like he had been gut-punched. There it was – the question that was birthed at the moment that each touched their pendants.

Are you going to be around Ruben? Or, are you still a tumbleweed?

He looked down the street into the distance, saying nothing for a moment. Then he locked eyes with her for the first time. "It would be the peak of hypocrisy to make you any promises."

His stomach wretched. Then he continued. "But I can tell you two facts that are as real as the playa we are standing on."

He paused, wrestling with how to express the thing he needed her to know.

"I'm done running. And, you're the first thing in twentythree years that's calling me to be something more than a piece of shit."

She stared back hard, as if trying to divine some deeper truth. Finally, she nodded. "I'll take that."

The tension that had gripped them vaporized like mist into the bone-dry air.

She side-eyed Ruben, then smiled at him. It was a weak indication that she might not hate him. "I'm going to take off. I need some downtime to work through everything that has happened in the last several hours, several days frankly." She turned and took a few steps away from Ruben. Then she turned and looked at him. "It might help to have a few conversations with my dad along the way."

The word felt weird. Foreign. But maybe... maybe it could become real.

Ruben's shoulders relaxed. "I've literally got nothing but time for you. Whatever you need. Whenever you need it."

"Good." She said evenly. She turned and headed back up Avatar.

She walked away. He watched her go. They'd found each other. And now they were learning how to exist in the same world.

Gordian Knot, 8:30 and Esplanade, 1:22 PM - Crawford

"The maze came down fast. The crew's muscle memory took over as everyone worked in silence. The speed surprised even Crawford. The crew had been at it for just over two hours, and all upright structures were now down and sorted into tidy piles of materials.

Jimmy pulled off a glove and slid his thumb and middle finger between his lips. The shrill whistle turned every head in the crew his way.

"Let's take a break before we load the truck," he called out. As one, the crew dropped what they were doing and drifted toward the shade of the common area.

Crawford followed, but paused when the satellite phone on his hip buzzed. He unhooked it and looked at the number. It read 'unknown'. He almost did not answer, but then thought better of it. "Crawford."

He listened intently for a moment, then asked, "What's his condition?"

Another moment of silence as he listened.

Then he asked, "Which hospital?"

After hearing the response, he ended the call with: "Thanks for tracking this down for me. I appreciate it."

He stood still for a beat, letting the weight of the news settle. His shoulders slumped, and he let out a sigh.

Then he started walking again, the heat and dust hanging close as he crossed to the dining area. Millie had prepared iced electrolyte drinks and cobbled together finger foods from the remaining supplies. She and Jimmy were chatting quietly as Crawford approached.

"Hey," he said, interrupting. "Glad I caught you both together." They turned to him, mid-sentence.

"Jimmy, can you finish the truck load?"

Jimmy nodded. "Yeah, of course."

"Thanks." Crawford's voice was steady. "I'm heading to Reno. We found the hospital where they took the kid."

Millie blinked. "What are you going to do?"

He looked at her for a long moment, his expression unreadable.

He thought about Randall. How no one had been there for him in the end. How he had not been there. He thought about the kid in the flames. His last words, "My family." He thought about standing and watching people fall.

Then he softened. "I'm going to be there." He paused. "Someone should be there."

He turned without ceremony and walked to his car. He didn't know if the kid would live. Didn't know if being there would matter. But he was done standing still.

Temple of Serenity, 12:00 and Outer Playa, BRC, 9:00 PM - Rachael

That Sunday had passed in liminal quiet. Camps packed in muted efficiency, conversations hushed. No news about the boy. The playa felt different; still beautiful, but haunted by what it had witnessed, a matured, somber version of itself. By evening, the remaining burners gravitated toward the temple, needing somewhere to put what they carried.

The crowd was quietly assembled around the temple in stark contrast to the frenzy of the Man burning. This was a quiet, sober occasion. Most of the gatherers wore work or street attire. No music played. The crowd was muted. This moment was for mourning and release.

A shape moved through the temple. Then a single flame flickered to life in the center. As it grew, a voice rose, unamplified and tender, singing soft Italian that unfurled into Desdemona's Willow Song from *Othello*.

Rachael had a new set of griefs to relinquish. She grieved for that boy who'd danced so joyfully before the flames took him, whose last word was "family." She grieved for all the years she'd armored herself against connection, against exactly the kind of vulnerability that had cracked her open this week. What had seemed vague and conceptual during her temple visit now emerged as layers of specific grief; the acute, trauma from the night before, her personal grief in shedding her old self to inhabit her own transformation, her anticipation of the end of her burn experience, all of the specific losses manifested in the many temple tributes. Her body still felt fragile from last night's collapse, but her tears flowed freely now. Sandwiched between Nathan and Elise, she let herself cry. She knew she would cry about this again.

She scanned the ring of burners and caught Justine's eye. The young woman stood with Ruben; her father, impossibly, and Harley's family. A quiet nod passed between them, carrying the weight of what they'd witnessed together. Farther down, she saw Emile and Liam, Emile's face wet with tears. The people who'd been there when the boy fell. When Crawford leaped into the flames. The people who'd formed a circle around tragedy and held it together. Most of them were here. Crawford was the only one missing, keeping vigil somewhere else.

As the aria ended, silence enveloped the crowd. The crackle of flame became the new soundtrack, absorbing all else. The temple structure slowly surrendered to the fire.

Rachael closed her eyes. For a breath, she let herself remember her first moment here, knees in the dust, grief leaking like smoke from some hidden rupture inside her. That time, she had sat alone. Now, she was held in a quiet community.

As the structure fell and turned to embers, the crowd began to disperse. Minor parties would flare across the playa tonight, but the big celebration was over. They had entered the long hush of goodbye.

Rachael stayed until the flames were just coals. She thought about the week; how she'd arrived so defended, how she'd left pieces of that armor scattered across the playa. How she had nearly died from forgetting to drink water, from a lifetime of forgetting to take care of herself. How people had caught her anyway.

And this time, she would not leave herself behind.

02 **Spins After the Man Burns**

Sparkleville, 3:15 and Chakra, BRC, 9:37 AM - Rachael

Rachael turned her car from the intersection, pulling into camp and parking in the spot where the carport and glitter pool had once stood. A few vehicles and tents dotted what had been a jam-packed landscape. Sparkleville was only slightly more populated now than it had been during her first visit early in the week.

She had spent Sunday replaying the Ataraxis event on loop; the boy walking into the flames, Crawford's leap, those final words: "My family." The temple burn had helped, but the images were still vivid, for a long time.

She opened the car door, watching dust rain down from the roof like sifted flour. Her travel clothes were already dustier than she'd hoped. There was no escaping it. The playa came with you.

She stepped out, she looked down at her feet, and kneaded her toes in her running shoes, comfortable, relieved to be rid of the boots.

No circumnavigation of crowded tents was required this time. She made a beeline for Leon's Vanagon. He was leaning into the side door, mid-pack.

"Hey there," she said.

He turned and smiled, standing up. "There she is." He gave her a bear hug and held her. She leaned in.

When they broke, she looked at him, tired, but content. "Thank you for taking care of me. I can't tell you enough what it means."

"Always, Rachael. You're family."

She paused, his words settling in. A wry smile crept onto her face. "I finally get that. I'll do better."

Leon laughed. "You just do you."

She clapped his shoulder. "I promise, my friend. I promise." She nodded thoughtfully, then added, "See you on the other side."

Leaving him to his packing, she crossed camp toward a standing tent at the far end. As she approached, the zipper slider skittered along its teeth in fits, ubiquitous dust making smooth action impossible. Bea stepped through the flap, a bag of clothes in each hand.

"Hi, Bea," Rachael said.

Bea looked up, surprise flickering to guarded anticipation. "Hey," she replied, caution in her tone.

"Do you have a few minutes to talk? Or, more to the point, to listen?"

Bea dropped the bags onto the playa and took a long breath. "Sure."

"Can we sit?" Rachael nodded at the camp chairs.

Without a word, Bea plopped into the nearest one. Rachael pulled the other around to face her.

"Thanks," Rachael breathed. "First... Let me apologize for getting my shit all over you. You didn't deserve it."

She saw Bea's shoulders visibly slump, tension draining from her face.

"Elise said something to me early in the week that's stuck. She was surprised I was struggling here, given my past. And it's true. I've thrown myself into far more intense, even dangerous, situations. But those were about proving something. A bottomless pit of rage fueled them. There was no option to quit. And it was all part of a facade... building myself into an indomitable man's man. My success just added more rage. A vicious loop."

"You mean your martial arts, your military?" Bea asked.

"Sure. That, and career success, engineering, marriage, mountaineering... all of it." She exhaled.

Bea nodded slowly. "Got it."

"This week has been different. I'm not building a facade anymore. I'm trying to be... me. Whoever that is. And I'm still learning how to untangle myself from the avatar I used to be."

She looked toward the jagged Black Rock peaks to the east, taking a breath.

"This week has been... God, Bea. Not physically hard. I've done harder. But every day I woke up less sure of who I was. Like the playa was stripping away everything I thought I knew about myself."

She turned back to Bea. "I realized that I've carried this chip on my shoulder since transitioning. This 'not-fitting' chip. Being trans, I'm used to that being the first and often the only thing that defines me to others. But here? It was the least interesting thing about me. Which left a terrifying question: If that isn't who I am... then who am I?"

Rachael smiled sheepishly. "To be determined."

"Oh, so many things," Bea said softly.

"I'll use you as a mirror," Rachael replied.

"Please do."

"I camped with one group, but barely spent time with them. I bounced between camps, orbiting without ever landing. I've been surrounded by thousands of happy, open people... and felt completely alone." She gave a bitter laugh. "You know where else I do that? Everywhere in my life."

She shook her head. "I finally shifted gears on Friday. But I did it clumsily, irresponsibly, almost too late. I hurt myself in the process."

"I heard about Burn night. I'm sorry you went through that," Bea said.

"It sucked," Rachael confirmed. "But maybe it needed to happen like that. I had to burn my soul to the ground, like the Man, so something new could rise from the ashes."

She paused, the silence between them making space for the metaphor to land.

Then she added more gently, "Which brings me to being your pet tranny."

Bea flinched.

"My words, not yours," Rachael said, holding Bea's gaze. "I don't trust people. I assume they want me for my usefulness. So I hold the reins tight. When people invite me in, I start looking for the angle."

She shook her head slowly. "When the Sparklites brought me in, asked for nothing, I assumed I was your novelty. Your token. It never occurred to me... that maybe you all just wanted to love me. Leon and our little Saturday night crew showed me that."

She hesitated, then: "Will you help me let myself be loved?"

Bea's tears began to fall, carving dusty trails down her cheeks. "Absolutely."

She threw her arms around Rachael. They held each other as long as the morning heat would allow, finally pulling apart, slick with sweat.

They stood, hugging once more.

"See you in the Bay Area," Rachael said.

"You can count on it," Bea replied, wiping the last of her tears.

Rachael turned and began crossing the empty stretch of playa back to her car. Halfway there, she paused, glancing over her shoulder at Bea standing in the silence.

The spot where the glitter pool had been shimmered faintly in the light, just a ghost of sparkle clinging to the dust.

"You know," she called out, "I think I'm finally ready to be here."

Magrathea Home Base, 10:00 and Divinity, 9:42 AM - Emile

The crew moved with unusual quiet. Thirty-three hours since the boy had walked into the flames. No word yet from the hospital. The joy of the week, Magrathea's joyous debut, sat uneasily beside the tragedy of Saturday night, and everyone felt it.

Emile walked to the side of the bus with Liam. They encountered a long scratch in the custom mural. Emile traced it with his fingers and then looked at Liam. He smiled. "Perfect."

Django swung the cargo door down. The belly hold was crammed so tightly that the door caught short of the frame. He leaned in, gave it a firm shove with his hip until it sealed, then twisted the handle and clicked the lock shut.

"Careful when you open it. She's packed tight," he called out.

The Magrathea crew gathered nearby, watching the final ritual. Their base camp had been stripped to the bone, just the hard playa, the bus, and the long road home. The SUV idled behind the trailer, Stanton running the A/C like a reward for surviving the week.

Emile stepped up on the stairs to get a better view of the group. He cleared his throat and raised his voice.

"Hey folks. Can I grab a moment before we roll?"

The crew turned toward him. A few looked up with polite curiosity, while others did so with a mix of fatigue and indifference. Only Dobbs looked like he was settling in for a show.

Emile scanned their faces, then took a breath. When he spoke, his voice was steady but carried something raw underneath.

"First off, thank you. Truly. You all crushed it this week, in spite of me stomping around, micromanaging, and generally doing my best to mess it up. You carried this thing. You made it beautiful."

A smattering of polite claps rose from the group.

"And... we also witnessed something terrible together. Saturday night. That boy." His voice caught. "I don't know if he's going to make it. But we showed up for each other at that moment. We held it together. That matters."

He cleared his throat. "I say this knowing we're leaving here changed in ways we didn't expect. Some good. Some..." He didn't finish.

Quiet nods from many crew members confirmed that the sentiment was shared.

"And look..." He paused, vulnerability creeping into his voice. "I owe you an apology. I've been a world-class asshole this week. There's no excuse. But I've spent the last few days staring some hard truths in the face, and let's just say... I've got *plenty* to unpack in therapy once we're back in Seattle."

He gave a sheepish grin, but his hands betrayed a slight tremor.

"Damn right!" Bedlam's fist shot into the air from the back of the group.

Emile laughed, the sound catching slightly in his throat. "Damn right," he echoed, nodding toward her.

That got a few genuine chuckles. The tension in the group started to loosen, and Emile felt something shift inside him, a wall finally cracking.

He paused, emotion tugging just behind his eyes. His voice dropped, more intimate now.

"I can't fix it all overnight. But if you're willing to stick with me... I promise I'll do better. I *want* to do better. For you. For this." His voice broke just slightly. "For myself."

A quiet beat passed. The crew stood still, absorbing the weight of his words. Several faces had softened completely.

Then:

"Fuuuuck youuuu!" Dobbs bellowed, hands cupped around his mouth like a bullhorn.

The crew broke into laughter. Not polite chuckles this time, but real, cathartic release.

"Fuck you, Emile!" Shimmer added, grinning with tears in her eyes.

"Fuck you, dude!" Misha chimed in, his voice full of affection.

It snowballed. One by one, voices joined in until it became a full-on chant:

"Fuck you, Emile! Fuck you, Emile!"

Emile laughed, affectionate warmth in his eyes. He raised his arms like a victorious boxer, encouraging the crowd. They kept it going, and for the first time all week, he felt truly connected to them. He dropped into an exaggerated bow, letting the moment wash over him, the acceptance, the forgiveness, the love disguised as profanity.

As he straightened, he caught Liam's eye across the group. Liam was crying too, smiling wide, proud, beaming with something that looked like hope.

And in that brief, sun-drenched silence between chants and departure, Emile felt something he hadn't experienced in years:

He was enough. Just as he was.

The road ahead stretched long toward home, but for the first time, he wasn't afraid of the journey.

Ataraxis Warrior, 11:00 and Outer Playa, BRC, 10:23 AM - Harley

Harley pulled up to the control station and killed the engine. Before the dust had settled, Cyan, Claire, and Ruben were out of the truck bed. Clarence shoved the stubborn passenger door open with a grunt.

Harley gazed up at Ataraxis Warrior. It no longer had the sense of resoluteness. Rather it appeared simply inert. Perhaps even resigned. "The Warrior's time has passed. You, my friends and family, are the death doulas, the mythological psychopomps. Shall we usher it to its next life?"

Without waiting for a response, he continued. "The crane will be here at 4 PM. Let's walk through what needs to be done so the operator can drop the structure. I prepped most of it this morning, but a few things are left."

He glanced, for the hundredth time, at the scorched spot where Cypher had lain, burning. The cracked playa there had hardened again, but Harley still saw it, the pain, the helplessness. He stepped closer, almost out of habit, then stopped. There was no mark to hold it. As soon as Ataraxis Warrior came down, the spot would vanish forever.

He crouched for a moment and gently touched the earth. Just a brush of his fingertips. Then he stood.

Clarence clapped a hand on his shoulder. "Not your fault, son. Not your fault."

"Yeah." Harley exhaled, not entirely convinced. "We have plenty to do. I'll deal with my guilt later."

"We'll all do that with you," Clarence said.

He stood, brushing playa dust from his hands. The warrior loomed above them, its time finished. In two days it had gone from triumph to tragedy to just another thing that needed dismantling. That was the playa. Nothing stayed sacred for long.

Cyan and Claire had already moved to the far side of the structure, beginning the prep work without needing to be told. They had not been here when Harley first erected it. But, now they would see it come down.

"Hey." They both turned to see Justine approaching, a small canvas bag slung across her shoulder. "I thought you might need an extra pair of hands."

Harley stepped in and hugged her. "We most certainly can use your help." As she wrapped her arms around him, her eyes found Ruben. He smiled back at her, hesitant, but open.

She pulled away from Harley and crossed over to him. "Hi."

"Want a hug?" he asked, voice softer than he expected.

She didn't answer. Just stepped in and wrapped her arms around him. He let her in, holding her carefully, as if afraid to break the spell. It didn't last long, but it was real. A threshold crossed.

When they separated, Ruben laid a hand on her shoulder, still getting used to the gesture, to having the right to touch her at all. "Do you know how to use an impact driver?"

She smiled, a mix of mischief and warmth. "I think I can handle that."

2:45 and Enlighten, 1:30 PM - Ruben

Justine assessed the small bus skeptically. "Not exactly the VIP ride that brought me here."

Ruben dropped Justine's bags next to the small bus and wiped his hands on his pants. This tacit connection, born in a moment of trauma, was a delicate bullet. "When will you be back in the Bay Area?" she asked.

Ruben looked at Justine. "Three weeks, maybe less. I'm helping Harley finish up, then DPW work until the city's down. Then I'm coming back." He paused. "For real this time."

She nodded. "When you get back, call me." She stuffed a sheet with her contact information into his hand.

He stuffed the paper into his pants pocket. "You can count on it." They hugged. "Have a good return to the default world." The default world was a burner term for life outside of Black Rock City. He turned to make his way back to the DPW ghetto.

"Dad!" She called out. He turned back.

The word hung between them, still strange in both their mouths.

"It's going to take me a while to get used to that," he breathed the words

"Me too." She held his gaze. "But I want to. Get used to it, I mean." He waited. Finally, she said, "Really. Call me."

He smiled. "Justine, other than sorting out work and a place to sleep, you're my only priority."

Her face became serious. "I'm not known for my optimism, but for some notion beyond reason, I feel hopeful. Like I can count on you."

His smile turned wan. "Before now, you would have been a fool to count on me. Now. I'm done running. I'll be there."

She smiled, picked up her gear, and boarded the bus. Ruben waved at her as they pulled away. She waved back. He watched the bus as it traveled down Enlightenment until it disappeared.

⓪③ **Spins After the Man Burns**

Ataraxis Warrior, 11:00 and Outer Playa, BRC, 3:23 PM - Harley

The two flatbeds moved away in unison. All that was Ataraxis Warrior was now the burden of those trucks, consigned to their destination. He watched after them. They pulled away to reveal a lone burly figure walking toward him. He watched as the tiny figure grew larger, unmoving. He was in no hurry.

When Ruben arrived, he reached out his hands and took Ruben's hand in a warm clasp. "Brother."

Ruben smiled back at him, a gesture that was both warm and worn. They had only known each other for days, but something had been forged between them: shared silence, shared grief, the quiet understanding of two men who'd both been barely holding on. Now they moved forward as brothers.

"I couldn't let you go without saying goodbye," Ruben responded.

Harley grinned. "Let's call it 'see you later.' This isn't goodbye."

"You heading out now?" Ruben asked.

"My steed awaits." Harley waved his hand behind him without looking at the old truck laden with a camper. "I'll give you a ride back, though."

"Good. It's a long walk," laughed Ruben. "Where are you taking the Warrior?"

Harley raised his eyebrows. "Wounded Knee. I'm taking it home." He paused. "No fire this time."

Ruben was surprised. "You going to move there?"

"Oakland's home now. The Knee is my past, my heritage. I'll be back in a few weeks."

"For some reason that comforts me," Ruben acknowledged.

"What about you?" Harley asked him.

"Frankly, I have no idea. The only thing I'm sure of is that I'm going to make up for lost time getting to know Justine, to the degree she'll let me."

Harley nodded. He was quiet for a moment, then cleared his throat. "How do you feel about building fancy ass gates for rich assholes? I have more orders than I can handle. A welcome problem that leaves me in the position of needing a trusted hand. I've been thinking... I could use help with the gate orders. If you're interested."

Ruben stared at him for a long moment. "You serious?"

"Dead serious. I can't wait to say nothing to you while we work together." They both laughed.

"I also have a spare room you can use until you get on your feet," Harley said.

Ruben was visibly shaken, almost confused. "Forgive me if this sounds like I am looking a gift horse in the mouth, but this feels a bit like charity. Or at least the most generous gesture I have ever received." His tone was laced with both wonder and skepticism. "Are you sure this makes sense?"

"I can see how you would see it that way." Harley paused. "I need to share a little secret with you. I know you offered me assistance to help yourself. You made that clear, and I was fine with that. What you need to know is that you saved my ass in two ways. Standing up the Warrior is obvious. But, you're the first person I've ever let help me. That opened a door for me. Without letting you in, I would not have been able to step across the threshold to let my family in."

"Whatever weird-ass playa magic threw you in my way. You're now my responsibility. I'm okay with that." Harley smiled.

"We are, at least at the moment, both traveling the same path and offering each other the same support. We've both been carrying too much for too long. Let's share the burden for a while."

Harley gestured at the pickup. "C'mon, man. You have a DPW shift to get back to. Let's get you back to Thud before she has your ass."

The two men walked to the pickup, climbed in, and moved away from the site. Neither looked at the spot where Cypher had lain.

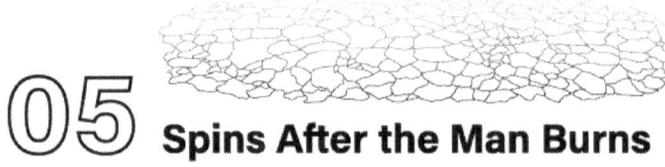

05 **Spins After the Man Burns**

7:50 and Inspiration, 9:32 AM - Ruben

Five days after the Man burned, the playa was nearly empty. It was nearly back to the condition that marked Ruben's first day. Ruben and Thud worked the cleanup grid in silence, cataloging what people left behind.

Thud pulled the DPW pickup to a stop at an abandoned camp. She let out a sigh of quiet exasperation. "Let's make this quick."

Ruben slid out and approached the collapsed tent. He pulled at the fabric, then stopped. Underneath: a sleeping bag, clothes, everything caked in dried playa mud. He brushed dust from a small cooler.

His hand froze.

Cypher was scrawled across its side in marker. Ruben sighed and muttered to himself, "Lord of the dust."

"Thud." His voice came out rough. "This is his camp. The kid from Ataraxis Warrior."

She came over, looked at the cooler, then at the scattered remains. Neither spoke.

Finally, Thud said, "Last I heard, critical condition in Reno. Burns over most of his body."

Ruben nodded slowly, still holding the cooler.

"I met this kid. Mixed up, lost, but trying to find something." Ruben explained.

Just like I had been.

"I'm going to visit him," he said. "In Reno. On my way back to the Bay."

"Yeah?" Thud ask.

"Someone should be there. He's a decent kid."

Thud nodded. "Alright then."

They worked in silence, carefully boxing Cypher's belongings. When they finished loading the truck, Ruben dusted off his gloves. He expected Thud to climb in, but instead she leaned against the side panel, looking at him.

"What?" he asked.

"You did good out here."

He blinked, caught off guard. Thud wasn't much for compliments.

"You showed up," she continued. "Not just for work. All the way."

"You gave me a place to show up to," he spoke in a hush.

After a pause, he said, "Honestly, I'll never be the same. I came here with literally nothing. I'm leaving here with ... everything. This place has left a permanent mark on me."

He stared into the distance, perhaps beyond the desert. Then he looked at her. "Harley said it best to me. I have playa dust in my soul."

She nodded, satisfied. "You did accomplish one great feat."

Ruben looked puzzled. "What's that?"

"You made me your friend." She gave him a lopsided grin.

He smiled back reflectively. "I'll take that to the bank."

She slapped the side panel and headed for the cab. "Let's get going." She moved toward the cab, not waiting for his response.

Ruben pulled his Nalgene water bottle, took a long drink, and studied its scuffed surface for a moment. What was once a foreign object had become part of him. He reholstered it and climbed into the passenger seat.

Thud said, "360 spins till the next burn." They both laughed.

Thud started the truck. As they turned toward the DPW Ghetto, the playa spread out before them – emptied, silent, already becoming a memory.

They rode in comfortable silence.

For the first time in twenty-three years, Ruben wasn't running. He was driving toward something tangible: a daughter, a job, maybe even a life. He didn't know if he'd be any good at it.

But he was going to try.

Appendix: The Playa Lexicon

A practical guide for the uninitiated, the dust-curious, and anyone wondering why everyone keeps saying "radical."

A Note on the Playa Lexicon

Compiled from field notes, dusty recollections, and late-night post-event debriefs. Facts may have been warped by heatstroke, dehydration, or transcendence. Use this guide with humility, hydration, and a healthy disregard for certainty.

Magrathea's Final Answer

A massive mutant vehicle and art installation; a roving stage, a dream, and a statement rolled into steel and light. Named after the legendary planet factory from *The Hitchhiker's Guide to the Galaxy*, it represents humanity's endless appetite to build beauty out of ruin. Also a magnet for chaos, revelation, and really bad decisions.

Ataraxis Warrior

A mythic concept, performance persona, and half-serious religion rolled into one. The Ataraxis Warrior seeks serenity through struggle; peace through motion, stillness through fire. On the playa, that usually translates to dancing until sunrise and pretending it's enlightenment.

The Gordian Knot

Crawford's labyrinthine art maze; a shimmering tangle of pathways, reflections, and ego. It's part installation, part metaphor: a problem built to be unsolved. Those who enter emerge dusty, dazed, and a little more honest than they intended. Or not at all.

The Ten Principles of Burning Man

The ethos that shapes everything from how people build cities to how they share water in a storm. These are not rules so much as operating myths — the loose code that keeps the chaos coherent.

1. **Radical Inclusion** – Everyone is invited. No velvet ropes, no VIPs, just dust for all.

2. **Gifting** – Give freely, without expectation. The value is in the exchange, not the object.

3. **Decommodification** – Commerce stays outside the fence. Inside, experience is the only currency.

4. **Radical Self-Reliance** – Bring everything you need and then some. The desert owes you nothing.

5. **Radical Self-Expression** – Say who you are, wear who you are, be who you are, preferably in glitter.

6. **Communal Effort** – Build together, lift together, clean together. No one gets through the dust alone.

7. **Civic Responsibility** – Even anarchy needs plumbing. Respect the community and the laws that sustain it.

8. **Leaving No Trace** – Take only photos (carefully), leave only footprints (briefly).

9. **Participation** – Spectating is not a verb on the playa. If you're here, you're part of the show.

10. **Immediacy** – Be present. The moment is the message, and it will never repeat.

Concepts

- **Default world**: Outside reality (mentioned once, worth expanding)
- **Decommodification in practice**: Why the coffee is free, why trading feels wrong
- **Radical self-expression vs. costume**: The deeper meaning behind the glitter
- **The gift of failure**: Why breaking down (like Cypher's camp) is part of the experience
- **Immediacy vs. documentation**: The tension of capturing moments

Common Playa Terms

Black Rock City (BRC)

The temporary metropolis that rises each year in Nevada's Black Rock Desert. Think *Mad Max* meets *Cirque du Soleil*, with better hugs and worse hygiene.

The Playa

Spanish for "beach," but here it's a vast, cracked lakebed made of ultra-fine alkaline dust that seeps into your soul, socks, and possibly your DNA. Once you've been there, you'll find dust in places science can't explain.

DPW (Department of Public Works)

The hard-living, hard-working crew that builds and tears down the city. Equal parts punk construction team and mythic cult of chaos. They live by grit, gallows humor, and caffeine.

DPW Ghetto

The rough-and-tumble neighborhood where DPW sets up camp. Part junkyard, part holy ground, and entirely its own world. If Burning Man were a body, the Ghetto would be its liver; tough, essential, and constantly processing toxins.

Burner

Anyone who's attended Burning Man and feels mildly superior for having survived it. Usually identifiable by goggles, a thousand-yard stare, and an unshakable belief in radical self-expression.

BMOrg (Burning Man Organization)

The official machinery behind the madness; event producers, administrators, dream-enablers, and red-tape wranglers. They balance spreadsheets and idealism with varying degrees of success.

The Man

The giant wooden effigy at the center of it all, ceremonially set ablaze in a fiery orgy of catharsis, fireworks, and questionable decision-making. "The Man burns" is both an event and a mantra.

The Burn

Short for Burning Man or the act of incinerating the Man. A collective release where tens of thousands scream, dance, and cry as the desert turns into a glowing vision quest.

Temple

A sacred structure built for grief, reflection, and letting go. The one place at Burning Man where even the most sarcastic DPWer gets quiet.

Art Car / Mutant Vehicle

Rolling, fire-breathing, LED-encrusted sculptures masquerading as transportation. A school bus might become a dragon, a ship, or a mobile dance floor. No two look alike; thankfully.

Esplanade

Main Street, Playa-style. The innermost, loudest, and flashiest ring of the city. It's where sound camps, spectacle, and sleep deprivation all collide.

Center Camp

The city's quasi-downtown; part café, part performance space, part spontaneous therapy circle. The closest thing BRC has to civilization.

Theme Camp

Neighborhood collectives that offer something, anything, to the community: pancakes, pole dancing, welding workshops, or existential dread at sunrise.

MOOP (Matter Out of Place)

Anything that doesn't belong on the desert floor, be it trash, feathers, or your abandoned emotional baggage. Leaving MOOP is the cardinal sin of the playa.

Leave No Trace

The sacred commandment: pack it in, pack it out, pretend you were never here. Even if your tent disintegrated in a dust storm, you take every scrap home.

Dust Storm

Nature's exfoliating gift. Visibility drops to zero, goggles become your religion, and everyone looks like a post-apocalyptic librarian.

Playa Name

Your alternate identity, bestowed by fate, friends, or tequila. Usually earned through embarrassment, heroism, or spectacular failure. ("Chainsaw," "Thud," and "Cheshire" did not come from HR.)

Deep Playa

The outer reaches of BRC, where art installations and strange encounters await. Go far enough and you might meet God, or at least a topless guy on stilts offering grilled cheese.

Rangers

Volunteer mediators and crisis whisperers. Equal parts peacekeeper, therapist, and desert Yoda.

Gate Road

The line you sit in for hours (or days) to enter Burning Man. A test of patience, hydration, and your car's cooling system.

Trash Fence

A miles-long barrier encircling BRC, preventing windblown debris; and metaphorical bullshit, from escaping into the wider world.

Fucko

A DPW term of endearment (or insult) depending on tone. Can mean "buddy," "idiot," or "you magnificent bastard."

About the Author

Sarah Marshall is a lifelong seeker shaped as much by landscape as by people. Born in Hawaii and raised in the Sierra Nevada foothills, her early years were marked by wide skies, deep forests, and regular visits to the Black Hills of South Dakota and Wyoming, where she lived and worked as a young adult. These places instilled an enduring reverence for nature, silence, and the subtle intelligence of land. They also seeded a restlessness that would become a defining trait: an ever-present curiosity about how people live, believe, build meaning, and find belonging.

That curiosity has carried her across six continents; not as a collector of destinations but as a listener, participant, and student of culture. She has lived and worked among many communities, learning to navigate differences with humility, adaptability, and respect. These experiences inform her writing deeply, particularly her attention to liminal spaces, chosen families, and moments of transformation that occur far from the center of conventional life.

Sarah's inner life is grounded in a longstanding personal spiritual practice, complemented by decades of study in martial arts, yoga, and dance. Movement has always been a language for her; a way of understanding discipline, surrender, embodiment, and connection beyond words. These practices shape both her worldview and her prose, which carries a physical, sensory awareness of the body moving through space, effort, and change.

She has participated in the Burning Man event more than twenty times, an experience that profoundly influenced her understanding of community, impermanence, creative devotion, and the tension between structure and freedom. The desert, the playa, and the temporary city that rises there are not merely settings in her work but living systems she knows intimately through years of contribution, leadership, and return.

Before becoming a novelist, Sarah served in the United States Navy and later built a career optimizing operations for growing organizations; work that taught her how systems shape human behavior and how culture determines what becomes possible. Throughout her life she has moved between worlds that rarely intersect: military and mystic, engineer and artist, strategist and wanderer. Writing has become the place where these threads are allowed to speak to one another.

She currently lives both close to nature and metropolis, still traveling when the road calls, still practicing, still asking questions that refuse easy answers. She is married and has an adult daughter, whose art adorns the novel. *Playa Dust in My Soul* emerges from decades of lived experience, patient observation, and a belief that transformation is not an event but a practice.